TRUTHS
I NEVER
TOLD
YOU

Also by Kelly Rimmer

THE THINGS WE CANNOT SAY
BEFORE I LET YOU GO

TRUTHS I NEVER TOLD YOU

KELLY RIMMER

GRAYDON
HOUSE

GRAYDON
HOUSE®

Recycling programs
for this product may
not exist in your area.

ISBN-13: 978-1-525-80465-6

Truths I Never Told You

This edition published by arrangement with Harlequin Books S.A.

Graydon House
22 Adelaide St. West, 40th Floor
Toronto, Ontario M5H 4E3, Canada
www.GraydonHouseBooks.com
www.BookClubbish.com

Printed in U.S.A.

For the women who carry infants in their arms
as they battle illness in their minds.

PROLOGUE

Grace
September 14, 1957

I am alone in a crowded family these days, and that's the worst feeling I've ever experienced. Until these past few years, I had no idea that loneliness is worse than sadness. I've come to realize that's because loneliness, by its very definition, cannot be shared.

Tonight there are four other souls in this house, but I am unreachably far from any of them, even as I'm far too close to guarantee their safety. Patrick said he'd be home by nine tonight, and I clung on to that promise all day.

He'll be home at nine, I tell myself. You won't do anything crazy if Patrick is here, so just hold on until nine.

I should have known better than to rely on that man by now. It's 11:55 p.m., and I have no idea where he is.

Beth will be wanting a feed soon and I'm just so tired, I'm already bracing myself—as if the sound of her cry will be the thing that undoes me, instead of something I should be used to after four children. I feel the fear of that cry in my very bones—a kind of whole-body tension I can't quite make sense of. When was the last time I had more than a few hours' sleep? Twenty-four hours a day I am fixated on the terror that I will snap and hurt someone: Tim, Ruth, Jeremy, Beth…or myself. I am a threat to my children's safety, but at the same time, their only protection from that very same threat.

I have learned a hard lesson these past few years; the more difficult life is, the louder your feelings become. On an ordinary day, I trust facts more than feelings, but when the world feels like it's ending, it's hard to distinguish where my thoughts are even coming from. Is this fear grounded in reality, or is my mind playing tricks on me again? There's no way for me to be sure. Even the line between imagination and reality has worn down and it's now too thin to delineate.

Sometimes I think I will walk away before something bad happens, as if removing myself from the equation would keep them all safe. But then Tim will skin his knee and come running to me, as if a simple hug could take all the world's pain away. Or Jeremy will plant one of those sloppy kisses on my cheek, and I am reminded that for better or worse, I am his world. Ruth will slip my handbag over her shoulder as she follows me around the house, trying to walk in my footsteps, because to her, I seem like someone worth imitating. Or Beth will look up at me with that gummy grin when I try to feed her, and my heart contracts with a love that really does know no bounds.

Those moments remind me that everything changes, and that this cloud has come and gone twice now, so if I just hang on, it will pass again. I don't feel hope yet, but I should know hope, because I've walked this path before and even when the mountains and valleys seemed insurmountable, I survived them.

I'm constantly trying to talk myself around to calm, and sometimes, for brief and beautiful moments, I do. But the hard, cold truth is that every time the night comes, it seems blacker than it did before.

Tonight I'm teetering on the edge of something horrific.

Tonight the sound of my baby's cry might just be the thing that breaks me altogether.

I'm scared of so many things these days, but most of all now, I fear myself.

ONE

Beth
1996

"What's the place...you know...where is the place? What...
today? No? It's now. The place."

Dad babbles an endless stream of words that don't quite make
sense as I push his wheelchair through his front door. My brother
Tim and I exchange a glance behind his back and then we share
a resigned sigh. Our father's speech sounds coherent enough if
you don't listen too closely—the rhythms of it are still right and
his tone is clear, it's the words themselves he can't quite grasp
these days, and the more upset he gets, the less sense he makes.
The fact that he's all-but speaking gibberish today actually makes
a lot of sense, but it's still all kinds of heartbreaking.

The grandfather clock in the kitchen has just chimed 5 p.m.
I'm officially late to pick my son up from my mother-in-law's
house, and Dad was supposed to be at the nursing home two
hours ago. We were determined to give him the dignity to

leave his house on his own terms, and this morning Dad made it very clear that he wanted to be left alone in his room to pack for the move.

Tim and I promised one another we'd be patient, and for four and a half hours, we *were* patient. He pottered around the backyard doing overdue yardwork—weeding the chaos around the bases of the conifers, scooping up the pinecones, reshaping the hedge that's run completely amok. Dad's house is in Bellevue, east of Seattle. Over the last little while he's been too ill to tend his own yard and we've confirmed my long-held suspicion that nature would entirely swallow up the manicured gardens in this region within just a few months if humans disappeared. While Tim tried to wrangle some order back to the gardens outside, I vigorously mopped the polished floors, vacuumed the carpet in the bedrooms and sorted the fresh food in Dad's fridge to distribute among my siblings.

But every time I stuck my head through Dad's bedroom door, I found him sitting on his bed beside his mostly empty suitcase. At first, he was calm and seemed to be thoughtfully processing the change that was coming. He wears this quiet, childlike smile a lot of the time now, and for the first few hours, that smile was firmly fixed on his face, even as he looked around, even as he sat in silence. As the hours passed, though, the suitcase remained empty, save for a hat and two pairs of socks.

"I can't…where is the…" He started looking around his room, searching desperately for something he couldn't name, let alone find. He kept lifting his right hand into the air, clenched in a fist. We couldn't figure out what he wanted, Dad couldn't figure out how to tell us and the more he tried, the more out of breath he became until he was gasping for air between each confused, tortured word. The innocent smile faded from his face and his distress gradually turned to something close to panic. Tim helped him back into his wheelchair and pushed him to the living room, sitting him right in front of the television, playing one of his beloved black-and-white movies on the VCR to distract him. I stayed in the bedroom, sobbing quietly as I finished the packing my father obviously just couldn't manage.

This morning Dad understood that he was moving to the nursing home, and although he'd made it clear he didn't *want* to go, he seemed to understand that he had to. This afternoon he's just lost, and I can't bear much more of this. I'm starting to rush Dad, because I've finally accepted that we need to get this over and done with. I guess after a day of getting nowhere, I'm ready to resort to the "rip the Band-Aid off" approach to admitting him to hospice care. I push his wheelchair quickly away from the door, down the ramp my sister, Ruth, built over the concrete stairs, down to the path that cuts across the grass on the front yard.

"Lock the wall," Dad says, throwing the words over his shoulder to Tim. In the past few weeks, I've found myself arguing with Dad, trying to correct him when he mixes his words up like this. Tim's told me not to bother—Dad can't help it, and correcting him won't actually fix the problem. My brother is definitely much better at communicating with Dad than I am. He calls back very gently,

"I'm locking the door. Don't worry."

"Sorry about that," Dad says, suddenly sounding every bit as weary as I feel.

"It's okay, Dad," Tim calls as he jogs down the path to catch up to us.

"No work today, Timmy?" *Tim* hasn't been *Timmy* for at least twenty years, except at family functions when our brother, Jeremy, wants to rile him up. Forty-two and forty-one respectively and with several graduate degrees between them, my brothers still revert to adolescent banter whenever they're in the same room. Today, I can only wish Dad was teasing Tim playfully the way Jeremy does when *he* slips back into that old nickname.

"I have the day off today," Tim says quietly.

"Are we going to the...that thing..." Dad's brows knit. He searches for the right word, waving his hand around vaguely in the air in front of him, then his shoulders slump as he sighs heavily. "Are we going to the green place?"

"The golf course? No, Dad. Not today. We're going to the nursing home, remember?"

We only realized Dad had dementia earlier this year, and at times like this, I'm horrified all over again that it took us so long to figure it out. He had a heart attack four years ago, and in the aftermath, was diagnosed with heart failure. His deterioration has been steady despite medication and cardiac rehab, and with the changes in his physical health have come significant changes in his personality and, we thought, cognitive function. He'd been losing words the whole time, but his mind seemed intact otherwise. And who doesn't search for a word every now and again? What exactly *is* the tipping point between "not as sharp as you used to be" and "neurologically deficient"?

Tim's an orthopedic surgeon, and given his years of extensive medical training he could probably answer that question in excruciating detail, but his eyes are suspiciously shiny right now as we walk Dad to the car, so I don't ask.

Dad sighs heavily and turns his attention back to me. He's on permanent oxygen supplementation now, the cannula forever nestled in his nostrils. Sometimes I forget it's there, and then when I look at his face, I'm startled all over again by the visual reminders that it's really happening—Dad is really dying. The evidence is undeniable now...the cannula, the swelling around his face, the sickly gray-white tone in his skin.

"Where's Noah?" he asks me.

"He's at Chiara's house." My mother-in-law worships my son—her third grandchild, first grandson. Today, when I dropped Noah off, she barely looked at him—instead she threw her arms around me and hugged me for so long that eventually, I had to disentangle myself to make a hasty exit. I like Chiara and we have a great relationship. It just turns out that I *really* don't like her feeling sorry for me, and that hug today was a strangely awkward experience.

"Visit him?" Dad says, immediately perking up.

"Another day, Dad. Soon," I promise. Between my siblings and our spouses, at least one of us will visit Dad every day from now on. My sister, Ruth, pinned a roster for the first two weeks of visits to the fridge in Dad's house, but for some reason, she's left me off it. Ruth has a lot on her plate so the mistake is understandable. I noticed it a few days ago. I just keep forgetting to call her to sort it out.

I help him from his wheelchair into the car, but just as I move to shut the door, he reaches up to hold it open. He pauses, frowning as he concentrates. I scan his face—those beautiful blue eyes, lined with sadness, lips tugged down. Tim helped Dad shave this morning and his cheeks are smooth. I'm suddenly besieged by a memory, of snuggling close to Dad for a hug after I'd fallen on this very path rushing out to meet the school bus one morning. I'd skinned my knee pretty bad, and Dad had waved the bus driver away, promising me he'd make it all better then drive me to school himself. I remember his cheeks were rough that day with stubble, but his arms around me were warm, and his gentle kiss against my forehead gifted me instant courage to deal with the blood that was trickling down my leg.

That moment feels like a million years ago. I just wish there was some way I could return the favor, to make him feel as safe as he made me feel so many times over the past four decades. But hugs can't make this better. Nothing can change the reality that our time with Dad is coming to an end.

"Come on, Dad—" Tim starts to say, but Dad shakes his head fiercely and he looks right at me as he says,

"Beth."

"Yes, Dad?"

His entire expression shifts in an instant—from determination to a sudden, crippling sadness. His gaze is pleading and his eyes fill with tears as he whispers,

"Sorry."

"You have nothing to apologize for."

"I do," he insists, and his gaze grows frustrated, presumably at my blank look. "I...the mistake and of course I didn't. Because I'm sorry and she's gone."

What strikes me first is simply how much I miss Dad being able to speak easily. His speech has been getting worse and worse over the past few months; most days now, it's just fragments of language that are, at best, related to whatever he's trying to express.

"Dad..." I'm trying to figure out what to say, but I can't, and Tim and I just stare at him in confusion for a moment as he tries to explain himself.

"I, when Gracie...alone. Remember? What's it called? When...and *she* came and I tried..." There are tears in his eyes again, and he looks from me to Tim desperately, as if we can help him somehow.

"That's enough now, Dad," Tim says firmly, then he adds more gently, "You're okay. Just relax."

Dad's language issues stem from a form of frontotemporal atrophy called semantic dementia. His memories are intact, but his language skills have been devastated. Tim sighs heavily and runs his hand over his salt-and-pepper beard, and I belatedly notice how weary my brother looks. For the first time all day, he seems to be struggling more than I am.

This situation is awful and it's been hard on all of us, but I know Tim, and it's not the stress of a sick parent that's giving him anxiety. Tim's habitual overresponsibility is slowly driving him crazy this week. Despite being the one to miraculously win Dad a place in the hospice ward of an amazing new nursing home on Mercer Island, he's still been trying to find some last-minute solution that would enable us to decline the placement anyway.

"We're doing the right thing," I assure him softly. We've been using a combination of at-home nursing care three or four days a week, supplemented with a rostered system of sleepovers for me and Tim and our siblings Ruth and Jeremy on the other days. This has mostly worked for the past seven months, but it was never going to be a long-term solution, especially now that Dad is well into the "end stage" of the heart failure process.

Tim's apartment is a forty-minute drive from here, in downtown Seattle close to his hospital. It's a lovely home, but it's on the twentieth floor of a high-rise tower—not at all a suitable place for Dad to live out his final days. Plus, Tim works insane hours, and his wife, Alicia, isn't exactly a nurturing soul. And Ruth has three children of her own *and* runs the family construction business. Jeremy is an earth sciences professor and when he's not teaching, he's traveling. Right now he's in Indonesia, reading seismic waves or something, and I know he's supposed to spend the second semester of next year teaching in Japan.

My husband, Hunter, and I probably were the only family members who could have cared for Dad given I'm at home full-time at the moment anyway. We already live nearby, too, so we could have just moved into Dad's house, or Dad could have moved in with us—either home is plenty large enough to accommodate us all. When Jeremy casually tried to hint at an arrangement like this, I just told him I was going back to work soon. That's a lie, but it was a necessary one. I've quietly extended my maternity leave by another six months, but I have no idea if or when I'll go back to my position as a child psychologist at a community center. I do know for sure that I simply cannot take on Dad's care full-time…especially knowing what's coming.

"I wish there was a way we could keep him at home," Tim says, for what feels like the one millionth time. "Maybe I should have looked into moving here…"

I step closer to him and slide my arm around his waist, then rest my head on his shoulder.

"Come on, Tim. Be realistic. The commute would have killed you." The commute or his wife. For the past seven months, Tim has been here with Dad at least one night a week—usually on his only day off, sometimes making the journey straight from a night shift. Alicia came with him a few times, then suddenly stopped helping out. As far as I can tell, she's very busy being a "media personality." Given she hasn't had an acting or modeling gig for at least a decade, "media personality" seems to mean she spends her mornings at the gym and her afternoons with her socialite friends, hoping she'll make it into the frame of a paparazzi photo so she can complain about her lack of privacy.

It's fair to say I was never Alicia's biggest fan, but her decision to sit on the sidelines while the rest of us struggled with Dad's care is not something I'll forgive anytime soon. Jeremy is newly single, but even his ex-girlfriend, Fleur, made an effort to help out a few times. And my husband, Hunter, and Ruth's husband, Ellis, have gone out of their way to help, too. Hell, even Hunter's parents, Chiara and Wallace, have taken their share of turns with Dad, especially after Noah's birth when I just couldn't get myself here.

It's been a team effort: Team Walsh Family and Friends— minus Alicia. And yes, I suppose it's possible I'm a little bitter about that.

"Are you okay?" Tim asks me suddenly. I grimace and nod toward Dad.

"I've been better."

"I don't actually mean about what's happening with Dad. I mean…in general." He says the words so carefully, it's like he's tiptoeing his way through a minefield. I raise an eyebrow at him.

"Do you realize you're deflecting?"

"Do you realize *you're* deflecting?" he fires back. We stare at each other, then at the same time, both break and reluctantly smile. "Look, everyone is busy, and we're all a bit overwhelmed at the moment. But I just need to make sure you know I'm here if you want to talk."

"I'm fine," I assure him.

"I can't tell what's going on with you, Beth. Sometimes I worry that you don't realize how little time he has left. Other times I worry that you're all *too* aware of that and maybe…not really coping with it?"

"There's a lot happening," I say, then I glance at my watch. "We really need to go."

Tim sighs, then gives me a quick hug before he walks around to slip into the driver's seat. I look back at the house one last time, aware that after today, it's no longer *Dad's house*, but *Dad's old house*.

Until this year when his speech started fading, Dad had a saying—*everything changes*. For as long as I can remember, those words have been my father's default response to pretty much everything that happened in our lives. He used the words so much when I was a kid that it felt like a corny, meaningless catchphrase—but there was no denying that my dad genuinely believed in the sentiment. *Everything changes* was his consolation when things were rough. It was his reminder to stay humble when things were good.

And now, as I sit in the back of the car and the house gradually shrinks in the rearview mirror, those words cycle through my brain on a loop—a simple but unavoidable truth.

The years have been rough and they've been kind and they've been long and they've been short…but everything changes, and the best and brightest era of our family's life has drawn to a close.

Grace
October 4, 1957

My baby girl turns one today. For some people, a milestone like this is bittersweet. After all, a first birthday marks the shift from helpless infant to inquisitive toddler, and inquisitive toddler leads to precocious preschooler and so on and so forth until that helpless newborn is a fully fledged adult who must leave the nest. A first birthday marks proof positive that the innocent days of parenting a child are a finite resource.

I don't grieve the end of the babyhood era. I won't miss the milky scent of her forehead, or the intensity of her gaze on my face as I feed her in the small hours. I won't be one of those mothers who laments the passing of time or coos about being broody, dreaming of going back and beginning all over again. No, I celebrate the closing of this chapter because if history repeats itself, it means that my life will soon improve again. For the sake of my marriage and my sanity, this day really couldn't have come soon enough.

We didn't have the money for a gift, which I feel so sad about. I'm sure for my first birthday my parents lavished me with toys I would have been too young to understand or appreciate, but my daughter's childhood circumstances are very different. She's growing up in a modest house in a modest neighborhood. She shares a room with her sister because although they constantly wake each other up, there are only three bedrooms, so in a family of six, everyone has to share.

I grew up in a house so large my sister and I never had to be in the same room unless we wanted to. This baby is growing up in public housing where just scraping by is the norm, and when she makes friends, many of them will be used to birthdays where a cake is about the extent of the expense spared. I grew up in a place where fathers were bankers and lawyers and politicians, and mothers outsourced the cleaning and cake baking so they could spend their days at the salon. My mother was busy with her charity work and herself, and while she was very formal at times, I can't ever remember doubting her love for me. She was steady and dependable in both mood and temperament, strong and capable as a mother and a woman. She wore the titles of wife and mother as a crown, not as an oppressive yoke over her shoulders.

If I could change anything about the life I'm providing my daughter, it wouldn't be gifts on her birthday or a nicer house in a better street. No, if I could change just one thing about our circumstances, I'd choose to change the mother in her scenario. I'm grateful for all of my childhood comforts, but I'm most grateful for the steadfast dependability I saw in my mother, and I just cannot offer that kind of certainty to my children. They deserve a better mother than the one God or fate or providence bestowed upon them, but I am selfish enough that I've prayed not to change for them, but for the courage to walk away. Motherhood has left me feeling both helpless and worn, and I am trapped here by my fears and failures. Like the skin on my stomach after all of these pregnancies so close together, I feel as if I've been stretched far too thin to ever go back to the way I was meant to be.

It feels hopeless. I feel hopeless. But feelings, even loud feelings, lie sometimes, and I know that all too well after the past three years. Beth is one now, and history has proven that a first birthday in this family means the beginning of the end of the seemingly endless chaos in my mind and my soul. I've held on this long—by the skin of my teeth this time, perhaps, but I have managed to hold on and when the misery breaks, I'll be proud of myself for that.

Just a little while longer and I should start to feel human again. Warm emotion will gradually seep back into my soul and color will come back into my world. Silent tears will give way to genuine smiles. Sobs will *give way to laughter. Fear will give way to hope. Rage will give way to calm. The urge to lash out and hurt will once again become a compulsion to love. If I can dam up the chaos…if I can hold back the storm…if I can just keep my* grip *on this life for a little while longer, the sun will come out from behind the clouds and life can begin again.*

Happy birthday, my darling Beth.

May this year be the year life really begins for all of us.

TWO

Beth
1996

It's Sunday, and Sunday has always meant an open invitation for dinner at Dad's house. Once upon a time, Dad would cook a huge roast with all the trimmings, and he'd sit at the head of the table and remain the center of the conversation. Today Ruth's done the cooking, and for the first time ever, Dad isn't even here. He's been unsettled since the move last week, and the doctors have asked us not to take him out on day-leave until he's adjusted to the new arrangement. In his place at dinner to-night is a heavy, awkward grief. I suspect everyone else is trying just as hard as I am to be brave, but conversation has been through a series of violent starts and stops ever since we arrived. We just can't get the chatter to flow the way it usually does... the way it should. There's a sporadic throb in the center of my chest. My gaze is constantly drawn back to that empty chair at the head of the table.

"I'm just going to put something out there," Ruth says suddenly, breaking a silence that stretched long enough for us to devour the meal she'd prepared. "Dad gave me and Ellis the company. The rest of you should decide what to do with the house."

Jeremy arrived back from Indonesia this morning and he's unkempt, jet-lagged and cranky. He sighs impatiently and stands to slide a bottle of merlot out of the wine rack Dad built beside the sideboard. Jeremy and Ruth are twins, and even now in their forties, they are close enough to fight almost constantly. Dad used to say they were "just too alike," and I think there might be something in that.

"What?" Ruth prompts him, snarky and defensive.

"Stop trying to be a hero," Jeremy says impatiently. He rummages for a bottle opener, removes the cork, then starts filling glasses in silence. As he moves toward me, I set my hand over my glass, and he shrugs and continues around the table to Hunter. "Dad gave you the business because you're the only one of us who worked there. You built that company almost as much as he did over the past few decades."

"*Walsh Homes* is worth a lot of money, and it's not fair that I should get that *and* a cut of the house," Ruth says stiffly.

"Well, it's also not fair that we should have to watch you play the martyr now, then listen to you complain about how put out you are for the next forty years," Jeremy says abruptly. I've been aware all night that there's a storm brewing among my siblings. I can see it in their stiff language...hear it in the way they are raising their voices. They're all looking for a reason to fight to distract us all from the empty space at the head of the table. I don't want to watch them quarrel, but if this is the only way to break the silence, I'll sit back and let them go for it. "Whatever we're doing with this house, we're deciding it together."

"*Whatever* we're doing with it?" Tim interjects, surprised. "Jez, there's only *one* thing to do with it. We have to sell it."

"We could keep it and rent it out," Jeremy says, frowning.

"And if we do that, how exactly are we going to pay for Dad's health care?"

There's a significant cost for Dad's care at this nursing home—it's a beautifully plush facility, but it comes with a mind-boggling fee to match, and his insurance is going to cover less than half of it. The first bills will come due early next year...maybe even sooner if Dad passes in the meantime. Dad *was* reasonably well-off, but when he retired he handed ownership of the business over to Ruth, and in the five years since, his savings seem to have evaporated. It was quite a shock when Dad signed his power of attorney over to Tim earlier this year and we realized just how little he had left. We're still not entirely sure where all of his money went. It's something Tim's "going to look into when he gets some time," but I don't really blame him for putting that task off—it's a pointless endeavor. Wherever Dad put that money, it's not coming back.

"We'll all chip in for the fees." Jeremy shrugs. "Between the four of us, I'm sure we'll find a way to come up with the cash without selling this place."

Hunter and I exchange a glance. I guess we could come up with some money if we had to, but we'd probably have to remortgage our place to do it. He's a junior partner at a law firm over in Seattle and he makes a good salary, but six years of expensive fertility treatments and now six months without my income have left us without any savings.

"I just don't think Dad would want us to do that," Tim says.

"But you really think Dad would want us to sell the house he built with his own two hands?" Jeremy snaps.

"He built hundreds of houses over his lifetime," Tim snaps back.

"Oh, come on, Tim," Ruth sighs. "You know this one is different. This one is *ours*."

"So you'd have us hold on to it, but then install complete strangers in it?" Tim snorts. "Makes perfect sense."

"Beth? What do you think?" Jeremy asks, and all eyes around

the table turn to me. Ruth and I have arranged babysitters for our respective children—Noah is with Chiara again; Ruth's kids are with her au pair. Alicia is supposedly coming, but Tim says she's running late, and I think we all know that means she didn't want to come but didn't have the guts to admit that to him. But Ellis sits beside Ruth, and Hunter sits to my left. It's Hunter my gaze goes searching for, because I don't have the energy to buy into this debate, and I'm hoping if I deflect the attention to him, I won't have to.

"Are there legal considerations?" I ask him, my voice small.

"I haven't seen Patrick's will," Hunter says. "But generally, after he passes, the house would go to all four of you unless he's specified otherwise. And in the meantime, Tim has power of attorney, so it's up to him what happens to the house."

"I wouldn't do anything the others didn't agree to," Tim says, aghast at the suggestion. Hunter shrugs.

"I know that. I think we all know that, Tim. But the law is also clear on this—the final say is yours."

"Beth, I wasn't asking you to ask your husband for his professional legal opinion," Jeremy interjects impatiently. "I was asking you what *you* think."

"Jez?" Hunter says, and he lazily shifts his gaze from me to my brother. Jeremy raises an eyebrow at him. "You're being a dick tonight."

Jeremy opens his mouth to argue, but then closes it again abruptly.

"Okay. Maybe I am." There's a burst of quiet laughter from around the table before Jeremy sighs and admits, "I'll be honest. I just cannot stand the thought of losing our last ties to this place."

"We're not losing each other. We're not even losing Dad. It's just a house…simply an object. What's actually precious to you is the bonds the house represents, not the house itself," I say automatically.

"Well done, Jeremy. You've knocked Beth back into therapist mode," Ruth sighs, but then she flashes me a wink. I offer her a wan smile, then divert my gaze back to my plate. If only there really *was* a therapist mode. I'd love it if I could press a button and revert back to the competent professional I used to be.

"You still haven't told us what you want to do with the house, Beth," Tim murmurs. "What *do* you think?"

I think that I'm over this dinner and over this conversation, but I have been since we arrived, and Noah isn't even here so I don't have an excuse to leave early. My feelings are muted on all of this—which is confusing, because everyone else is frothing at the mouth about what we should do next. Tim obviously wants to sell, Jeremy and Ruth obviously don't, Hunter and Ellis will keep their opinions to themselves because although they are definitely part of the family, it's really up to the four of us.

I start to think it all through—what it will look like to prepare the house for sale or lease, the packing and the cleaning and freshening up the paint and fixing the garden. It's a big job. No, it's a *huge* job, and an awful one. It's a job that no one has time for, although one of us could, theoretically, make time. And one of us is most definitely stuck in an odd rut at the moment, so…

"We'll need to get the house ready either way," I say slowly. I skip my gaze around the table, but this time avoid my husband's eyes. "We can get help in for the painting and the gardening, but sorting through Dad's things is going to be the hardest part. Maybe I should take that on, since you're all so busy."

"Wait—aren't you going back to work soon?" Jeremy asks. I *knew* that lie was going to come back to bite me.

I clear my throat and say noncommittally, "Soon. But not quite yet."

"You can't do the whole house, Beth. That's not fair." Tim frowns.

"I…" I glance quickly around my siblings, then back to my plate as I shrug. "I'm the only one of us who can make time. And I kind of want to do this. For Dad."

"You'd have to let us all help around work," Ruth says. I glance up at her, and find she's staring at me. I don't like it. She's too sharp and it feels like she's looking through me. I pick up my fork and begin to push the food around on my plate, just so I can avoid her gaze. "And of course, when you need contractors, I can arrange them."

"Good," I say, still looking down.

"Are you sure, Beth?" Tim asks, very gently. I nod firmly then force a smile before I raise my gaze to look at him.

"Noah is five months old, guys. I'm ready for a project."

Now everyone is looking at me. I feel my cheeks heating.

"It's just...you're sure you're up to this, Beth?" Jeremy says eventually. The words drip with awkwardness, and I scowl at him.

"What? Of course I am." *Oh, God, please let me do this. I just want to feel useful again.* "I had a baby, Jez. I'm not the one with the terminal diagnosis here."

"Hunter?" my sister prompts carefully, and I gape at her.

"Seriously, Ruth? Did I time warp back to the 1950s? Did you *seriously* just ask my husband to give me permission to do something?"

"Of course she didn't," Hunter sighs. "Let's talk about this later."

"No, Hunter," I say flatly. "Let's talk about it now."

"Talk about it all you want, guys, but I'm too jet-lagged to watch you two battle it out tonight, so can you do it at home?" Jeremy interjects.

"Like you can talk," Tim snorts. "You're the one who's been picking fights all night."

"Jesus *Christ*," Ruth groans, rubbing her eyes wearily. "If this is how family dinners are going to be without Dad, can we just forget about the tradition altogether?"

The reminder of that empty chair is the slap in the face we all needed, and the squabbling stops immediately.

"Sorry," I whisper, after a while. Around the table there are echoes of *me, too*, except from Ellis. I'm pretty sure he's actually reading, because although he's still sitting with us, he's been silently staring at his lap for a long while now and every now and again I hear the faint rustle of pages. It wouldn't be the first time he's mentally checked out of a family function to disappear into a book, and I guess that's what Ruth gets for marrying a librarian.

"So the plan is that we clear out the house, tidy things up… then decide what to do with the property once it's all done?" Jeremy asks quietly.

"In the meantime, we can all think about whether or not we can chip in to cover Dad's health care bills," Tim suggests.

"Andrew's confirmation service is at St. Louise's next weekend," Ruth says suddenly, speaking about her eldest son. "Let's have one last family lunch here after Mass."

"We can bring Dad back for that, if he's ready for a day-leave by then," Jeremy says, and that reminds me…

"Ruth, you left me off the roster this week. When do you want me to go visit Dad?"

My sister stiffens again, then offers me a thin smile.

"I thought you might like a little break before you dive right into all that."

"What? Why?" I ask blankly. It was *deliberate*? That makes no sense at all. If the doctors are right, we don't have much time left with Dad. And even if they're wrong, I've seen how fast he's declining. God only knows what his condition will be in two weeks. Besides, Dad and I are incredibly close. He's going to notice if I don't go in to see him.

"We should get going," Hunter says quietly as he rises. "We said we'd pick Noah up from Mom's by nine."

"I want to go see Dad," I say stubbornly. No one says anything, and I sigh impatiently. "Look, I'm going in with or without your approval and I know you're all busy so you may as well swap."

"Go on Wednesday in Alicia's place," Tim says eventually. I

nod at him curtly, and then rise beside my husband. I glance at my sister again, and find she's staring at her wineglass.

"I'll start straightaway on the house, but I'll pack up this room last," I say with a frown. "In case he comes home for lunch with us next week, we should try to keep things nice and normal for him."

"It's settled, then," Ruth sighs, resigned. "You start the process, but promise me you'll call us for help when you need it."

"Fine."

I glance at Hunter, and I'm wholly unsurprised to see him staring into space, his face set in a grim mask.

"What are you thinking, Beth?"

We're on our way home. Hunter is driving, his face set in a stony mask as he stares ahead at the road. It's raining heavily, and now isn't the time for an argument because he needs to concentrate on driving. I keep my tone mild as I reply.

"It's just that someone has to get the house ready, that's all. The others are all so busy——"

"And so are you."

"Not really," I say. "Not compared to them." I pause, then can't help but frown as I ask, "And what was all of that about anyway? Since when does everyone treat me like I have leprosy?"

Hunter sighs heavily, then runs one hand through his hair. His hairline has just started to recede, something he's philosophical about. When we first noticed the hair loss eighteen months ago, we were in a very different place. I remember tentatively raising the issue as we were getting dressed in the bathroom one morning, and, shirtless, he'd flexed his muscles and told me not to worry, he'd still be just as irresistible once he was bald as a bowling ball. When I laughed, he chased me into the bedroom, his cheeks still covered in shaving cream, cornering me near the bed and kissing me playfully. I washed my face and reapplied my makeup but I smelled like his shaving cream all day, and between appointments with my clients, I'd pause to enjoy the scent and think about him.

"Are you feeling any better?" he asks me hesitantly.

"Better than what?" I scowl.

"Beth. You haven't been yourself for months, and whenever we ask if you're okay, you change the subject."

"We?" I repeat, eyebrows drawing down. "Who is this 'we'?"

"Me and Ruth. And the boys. Everyone can see it. Is it your dad?"

"Is *what* my dad? I just had a baby, Hunter. I'm allowed to be tired."

Hunter doesn't reply. Instead, he drives in silence for a while. Part of me wants to argue more, but I'm not sure I want to delve into this too deeply. I'm not myself, but I'm definitely not ready to explain to him where my mind is at. When we're a few blocks from home, he speaks again, so suddenly that I startle.

"I assume, since you're so keen to sort out your dad's house, you really think a project is going to help?"

"There's nothing to help," I sigh impatiently. "I'm fine. But I do want to do this for Dad and it's not a big deal. It needs to be done, and if someone doesn't take it on, the task will linger for months."

"I've been thinking that maybe you should see someone."

"See who?"

"See a psychologist, Beth," he says. I gape at him.

"Do you want to ruin my career?" I ask him incredulously.

"Do *you*?" he fires back.

"If the directors knew I was in therapy, I won't have a job to go back to."

"Come on, Beth. That's hardly—"

"That's the reality of it, Hunter!"

He pauses, and I think he's going to try to debate with me about whether or not there's a stigma around mental health professionals seeking mental health treatment. I'm getting ready to point out to him that he's a *lawyer*, and what would he know, but he draws in a sharp breath, then asks very quietly,

"So if your career wasn't a factor, you would talk to someone?"

The question catches me off guard, and I stare at him, momentarily unsure how to answer. My problem is my circumstances, not my thought processes. And maybe I'd love to talk through the tangled mess of worries I'm drowning in lately, but I just don't have the energy, and even if I did, I can't bear the thought of admitting aloud to another human being some of the stupid things that have been going through my head.

"No," I say stiffly. "You're wrong about this. I don't need therapy. I just need time."

There's a terse, awkward pause, then I relax as Hunter softens his tone and changes the subject again.

"So you're going to pack your father's house up this week? And next, I guess. It'll take a while."

"Yes, I think that's for the best."

"And are you taking Noah with you, or were you planning on asking my mom to babysit him for days on end?"

I turn to stare out the window, embarrassed that he's seen right through the reason I was so quick to volunteer for this arduous and painful job. I like it when Chiara takes Noah for a few hours. She's an amazing mother and she's incredibly comfortable with him—so much more capable than I am. I feel like he's safer with her, but there's no way I'm going to admit that to Hunter. Now it's my turn to fall silent, and I stare sullenly out the window, planning a hasty retreat into the bathroom as soon as we get home. I'm not much of a crier, but I feel pressure and heat behind my eyes, and maybe I do need to leak a few tears tonight.

When we pull into our driveway a few minutes later, Hunter reaches across and rests his hand on my forearm. I'm not sure the expression on my face won't entirely give me away, so I don't turn to face him.

"Just think about talking to someone, babe. It seems like you really don't feel like you can talk to me," he murmurs. I open my mouth to deny this, but then I close it again. Once upon a time, I had no filter when it came to Hunter. I'd share any thought that crossed my mind, and I'm pretty sure he felt the same way. There's no denying that's changed since Noah was born. Hunter's hand contracts around my arm, gently squeezing. "If you're worried about your clinic finding out, I'll help you find somewhere you can be anonymous. Whatever you need, we'll make it happen."

"I don't need therapy," I whisper insistently. "I know exactly what a therapist would say, and I can say those things to myself for free."

We sit in silence for a moment, and then Hunter asks, "Well… what would you say to yourself, then?"

"Time," I croak automatically, as, at last, I turn to face him. "I'd tell myself to just give it more time."

Hunter nods, kisses me on the cheek and leaves the car. As I swing open my door and step out, I force a brutal moment of internal honesty for the first time in months. I don't treat adult patients anymore but I did early in my career, and I can easily picture a client sitting in my office voicing my recent struggles. I see myself as an impartial third party, listening and mentally planning my response.

My gut drops when I finally admit what I'd actually say to that client.

It sounds like you're totally overwhelmed and out of your depth. It sounds like you're struggling with your dad's situation, but that's not the biggest issue you're battling. It sounds like you're actively looking for excuses to avoid your son, and you're not coping at all when you are alone with him. You're terrified that having Noah was a mistake you can't undo. Is avoidance really the solution here, though? Let's talk about other strategies you can employ.

On the porch Hunter and his mother embrace and then I see them talking quietly. As I step out of the car, Chiara flashes me a warm smile and a wave, and I wave back, fixing my brightest smile in return. I'm certain it's convincing, despite the fact that I've just dropped a mental bombshell on myself and my gut is churning. I'm so desperate to get behind that locked bathroom door it's all I can do to stop myself from sprinting for it. Luckily, the one thing I am quite good at these days is putting on my game face.

"Sweetheart," Chiara greets me as she takes me into her embrace and kisses both of my cheeks. "Hunter was just telling me you're going to pack up Patrick's house over the next few weeks. Of course I'll watch Noah for you."

Hunter is watching me closely. Is this some kind of trap? Even if it is, the offer is too enticing to refuse. So much for changing strategies from avoidance.

"Chiara, that would be amazing. Thank you so much."

Once Chiara is gone and Hunter and I are alone in our living room, I turn my gaze to him.

"I got the impression when we were in the car that you *didn't* want me to ask your mom to watch the baby while I'm at Dad's."

"You said you need time," Hunter says, cheeks coloring. "I told you, Beth. Whatever you need, I'll make it happen."

I guess if eleven years with Hunter should have taught me anything, it would be that he has my back at all times.

I just can't help but wonder if he'd still be Mr. Supportive if I told him the truth: that we spent half a decade trying to become parents, and after just five months, I'm convinced it was the biggest mistake of our lives.

Grace
November 2, 1957

I don't know what I intend to achieve with these little notes. The first time, I actually sat down to write a letter to Maryanne, just as I'd done so many times before. This time I was going to do something new: I was going to tell her the truth. I've painted such rosy pictures of our life here over the years, but in this new slump, I was determined to reach across the divide with something real...something raw.

The problem was that when my pen hit paper, I couldn't bear the thought of my sister knowing. *Even after all of this time and even after all of my failures, I'm still proud enough to want her to think I made the right choice in Patrick. I suppose that's why what came out of my pen that day was more like a letter to myself. I've decided it's for the best. I don't doubt that if Maryanne knew how bad things are for me, she'd blame him and him alone—she does so love to blame men for everything. In this case, she'd feel he's proven her right, because she tried so hard to warn me against this life.*

I chose Patrick anyway, and that decision has forced a distance between Maryanne and me that I've never figured out how to close. In some ways over the past few years, that distance has been a necessary evil. If she knew, she'd probably try to intervene, and I might not have much these days, but at least I have my pride. Plus, I love that Maryanne thinks I'm a good mother. I can't bear for her to know the truth.

Even so, I had the urge to write to her because although there have been so many things about the past few years that have been difficult, the isolation has been the hardest. The irony of course is that I haven't been truly alone in well over two years now, given I haven't had so much as an hour without some company since the twins were born. It's not even silence I crave. I'm starving simply to be present with someone who doesn't want something from me. I have reached the point where I don't fantasize about making love or relaxing or even sleeping anymore. Now I daydream about sitting down with someone who will listen to me—who will understand me. And, these notes have somehow tricked my brain into thinking I'd been heard by someone, at least for a little while, and I have been doing so much better. Ordinarily, it takes me a few months to rise out of the funk, but after I wrote those notes, something immediately felt a little lighter inside.

Until today, that is. This relapse hit without warning, and it took me back to my very darkest months. Ruth has a bit of a cold and kept waking up because her nose is blocked. I got even less sleep than usual, and maybe that's what triggered it. All I know is that I was buttering the toast for breakfast and Jeremy and Ruth were fighting and the noise rose all around me like a tidal wave until it took up too much air and suffocated me.

I asked the children to be quiet. I told them to be quiet. I shouted at them to be quiet. I shouted at them to stop. And then I screamed at them to shut up.

That's when the thoughts came back.

I looked at the knife in my hand and I pictured myself dragging it across the smooth white skin of my wrist. I imagined the dark red blood bubbling up and the silence rushing in. I don't know how long I stood there, but when those god-awful thoughts finally cleared from my mind, I was standing beside the table in front of my four babies, who were all sitting in terrible silence, staring at their breakfasts with the kind of desperate intensity that only comes from being completely petrified.

I didn't actually hurt myself this time. I've never done something as drastic as cutting my wrists, except for that one night when I—no. I don't think about that night; it's too dreadful and too hard. Instead, these *days when I feel this stretched, I have developed a coping mechanism, as awful as it may be. I sneak away to the bathroom and I scratch myself, as if breaking the surface of my skin will let all of the frustration bleed out. I always scratch beneath my clothing because I have no idea how I'd explain such a thing. It was bad enough when Patrick saw a mark on my breast and I had to lie and say that Beth had done it when I was feeding her. I was lucky that time, because it was just the smallest little thing. Other times I've scratched so hard and so long that my breasts and my belly have been speckled with blood and black-and-blue with bruises. Anything to let the frustration out. Anything to let the sadness out. Because if I bottle it up inside, it finds other ways to burst out of me…like that moment today in the kitchen.*

I hurt my children today—not with the knife, but with the threat of it. My frustration and irritability and this pervasive misery drowned me in that moment and I was hopelessly out of control. Even after all these years, I don't actually know what those moments are…the moments when I can't outrun the bad thoughts. I don't see images with my eyes, more with my mind, but they swamp me anyway. Are they hallucinations? Visions? Prophecies? Whatever those thoughts are, they are vivid and real and worst of all, they are stronger than I am.

I set the knife down on the cracked white vinyl of the table and I stepped away from it. I spoke to my children in a voice that had become artificially high with panic, and I called them "my darlings" because I always call them that when I'm well, and I gently ushered them out to play. Once they were all in the yard, I locked the back door and sank to the linoleum and curled up in a little ball—my back pressed heavily against the door as if the kids could push hard enough to break the lock.

They were fine out there at first, climbing the pear tree and riding their tricycles, but the hours went on and I just kept thinking about the knife and the frustration and their scared little faces, and I couldn't convince myself to get up. Soon, Beth was crying at the door because she was hungry again. My fear and my rage had faded, but a paralyzing guilt and numbness had taken their place. I stayed on the floor, and when I didn't answer their increasingly insistent knocks and calls, Tim climbed through a window, fetched some bread from the kitchen and ferried it out to his siblings. He's such a good boy. He deserves so much better than the life I give him.

What scared me wasn't the vision or my rage or the mood I was in. It was how unexpected the resurgence of the madness was. I've walked this journey before—twice before, and the end doesn't go like this. With my first two births, as soon as I felt better, I really was better—there was no sinking in and out of funks once the babies were toddlers and the darkness had cleared. So was this just a one-off bad day, or is it a sign that I'll never truly be able to trust in my stability, not ever again? How exactly is a person supposed to live if she can never trust in her sanity?

That's why I'm sitting down with this notepad tonight. I'm hoping and praying that once these thoughts are on paper, they will break the endless echo chamber of my own mind. Left to my own devices my thoughts get louder and louder and louder, until I can't eat or sleep or do anything except think.

I need to prevent the spiral that leads to the quicksand thoughts, because once I'm submerged, I don't know how to climb out.

THREE

Beth
1996

The next morning I park my car in Chiara and Wallace's driveway on Yarrow Point. A few years ago they sold the family home in Bellevue where Hunter and his brother, Rowan, grew up, and we all thought the plan was to downsize. Instead, they bought this place—two magnificent, opulent stories on the shores of Lake Washington.

I have no idea how long they'll live here—it's hardly the most practical house for an aging couple. The house is beautiful and glamorous, but it's certainly not child friendly. Rowan's girls are old enough to navigate the various hazards, old enough to stay away from the unfenced waterfront when they play in the backyard. It'll be years before Noah reaches that level of maturity—how will we keep him safe?

This is one of the many things I've been worrying about that I didn't yet need to worry about, and also, one of the many things

I've been worrying about over the past few months that *might* just be worked out in a two-minute conversation—if I could only motivate myself to start it.

"Good morning, you two!" Chiara calls as I let myself in with my key. Chiara's house always smells amazing—there's a lingering scent of vanilla and coffee in the air. She rises from her overstuffed leather chair to greet us, and my gaze skims over the roaring fire on the open hearth, and the steaming cup that sits on the edge of her coffee table.

Yep. Babyproofing this house is definitely going to be impossible.

"Hi, Chiara," I say as I sit the diaper bag down by the hall table. "Thanks again for doing this."

"It's nothing," she says, waving a hand toward me. Chiara retired a few years back and sold her restaurant, but Wallace will have left for work hours ago. He's a lawyer who works in Seattle just like Hunter, except Hunter works in family law at a very small firm, and Wallace is a partner at one of the big commercial firms...hence the multimillion-dollar home. "I love spending time with our little man. Did you bring milk?"

"There's enough for the whole day," I say, motioning toward the baby bag. Chiara looks from the bag to Noah in my arms, then offers a cautious smile.

"Beth, I just have to ask you. How on earth will you keep up with pumping milk if you're busy at your father's place all day?"

"I've managed fine so far when you've babysat in the past." I shrug.

"Yes, but that was only here and there... Hunter said you're planning on spending a lot of time at your dad's over the next few weeks. I'm just worried about you, sweetheart. You're making all of this so much harder than it has to be."

"It's just better this way. I've got the pump in the car. I'll just stop to express the milk while I'm at Dad's, then bring it here for you for the next day. It'll be easy."

"Not nearly as easy as just weaning him. He's five months old now. That's plenty long enough. *No one* breastfed back in my day, and look, your generation turned out just fine."

"I'll think about it," I say, even though I've already made up my mind. The *only* part of parenting I've mastered so far is breastfeeding. It's the one thing that's working, the only way to get Noah to sleep sometimes…the only reason I remember to *hold* him some days. The reality is, breastfeeding is providing all the structure to my parenting at the moment and I'm pretty sure if I remove that, the entire operation is going to collapse.

"But we could pick up a can of formula at the supermarket, and it will just make your life so much easier—"

"I said I'd think about it, Chiara. That's the best I can do." I cut her off, and her face falls. She closes her mouth delicately, then offers me a weak smile and motions to take Noah from my arms. I hand him over, then turn to leave.

"Aren't you going to say goodbye to your son?" Chiara prompts me, pointedly but not unkindly. I squeeze my eyes closed, take a deep breath, then turn back to her, smile fixed in place.

"Of course. Silly me. Goodbye, Noah," I say, then I brush a quick kiss on his forehead before I escape out the front door, into the safe silence of my car. As I reverse into the street, I don't look back. I know Chiara will be sitting by that fire, toasty and warm with Noah on her lap, staring down at him with adoration, cooing and talking and generally just loving on him.

When my friends meet Chiara, they inevitably tell me I've hit the mother-in-law jackpot. She's caught up in a passionate love affair with cooking so she's constantly preparing the most amazing food. Even so, she's humble about her culinary skills and is always enthusiastic at my own cooking attempts, even when I inevitably under or overcook the dish. Chiara is generous and gentle and kind, even if she can be just a little over-bearing sometimes. She's patient and sweet, and she seems to genuinely like me, which I find to be very strange, considering

I'm still not sure how I'm supposed to relate to the woman. Is your mother-in-law supposed to be a friend? Like a close aunt, if your aunts had a vested interest in your spouse? A parental figure...a second mother?

I think that last one is why I'm still so confused. While I hold a handful of precious memories of Grace Walsh, I hardly had the chance to *know* her. I do have a few memories of Dad's aunt Nina, who helped care for us for a few years after Grace died, but she was old and frail and distant—often caring for us with the help of one of the babysitters Dad hired.

I've never *really* had a mother figure, and if the dynamic that exists between Chiara and me is what a motherly relationship should feel like, it's bewilderingly alien to me, even after a decade.

In all those years Hunter and I spent desperately trying to achieve parenthood, I just wish we'd stopped even once to consider the possibility that a motherless woman might not know how to be a mother.

I stop off for some packing and cleaning supplies, then head straight to the house. I park in the drive, and as I begin to walk toward the front door, I take a trip down memory lane. I remember the way that Tim and Jeremy dumped their bikes on the path as they ran. I remember sitting on the steps with Ruth eating Popsicles late on hot July nights. I remember kissing Jason White, right on the stoop after our first date.

I remember opening the front door after that kiss, and finding Dad standing in the hallway, lurking just where he thought I wouldn't notice him. And when I ran to the toilet and threw up, he was right on my heels, making sure I was okay. I've always been a nervous vomiter. That night with Jason was probably one of the most terrifying nights of my life—he was the student council president, popular and handsome, creative and clever... And there I was—pale, quiet, *way* out of my depth. It was a great kiss as far as first kisses go, but it's not all that surprising that I lost my dinner afterward.

Dad and I sat in the kitchen after I emerged from the bathroom. He'd perfected a recipe for apple cake that summer, and every time we ate our way through a cake, he'd immediately whip up another. That was one of Dad's quirks—he wasn't the world's greatest cook, so when he got the hang of a dish, we'd eat it ad nauseam until he found a new recipe. That night he'd just finished baking, so the kitchen air was heavy with cinnamon and apple and I perched beside Dad at the breakfast bar for a talk. I nibbled at my cake and sipped the overly sweet tea he liked to make in times of crisis, and in his subtle way, Dad made sure I was okay. He was a man ahead of his time when it came to parenting. He made sure that Ruth and I understood that we were our own people—he taught us to stand up for ourselves and to make decisions that we could be proud of.

As I step into the house now, I open my mouth to call out to greet him—then I remember that he's gone. I feel that knowledge right in my chest—a dull ache that I know I'll have to adjust to because Dad isn't coming home, and the pain is going to get much, much worse before it gets better.

I walk along the hallway, peering into the rec room on the left, the study on the right, and then the massive, window-lined living area at the back of the house looms before me. It's as tidy as it always is. I can't ever remember seeing this space messy, except on Christmas mornings. Especially since Dad retired, he liked to run a tight ship. He baked his own bread, made his own beer, grew an extensive garden in the backyard…and everything always had a place, and everything was always *in* its place. Even this past year when language began to deteriorate, he only became more regimented—almost compulsive. On the one hand, that was going to make packing up the house a lot easier.

On the other hand, moving those things from their special place, putting them into boxes and giving them to charity or distributing them to my siblings…that is going to feel all kinds of wrong.

But it has to be done. So I make myself a hot cocoa, I set up some boxes and then begin the task of dismantling my childhood home.

It's not long before I have a plan in place to pack up Dad's house. I'll work through the bedrooms and the attic over the next few days, then deal with the living areas after Christmas.

I start with the main bathroom because it's the least nostalgic place in the house. I imagine the real estate listing as I clear out the extra shelves Dad installed over the years. *Unique and much loved family home on a quiet, leafy street. Five generously sized bedrooms and three large living areas. Generous storage. Actually, so much storage, it's bordering on ludicrous.*

In the end, I pack every movable item in that bathroom into boxes, and then marker in hand, I take a deep breath and write *Trash* on every single one. I have to be ruthless with this process, or my siblings and I are going to drown in needless memorabilia and maybe nostalgia, too.

One room down already, I decide I'll reward myself by wandering through the rest of the house and daydreaming a little. My bedroom was the closest to Dad's, probably because I was the youngest and likely still waking up at night when we moved in. There are posters of The Monkees curled and yellowed but still fixed to the wall, and the duvet cover on the bed is a ghastly orange, green and aqua pattern that I remember falling headlong in love with when I was fifteen. My shelves are all full of what I suspect will be intensely dusty books.

I wander into Ruth's old bedroom next. Her walls are bare—she was never one for obsessing over bands or movie stars. There aren't any books in Ruth's room—instead, there are half-finished wooden creations. Dad was nervous about a teenage girl taking on a carpentry apprenticeship in the seventies, but Ruth being Ruth there was no deterring her, and it turned out she didn't care one bit about being the only woman on the team for most of her career.

Jeremy's bedroom is by far the most chaotic. His shelves are lined with rocks and gemstones, and even a few vials of dust he'd deemed necessary to keep after research trips. Jeremy lived at home far longer than any of the rest of us because he commuted right up until he finished his undergraduate degree. He had no interest in supporting himself with a part-time job as the rest of us did during college. Instead, he was content to live with Dad for free and use the hour-long commute each way for reading time. Dad always said that if Jeremy hadn't fallen in love with science, he'd probably have wound up in jail. Jez had made something of a career of mischief until he belatedly found some ambition when he reached his sophomore year of high school. It's fair to say that the only discipline my brother has ever taken to is of the academic variety.

Tim's bedroom is going to be the easiest to clean out. Much like Tim himself, it's orderly and neat. He's the oldest, and he's always taken a somewhat parental role over the rest of us. I can remember him threatening to ground me when I was nine or ten because I hadn't taken my dirty clothes to the laundry room so he could wash them. My parents had us in quick succession, and Tim is only three years older than I am, but he always related to us as if he were the adult in the group.

I don't go into Dad's bedroom. I'm not ready to think about that room being empty. Instead, I head to the stairs that lead to the attic.

The massive attic was one of the most unique features of our family home. It was unfinished storage space when we moved in, but Dad converted it into a huge, usable room that runs the entire length and breadth of the house. There are peaked windows all along the walls, a high cathedral ceiling, and highly polished floorboards on the floor, dotted with several mismatched rugs that had been purchased over time in attempts to reduce the echo in the room. When he retired, Dad converted this space into his art studio, but as his heart function faded, so did his ability to walk up the stairs, and I'm pretty sure he hasn't painted in over a year. As I mount the final steps, I wonder if I should take some brushes and paints with me when I visit him tomorrow.

I put my hand on the doorknob and turn it, then bump into the door—completely caught off guard when it doesn't budge at all. I twist the handle hard, and push my shoulder against the door, but when this makes absolutely no difference, I look down at the lock and frown. This is a new handle—and it sports a seriously heavy-duty deadlock.

But why would he need to lock the attic? Dad must have installed this lock when he lived alone—otherwise we would have noticed. Was he locking himself in, or locking the world out? It was almost certainly during the period when we didn't realize he was developing dementia. I can't stand the thought that Dad might have been afraid of something and completely alone with that fear.

There's no avoiding Dad's bedroom now—it's the logical place to find the key. I wander back down the stairs to his room but I pause at the door, then take a deep breath and force myself to go inside.

Here, more than anywhere, I feel his absence. The room smells like Dad—his aftershave and deodorant linger in the air. This scent is warm hugs on sad days, and laughter over the breakfast bar, and suffering through the sheer boredom of the old black-and-white movie marathons he so loved to inflict upon us on rainy weekends.

Dad. Oh, God, Dad, how am I ever going to survive without you?

My sadness swells again, but I can't let it distract me—I have to focus on finding the key. Dad's furnishings have always been about function and comfort, with no consideration for style, and that's never been more evident than when I consider his bedroom. The dresser doesn't match the bed frame; the curtains are the tattered remains of a coarse, cream-and-brown gauze.

I pull the curtains open to let some sunshine in and turn to survey the room. Every surface is pristine; not a speck of dust can be found. I open drawers and find perfectly folded clothes, exactly in the right place, but I looked through these same drawers last week when I was packing for Dad and I didn't notice any loose keys. Then again, I wasn't actually looking for a key, so I'll have to search again.

My efforts become steadily more vigorous, but I'm trying not to make a mess, as if Dad might find me rifling through his things. After a while, though, the reality sinks in that Dad is likely never coming back to this room, and I begin to take clothes and objects out of drawers and shelves and to rest them haphazardly on his bed. When I've searched his entire room, I shift my attentions to the rest of the house.

Another hour passes, and now I've given up on keeping the place pristine and I've made a huge mess. I've tipped out drawers and dumped the contents of shelves onto the floor and benches. I'm frustrated, and when I finally concede defeat, I belatedly realize that I'm sweaty, dusty and exhausted. I pour a glass of water and walk to the phone to dial the first number I ever learned by heart.

"Walsh Homes," a chirpy voice on the other end says.

"Hello there, Janet, it's Beth. Is Ruth available?"

Predictably, I wait almost ten minutes for my sister to pick up. I'm important to Ruth...but everything is important to Ruth. She's become the kind of woman who habitually juggles an improbable number of balls, makes it look easy, and then unwittingly shames everyone who can't quite manage the same feats of endurance. School wasn't Ruth's forte, but everything else in life seems to be. Ruth is the perfect mother to three unruly sons, but to hear her speak about them, you'd think she was purposefully crafting them that way. Ruth has the world's most perfect husband in Ellis—a man who genuinely seems to live and breathe to make her dreams come true. Ruth has a magnificent family home, one that she designed herself, and then of course, she managed the building herself, too.

Even now, at almost forty, I sometimes feel like a miserable failure compared to Ruth. She has shiny, chestnut hair, beautiful amber eyes and a figure most women would die for. I've been breastfeeding for five months but I'm still somehow flat-chested, and my frizzy, dark brown hair has been even harder to tame since pregnancy. I have the most ordinary set of blue eyes that you've ever seen and my skin tone is either porcelain white or sunburned—there is no in-between. There isn't enough mascara in the world to give me decent eyelashes, while Ruth's have always seemed unnaturally thick, unnaturally long. Despite years of working on building sites with teams of less-than-sophisticated tradesmen, Ruth is still so *elegant* and capable. Worst of all, she has the audacity to be funny and kind, too. Except when she's reminding me how utterly busy she always is—and when she finally answers the call, that's exactly where the conversation begins.

"Beth, I'm so sorry it took me so long to get off that other call. It was a supplier who's been messing us around on roofing gear and honest to God, I just tore him a new one, so hopefully that's the end of that for now. Things are crazy here. Crazy! But seriously, I'm *so* glad you called. I've been trying to—"

"Ruth, take a breath, for goodness' sake…" I sigh, already exhausted by the call. I hear the sound of her sharp inhalation as if I'd deeply offended her, and I groan inwardly. Ruth and I have always been close and I love her more than just about anyone. At the moment, though, there's something about her too-perfect life that grates on me. It's possible that I've been avoiding her a little lately…but I really need help today, and Ruth has access to the resources I need.

"Of course, I'm sorry. What did you want?" She's speaking *too* slowly now. I appreciate the effort.

"Did you know Dad installed a lock on the attic door?" I ask quietly.

There is a pause, and then Ruth murmurs, "No, that's awfully strange."

"He must have done it ages ago, but we haven't had cause to go up there since he got sick."

"Are you sure it's a lock? The door's probably just jammed."

I stifle my impatience but can't quite manage to swallow my sarcasm.

"I'm not a carpenter, Ruth, but I do know what a lock looks like. Someone has installed a new doorknob and I can't find the key anywhere. Can someone come help me get in there?"

"I'll send some of the boys around tomorrow morning. That's really odd. How's the rest of the house? Have you got much packing done? Is everything else normal?"

"As normal as it could be, given the heart of the house is dying."

We sigh at the same time, and I know that at least when it comes to Dad, we feel exactly the same way.

At three o'clock the next morning, I find myself awake, sitting in the rocking chair in Noah's room. He's been up and down all night tonight. I know that my best shot at getting him back to sleep is a tummy full of milk, so as he fusses at my breast, I keep placing my nipple back in his mouth, hoping to convince him to drink. When he finally makes a halfhearted effort at latching on, I let my mind wander. The television is on but the sound is muted. Scenes from a romantic comedy play out before my eyes, but for the first time in a long time, my thoughts travel back in time.

I've long wished I could have known Grace Walsh. I've sometimes felt uncomfortable thinking of her as *Mom*, maybe because I never got to call her that. And for most of my life Dad fulfilled the role of *Mom* for me. I don't ever remember him being a stereotypically clueless single father. Perhaps the one exception was when Ruth got her first period, and the school called him to ask him to bring supplies. He panicked and instead he picked her up and took her to our family doctor, so that she could explain what was happening. He did much the same thing when I got my first serious boyfriend—leaving it to Dr. Lisa to talk to me about birth control.

Even so, my father did an excellent job of parenting us. As a result, until this year, I've been an exceedingly confident woman, never doubting my ability to navigate my world.

In fact, the only real struggle I've ever faced has been motherhood. It was a struggle to achieve, and now it's a struggle to master and in these small, dangerous hours when I'm alone with my thoughts, I can't help but wonder if any of this would have been easier if Grace Walsh were here to guide me. I hold a handful of precious memories of her—and particularly over the past few months since Noah was born, I replay them. Even the thought of those moments with her brings me comfort, and that's something I sorely need. I'm utterly exhausted, physically and mentally, yet I'm here, wide awake at 3:15 a.m. My failure to master this role feels so obvious and shameful that I'm sometimes confused why Hunter trusts me to care for Noah at all.

Right now I'm nursing a son that I can't even convince myself to look down at. I'm pretty sure no one has noticed that when I feed Noah, I shove my nipple into his little mouth and look away as quickly as I can.

It's so much easier to look away than to gaze down at him and come face-to-face with all of the ways my feelings for him just don't add up.

Grace
December 1, 1957

Patrick is late again. He said he'd be home right after work, but here I am, sitting at the dining room table waiting and wondering. I could go to bed, but why bother? I won't sleep—I never do on days like this. Mother and Father gave us the television set for a wedding gift, and when Patrick comes home late, I always leave it on. Even after the broadcast finishes for the day, the static comforts me. For all of their flaws, I do miss my parents since they stopped talking to us last year, and the television always reminds me of them. Maybe that's why mindless static is better than silence. Maybe that's why, when I try to cope with the quiet, I hear unbearable echoes of my loneliness.

It wasn't always like this. Patrick is a good man, deep down somewhere inside. Sometimes I glimpse that young boy I fell in love with… the boy he was five years ago, instead of the man he's never quite figured out how to be. Tonight, when my disappointment feels so immense, back then *is where I want to take my thoughts.*

When we first met, Patrick was an apprentice, helping his boss, Ewan, build the extension to Mother and Father's house at Medina. The house is beautiful and lush, but nevertheless, it was a sensible size when my grandparents built it—they had eight children so they needed a lot of room. Father eventually inherited the house and he and Mother moved in after their wedding, planning to fill the enormous residence with their own brood. Maryanne was born first, and then me two years later, but something went wrong during my birth and Mother had to have a hysterectomy. That meant the four of us were destined to rattle about in all of those rooms, and for my entire childhood, that's what we did.

After Maryanne left, the giant house seemed especially absurd, so I was utterly horrified by Father's decision to extend *the living areas and add on a rec room for a billiards table I knew we'd never use. He said we needed the additional space so he could entertain executives from the bank. I was convinced he was enlarging the house only because Mr. Nagy across the road had just added a bedroom and now our place was the second largest on the street.*

But not for long. Father's renovation would fix that right up.

At sixteen, I finished my last year of high school. It was summer vacation, so I was waiting around for secretarial college to begin—and that meant endless hours to spend with friends, or sit at home to read. God, I long for the blissful, eternal emptiness of those days. Did I really live that life? I did, and the worst thing is, I didn't even appreciate it at the time. I was too busy feeling paranoid, convinced the builders were quietly laughing at how ludicrous our extension was. I found myself sitting on the window seat in my bedroom, looking down on the contractors as they worked, assuming their bursts of sporadic laughter were directed at us.

I still remember the first time I saw Patrick. He was carrying a long beam of wood, and the sun was in his eyes so he was squinting. It was so hot that day, a patch of sweat had soaked right through the back of his shirt. He sat the beam down on the grass and then turned around to the rest of his team. But then he paused, raised his hand to shield his eyes from the sun, and to my shock, looked up. Our eyes locked, and he smiled. When Patrick Walsh smiles, the harsh angles of his face are transformed into something gentle and joyous and magnetic. Watching that transformation for the very first time, my stomach flipped, and my heart began to race.

That's all it took. Maybe it was just the intensity of my first taste of romance, but I truly believed I loved that boy right from that moment. Suddenly, even the patch of sweat on his shirt seemed alluring, as if his strength and his masculinity were seeping through his clothing.

Over the next few days, Patrick and I played a kind of game. I'd sit in the window and stare at him, and convince myself that I knew him, just on sight. I saw strength of character in the muscular set of his body, toned and taut from the physical labor commanded by his job. I saw attention to detail in the way he shaved his head so close around the back, but slicked the longer strands on top to the side with pomade. It's certainly true, even now, that Patrick is handsome, but it's also true that he can be ever so playful. He'd catch me staring and he'd give me that flirty smile and motion that I should come down and join him. But I couldn't possibly socialize with one of the contractors. *My father would have thrown a fit. So instead, I'd smile back and shake my head. But I didn't stop sitting in that window seat. And no matter how hard I tried, I couldn't stop staring down at him. It was as if I were drawn to him by some magnetic force too bold to be contained.*

On the fourth day, my parents were both out of the house and I was home alone. I was starting to think about creeping down the stairs... slipping into the kitchen for some ice-cold water and taking it out to him. But just as I decided to do this, I realized I hadn't seen him in a while. Had he finished his portion of the renovations? Was he going to disappear before we'd even exchanged a word?

Then I heard the creak of someone on the stairs. I dropped my book onto the floor, stumbling in my haste to see who was inside the house. And when I reached the door, there he was, right in my hallway. I was never going to invite him into my bedroom but I was frozen—too nervous to suggest we move downstairs and so we stood there, him in the hall, me in my doorway. We started to chat—well, he *started to chat, and I croaked out monosyllabic responses whenever my voice actually worked. His was exactly as I'd imagined it—manly and deep and smooth. He smiled that crooked smile, and his scent had filled the hallway...cologne and sweat and sunshine. Shivers raced all up and down my spine, and his proximity was almost too much. My entire education had been spent at the Catholic all-girls' school down the road. Most of my encounters with young men were at the bank Father manages, and those boys were refined and polished and probably more important,* utterly *terrified of me.*

Patrick was none of those things. He was confident, suave and bold, and when he said that his break was over and he had to return to work, I didn't want him to go. That's when he asked me to have a milkshake with him on the weekend.

I wonder what I'd do if I could go back and make that decision all over again. Would I rebel, and lie to my parents for the first time ever, telling them I was going to the pictures with my girlfriends but instead, meeting a boy? Or would I refuse, and retreat into the family life I'd always known? For all of his flaws, I know Patrick would have honored a refusal. I guess what might have been doesn't even matter now, because I did sneak out of the house. We shared a malted milkshake, and from that night on, he was mine and I was his.

FOUR

Beth
1996

Noah remains unsettled for the rest of the night, and so do I. Not just because I am suffering through the hell of a screaming baby waking me up every hour, but also because I can't sleep even when it's quiet.

I think about Grace for a while, replaying my memories of her, seeking the blissful comfort that sometimes steals over me when I bring her to mind. But tonight I'm too wound up for that, and I start thinking about the door and the attic, and what might be waiting for us upstairs. I consider innocuous possibilities: opening the door and finding Dad's art supplies neatly organized, or discovering he's packed up the studio and converted the attic into storage for his immense tool collection. I consider humorous possibilities: maybe there's a stash of adult material up there, or maybe he's converted the entire space into shelving "just in case" he needs it one day.

I briefly consider desperately dire possibilities, and for a while, panic actually claws at my throat and I have to get up to make a tea to distract myself. What if there's some evil side to Dad we never even suspected existed? What if I open that door tomorrow and there's something utterly sinister behind it?

I eventually convince myself that this is nonsense. The man who has been my guiding light for forty years has no skeletons in his closet...or attic, as the case may be. I refuse to even consider the possibility that he's ever been anything other than the incredible human being I know him to be.

So I cycle back again to wondering what else might be in there, and my mind is the needle on a record player, stuck in a groove, circling round and round, rehashing the same thoughts. I eventually fall into an uneasy sleep an hour or so before dawn, and wake when I hear Hunter turn the shower on.

I stumble through the morning with Noah, then when I drop him off at Chiara's house, she greets me with an announcement that she can't babysit all day, because Hunter's brother, Rowan, has asked her to attend his daughter's dance recital and it starts at four o'clock. This irritates me, and I *hate* my entitled, spoiled reaction, but I can't seem to shake it.

I'm frazzled and running late by the time I arrive at Dad's house, and then I'm quickly confused, because there's a *Walsh Homes* van at the curb, as expected, but my sister's BMW is also parked in the drive.

"Sorry!" I call as I step through into the hall. At the other end of the house I see Ruth in the dining room, sitting at the table, reading the newspaper. She looks amazing, her hair smoothed back into a flawless bun that would put a ballerina to shame, her black trousers and emerald-green *Walsh Homes* collared shirt are crisply ironed, her face carefully made up. It's entirely possible that my sister could have been a model if she'd chosen a life of fashion and makeup instead of sawdust and tradesmen.

"Sorry for what?" Ruth calls back. The click of her heels

against the floorboards echoes down the hallway as she walks across to the countertop. "Want a coffee?" I'm in the living room now, and she's already got a mug in hand by the time she asks the question, so it appears she thinks she already knows the answer.

"Tea, please." I'm still nervous to drink coffee, even when I'm exhausted. I'm desperately craving a jolt of "wakeup juice," but I'm equally sure the caffeine in my milk wouldn't be good for Noah. "I'm sorry I'm late. Did you have to let your workers in?"

"Well, yes. That, and I'm here to talk to you."

"Oh?"

Ruth gives me a wry look.

"Do you want the careful, diplomatic approach, or can I just be blunt?"

"Be blunt," I say stiffly, instantly on guard.

"Beth, you've been acting so weird lately. Everyone has noticed it, and frankly, we're all worried."

"I'm not really sure what you're talking about. I'm fine."

"You're *not* fine. What you are is withdrawn, cranky and defensive."

"I know you're no therapist," I say, after a pause. "But if you want someone to open up to you, generally the accepted practice would be to avoid starting the conversation by accusing them of being *cranky and defensive*."

Ruth laughs and turns back to the kettle as she says, "The thing is, *catch up with Beth* has been on my daily to-do list every single day since Noah was born, but I've been so busy with Dad and work and the boys…and to be honest, I kind of assumed you'd come to *me* if you needed to talk." It's obvious from the way her voice drops as she says this that she's hurt I haven't. I don't know how to explain to her that she's the last person on earth I could have talked to about my current situation—Ruth Turner, the very concept of The Perfect Mother, in human form. "So anyway, I just thought we'd have coffee and a chat while Gus and Harry bust past that monster lock Dad installed."

I dump my bag on the table and don't quite manage to hold back the sarcasm as I ask,

"So the door wasn't jammed?"

"Sorry," she says ruefully, glancing back at me as she makes my tea. "But you have to admit, it doesn't make much sense. Why on earth would he install a lock like that? It's a dead bolt designed for an external door. I'm a little nervous about what's in that attic now, to be honest."

"Me, too," I admit. "I was up half the night thinking about it." At least it was partly Dad's mystery attic that kept me awake. I've been sleeping less and less and the insomnia isn't always so easy to explain.

"How did we miss it, Beth?" Ruth sighs suddenly. I look at her in alarm, thinking she's referring to *me*, but then I realize she's still talking about Dad.

"I don't know," I admit. "I think we were so focused on the heart issue, we didn't realize there was another condition at play. We noticed he was different after his retirement, remember? You even asked me about it—you all did. I just thought it was him coming to terms with the changes in his physical health... adjusting to the new stage of life."

Dad founded *Walsh Homes* when he was a single father with four young children. He worked with his hands and built houses and eventually a business that supported our family in a comfortably middle-class lifestyle. Given that I'm struggling to keep my head above water with one kid, I just have no idea how he managed. He outsourced the cleaning every now and again and we had help from Aunt Nina and a part-time nanny until Tim was old enough to supervise us after school, but for the most part, Dad handled every aspect of our household on his own.

I hope he thinks it paid off. I never doubted that we'd made him proud, but lately I've been feeling so guilty. The result of all of Dad's nagging about school is four grown children with solid educations, two of us health professionals, yet not one of us smart enough or at least aware enough to notice that it wasn't just his heart that was failing; his mind was going, too.

"I feel so guilty," Ruth admits, her voice husky. "We took the kids to see him yesterday and he's completely lost. I just wish I'd pushed his doctor to do some more tests after the heart attack. I suspected something was up then. It was hard to put my finger on what was wrong."

The heart attack came out of nowhere. Dad was swinging a hammer with the team on a job site when he collapsed, and at first, it seemed he'd just need medication and some lifestyle changes. It soon became apparent though that his heart was damaged, and we were all in for a second fright because the cardiologist soon determined that Dad was in heart failure. Still, the doctor seemed optimistic that we had years and years left with Dad if he looked after himself. Dad had been cleared to go back to work and he seemed excited to do so. His sudden retirement came as yet another shock.

I still remember that day. I'd just arrived home from work to the phone ringing, and when I ran to pick it up, Ruth was sobbing on the other end. At first, I thought the worst—maybe another incident with Dad's heart...maybe a more serious heart attack this time. Instead, Ruth told me he'd given her the business and had decided to paint full-time.

"Paint?" I repeated. "As in, paint houses?"

"No, Beth. Paint. As in, paint abstracts or landscapes or... I don't know. Something like that."

"But... Dad doesn't paint."

"Well, apparently he does now."

Dad loved his job and he loved his company, and that's when we tried to talk him out of retiring, even Ruth, who stood to gain ownership of the family business. But Dad, he was adamant. He said he needed a quieter lifestyle, and that giving up work would mean less stress on his heart. This was what he needed for the next chapter of his life, and in the face of such determination and logic, who were we to argue? He'd certainly worked hard enough to be entitled to rest if that's what he wanted to do.

And it actually seemed Dad had been hiding an extraordinary talent. He'd never been trained in visual art, but soon he was prolific. He was painting all kinds of things—abstracts, portraits, landscapes—his talent seemed endless. Hunter even has a series of Dad's artwork on the walls at his law firm, a collection his boss commissioned. They are vivid and clever and layered. That commission seemed to represent the start of a whole new, if somewhat unlikely, career for Dad.

But the reality is, Dad's sudden interest in art was an early symptom of a neurological condition rather than a long-hidden talent, and it was just the start of his decline. Ruth's right—it *was* hard to identify exactly what was wrong, but his presence and his world just seemed to shrink. He slowly disconnected from his friends, and while he'd always liked to keep the house tidy, cleanliness gradually became an obsessive focus. I remember Jeremy telling me that when he'd come for a visit, before he'd even set his beer glass down after the last mouthful, Dad took it right out of his hand, washed it and put it away. Tim expressed concern about Dad's weight gain. Ruth was still confused about Dad's sudden retirement, convinced it wasn't an empowered, smart way to live out his later years, but a sign of an irrational impulsivity and an indication that something was drastically wrong.

I'm the psychologist in the family, so it was me they called when they were concerned, and I dutifully assured them Dad was fine. He'd gone from sixty-hour weeks at the helm of his own company to endless days with no set agenda. And Dad *was* facing a terminal diagnosis—despite the excellent chance he'd survive for years, the confirmation of his mortality was likely still playing on his mind. Of course these things were going to have a psychological impact. Of course he'd need some time to adjust. I tried to help my family focus on the positives, not the negatives. I even remember telling Hunter that it was nice to see Dad talking less and listening more now that his life had slowed down. Dad and I have always been particularly close, but after his retirement, he seemed to have endless time to listen to me, gazing at me with patient, quiet wisdom.

In hindsight, I was seeing what I wanted to see.

He started forgetting words, which was easy enough to ignore at first. It wasn't as if he wasn't communicating—he'd just pause midsentence and often ask, "What's that word again?" Or he'd wave his arms vaguely while he talked about the "thingy" or "you know, the whats-it." But it got worse and worse over time, and soon he was confusing nouns—saying chair when he meant table, tiger when he meant cat. But he seemed happy, so much so that he'd developed this adorably innocent laugh. It's hard to accept that someone might need some kind of additional medical intervention when they are utterly delighted by every aspect of life. And Dad really was so *smiley*...so quick to joy and laughter.

Then one Tuesday evening he came to visit me and Hunter. Five minutes after he left to go home, I opened the door and Dad was there on my doorstep again, overjoyed to see us, completely unaware that he'd only just said goodbye. When we explained that to him, he chuckled at himself and insisted he was just having a "senior moment." He didn't seem concerned about what happened...and he didn't seem embarrassed. But Hunter and I were nervous, and so we drove Dad home and then I called Tim. We made plans to get Dad over to Tim's hospital for a checkup later that week, but Dad's health crisis couldn't wait that long. The very next day, the straw house of explanations we'd built around Dad's personality changes collapsed entirely.

I was six months pregnant with Noah and I was having a bad day. I'd had a series of awful appointments with my clients—a child who was developing an eating disorder, then one who'd been abused by a parent, then one who was self-harming. Such a lineup wasn't unusual, but something felt off in the way I engaged with each child. I was already becoming uncomfortable as the pregnancy progressed and I knew I was increasingly distracted. I wasn't giving my patients my best—something I'd always prided myself on. I wondered if I should think about going on maternity leave early and I called Dad for his advice.

But when he picked up my call, I could hear that something was wrong. He wasn't calm or wise, he was confused—the pattern of his speech sounded fluent, but the way he was using the words made almost no sense. I wondered if he was having a stroke. I left work and went right to his house, but Dad was inexplicably beside himself, babbling and crying, and as hard as I tried, I couldn't calm him down.

I called Tim again, and he met us at the Overlake Medical Center. Tim broke all the rules that day—not just the speed limit, but by insisting that the staff at the hospital let him do Dad's cognitive assessment. By the time he'd finished, I knew Dad was in serious trouble. Even if my own training as a psychologist hadn't given me *just* enough understanding of neurology to interpret some of the results, the look on Tim's face would have said it all.

From there, it was days of more formal testing before the consultant neurologist sat us down and confirmed what we'd finally figured out for ourselves. The dad we knew and loved was already leaving us, brain cell by brain cell. His language skills were in significant decline, and what I'd thought of as patient listening was actually Dad disconnecting from our conversations. What we'd thought of as him becoming house proud was actually obsessive behavior. That stubborn change in his diet was a symptom, too, and we soon came to suspect he'd been existing on that one roast meal with us for Sunday dinner, supplemented by endless caramel ice cream over the rest of the week—his freezer full of dozens of tubs of the same brand and flavor.

Even the overnight emergence of artistic skill was no late-life crisis brought on by the heart attack. It turns out that sudden visual artistry is a recognized symptom of his particular type of dementia—and this particular type of dementia is known to happen sometimes in patients suffering heart failure.

We'd all missed it, even as Dad walked through years of decline alone, right in front of our eyes.

"I should have listened to you guys," I say suddenly. "I shouldn't have been so quick to justify the changes in his behavior—" I trail off at the sound of footsteps in the hallway. Two young men appear, one carrying a toolbox.

"Excuse me, Ruth," the taller of the two says. "The door is off." He shifts, then scratches his neck and stares at the floor. "So is there anything else?"

Ruth sits up straight and clears her throat.

"No, thanks, Harry," she says, then she nods. "I'll see you boys back at the office."

We sit in silence until the front door closes behind them, then I stand.

"Let's go check out—"

"Just wait a second first, Beth," Ruth says, her voice coolly professional. I bristle a little, but remain standing. I was very much hoping to avoid the intervention Ruth seemed to be building up to, and as awful as the detour was, I was relieved to focus on Dad's illness for a few minutes, instead of letting her focus on *me*. But she gives me a pointed look, and I know distracting her isn't going to be easy.

"Aren't you curious?" I ask, giving it one last shot. I even go as far as to take a step away from the table and add, "I'm dying to see what's up there."

"Of course I am, but it can wait a few minutes." When I don't move, she gives me an exasperated look and points to the chair. I guess lifelong training at the hands of a bossy older sister has left me with some ingrained habits, because I sit heavily. "*What is going on with you? Are things okay with you and Hunter?*"

"Everything is fine," I say impatiently, and I motion toward the hallway. "Let's—"

"Is it Noah, then?"

I shake my head, and give her a desperate look.

"Don't you remember what it's like with a newborn? I hardly sleep, I'm basically a walking milk machine. It's hard. It's *supposed* to be hard."

"Sure," she says, shrugging. "It's hard, and I had days here and there with each kid when I felt like it was too hard. But I didn't disconnect from you, did I?"

"I haven't disconnected from you." It's a complete lie, and an unconvincing one at that.

"It's like you're here, but you're not really *here*," Ruth murmurs. "You come to family dinners, but you don't say much, and you're dragging Hunter out the door as soon as we finish eating. You've been doing more than your share of the heavy lifting with Dad, but as soon as anyone else arrives to help, you leave. Jesus, Beth. You even left Noah's baptism early."

"Well, he was crying—"

"And Chiara and half of her family and Tim and Ellis and I, and Fleur and Jez and even damned Alicia all offered to help you, but you wouldn't let us. It was like you were looking for an excuse to leave."

I scowl at her.

"Come on, Ruth. It wasn't like that. It was hot that day and he was miserable. We had to get home so he could sleep."

"Chiara locked herself in her bedroom and cried for an hour after you left. You hurt her."

"Well, that certainly wasn't our intention—"

"Stop talking about that day like Hunter wanted to leave," Ruth interrupts, exasperated. "He was trying to talk you into staying right up until you snatched Noah up and put him in the car. Hunter left with you, but only because you gave him no choice."

I pause, frowning as I try to remember.

"That's not how it was at all."

"That's *exactly* how it was, Beth." Ruth doesn't exaggerate, and I can see she's telling the truth. I remember feeling so removed from the festivities that day, watching myself through a thick pane of glass, so tired and frustrated I could barely force myself to sit through the ceremony at the church. "And what's really happening with your job?" she adds now, apparently not done yet. When I'm feeling better, I'm going to give my sister a few tips on how to guide someone through a psychologically difficult time, because she's really making a mess of this intervention. The last thing I want to do right now is open up because with every second that passes, I feel more attacked. "You told me you were taking another six months unpaid leave. You told Jeremy you're going back anytime now. And Tim said he asked you last week and you changed the subject. Is there a problem at the clinic?"

"I thought this was a welfare check, Ruth. I didn't realize it was an interrogation," I say defensively, and I rise again. The last thing I want to do is admit to Wonder Woman that I've put off my return to work not because I want to, but because I don't trust myself with the welfare of innocent children right now.

"Just answer one question," Ruth asks, pulling back all of the accusation in her tone and speaking to me very gently. "Yes, this stage of life is hard. And yes, it's tiring. But it shouldn't break you. It *can't* break you, because I know you're used to being responsible for other people's welfare at work, but what you're doing now is literally the most important role you'll ever take on. Are you coping okay?"

One day Noah was screaming and I couldn't bear the way the sound pierced my ears. It grated and grated and I suddenly realized I couldn't bear it for another second. I walked out the door and down to the coffee shop on the corner of our street. I zoned out completely—I'd actually ordered a latte before I even realized what I'd done. I ran home and sat next to his crib but I still couldn't convince myself to pick him up and comfort him. He cried himself to sleep. I sat on the floor beside him and I sobbed for hours. I still can't explain what actually happened that day and I'm too scared to talk about it because I don't want everyone to panic.

"I'm *fine*," I say, and when she opens her mouth to talk again, I lean back to snatch my teacup from the table and head toward the hallway. "Honestly, Ruth, you're being ridiculous. Come on, let's go see what's in this attic."

Ruth sighs and rises. As she follows me along the hallway toward the staircase, she murmurs, "It was hard for me at first. I missed having a mom so much. There was no one around to ask for advice and I had to figure it all out for myself and it felt so *lonely*. If you're feeling like that, I really want you to remember that you've got me, and you've got Chiara. You've even got Elena and Harriet. I *know* they'd be happy to be there for you if you let them."

Elena and Harriet are friends from college, with six kids between them. But just like Ruth, Elena and Harriet had babies and made it look easy. God, I remember Elena putting off her return to work for an extra six months not because she didn't think she could cope but because she was *enjoying* motherhood so much she couldn't bear to be away from her kid. Sure, they might have practical experience, and maybe they could offer me advice about diapers or pacifiers or feeding, but that's not actually the kind of advice I need right now.

What do you do if you find yourself as a new mom and you realize you're just not capable?

"Maybe I'm just finding my footing," I blurt. Ruth frowns. "I just mean, I still don't know what I'm doing. When does it start to feel natural?"

"What on earth are you talking about?" Ruth says, blinking at me. "He's five months old. You're already doing everything you need to be at this point. Feed, change, play, cuddle. That's it."

"I know, I just..." She's looking at me as if I've suddenly grown a second head and if I could go back in time a few seconds, I'd have kept my mouth shut. *This* is why I haven't talked to anyone about this. I knew they'd look at me like Ruth is looking at me now—as if it doesn't make any sense, and that's a perfectly reasonable response, because the way I've been feeling *doesn't* make sense. I straighten my chin and try to backtrack as much as I can. "If I seem stressed, it's just because my life is so different now. I'm still adjusting."

Ruth doesn't seem convinced. She touches my elbow gently, trying to stop me as we walk toward the staircase.

"Are you *sure*—" she murmurs, and I flash her a look.

"You asked. I told you I'm fine, just getting used to things. You need to drop this," I say flatly. Ruth sighs again and opens her hands in surrender, and we continue down the hallway in silence.

Grace
December 5, 1957

It was so much easier for Patrick and me to meet once I started secretarial college. I had a newly minted driver's license but was anxious driving in the city, so I caught a series of buses to get to my campus. The buses could be unreliable, and sometimes I'd be studying late…at least, that was the story my parents heard. In reality, I was always finished by four o'clock, and the buses ran like clockwork. But Patrick finished work at four during the winter when the days were short, and we'd sneak a precious hour together before he dropped me off at the corner so my parents had no way of knowing I hadn't taken the bus.

In the same way that I now obsess over the dark thoughts that swirl through my mind, I once obsessed over all there was to love about Patrick. He was attentive and affectionate and kind, and flirty and fun and cheeky in the best kind of way. Sneaking around only added to the fun of it, at least at first. My sister, Maryanne, was a defiant child, always reveling in the opportunity to do the unexpected, but I was the exact opposite, quiet and compliant, determined to please and to obey. Certainly part of the allure of Patrick Walsh was that being with him was my first rebellion—and the danger was delicious. Perhaps that's also why I didn't even tell Maryanne about my secret relationship. I knew she'd understand my desire to rebel, but I was also quite certain that my bookish, fiercely independent big sister wouldn't have a clue about how it felt to tumble headlong into love, and I couldn't bear her disapproval. We spoke on the phone every few weeks over that first year and I didn't say Patrick's name to her once.

But soon enough, my year at the secretarial college was coming to an end, and my father talked about a phone operator position at the bank. I didn't mind the idea of a job with Father, but there was another possibility that seemed even better: marrying Patrick. I knew it was either the job or the wedding, because Father's bank operates under the marriage bar, and once a girl is married, her employment is terminated.

It was another crossroads, I suppose—another moment when I could have walked away, another opportunity to correct my course. Instead, Patrick and I decided it was time to come out from under our cloak of secrecy. I invited him to join us for Mass, and then afterward as we mingled on the church front lawn, I introduced him to my parents as a friend. Patrick didn't go to our church normally—he sporadically attended Mass in downtown Seattle, near the apartment he shared with two work friends. But ours is a very large congregation, and my parents had no idea that he wasn't a regular attendee. We tried to ease them in gently—Patrick attended the same service as my parents and me for a few weeks, and then one Sunday I quietly mentioned to my parents that he'd asked me out on a date.

Father just grunted. Mother reacted with shock.

"But... Grace! Do you even know who his people are?"

"He's an orphan, Mother. His aunt Nina raised him, but she lives in Bellevue and doesn't see him often. He's all alone in this world."

I hoped that would endear Patrick to them, and that some sense of sympathy might soften the coming blow, because I knew what Father's next question would be. I was totally unsurprised when he asked, "And what does this boy do for work, Grace?"

Any lie would be revealed eventually, so I had to tell the truth. I felt sick as I said it, because I knew that we'd reached the point where my loyalties would be tested.

"You're not dating a contractor," Father said as if that settled the matter. He caught my eye and sighed. "Just think about it, Gracie. He likely *only asked you out because he knows that we have means. It's best that you don't see him again."*

I'd rarely argued with my parents over the seventeen years that preceded that Sunday, but for the week that followed, I found myself making up for lost time. Every time Patrick came up in conversation, Father would go red in the face, and Mother would reach for her pills or glass of wine as if we were stressing her beyond what she could bear. Sometimes when Father was at work, she'd sit me down to try to convince me of the error of my ways.

You don't want to tie yourself to a man with low ambition, Grace.

Date if you must, but be sure to choose boys from our neighborhood. Or what about one of the boys from the bank? Perhaps once you start your new job you'll meet someone nice there.

Gracie, darling, just think about it some more. I mean, what kind of life could he even offer you?

I'd thought about it plenty. My head was full of dreams about the life Patrick and I might share, and I was determined to reach for it. A few days later Patrick arrived unannounced with his hat tucked against his chest. Father slammed the door in his face. But the more vocal my parents became, the more I convinced myself that to choose anything but Patrick would be to betray the very love of my life. I walked out of their lavish home for the last time that night and went to stay with one of my college friends.

For the first few nights I felt brave and bold. That wore off quickly, and soon I found myself feeling miserable and lonely in my friends' guest room. I wrote to Maryanne and told her what was happening, and of course, invited her to come for the wedding. In my heart of hearts, I knew she'd disapprove, but I felt so lost, and I had hoped she'd surprise me and I might be consoled by her support. When her letter came, her disapproval was every bit as vehement as our parents' had been—but Maryanne didn't care about the specifics of Patrick's situation. She'd have begged me to reconsider even if I'd been marrying a prince.

Grace, you're being wildly impulsive and you're going to sorely regret it. Put aside these foolish thoughts of marriage, especially at your age! What you need to do is to reach for a better life, and I'll help you do just that. You must cancel the wedding for now, and instead, catch a train down here and clear your head. Who knows? You might even want to enroll in college once you see what the lifestyle is like. You're a bright girl. You could handle the coursework— and imagine the fun we'd have! Otherwise, what are you signing up for? A life of laundry and housework? You are meant for so much more. Do not let the haze of young love ruin your future, Grace. Perhaps this boy gives you butter- flies, but if you stop for a minute and think about it, I'm sure you'll agree that a few butterflies are no compensa- tion for the ability to direct your own future.

The scornful, arrogant way my sister spoke of marriage and house- wives and "uneducated women" always confused me, but when I read that letter, I realized just how different Maryanne and I really were.

Our ideological differences always existed in the space between us—but they were impersonal, vague. Now Maryanne's inexplicable dislike of all things traditional had a face and a name. Her scorn was directed at the love of my life, and by extension, at me. For my sister, a union between me and Patrick was a tragic ending. To me, it was an exciting beginning.

A fracture appeared in my relationship with Maryanne for the very first time. She'd been living in California for several years but I still considered us close—yet her harsh letter damaged us in a way that even geographical distance had failed to do. I wanted so desperately for her to be happy for me and to understand that I wasn't; I was actively achieving the life I wanted. I wrote her back, my pen strokes hard, my words unwavering.

This is my life, Maryanne. You do not have the exclusive right to make your own decisions regardless of what others think. Whether you and Mother and Father like it or not, I will marry Patrick next month, and I'll be happy, even if my choice costs me my family.

Patrick and I had booked the beautiful St. Joseph's Church on Capitol Hill. I steeled myself as the day approached—lonely and sad, but even so, determined to marry the love of my life with or without my family. But the day before the ceremony, Maryanne appeared on my doorstep, fresh off the train from UC Berkeley. She held my upper arms in her hands and she stared at me.

"You're sure this is what you want?"

"It is."

"Then tell me how I can help."

"You're here," I said, and then I burst into tears and embraced her. "That's enough."

Despite her last-minute arrival, Maryanne stood as my bridesmaid, and she was such a picture in that powder-blue dress that I couldn't help but feel sad that she'd never be a bride herself. As I followed her down the aisle, I was startled to find my parents sitting right there in the front row. I'd sent them an invitation, although never in my wildest dreams did I expect them to attend. Only later would I discover that their quick change of heart hadn't exactly been spontaneous—rather, Maryanne all but bullied Father into reconsidering his stance. I rarely understand my sister, but I can't help but admire her moxie.

Patrick and I couldn't afford a reception dinner, but Ewan's wife, Jean, made us a cake for morning tea afterward. We cut the cake in the church vestibule and basked in the congratulations of my friends from secretarial college and Patrick's colleagues. Aunt Nina surprised us with an envelope stuffed with crumpled notes—later we discovered it amounted to several hundred dollars—a fortune by Patrick's standards. Mother asked us to join her out at the car, and that's when she gave us the television. It was a shocking act of reconciliation. That gesture was almost as important to me as the ceremony itself—an acknowledgment that although Patrick wasn't the husband they'd hoped I'd find, they still supported my decision.

I pictured Patrick and me in a humble but beautiful home, building a humble but beautiful life. In the end Patrick's salary wasn't nearly enough for us to rent anything, and it didn't seem right for us to continue to live with his apprentice friends now that we were married. We were lucky, though—a public housing apartment in Yesler Terrace became available and because Patrick's apprentice salary was so low, we were eligible. When we picked up our keys, the super dropped some none-too-subtle hints about how handy Patrick's building skills would be, given the apartment had housed some less-than-respectable tenants and was in dire need of love and care. Patrick, my smooth, charming new husband, was only too happy to promise to fix it all up, given that we were so very lucky to get it in the first place.

Initially, Patrick did seem to delight in showing off his skills. We had that wad of cash from Aunt Nina and no idea what to do with it. I wanted to put it in the bank, but Patrick felt it would be wiser to have it safely on hand, so he spent weeks building a heavy wooden chest to serve as a coffee table for our living room, then proudly showed me the hidden compartment he built into the bottom. But his energy for at-home construction and maintenance quickly waned—and that easy access to the money was probably the worst decision we ever made, because it all evaporated, right along with Patrick's desire to work around the house.

Four years later I'm still waiting for him to make those repairs he promised. This apartment is only a little larger than my bedroom was back at my parents' house—three small bedrooms, the world's smallest, dampest kitchen, a living area, an enclosed veranda and a roof that leaks when it rains. For the first three months we slept on a mattress on the floor in the living area because it was winter and that's where the heater happened to be.

Mother called every few weeks, and we'd share a stiff, slightly awkward catch-up. Maryanne called sometimes, too, and sometimes she wrote. But despite her efforts, something had changed between us, and that became more obvious with every stilted conversation. Our chats were no longer smooth, and the connection between us no longer reliable. When the gap between her calls and letters began to grow, I was both disappointed and resigned. Perhaps it was inevitable that at this adult stage of my life, my sister would play a less vital role.

But despite the challenges, those early months of marriage were bliss anyway. Patrick and I were in love and building a life together. I looked after the house, and Patrick worked, and we spent our evenings and our weekends enjoying one another. Life was good. And it seemed even better when I realized that my time of the month hadn't arrived for some weeks.

We were pregnant with our first baby, and everything was going pretty much according to plan.

FIVE

Beth
1996

By the time we reach the top of the stairwell, Ruth has over-taken me. I'm uncomfortable after the confrontation, so I let her take the lead, mainly so I can compose myself before she realizes how on edge our chat has left me. I'm so caught up in my head, I've almost forgotten where we're headed and why... until Ruth reaches the top and lets out a horrified squeak. The door is resting against the wall at the top of the stairwell, and behind it, chaos waits.

I stand at her side as we take in the attic space. What was once a pristine studio is now a tableau of utter madness. Overflow-ing cardboard boxes are stacked almost to the roof in places, surrounded by heaping baskets and piles of papers and candy wrappers and discarded items of clothing, dirty bowls and soda cans, and half-built shelves upon half-built shelves. It's a massive space—big enough that when we were kids, we could rough-house and run around with our friends and it never felt cramped or crowded. Now this room is full to bursting. There's so much junk up here that Ruth and I can't even step into the room. Random junk is stacked or dumped or dropped at least waist height on every single square inch of space. I know there are floorboards and rugs under there somewhere, but I can't see even a sliver of either.

There's a bewilderingly confused scent hanging heavily in the air. It's stale food and mold and paint and dust, and as it registers, I cover my nose and mouth as if that will help. When I glance at Ruth, she's white as a ghost, also holding her nose. The sight of the messed up attic is upsetting, but watching Ruth react is almost worse. I can't remember the last time I saw her cry, but right now there's a definite shine in her eyes.

I look back to the piles of trash, skimming my gaze over it all, trying to understand. At first glance, the only objects in the attic that don't appear to be trash are the paintings. Some are colorful, and some are dark. Some feature color palettes which seem completely random—jarring clashes of color without rhyme or reason. Some are done in acrylics, others are watercolors; one is a mosaic of tiny cubes that I suspect are tile. Some are simply lying flat on the other junk, some mounted on the walls; one is on an easel. They are differing sizes and shapes—most are rectangular, but two are square.

My sister fumbles for my hand and squeezes it, hard. "Jesus Christ, Beth. What *is* this?"

"I don't know," I whisper back. It's like we're both afraid to raise our voices, in case we stir up more trouble in this once-innocent space. Maybe there's even some logic in that. "There's got to be mice up here. Maybe even rats. Or snakes. Or all three."

"There might be some mice," Ruth concedes, tentatively tipping a box over with the tip of her shoe. "But probably not snakes. I mean, they'd be hibernating at this time of year anyway. Right?"

"Yeah. Hibernating in this vast sea of undisturbed trash," I shudder.

"We'll soon know. If there are droppings…" We pause, stare at each other, and then faux-gag. My sister and I will merrily deal with even the most menacing spider, but we both *hate* snakes with a passion. "I can't let you pack this up on your own. I'd never forgive myself."

"I'm not really giving you a choice," I mutter, wrapping my arms around my waist. "I have time, you don't. It's simple."

"Are you really going to bring Noah here while you clean this up?"

"Chiara offered to watch him."

"This will take days." She puffs out a breath of air. "Hell, Beth. It might even take weeks."

I shrug, and Ruth sighs.

"At least let me get a dumpster. No, we'll need at least two, and we'll put them on the lawn out in front. And I'll get some laborers to help ferry the trash downstairs."

"Let me sort through it first," I sigh, gingerly kicking a box right side up with the very tip of my shoe. Beneath it I find an unopened packet of paintbrushes and a moldy coffee cup. "Who knows what family mementos are lost among this chaos?"

"It looks like Dad used this as a trash room," Ruth says. "I have a feeling you won't find anything of value up here. You know what Dad was like. He was so *precise* with the things he loved."

"Maybe. I'll start sorting through it, and if it is all just trash, I'll call you for help."

"What do you make of the artwork?" she asks.

"Maybe he was trying to perfect an idea he could see in his mind."

"Is it a letter? Half of the letter B?"

I tilt my head to stare at the nearest canvas, then shake my head. "Oh, I see what you mean. I don't think so—why would he paint the curves of a letter like that?"

"Well, what do you see?"

"I didn't see anything at first—just abstract paintings. Now that you've pointed it out, though, I do see that they all have something in common." I skim my gaze around the paintings, squinting at them. "They're all so different, but every one does feature a similar shape. It's like a little curve, then a big curve right beneath it, right?"

"I see why you're not an art critic," Ruth laughs softly. "I meant how do you interpret it?"

I stare around the room and think about it in the context of the house, then I wrap my arms around myself, feeling suddenly chilled.

"I honestly have no idea what—if anything—the paintings represent. But I suspect that Dad was deeply ashamed of what he's left up here—that's the only explanation for the lock. And if you think about what he left on display—how pristine the rest of the house always was, it kind of makes sense that he'd lock away *this* mess." I hesitate, then suggest, "It's like we're seeing inside his head, if you know what I mean. He managed to hide the problems he was having for *so* long, until he just couldn't hide them anymore. This attic is kind of the same."

"Maybe this is where his savings went," Ruth says suddenly. "I don't know how expensive art supplies are, but surely this junk represents a lot of wasted money."

"Maybe that's part of the puzzle," I sigh. "But Tim said there's hundreds of thousands of dollars missing—pretty much all of Dad's retirement savings. There's not that much paint up here."

Ruth shakes her head slowly.

"Sometimes I feel like I can't bear to watch Dad fade away. It's almost too much to bear, but at the same time there's just no way to escape it, because the signs of his illness are everywhere now." She suddenly, furiously kicks an empty soda bottle.

It flies across the room and hits an exposed beam, then drops and disappears into the mess below. "Even in the damned attic."

I disentangle my arms so that I can link my elbow through hers, and rest my head on her shoulder.

"I know, Ruthie. I know exactly what you mean."

In this pain, I can connect with her. This is our family's tragedy, and we each play a part in the suffering. By sharing it, we can survive it, because we subconsciously remind one another that one day soon, this will end, and we'll still be standing side by side. Dad will be at peace, and Ruth and I—and Jeremy and Tim—will all still have each other. We are his legacy, and despite the tragedy of his current circumstances, that's actually a pretty spectacular thing to have in common.

But just like Dad's locked attic, there's a whole other world inside my mind that I have to keep separate from Ruth at the moment. I can't bear to talk about what's going on in the quiet moments when I'm alone, or worse, when I'm alone with my son. I don't have the language because I haven't made *sense* of it myself.

If Ruth wants to support me through that world of pain, she'll have to be patient with me…just as I'm trying to be.

Grace
December 15, 1957

I used to think every woman was born to be a mother. I thought the first time I held my child would be a moment of perfect clarity and purpose. This wasn't a one-off moment of romanticism from a girl too young to know better—no, I was expecting that swell of meaning and beauty right up until they lifted my bloody, screaming son from between my legs and rested him on my breast. After twenty-eight hours of back labor, a roughshod episiotomy and a less-than-sympathetic obstetrician who was irritated to miss a golf date, I was ready to stare down at my baby's little face to be reassured that it had all been worth it.

So you can imagine my surprise when I looked down at Timothy's perfect features and felt nothing but relief that it was all over.

Labor seems like an ending, the full stop on the sentence of nine long months of anticipation. In reality, labor is the beginning of an endless journey. Even when I am gone, my children will still walk the earth, and the journey will continue.

I was fine for the first few days after the birth, even if bewildered by the disparity between my physical reality and my inner world. I was still in a great deal of physical pain, although I felt strangely numb on the inside, and was dreadfully confused about why the rush of love I was supposed to feel still hadn't arrived. The "baby blues" landed with full force on day three, the same day that Mother came to the hospital to meet Tim for the first time. She handed me her carefully embroidered handkerchief and assured me that the blues were a normal part of having a child, and that the tears would pass within a day—just a sign that my milk was coming in. She was right about that at least: by midnight that night, my breasts were painfully engorged. She was wrong about everything else.

I wasn't allowed to leave the hospital bed for ten days after the birth and other than a brief shower each day, I was expected to remain on bed rest. Between the agony of learning to breastfeed, the agony of my stitches and the indignity of trying to use the bedpan, I felt like my whole life had become suffering, and I was stunned by how blasé *everyone was about my situation. I was in constant pain and my body seemed to have been damaged beyond recognition, and no one at all seemed concerned about any of that. I felt like shaking the doctor when he'd assure me in that condescending tone that "this is difficult for all young mothers." Patrick came to visit during the allotted hour each day, but he spent a lot of time staring at the baby with a confused mix of pride and terror, and seemed to have little energy to inquire about* my *welfare. Most of the nurses were brisk and unsympathetic—run off their feet, and I suppose they become hardened after a while. That entire week was so draining, but I clung to the hope that I'd feel better after some sleep, and once I was home and back to my own bed.*

When they finally discharged us, I remember walking down the steps from the hospital ward with Timmy in my arms, looking back at the doors cautiously. I was certain someone was about to tell us they'd made a terrible mistake and we needed to come back inside. Even as I slid into the car, I was confused. Were they really going to let us just walk out of there with a baby? I had no idea what I was doing. How was I ever going to keep him alive? There seemed to be some great assumption that I had some experience with babies or even maternal instincts that would kick in to help him thrive, but that just wasn't the case. I was the same clueless woman who'd walked through those doors in labor eleven days earlier, just slightly thinner, significantly sorer, and now holding another life in my hands. I cried all the way home, and Patrick just kept shooting me bewildered stares. I'm sure he thought I was being overly emotional, and maybe I was. But it wasn't his *responsibility to care for that baby.*

He'd be going to work for ten hours a day, leaving me at home with his son, and overnight my *work had become a job I'd never been trained to do.*

No one at the hospital had mentioned anything to me about Timmy waking up through the night, and I felt sure that they would have, because I was certain that behavior wasn't normal. Still, now that we were home, Tim was crying every few hours, demanding milk. This worried Patrick, too, and we were both convinced that something was wrong. We scraped together the money to take the baby to the doctor, who told us that my milk was too thin. He said that formula was better for the baby, scientifically developed to help him grow and sleep. So we switched to the bottle, and it made no difference. If anything, things got worse, because now I was up fumbling with bottles in the middle of the night and Timmy was constantly constipated.

It was several weeks before Patrick's aunt Nina came to visit, and when I mentioned how worried I was about Timmy's inability to sleep through the night, she laughed and laughed. Aunt Nina found it hysterically amusing that Patrick and I didn't even know enough to recognize typical newborn behavior, but how could we know? This was like the shock of labor all over again. I had been so caught off guard by the pain of those first few contractions I actually felt cheated—because someone should have warned me. *Childbirth and the early days of childrearing are a shameful business, spoken about only in hushed whispers when the men aren't around. The scant knowledge I did have came courtesy of Maryanne. Our cat had kittens when we were younger, and she'd whispered to me quite scandalously about what had happened.*

So there I was, in our ramshackle apartment, miles away from my parents, alone for sixty hours a week while Patrick built houses, with a baby who cried all day and night, and gradually, I began to lose my mind. People can use those words so flippantly, but I mean them in their truest, darkest sense: I felt like I had lost the essence of myself, and the new creature I had become instead was worthless and useless. Mother-hood changed me—it had sucked the very life from my bones, and now I was an exhausted, empty shell. It was the strangest thing—the way my thoughts about myself evolved, until I held nothing but disdain for the person I'd become. I cried from morning until night, and sometimes, Timmy did, too. Sadness drenched me to my core, and I was so lost in my confused thoughts, I couldn't stop to wonder if this was the way it was supposed to be.

Somewhere during the blur of this, I realized that Patrick was stay-ing out longer after work. In hindsight, I can see that our domestic real-ity didn't match the picture he'd had in his mind for our life together, and so instead of trying to fix it, he ran from it.

I can't say I blame him. If I'd had the option, I'd have run, too.

SIX

Beth
1996

Once Ruth goes back to work, I fetch heavy gloves and some trash bags from downstairs, then pick my way cautiously across the carpet of junk. First order of business is to remove anything that looks like it was once food, and to air the place out. I climb over the trash, gingerly at first in case I disturb any rodents, and open the windows. It's windy outside and it's going to be cold up here, but that's still better than dealing with the smell.

I do one pass of the room, scooping up plates and bowls and packets of what once contained junk food. I'm becoming less anxious about disturbing critters, and a little bolder as I move about the place, trying to formulate a plan. My gaze lands on one of the canvases, and I'm suddenly drawn to it, almost on autopilot.

This one falls somewhere in the middle of the color spectrum that Dad used—neither dark nor bright. It's composed of muted shades of blue and green—the colors of the ocean on a cloudy day. I lift the painting, revealing the surface of a table beneath it. Ruth's crack earlier isn't far off the mark—I wouldn't make much of an art critic and I don't have an eye for visual aesthetics. Even so, I stare at the image for a while, trying to figure out what it means.

I *can* see part of a capital B in this painting, but I'm not convinced that's what he was trying to represent. It could be almost anything—it could be nothing. I gaze around the room, taking in the other artworks, finding that same mysterious shape in all but one. I'm suddenly struck by the way this collection is different from the other pieces Dad produced over the past few years. Even when he painted a series, each piece was unique. Most of these canvases seem to represent a manifestation of an idea that captured my father's imagination and refused to let go.

What on Earth am I going to do with them? Even before I start digging through the piles of trash, I can see at least half a dozen canvases scattered around the attic. I decide to clear a space and pile them up out of the way. I don't want to damage them, so I go downstairs and retrieve some towels and sheets from the linen closet. Then I sit that first painting down on a table, facedown, resting on a towel.

That's when I notice the date.

It's written on the back of the frame, right at the top in the center. It's been scrawled with a blue ballpoint pen, but my father obviously pressed too hard, and he's etched the numbers into the wood. I recognize Dad's awful handwriting. It's a running joke in our family that Tim might be the doctor, but Dad has the doctor's handwriting, because Tim writes with a beautiful, almost feminine, script and Dad's handwriting is consistently close to illegible.

December 5, 1957.

I turn the painting over again, even more intrigued. I set it on the table and walk to pick up one of the other canvases. When I turn the second one over, there's another date. This one is later, *December 28, 1957*. It's noticeably darker. But now that I really think about it, if I were to line these paintings up in just the right order, the colors might shift gradually, like frames from an animation, or a series of time lapse images. And maybe that movement starts with the bright image mounted on the wall near the door, gradually shifting through to this calm blue/green, and working its way through to the darkest, angriest color—the black, white and gray visible on the canvas resting on an easel at the other end of the room. The colors are just so *bleak*.

After that I climb around the room like a madwoman, picking up every canvas and ferrying them back to the table. The dates are in the same location on every painting. On all but one, the motif is identical—two mismatched, slightly offset semicircles.

The one exception is a canvas I find behind a basket at the back of the attic. It's less skilled than the others—perhaps it's unfinished. On a silver background, he's painted a white circle, with a burst of light blue at the top—like a blue sunrise over a hollow earth. This canvas has a date on the back, too—but it's much later than the others.

January 1961.

Over the period when Dad painted these paintings, his handwriting changed, but I'm sure he painted them in order. I can track the deterioration in his mind, not just through the darkening colors in the images, but by the way the numbers on the back on the frame become more slanted, etched deeper into the wood, harder to read.

There's another particularly dark painting, and as I approach it, something gives me pause. As I step closer to pick it up, I notice a note pinned to a clipboard on the table beside the image. The handwriting is beautiful—at first, I think Tim probably wrote it. But this couldn't have been Tim; the date at the top of the page is *March 24, 1958*—Tim was only four years old. I pick up the clipboard and scan the words.

I've spent the past few weeks considering my options. Grieving, never once celebrating. I've realized that there is only one thing left to do but it is the worst, most drastic option. I just need to escape—I simply can't face this again. The fear looms big and bold, and I cannot even convince myself to live in its shadow.

There is only one way to outrun it. There is only one way to peace. It's bad enough that I've come back to this place—my children deserve for me to choose not to stay here. Even Patrick deserves better than this.

I know it is a mortal sin, and I have no idea how I'm ever going to convince myself to go through with it when I can't even bring myself to write the word, but I have run out of options, haven't I? It's death, one way or another, and at least this way I have control.

May God forgive me for what I have to do.

I drop the clipboard. It clatters against the tabletop then falls with a thump to the floor, but it lands right side up and I can't take my eyes off the page. Even so, I take a panicked step back.

Who the hell wrote that note?

It mentions Dad.

It mentions Dad.

My foreboding grows as I step toward the dark canvas. I turn it over, and there's a *whooshing* sensation in my gut as I confirm that the date on the top of the frame matches the date on the note.

My mother wrote this note. My mother wrote this note and this looks like a suicide note.

My father always marked my mother's death every April 14. At first, he took us kids to the Lake View Cemetery to leave her flowers, but as the years passed and we all started to grow up, it became more and more difficult to convince us to join him. By the time I was a preteen, he'd changed tactics; instead of dragging us all to her grave, he'd bring out a framed picture of her and we'd say a little prayer for her soul before a special dinner at home. So I've always known the *date*, but over time, I've forgotten the *year* it happened. But I do know she can't have died in 1958, because I was only eighteen months old then—far too young to retain memories, and I *can* remember Grace Walsh. Besides, Dad, understandably, didn't like to talk about her death, but he did tell us that she died in a car accident.

Maybe she was contemplating taking her own life, but she didn't go through with it. I try to draw some comfort from this realization, but I can't, because the broader implications of this discovery are just starting to sink in.

I cover my mouth with my hand as I spin back to the pile of canvases. *Twelve other canvases so far, and each one has a date on the back.* Do they *all* represent notes from Grace Walsh? I can barely remember where the canvases were originally. Are there other clipboards…other notes? I didn't see them if there were, and now I don't know where to look.

What if there are notes buried in all of this chaos? I'm going to have to sort through every single article of trash individually and with extreme care. What was already a mammoth job has now become utterly overwhelming.

I exhale then inhale, breathing in the scent of paint and dust. I could drown in panic right now—the task seems *impossible*, and I feel completely alone with it.

Ruth will freak out if I tell her about the note. So would Tim, and Jeremy, too, most likely. They'd insist on getting involved, or maybe even try to take over the task completely. If that happens I'm right back where I started, at home with Noah alone every single day, wishing away the hours and struggling to figure out how to manage.

No, I'll keep the note to myself, at least until I know if there are others. It's the smartest approach, for sure.

I'm lost in my own world as the afternoon passes. I set a goal of sorting through one particular section of mess before I go home for the day, and I dig into the task with gusto. It takes longer than I thought it would—mostly because I'm now sorting past each item as if there might be a precious, fragile note lost among the clutter. Sometimes I throw pieces of trash into the bin, then panic and fish them out to double-check. I'm so focused on the work that when I hear the front door downstairs slam, I almost jump out of my skin.

"Hello? Who's there?"

"Jesus Christ, Beth!" Ruth calls back, frustration and anger ripe in her voice. I scramble to my feet, glancing at the windows in the attic as I rise. The sun is surprisingly low in the sky, and just like that, I remember that I was supposed to be back at Chiara's place by two-thirty. I look down at my watch.

4:30 p.m. Oh, shit.

"I lost track of time," I exclaim, skipping down the stairs to the hallway. "I was supposed to be back at Chiara's by—" I trail off when I finally reach the hallway and see Ruth standing there with my son on her hip. "Oh, no. Was she mad?"

"She missed Tia's recital. She convinced herself that you'd slipped and banged your head and knocked yourself out cold or worse. She called Hunter at work in a panic, because she doesn't have a car seat in her car so she couldn't come check on you herself. Hunter was in court and couldn't come home, but his secretary got a message to him, so he panicked, too. Chiara then called me because she'd run out of other options. And yes, *I'm* mad at you, too, because I tried to call you, and you ignored my calls as well."

"I didn't hear the phone," I protest, craning my neck to peer toward the living area. The answering machine is flashing a bold angry *18 messages* on the screen, and I groan. "You know it's hard to hear the phone up there. I'm really sorry."

Ruth passes Noah to me, then runs her hand over her hair in exasperation before she points at my chest.

"Bethany Evans," she says abruptly. "Take your son and go

home. Get a good night's sleep, and if Chiara *ever* agrees to babysit for you again, take the goddamned cordless phone upstairs with you."

"I will," I promise. She still looks a little frantic, and I take a step toward her to rub her upper arm gently. "Honestly, I'm sorry to scare you."

"It's not just me," Ruth says, abruptly pulling away. "Chiara is worried about you, too. See? It's not just me being paranoid. We can *all* see something is up with you. When you didn't answer the phone today…"

I frown at her, then my eyes widen as I long jump to a conclusion, the note upstairs too fresh on my mind.

"Seriously? You thought I'd *killed myself*?"

"What?" Ruth gasps, hand flat against her chest in horror. "Have you thought about doing that?"

"No! Of course not! I just…why else would you all be so worried?"

"Jesus." Ruth slumps a little, then shoots me a fierce look. "Because you're acting *weird*, Beth. You won't tell us what's really going on, and we're all trying to keep an eye on you until you're ready to explain. So *be more careful*."

"I will. I'm sorry."

"I have to go," she sighs.

"Sure," I say, motioning toward the doorway. I want her to leave before me, mostly because I *don't* want her to go upstairs and stumble upon the note. "Go ahead, I'll lock up. Talk to you soon."

"Talk *tomorrow*," Ruth corrects me, still frowning. "I'll call you tomorrow."

"Okay," I say, nodding. "I'll talk to you tomorrow."

When she leaves, I leave, too, locking the door behind me. But before I start my car and pull out of Dad's street, I peer up at the windows that lead to the attic, wishing I could go right back to untangling its secrets.

*   *   *

By the time Hunter gets home, I have Noah bathed and in bed, and I'm busily cooking pasta for dinner.

"You really scared Mom today," Hunter says as soon as he steps into the house. He sounds pissed, and that's not an easy feat. My husband is so laid-back, it's rare for him to react with anger to anything. Even so, I'm distracted, and only half paying attention to him as I stare down at the pot I'm stirring.

"I know, Ruth told me. I don't know why she overreacted like that. I just forgot she had to go out, and I didn't hear the phone," I murmur.

The note. Did she really write the note? It has to be her. Who else would talk about "Patrick" like that? Why was Grace so distraught? Did she actually kill herself? Would Dad have lied to us? Is it too late to ask him?

"Mom didn't *overreact*, Beth," Hunter says abruptly. "You went AWOL on her and she had no idea where you were. Anything could have happened to you, for God's sake! You knew she had something important on. Shit, the whole reason she panicked was that she assumed for you to be late like that, something drastic must have held you up."

I wince, shaking my head.

"I know. I didn't mean it like that. It was just... I just spoke without thinking."

Hunter scoops up a slice of tomato from the salad on the table and pops it into his mouth, then raises his eyebrows at me.

"So I assume you've called her to apologize?"

"You always take her side," I blurt. His eyebrows draw in and his mouth opens in surprise. It's kind of true—Hunter does adore his mother and he'd defend her to his last breath, but it's also not at all true, because Chiara and I get along and I'm a peacemaker by nature, so even when she's a little pushy, we never argue. After eleven years, there's been no real cause for him to take sides at all. I feel my face flush, because I have *no* idea why

I just said that. I just feel so defensive, and I don't really understand why they all panicked just because I lost track of time. "Just... I'll call her. Okay? *Christ*." I drop the ladle heavily into the sink, spin on my heel and leave the room.

"Where are you going?" Hunter calls incredulously.

"To *bed*," I snap. "Don't worry. I'll call your mother first."

I slam the door to our bedroom. I flick the lamp on, change out of my clothes and into pajamas, and then I sit on my side of the bed and pick up the phone.

But half an hour later I'm still sitting on the bed staring at the handset. I just need to dial a number I've known by heart for years and years and I only need to say two simple words. It should be easy. I *am* genuinely sorry I messed up Chiara's schedule, and I only need to dial and tell her that.

So why does that tiny task feel as challenging as tackling a marathon on a day when I lack even the energy to climb stairs?

I put the handset back on its cradle, turn off the light and stretch out on the bed in the darkness, knowing that I'm not going to sleep.

Grace
December 28, 1957

Patrick seemed so confused about my attitude toward Timmy, and that made two of us. He seemed to think telling me this was supposed to be the happiest time in our lives would help. He was constantly pointing out what a beautiful baby Tim was or reminding me that this is exactly what we talked about: a family of our own, a child born of the love that we shared.

Sometimes I felt that Patrick assumed that childbirth had left me quite stupid and in need of someone to point out the obvious. Other times I was bewildered by the way that he seemed cheated by how much I was struggling to adapt to early motherhood. When I tried to talk to Patrick, he'd make my confused sadness all about him. All of his insecurities had come to the fore: Wasn't he providing enough luxury for me? Did I miss the gilded cage of my parents' home? Did I wish I'd married one of the rich boys from the bank? Why couldn't I just be happy with the humble life he was trying to give me?

One day I tried to explain that I was happy, that I was just overwhelmed and tired. That wasn't strictly true and I didn't like lying to him, but I was also trapped, because I had to say something and I couldn't exactly explain what was really going on. I did love Tim, but some days I felt such an emotional distance from him, as if I loved him in an impersonal way, as if I loved him through glass.

Patrick and I were supposed to be partners in the big picture of our family life, but our roles were completely distinct: his was to earn the money, and mine was to raise Tim and keep the house. There were clear, stark boundaries between those roles and that meant that at all times, Tim was my responsibility, and the weight of that was more than I'd ever ex-

pected to bear. If Tim had a bad day, I had a bad day, and the inverse was equally true. But if Patrick had a bad day at a building site, he'd have an extra beer at the bar during the six o'clock swill, and the world would be righted for him by morning.

I was utterly alone with Tim all the time, because the worse I felt, the more I began to withdraw from the shaky social circle we'd established since we moved to Yesler Terrace—mostly the wives of Patrick's work friends, all women who seemed to take to motherhood like ducks to water. I couldn't manage to get myself and Tim dressed and out the door to the park, especially when we were to meet those women. I'd show up— stains on my blouse, hair half-done, too poor to buy makeup, and I'd look at those women with their perfectly coiffed hair and beautifully dressed children and feel small and insecure. I became increasingly nervous about my unstable composure—imagine if I cried in front of them! I couldn't stand the idea of it, and so I stayed home. I'd wait for the mailman with a mix of hope and trepidation. More often than not, he'd deliver an over-due notice or a bill and the mail delivery would only worsen my sadness, but I watched for him anyway, because every few months, he'd bring me a letter from Maryanne.

That year was the first time I lied to my sister.

Timmy is growing so big now. He's such a smiley child and his whole face lights up when Patrick comes home. I know Mother and Father were horrified when we moved into public housing but it's not so bad. The women here are so kind to me and I've made such good friends in the community. Patrick is such a doting father, too. Mother-hood is everything I hoped it would be, and so much more.

I was too stubborn and proud and cowardly to put the truth onto paper. And in those days I still hoped I could outrun it. I still hoped I could fix it. And writing down the reality of my thoughts would have made them concrete and real.

Maybe you were right. Maybe this life isn't for me. I don't know how much longer I can live like this. I'm trapped here and I don't know what I'll do if it's too late to save myself.

I thought having a baby would be my contribution to the world. I thought it would be my way of expanding the world and making it a better place. Instead, the birth of my child had narrowed my existence, until that screaming baby was all that I thought about.

When Tim was three months old, Patrick asked me to come back to our bed. I couldn't bear the thought of him touching me—sometimes he'd hug me and I'd feel such irritation that I'd snap at him. I feared so many things—would it hurt after the trauma my body had been through in that delivery room? Pregnancy and childbirth had changed me so much—would he still find me attractive once he saw me without my clothes again?

Would I be able to stand to have so much skin against mine, when sometimes even holding my baby seemed to be too much?

And most confusing of all, why was I avoiding intimacy with Patrick with every ounce of energy I had, when I felt so utterly alone, and his touch might offer comfort? My mind was a mystery to me. I just floated through the days in a miserable haze of self-inflicted loneliness, misery and shame.

After only a few weeks of resisting Patrick's invitations, he looked at me with such sadness and longing in his eyes that I knew I could hold out no longer. When he kissed me that night, I was comforted by the sweetness of his love, and I was glad to have acquiesced. I was still tired and con-fused and sad, but as I cuddled in his arms afterward, I felt less alone, at least for a little while.

Besides, I thought at the time, it was far too soon for me to fall preg-

nant again and my life was so devoid of pleasure in those days, I should let myself enjoy Patrick's attention. At least while I was in his bed, I felt like less of a failed mothering robot, and more of a woman again.

It turns out there's no such thing as too soon *to fall pregnant. Within no time at all, the undeniable baby bump had returned...and this time, it was twins.*

SEVEN

Beth
1996

Chiara couldn't take Noah today. Hunter said she had a doctor's appointment, but he was so cagey when I asked if she was okay that I'm pretty sure she's just angry with me about yesterday. I guess that's fair enough—especially since I still haven't called to apologize.

I'll do it today. I'll definitely do it today...later.

Chiara's sudden unavailability means that Noah is with me today. He's lying in his playpen in the attic at Dad's house, kicking his chubby legs, staring up at the ceiling as if it's fascinating. I had to kick clear a space for the playpen. It's windy again, and I left the windows open all night to air the room out. The smell is much better now, but even though I've had the windows closed and the heat on for hours, it's still cold up here. We're both bundled up and Noah seems content enough, but every now and again I worry that he's too hot or too cold, and

I hover over him, unsure of how to *be* sure. I keep coming to the same conclusion: I'll know he's uncomfortable if he cries.

It's just that I *hate* it when he cries.

I'm not altogether sure that having my infant in this dusty, filthy space is safe. In fact, I'm fairly sure it's a bad idea. But I'm also too impatient to wait to keep looking for notes, and I don't have an alternative for childcare.

I force myself to stop fussing over the baby and get to work on clearing the space beside him. I'm cursing the stairs as I sprint to ferry trash down to the enormous dumpsters Ruth had delivered onto the front yard, and cursing the stairs again as I sprint back up to check on Noah. Every second I'm away from him feels *wrong*—my heart races, and I have to remind myself that he's in a playpen, that I haven't seen any rodent droppings, that there's no way he could hurt himself up there.

It's uncomfortable and stressful, but this is the best I can do given Chiara has taken herself out of service today.

There are several large piles of assorted chocolate bar wrappers in the attic—Dad's sweet tooth must have kicked in earlier than we realized—and today's goal is to completely clear them out. I'm scooping handfuls of crinkly plastic into a trash can, and soon making good progress. The bin is almost full when I happen to glance down between armfuls and see, crushed among the pile, the same shade of yellowed paper as the first note.

I'm immediately panicked at how close I came to missing it. Another second or two, and that note would have been completely buried in plastic.

I drop the armload of wrappers back to the floor, then I dive toward the bin to retrieve the note, but I'm clumsy in my haste and my elbow collides with the steel of the trash can. Between the sharp *clang* of elbow versus trash can and the loud curse that I shout as the pain rockets up my arm, sound echoes all around, suddenly shattering the silence in the room.

Noah gives a squawk, then a cry, which quickly becomes a

bellow. I know exactly what needs to happen here: I need to tend to Noah and to fetch that yellowed paper from the bin and check if it's a note and I also need to take the trash can downstairs to empty it into the dumpster. But I don't know what to deal with first, and my heart is now thumping painfully against the wall of my chest as I stare down another *nothing* decision—the kind of thing that should be easy to organize in my mind.

It's really a very simple exercise in sequencing, but I just can't figure out *what* is the right order for those tasks, and because I don't know where to start, the decision seems to swell in my mind until it looms ominously at the forefront of my thoughts. It's a confusing form of procrastination for tasks so minor I should be able to complete them all without a single conscious thought.

"Just *shhh*," I plead with Noah, who only bellows louder in response. I bend down to tip out the trash can onto the floor, and the note falls out and blessedly lands near the top of the pile. I snatch it up and smooth it out, then peer down at that beautifully scripted handwriting:

I am alone in a crowded family these days, and that's the worst feeling I've ever experienced. Until these past few years, I had no idea that loneliness is worse than sadness. I've come to realize that's because loneliness, by its very definition, cannot be shared.

Tonight there are four other souls in this house, but I am unreachably far from any of them...

The letter is dated September 14, 1957. I might not know how to soothe my son or clean up trash efficiently, but I do still have a mind for numbers and I know without checking that this very same date is on one of the canvases. I also have more evidence here that Grace Walsh wrote these notes. *Four other souls? Was I one of them?* And maybe that's why I can't bring myself to finish reading. I sit the letter down on the floor beside the trash can and I walk out of the attic, down the stairs to the kitchen.

Noah's cries seem much fainter from down here, but I can still hear them, and even with the distance, the sound grates on me until my ears ache. I can't stand it. I just can't stand that sound right now, and I'm panicking as I fill the kettle and set it on the stovetop. The faint sound of the gas heating the water drowns out the baby's cry a little more, and as I sink into a chair at the dining room table, I hold my head in my hands.

I'm losing it. That's what this is. It's a panic attack, or maybe a good old-fashioned nervous breakdown, and maybe I'm hallucinating those notes. I do feel a little disconnected from the world, and hallucinations are as good an explanation as any. I'm going to have to leave Noah with Hunter and go into a hospital before something unthinkable happens. *Crazy.* It's an awful word, one I'd never, ever let myself use to describe another person. But I feel crazy right now, and I'm so ashamed that I start to cry.

The letter needs my attention and the baby needs my attention and the canvases must match notes from her and all of this obviously means something and the attic is a mess and Dad's really going to die. It's all just too much.

Breathe, Beth. What would you tell a client?

The kettle is boiling now, and I rise to flick the gas off. As the sound recedes, I hear Noah's cries, draw in a deep breath, and rush back up to tend to him. His face is red and purple and there are tears all over his cheeks, but when I peek over the edge of the playpen, he quickly calms, so I know it wasn't anything too serious. By the time I've scooped him back up and into my arms, his sobs are fading to shuddering whimpers.

"I'm sorry," I say numbly as I pick my way across the mess, back towards the trash can, where the letter rests on the floor. I remember seeing an ornate wooden chest nearby, one I vaguely recall Dad used as a coffee table in the living room for a while, one I'm pretty sure he told me he built himself. It's buried beneath a stack of drop sheets, so I kick my way toward it and use the side of my foot to clear the sheets from the top, then I sit heavily on it. Noah is fumbling at my tank top, and it occurs to me that he's probably hungry, so I set him up to nurse and then I draw in a deep breath and read the letter.

Tonight there are four other souls in this house, but I am unreach-ably far from any of them, even as I'm far too close to guarantee their safety. Patrick said he'd be home by nine tonight, and I clung on to that promise all day.

I'm shaking so hard I can barely continue reading, but I force myself to persist. When I finish, I look down at Noah. I *really* look at him, maybe for the first time in weeks. His eyes have fluttered closed, and his hand has curled into a fist against my skin. I stare at him until my vision blurs, but the whole while, I feel numb.

But she held me like this. She dreaded my cry, just as I dread his. Maybe she felt numb, too. She certainly seemed to think about running away, just as I have.

Perhaps some people would be upset to know that their mother struggled to care for them, but I'm nothing like *upset*. More than anyone, I understand that a mother can love a child desperately, and simultaneously find themselves broken by the endless demands of parenting.

I actively seek ways to avoid my son because I just don't feel I'm up to the task of nurturing him the way he needs and de-serves to be nurtured. Not only have I never said that aloud, I've also never even let myself think those words explicitly before.

I look back to the letter, and I see my struggle reflected in the beautifully scripted handwriting of a woman who's been gone for decades. Until five minutes ago, all I had left of her was a handful of precious moments that I replay in my memory when I'm feeling lost.

But for the very first time since Noah's birth, I don't feel iso-lated. I didn't just discover a letter from the past. I found a voice that expresses what has been caught in my throat for the past five months—emotions and thoughts that were shapeless specters, now have words to define them.

I nurse Noah as I ponder this, and when he's fed and content, I settle him back into the playpen and move to set this new note next to the original one.

Any shred of comfort I might have gained from Grace's new note disappears when I move to pin it to the clipboard, and again see the words of the first note. Together, these notes carry a message that simply cannot be ignored.

Dad has always said she died in a car accident, but what if he just couldn't bear to tell us the truth? Maybe Grace Walsh did walk this same path I'm walking, but even if she did, there's a real chance it eventually lead to tragedy.

As I tear through the junk looking for more notes, I'm moving as fast as I can, but trying to stay cautious enough to avoid accidentally throwing one out like I almost did this morning. It's hard work finding the balance between impatience and care. Fortunately, Noah takes a long nap, and then wakes in a particularly content mood. I set him up in a bouncy chair and he has a one-sided conversation with his fist while I work.

Early afternoon I hear the faint trill of the phone as it rings downstairs. I scoop Noah up and take him with me as I rush down to answer it. I'm completely unsurprised to hear my sister's voice at the other end of the line.

"Beth?"

"Hi, Ruth," I sigh, settling Noah on my hip and bracing myself for another clumsy interrogation.

"Have you been to see Dad yet?" she asks me instead.

"Dad?" I repeat, then I scowl. "Ruth, you left me off the roster for two weeks, remember?"

"Actually, Beth," she says pointedly, "*you* swapped with Alicia for today. We talked about this on Sunday night. Remember?"

"*Shit,*" I groan. "I'll go now."

"Beth—"

I didn't intend to hang up on her—I just realized too late that she was still talking. I hover, debating whether I should call her back, then decide against it. I scoop up my handbag and Noah's things, and drive straight from Dad's house to the nursing home. The facility is in a brand-new, state-of-the-art building, walls painted in a soothing array of blue hues, each room decorated with homey furnishings and indoor plants. Dad's room opens out to a garden, and I find him seated in an armchair, staring out through the window at the plants. There's a television on a dresser nearby, and he has it on, a black-and-white movie playing with the sound turned down low.

"Hi there, stranger," I say, forcing cheerfulness into my tone as I step into his room. Dad glances at me, and his entire demeanor brightens. He pushes himself into a standing position and, forgetting all about the gas line that connects him to the oxygen outlet on the wall, takes a step toward me, already extending his arms to hug me. The cannula drops out of his nose and he catches it awkwardly, then looks back at me, his eyes suddenly swimming in tears.

"Maryanne!" Dad exclaims desperately. He's confused names before, but never mine, and this is almost more than I can bear.

"Who's Maryanne?" I croak. Dad blinks at me. "I'm *Beth*. Your daughter. You know who I am, don't you?"

"Yes. Beth. That's what I meant. Beth. Beth Walsh. No, it's Beth Evans now. That's what I...what's the word? I..." Dad gives me a pleading look as he rights the cannula. It's clear that although he might have just called me by the wrong name, he's well aware how much that hurt me, and now he's hurting, too. This would almost be easier if he *didn't* know. "I'm please. I'm please, Beth."

He means *sorry*. I don't bother correcting him. There's no point, and it would only embarrass him more.

"It's okay, Dad," I say dully. I know he can't help it, but that doesn't lessen the ache. Dad's finally noticed Noah—and he

opens his arms for a cuddle. I pass him the baby, but as I do, I'm
pushing Dad gently back down into his chair.

"How are you settling in?" I ask as I take a seat opposite him.

"The plates," Dad mutters, raising his gaze from Noah's face
to mine and frowning. "And...the juice. I don't like the juice.
The..." He motions toward the tray beside his bed, which con-
tains a plate full of food, and an empty coffee cup. I'm guessing
he means *coffee* when he says *juice*, because there's no sign of anything like juice here. The coffee is probably drip, and Dad always
preferred espresso, so that makes sense. But as for the plates...

"What's wrong with the plates?" I ask. He hasn't touched his
food, but the plain white dishware appears entirely unremarkable.

"Not enough salt," Dad says, then he clucks his tongue. "I
need garlic and salt, Beth. A man can't live off plates like this."

Ah. So by *juice* he means *coffee*, and by *plates*, Dad means *food*.
I smile gently.

"You're not supposed to eat salt, Dad. And I have a feeling
your nurses will notice if I bring you garlic."

Dad actually laughs, and a gentle smile eases the stress lines
in his face as he looks down at Noah. When he speaks again,
the words flow beautifully.

"Thank you for bringing the baby. Everything feels better
with a baby in your arms."

Once upon a time, I might've said the same. It didn't even
occur to me how much different it would feel when the baby
in my arms was my own.

"Daddy," I say gently. "I'm cleaning out the attic."

Dad keeps staring at Noah, but I see his arms contract a little
around my son as if he's holding him just a little closer.

"You found the..." Dad squints, concentrating hard. "What
is the word? What is the...you know the thing..."

He adjusts Noah's position on his lap, shifting the baby over
to his left side, and then he raises his right hand in a fist. It takes
me a moment to realize that this gesture is the same one he made

the day we took him from the house. Now he rotates his fist and I finally realize that he's miming a key. His agitation that last day makes sense. Maybe he *did* want to get up there to pack some art supplies to bring to the nursing home.

"No, Dad, I didn't find the key. Ruth had the boys from your office bust through the door."

For a minute Dad looks impressed, but then I guess he remembers what was behind the door. His entire expression changes, and he curls forward around Noah as if he's protecting him. Dad rocks a little, reaching with his right hand to gently touch Noah's face.

"Shouldn't have," he mutters.

"Dad, we had to. But can you tell me about the paintings?" Dad doesn't react, so I prompt him gently, "The paintings are about the notes, right? And...she wrote the notes? Grace? Mom?"

He purses his lips, then looks up at me, concentrating fiercely. I know he's searching for words, and I'd do anything to make it easier for him, but all I can do in this case is wait. Seconds pass, and then minutes, and soon his breathing becomes more labored and I cannot stand to watch him suffer like this.

"It's okay, Dad," I whisper. "It's okay. I don't need to know."

Dad gives me a helpless look. "I can't remember what it's..." Dad clears his throat, then shakes his head. "You know, the word. I can't remember what the word is. Grace is dead but it was an accident." He opens his mouth, then licks his lips and makes a grunting sound.

"That's right, Dad. Mom died in a car accident."

"No, *not*..." He gives me a frustrated look, then rubs his forehead. "What's the word? She's *gone*. And you need her now that I'm...sick." He looks at me expectantly as if this news might shock me. God, why did I insist on visiting him today? I was already feeling off-kilter and this conversation would have been pure hell at the best of times.

"She's *dead*, Dad. Can you at least tell me if she wrote the notes in the attic?"

"Grace was beautiful in the place. You know, the place with the roof. I built the place with the roof for her uncle. Her…*no*. Her father. But she was beautiful in the window, like an angel with her…the paper thing…sitting behind the glass in the window seat."

"Dad. The notes."

"Maryanne at the table. In the nightgown. Remember… beautiful with the food and my…" He looks down at his hand, then holds up his forefinger. "With the rock. I need to tell her sorry. I was wrong."

"Dad. Did Mom write the notes?"

"She…" Dad tilts his head this way and that, concentrating fiercely. "Yes. Letters. She wrote the letters with the scissors. Right?"

"With a *pen*?" I prompt. Dad looks at me blankly as if he's completely unfamiliar with the word. And maybe, today he is. I grit my teeth and I blink as fast as I can, but I can't quite shake off the tears that rise. I turn my eyes toward the ceiling, trying to stop the moisture from spilling over. "Daddy," I choke. "I'm feeling so overwhelmed at the moment and I don't know what to do. Everyone is worried about me but I don't even know how to talk about it."

Dad shifts Noah higher into his arms, and then leans forward and rests his hand on my forearm. I blink away the tears and look at him. He's staring at me with visible concern, but also, the gentlest of smiles. Here's a hint of the Dad I've always been able to rely on, and this throwback couldn't have come at a better time. Even now, when everything else is failing, my dad finds a way to come through for me.

"You're a good girl," Dad says, very quietly. Right now, but for the heavier rasp of his breathing, he could almost be well— his gaze is focused on me, and he appears to be completely present. "And what do I always tell you?"

"Everything changes," I whisper unevenly. Dad nods, satisfied.

"That's right, Maryanne. Everything changes, so you just hold on for a while and see what happens next."

I close my eyes again. The tears spill over, and I can't suppress the sobs when they rise. Dad's looking at the TV now and he doesn't seem to notice I'm distressed. Whatever moment we just shared has already passed.

"Can I stay here awhile, Dad?" I ask him through my tears. "We don't have to talk anymore. I just don't want to go home yet."

"Of course," Dad says, effortlessly shifting Noah, so that the baby rests against his shoulder. "You can always come home when you need me."

That has always been true, but the miserable reality is, it won't be for much longer. I'm almost forty years old—but sitting in that hospice room with Dad, I'm suddenly overwhelmed by the realities of adult life, and in particular, facing adult life as an orphan. There's comfort in having a living parent that I'd never appreciated, but soon I'll be on my own. Married—a sister to three close siblings—and a mother, so not totally alone, but even so, *parentless*. Just the idea seems terrifying. I'm not ready to lose Dad, not nearly ready to navigate life without his calm presence, certainly nothing like ready to parent my own child, let alone without his support.

Dad sinks into one of the wretched, desperate coughing fits we've all grown so used to over these past months. I take Noah and rest him in the stroller, then rub my father's back. Dad coughs and wheezes, and I sob, and the hours drag past until a nurse comes to help Dad into bed.

"We'll call you if he needs you," she tells me kindly, and as I push Noah out toward the car, I can't help but wonder who I'll call if I need him.

Grace
January 1, 1958

I went into labor with the twins on a stormy night in early 1955. Tim was only thirteen months old, and despite their horror that we were living in public housing, Mother and Father still hovered at the periphery of our lives. We planned for Tim to go to stay with Mother while I went into the hospital, but the twins came five weeks early, Mother doesn't like to drive and Father was away on business. When it became apparent that I had to go to the hospital now, *Patrick rushed next door to what we always referred to as "the old people's place." Mrs. Hills doesn't sleep much, apparently, and despite it being 5 a.m., was wide awake sipping a cup of tea. She wasn't exactly delighted to babysit for the strangers next door, but she did agree.*

An hour after we arrived at the hospital, Ruth burst into the world, followed a few minutes later by Jeremy. Seven days later we brought the new children home and I began living in the peculiar hell of having three children under the age of two. I don't remember much of the early months—it's all a blur of sleep deprivation and laundry and feedings. One day I was cooking dinner and making myself a cup of coffee, and only when the house filled with smoke did I realize that I'd put the roast in the fridge and the milk in the oven. I lived an infinite monotony of days like that, and it was rarer for me to be dry-eyed than it was for me to cry. But who was to say what was normal and what was not under such circumstances? Anyone would be broken by the endless demands. We were struggling financially, always behind on our bills, and the more stressful things were at home, the less Patrick was around.

When the twins were six months old, Mother called and announced that she was coming for a visit. I raced around trying to bring the house into something like order, and managed to pull on a clean dress before she arrived. Mother sat awkwardly on the very edge of our sofa, lip curled in disgust at something. When I asked her why she was there, she announced with some fanfare that she and Father had made a decision.

At one of the worst times of my life, my mother offered me a refuge in her home, with promises of her housekeeper to manage the laundry and the cleaning, and a night nurse for the twins. At first, I saw this as an olive branch…perhaps, a lifeline. She offered me a utopia of assistance and respite, and yet it soon became very clear that in order to take it, I had to betray Patrick, because he was no longer welcome in their home… and nor would I be, as long as I was married to him.

"It's a sin to divorce," Mother told me. "But I talked to Father Mc-Williams. He said perhaps they could annul your marriage, given Patrick has failed to uphold his vow to provide for you."

As alone as I felt…as broken as I felt… Patrick was still mine, and I was still his. I didn't see the lout my parents saw—I still believed in the father I knew he could be. I'd see concrete flashes of a responsible, attentive man every now and again on the weekends when he'd play outside with Tim, or he'd arrive home from the bar with a bunch of flowers and a teary, drunken apology for all of the ways he was letting me down.

"He can do better," I told my mother. "He can be better."

"You've been married for two years now, Grace," Mother said stiffly. "You're still…" She looked around the room slowly, then gave me a helpless look. "Darling, you're still living on the breadline, even with all of the help we've given you. Besides, did you really expect us to support you forever?"

I blinked at her, bewildered.

"What are you talking about? I've only borrowed money off you a handful of times, only when we were desperate."

Frustration twisted my mother's features.

"I know, darling, but surely you know that Patrick asks for money, too." She paused, then pursed her lips. "He calls constantly, Grace. Every month, at least."

I opened my mouth to argue, but I could see from the tension in her gaze that she was telling the truth. My shoulders slumped. I was well aware that we were struggling, but Patrick handled the finances. Until that day, I had no idea how bad things really were.

I'd been prepared to sacrifice my relationship with my parents for Patrick in those early days, when my eyes were alight with stars, and I believed love would conquer all. Things were different by the time the twins came along. I was sorely tempted to flee to the refuge of my parents' home. In the end, I stayed with Patrick because I had survived those difficult years only by maintaining some desperate hold on something like hope. Hope that Patrick could turn things around. Hope that we could be the family he and I had dreamed of. Hope that I could do better, on my own—that I would find some hidden reserve of strength and rise at last above my circumstances.

At least by then I had Mrs. Hills. She would hardly be my first pick for a stand-in mother figure. She has a voice like nails on a chalkboard and what she called a "bung hip"—I'm still not exactly sure what that means except that she walks with a cane and a pronounced limp. Her husband, Mr. Hills, seems to be perpetually close to death—he's rail-thin and weak and quite hard of hearing. Mrs. Hills is all loud opinions and she seems to know everything happening in the entire neighborhood, which I think is necessary because she's made a full-time job out of disapproving of everyone else's decisions.

But after Mother left, something inside me seemed to break. Several more days blurred past where I just could not motivate myself to get up out of bed. I wasn't even sure why I was crying, except that the babies were all crying and Patrick was never home. Things got worse and worse, until Mrs. Hills caught Patrick by the ear one night and told him I had to see a doctor immediately. The next day he took me into the clinic and I sobbed as I explained to the doctor that I didn't mean to cry and that I was trying my hardest but that I just couldn't keep up with everything that was happening in our lives.

"What did you expect, Mrs. Walsh? That these days would be easy? You have three young children and a husband to care for. You simply have to pull yourself together."

I resolved that I would indeed "pull myself together." I promised myself I'd do better. I made a decision that I would no longer cry and that I'd keep the house tidier and I'd go to the park with the other mothers again and that I'd give Patrick and the children all of the love and care they deserved.

Patrick dropped me home so that he could go to work. But once I was alone in the house with the children again, all of that firm resolve disappeared. I think I spent most of that day sitting on the floor in the laundry, locked away from the children so that I could think, barely registering the sounds of their cries. The whole time I wondered if there was some way—any way—that I could run away from it all and be free. It was a fantasy—I had an open door at Mother's house, but even as I daydreamed about escape, I knew I'd never leave. I simply couldn't, because Patrick would never cope without me.

That's how the rest of that year went. I have no idea how the children survived—I gave them all the bare minimum. Patrick was always frustrated at the mess in the house and he'd complain about the children crying and I'd wonder, does he think I like living like this? But I was so miserable I couldn't even argue with him—I floated around the house a shadow of my former self, trying to do just enough to keep us all alive.

The twins turned one and I baked them a cake and Timmy and I made a little party for them in the backyard. And ever so gradually, the sun came out from behind the clouds, and I again found the energy to read the children stories and to walk them to the park and to smile again.

I promised myself: no more babies. I told Patrick as much, and he seemed bewildered. But we wanted a large family, he said. I know, I told him, but that was before I knew what it was like. Besides, I asked him, do you really think I'm doing a good job? He told me I was doing fine. Contraception is a sin, he reminded me, as always, deeply religious but only when it suited him. Besides, we couldn't afford rubbers or a diaphragm even if we could figure out how to access such a thing. Given that, how could we avoid another baby? Did I intend to stay out of our bed forever?

I missed him, and now that I was feeling alive again, I wanted to move back to his bed. We went back and forth on all of this for days, and what started out as frustrated squabbling soon became more urgent. We wanted to reconnect so badly, but I knew that if I gave in, another pregnancy might just kill me. This was the one aspect to my life I was both desperate and determined to control.

In the end, Patrick came up with a solution: I'd come back to our room, but he would be sure to finish away from me. This was still sinful in the eyes of the church—but as Patrick grudgingly acknowledged, the church wasn't going to feed and clothe another baby if we did have one, so surely God would forgive us.

I went back to Patrick's bed that night, and we lived through another of those honeymoon periods when things were peaceful and blissful. I managed better, I smiled again, I'd laugh at Timmy's antics and the twins' growth began to delight me, and instead of Mrs. Hills bringing baked goods to our door because she pitied me, I grew a garden and repaid the favor.

In those months I finally discovered that the love I have for my children is the most powerful thing on earth. It's fierce and determined and an absolute force to be reckoned with. I would do anything for them.

On a good day I know that I am far from a perfect mother, but I am all they have, and all I can do is to make sure that I expend every breath trying to do my best.

But the bad days seemed to stack up in a row after I give birth, and when that happens, the same powerful force of love turns inward. All I see are my failures, and it paralyzes me. The love I feel for the children and the perfection I wish for them become a force of destruction and my mind becomes clouded with lies, until I see my existence as a liability, not a strength.

Just as the love I have for my children is a powerful force, the relentlessness of nature cannot be controlled and it will not be denied. Patrick and I are drawn together, and there's life and love in our union.

I realized I was pregnant again when the twins were thirteen months old. Whether I liked it or not, our family was about to expand again. I was going to face another storm in my mind, this time with four tiny children in tow.

EIGHT

Beth
1996

I call Jeremy as soon as I get home, partly to ask about the art supplies for Dad, partly because I can't stand the silence in my house. He rambles for forty-five minutes about some research results that I can't even begin to understand. I try to make noises at the right times, but mostly I'm just glad to have his voice in my ear.

"I better go," he says eventually, sounding pleased by my interest in his work.

"Oh," I say, disappointed. "Right. There was something else..."

Jez is happy to take painting supplies on his way to the nursing home tomorrow, but he probably won't have time to go all the way to Dad's house to get them, so he'll just stop at a store near his campus. Then he asks about the house, and I tell him I'm making progress. When he hangs up, I call Chiara immediately, unthinkingly, just to fill the silence. It's only when she answers that I remember she's angry with me.

"I'm sorry," I say as soon as I've identified myself.

"Beth, of course I forgive you," my mother-in-law coos, because she's a living saint. "I'm just worried about you. It's not like you to be absentminded. Are you quite sure you're okay?"

"Just a lot happening at the moment," I murmur. My eyes still feel puffy from my crying at the nursing home. It feels like every corner of my brain is full of worries, and I'm worn out by the bombardment. It's hard even to summon the energy to dismiss Chiara's concerns.

"I know I'm your dreadful monster-in-law," Chiara says after a pause. She's trying to make me laugh. It's not funny at all, because she's perfect, and if anyone is the monster here, it's me, but I force a chuckle. "After all these years, I also hope I'm your friend, and I love you like a daughter. If you need to talk, I'm here. Anytime. Day or night."

I mumble another thanks and get off the phone as fast as I can. I take a similar approach to Hunter when he comes home. He's pleased because I apologized to his mother, and he's animated because he had a win today in a messy custody case. Hunter suggests we watch some television together but I have a sudden urge to retreat from him—he's in such a good mood and I know that my bad mood will sour him if I don't leave. I tell him I'm tired and turn in for an early night but I'm still lying wide awake when he joins me in bed at eleven. I pretend to be asleep as he wraps me in his arms. At first, I'm comforted by the warmth of his body against mine, and for a while I feel sleep softening the edges of my consciousness.

But it's not long before Hunter's breath is deep and even in my ear, and rest is eluding me. I really thought five months of parenthood had taught me what sleep deprivation felt like. Since Noah was born, I've survived on short stretches of rest, which of course is far from ideal, but I've always managed just enough sleep to function.

Now, though, when I close my eyes, Dad's paintings appear

and the images chase away sleep altogether. The colors cycle through my brain, the imagery flickering through shades, but always vivid. The shape of the motif represents intrigue and mystery and a puzzle my mind seems convinced it can solve if I just focus on it hard enough, and so I concentrate and I wonder and I analyze. The hours tick by, but even though I drift toward sleep, I don't sink beneath it. My mind is too active and I can't shut it down. I'm completely stuck on the notes and the paintings and hard as I try, I *cannot* think of anything else.

I get up for a cup of tea, feed Noah, and then return to bed. It's now 3 a.m. and I can't even close my eyes. I'm wired as if I've had ten cups of coffee, so wound up I can't lie still. Images again take shape in the darkness above me, but this time it's not Dad's paintings I see. Instead, I'm replaying memories of Grace.

It makes sense that my mind would go here when I'm agitated. The mere thought of her has made me feel safe and secure in a way that's hard to replicate in the adult world.

I'm small all of a sudden, small enough to curl up on her lap and stretch my hand up to touch her dark hair. It's soft against my fingers, and I love the way she smells—like flowers and cake and sunshine—like *all* of the best things in life. She finishes the story and I beg her for another, and she laughs to herself and reaches for another book, and another, and another. And of course she does, because I know that this is our pattern each night. *Just one story, sweet girl*, she tells me, but it's always five or six or if I've been really good, more.

Then she's tucking me in, and she bends to kiss my forehead, and maybe I almost drift off to sleep then—but in a heartbeat I'm startled awake again. Am I here, or am I there? The line between the vision and dreams and my reality becomes thinner.

Now I'm standing with my siblings in the cold morning light of a living space I don't know, but I do know it's ours, because the heavy chest from Dad's attic is there, and Dad is sitting atop it. Jeremy and Ruth are sobbing and so am I, but Tim is gone—

I think he's hiding behind the sofa. I throw myself at Dad at the same time Jeremy and Ruth do. Dad's crying along with us, and I sense his panic as he tries desperately to comfort us. He's holding me awkwardly—I'm half across his lap, squished beside Ruth, and now my hands are resting on the carvings on the top of the wooden chest.

I can *feel* that wood beneath my hands. I run my fingers through the engraving, tracing patterns and shapes. I miss Momma so much, I don't think I can survive it. Where is my safe place now? The entire world has changed simply because she is gone.

I startle and then it's gone—all of it is gone, and I'm staring at my ceiling in the predawn light, bewildered and more than a little unnerved. I tell myself I was just dreaming, but those moments I relived were *real* moments. Can you dream your memories?

Maybe not, but you can definitely hallucinate them.

The more I think about that, the more distressed I become.

"Hey," Hunter murmurs sleepily in my ear. "Are you cold? You're shaking."

"Can you meet me at Dad's after work?" I blurt.

"Sure?"

"Maybe Wallace could come, too. There's something I want to bring home and we're going to need help carrying it."

I leave Noah with Chiara this next morning and get back to work on the attic, but despite making some small headway in the chaos, I don't uncover more notes. I do, however, organize things so that we can get the chest out. I can't lift it on my own—it's far too heavy—but I clear a path so that by the time Wallace and Hunter arrive, they are able to get into the attic and lift the chest out, without climbing over piles of trash to do so.

"You should have told me how bad it is up here," Hunter mutters as he passes me with the chest.

TRUTHS I NEVER TOLD YOU

"I told you it was a mess," I protest. He gives me a pointed look.

"This isn't a mess, Beth. This is a disaster. You shouldn't be doing this on your own."

Wallace withholds comment, but he's a softhearted guy and he and my dad have been close friends for years, and I'm not surprised to see him on the verge of tears as he looks around. They manage to get the huge chest down the stairs with a bit of persistence and patience, and Wallace then drives it back to our place in the back of his SUV. Hunter puts it right into place in the center of our living area and comments that it fits beautifully.

"When did he build this?" he asks.

"Long before we moved to Bellevue. It's been in our house for as long as I can remember."

"He was an artist long before he learned to paint, wasn't he?"

I think this is why I simply had to retrieve this chest today. It's a piece of Dad's talent, something physical I can touch that ties the memories of my childhood to my present. After we've eaten and put Noah to bed, Hunter retires to his study to catch up on some work, and I get cleaning supplies out.

I wipe the layers of dust from the intricate carving on the lid, oil the hinges and polish the outer wood back to its once-gleaming shine. I have no plans for the chest beyond cleaning it up, so I open it and peer inside, wondering what I might store in there. The obvious options are blankets or maybe Noah's winter clothes once it warms up, and so although the inside isn't particularly dusty, I decide to clean it out, too. As I'm wiping inside, I feel the base give a little against the pressure of my hand. When I press harder, the base pops up, and I can lift it out of the chest—revealing a cavity beneath. I'm frowning as I stare down at what I find: a beige photo album and a blue velvet ring box. I reach for the ring box first, and open it to find a tarnished pair of rings—both silver, one adorned with a chip of a stone, the other plain.

It's the first ring that catches my eye, and I shake it out of it's box and into my palm. It's hardly an elaborate piece of jewelry, but it is somewhat unique. The setting is simple, four prongs that hold the stone against a rounded band. I polish it on my clothes, and hold it up to the light. As I turn it so that I'm staring at its side, I suddenly realize I'm looking at the very object Dad's tried to capture in the last painting in his series—the one from 1961. From the side, the ring is simply a round circle with a blue burst of light at the top. All that's missing from my view is the silvery gray of his background, but there's no denying that this was his inspiration. It has to be my mother's engagement ring, and I feel an awful, miserable clench in my chest at the thought of Dad keeping this for all these years, locked away where it was safe.

The album is plain and I have to guess which side is the front. Before I open it I know that it will be full of photos of Dad and Grace, and when I turn the face page, I see that I'm right. It's snaps from a simple wedding ceremony. Dad is instantly recognizable, as is my mother. She's reed-thin, wearing a long-sleeved wedding gown, with an illusion neckline and collar, and overlain with lace detail. There's a lace cap pinned into her dark hair, with a long veil trailing off, falling around her shoulders.

Both Grace and Dad look far too young to be married—but their expressions are joyous, the shining hope in their eyes almost painful to think about when I consider they had only a handful of years together, most of which were focused on us kids. They were probably short on money when they married—the last few photos have them cutting a homemade cake in what looks suspiciously like the church vestibule, and there's only a handful of guests.

Wedding photos only take up a few pages, and then I turn the page to find a yellowed piece of paper has been folded and placed loosely against the next page. I open it and nearly drop it when I discover it's my mother's death certificate. There are so many fields—most typed, some scrawled in ink. My gaze flies over the page, soaking in the details.

Grace Vivienne Walsh—nee Gallagher.

Mother's name: Vivienne Mary Gallagher.

Father's name: Francis Ian Gallagher.

Spouse: Patrick Timothy Walsh.

Mother of Timothy, Ruth, Jeremy, Bethany.

Date of death: Undetermined. April 1958.

That simply cannot be right. How on earth could the date of death be undetermined if she died in a car accident? And if Grace died in 1958, I was only eighteen months old when we lost her and it is highly unlikely I'd remember her at all. But I *do* remember her. Even now, if I close my eyes, I can summon the feeling of being held in her arms. My God—the thought that I've manufactured those memories leaves me feeling physically ill.

Those memories are a part of how I understand myself. I was loved by Grace. I was nurtured by Grace. On some level, I know myself as someone who began her life in the arms of a woman who adored her.

What if I made it all up?

I don't believe it for a second—the memories are far too vivid. I'm about to fold the paper and to set it aside when a new thought strikes me, and I scan down the page again, looking for a cause of death. I fully expect to be at least partly reassured by the words *motor vehicle accident* or something similar, but that's not what I find.

Unable to confirm due to decomposition of body.

I fold the paper carefully and set it down on the floor beside my legs. I'm dizzy and confused, not sure what to make of my discovery. It was obviously some time before Grace's body was found. This definitely doesn't fit Dad's story about a car accident, but it also doesn't indicate that she died by suicide. Unless she ran away somewhere before she ended her life…?

Another wave of nausea hits me. *Poor Dad. My God. Poor Dad.*

The room is spinning so I close my eyes, trying to calm myself down. Just then I hear a sound in the hallway and I realize that Hunter is probably done for the night. He was already hesitant about me cleaning out that attic, even just upon a single glimpse of the mess. If he sees this mind-blowing discovery, maybe he'll try to insist I leave the job to my siblings. He loves me—he's trying to protect me—but more than ever, I need to get to the bottom of this.

I stuff the ring box and the album back into the bottom of the chest and slip the base back in place, and despite my shaking hands, finish closing the lid as Hunter returns to the room.

"Want to watch a movie?" he asks me, sniffling a yawn. "I don't feel like working tonight after all."

"Sure," I say. My heart is racing and my palms are sweaty, so I scramble to my feet and flash him what I hope is a convincing smile. "Let me just go wash up. I'm all dusty from cleaning this thing."

Grace
January 9, 1958

When I went into labor with Beth, I tried to pretend it wasn't happening.
I stayed at home as if that would stop the inevitable—but I was foolish,
because of course, a baby doesn't care if the mother is in a birthing room
at the hospital or in her own laundry. When she is ready to be born, she
will be born.

When the urge came to push, I panicked, because I was at home with
Tim and the twins. I called out for help until I realized it was pointless:
the McClarens on the west side of our house wouldn't come even if they
knew I was being murdered, and even though Mrs. Hills isn't quite as
deaf as her husband, her hearing isn't as sharp as it once was.

In the end I sent Tim next door to Mrs. Hills, despite the fact I had
no idea if my two-and-a-half-year-old son would successfully make
that journey or get lost in attempting it. I sat the little ones in front of the
television and told them not to come into the laundry.

By the time Mrs. Hills came, I was sitting on a towel beside the
washing machine, and Beth was already in my arms. My third birth
happened all by myself, on a floor I hadn't cleaned in forever because my
belly was so big. Even so, my third birth was my best birth, because yes,
I was alone and scared, but no doctor cut my body to ease her entrance,
and no doctor was pulling my legs apart and yelling at me, and no nurse
was holding me down, forcing me to lie on my back.

Instead, I let instinct call the shots. I squatted and I breathed and I
let my body take over, and then I guided her into the world myself, then I
lifted my beautiful little girl up onto my breast and I sank back onto the
floor in shock. She had a thatch of dark hair slicked against her head and

the biggest, bluest eyes I'd ever seen. She cried until I cuddled her, and then she settled and stared up at me with wonder in her gaze.

It was all so peaceful. It was certainly still painful, but the pain was bearable—perhaps because I could shift myself around when I felt the urge. Once Beth had settled in my arms, I felt an astounding euphoria rise and by the time Mrs. Hills arrived, I was weeping tears of pure joy. That birth was one of the best experiences of my life, at least in part because for the first time, I was in complete control of my body.

Even so, Mrs. Hills was horrified and she chastised me for not calling Patrick—what if something had gone wrong? I guess it was risky and silly to delay the hospital visit, especially when we had no phone …it had been cut off months earlier because we hadn't paid the bill. Mrs. Hills called an ambulance, and as Beth and I were swept away to the hospital, I let myself hope. Her birth had been so much easier, and those precious early minutes felt like bonding. Maybe this time would be different?

The optimism lingered that first week in the maternity ward, because it seemed I'd produced the world's most relaxed infant. Beth slept when I needed her to sleep; she fed on a reasonable schedule right from birth; she was content to be ignored for a little while if she was in my room during the day and I didn't scoop her up right away. Even once we went home, Beth settled right in. I was now in the tenuous position of having four children under three, but at first, it was almost okay. I established something of a routine with the oldest three children when my mood was good, and now that Beth had arrived and proven herself to be the kind of easygoing baby that every mother dreams of, I thought I had a shot of getting through the first twelve months unscathed.

By then, I should have known that however confused my mind became in the months after childbirth, it was a temporary torture. I had emerged from the fog twice, and so I should have known that if I got sucked back in, all I had to do was hold on and wait. Even so, when Beth was six months old and I felt the tide of misery seeping back, I couldn't think about how this too would pass. *All I could think about was the stretch of hopeless days that I knew I'd have to march through.*

I feared it would be bad—but I had no idea just how bad it would get. Some combination of the monotony, the endless demands, the loneliness, the isolation and the exhaustion left me feeling like I was standing outside my body, watching another woman fail the world's most wonderful children, again and again and again. When the dark thoughts began, and the swirling torrents of torment started, and when the exhaustion seemed irreparable rather than something easily fixed by a stretch of decent sleep, I convinced myself that the only way forward was to find an escape.

I don't remember picking up the keys to Patrick's car that night, and I don't remember walking out of the house. I don't even remember reversing out into the street or driving away. The first I really remember, I was standing on a bridge over water. It was deathly dark—hours still before dawn, and I was miles and miles away from home, at a place I knew on some level was the Aurora Bridge. I had zoned out, and taken myself automatically to the a place in Seattle infamous for suicides.

I wasn't consciously thinking of what would come next. I was calm as I walked along the pedestrian path, marveling at how quiet the road was at the early hour. My feet moved without permission. They carried me right to the edge of the path and over the handrail…to the very edge of the bridge, slippery from the rain. I stared down into the dark water and it called to me, promising peace and rest.

I knew what I was about to do was a mortal sin, and I had a desperate urge to explain myself to God. I was simply going to tell *Him* that I couldn't go on—that I'd reached the absolute end of my rope and besides, Patrick and the children would be so much better off without me. For a moment, I felt utterly certain that any reasonable person or deity would agree with me—that it was all too much, that I was failing too *miserably, and that the water offered the sensible path forward. But as I opened my mouth to speak to the endless nothingness of the night, I suddenly realized how close I was to that drop into the water and how close I'd come to my worst mistake yet. I panicked, and I clambered over the rail and threw myself forward in my panic. I hit the concrete path as a dead weight, breasts and stomach and knees and elbows and shins colliding and skidding over the rough surface, winding and bruising and scratching me. And even though the concrete path had caused me such pain, I clung to it as if it was my savior. The physical pain was intense enough to penetrate the fog in my mind—the first feeling other than frustration and sadness that I'd been conscious of in weeks.*

And when my breath returned, it came in desperate gasps between huge, rolling sobs that went on and on—tears that burned as they cleansed. The sobs were cathartic—the relief that I hadn't jumped without even thinking reminded me that I did desperately want to live, and that the way I'd been thinking about my death was yet another lie that my mind was telling me. I was glad to be alive, and in the momentary joy of the close call, promised myself I'd remember that moment forever.

I cleaned myself off. Shaking with fear and cold and confusion, I went back to the car. I knew that even if I made it home before sunrise, before Patrick even noticed I was missing, I would have to explain the drained gas tank in the car and the mess I'd made of my body. My chin was scratched raw, as were my hands, knees and forearms, and I had bruises everywhere.

Even so, I had faced death that night, and I had found the strength to refuse it. I told myself that despite the misery I had been ambling through for months, there was some bravery left in the depths of my soul, and I must never again forget that. If I had the courage to pull away from that water, I surely had the courage to face another few months of the depression until it lifted. As I drove home that night, I made myself a solemn vow: I would never again fall pregnant. Every time I'd faced the depression it was worse than the last, and a fourth bout would surely kill me. The years of helplessly bearing child after child had taken something from me, some last reserve of inner strength that was now all but gone. I had to protect that last sliver of myself, and if that meant never returning to Patrick's bed, he and I would simply have to pay that price.

I made it home just as the sun breached the horizon. Tim was already awake, playing with a wooden train on the floor of the living room. Patrick he was asleep in our bed, and the younger children were asleep in their beds, and somehow, they had all survived without me.

When Patrick woke and stumbled into the kitchen seeking coffee, his face puffy from sleep, a crease from his pillow over his chin, I felt my heart beat faster—both from fear, and from love. I wasn't afraid of Patrick, rather, his reaction to my physical injuries, and the desperate love I felt for him right from that first day at the window seat seemed to breathe fresh life into my tired, aching body.

Patrick noticed the bruises and scrapes right away. He kept asking me what happened, and although I'd come up with what I thought was a convincing story about slipping on the back steps in the night, he wasn't buying it, and it didn't explain the empty gas tank.

Maybe he'd been useless to me over the lonely months that had passed before, but that morning gave me hope. He prepared the children's breakfast, then led me away to the living room and sat too close to me on the couch. His hands shook as he brushed the hair back from my face and then he pulled me into his embrace and begged me to tell him what had really happened. I cried, and although the best I could do was to tell him that I had been feeling so lost and lonely, it seemed to be enough for him to understand that we had come very close to losing one another that night.

"I'll do better," he promised as he cupped my face in his hands and he kissed me around my injuiries. "I'll do better, Grace. I promise I'll do better."

And for a while, he did. I saw frequent flashes of the man I always hoped he could be for a while. He came home on time and he didn't complain when I fell behind with the laundry. He was drinking less, so we had the money to catch up on some of the bills. But of course it didn't last, and by Beth's first birthday, he was coming home late every night again, and the milkman was angry because we hadn't paid him for weeks and the roof was leaking again but Patrick never seemed to have the time to fix it.

These days, he's back to the man my parents think he always will be, and at long last, I'm starting to feel resentful. Funny how we can't afford to have a phone anymore, but Patrick can afford to go out for beer with his friends almost every night. It's funny how the money he gives me for housekeeping keeps shrinking and the bills go unpaid, but we're never too short for a bottle of whiskey each week.

He says he's stressed and he needs time to himself. He says he misses his freedom and I need to let him be for now. He says I shouldn't question him. After all, he's the man in this household, and he's working so hard supporting us all.

I haven't written to Maryanne in months because I haven't had the energy to pretend things are okay, but if I did find the courage to write her and tell her the truth, I know that Maryanne would insist that things don't have to be this way. She'd say they need to change, but she may as well be asking for the moon. It seems that this is the natural order of things: women are born to nurture and to care for the home, and men are born to lead and dominate. I love Patrick with a depth that still surprises me, but I'm not sure he has the capacity to love me back the same way.

The only thing I can't decide is whether it makes me an optimist or a slow learner that I'm only just figuring out that I care about Patrick a lot more than Patrick cares about me.

NINE

Beth
1996

I try to consider every possible explanation that night when I finally give up on sleep.

In her note Grace talks about Dad being unreliable, but the Dad I know has never been unreliable in his life. Maybe her perspective was warped. She was probably seriously depressed. Maybe she had a serious mental illness. A delusional disorder? Manic depression?

It does look like Grace was suicidal when she wrote that note. How does that tie in?

Oh, my God. If the date on the death certificate is correct, she wrote that note just weeks before her death.

I can't think about that now. I need to think about something calming. Maybe try to visualize those moments when she held me in her arms—

But did she hold me in her arms? How could I remember if I was only eighteen months old when she died?

This is it, Beth. This is the moment when you lose your mind altogether.

When Hunter climbs out of bed for his shower at six, I'm still every bit as awake as I was when I got into that bed eight hours earlier. I don't think I've closed my eyes for more than a minute. I'm so exhausted now that I'm battling tears as I try to get ready to drive Noah to Chiara's house for the day.

"Beth," Hunter says, abruptly breaking a lengthy silence as we eat breakfast in the kitchen. I drag my gaze from my untouched toast to his face. His lips are pursed, so I know he's about to say something I won't like. "I don't think you should go to your dad's place today. Stay here and try to rest."

I know his suggestion comes from a place of love, but it feels paternalistic and I bristle. I try to take some deep breaths to stop myself from snapping at him, but anger and irritation are fierce beasts, just waiting for a chance to pounce. I open my mouth, but he holds up a hand before I can even say a word, and now Hunter is impatient. "Will you please just listen to me for once? I'm worried about you, Beth. You're wound up like a spring. Packing up your dad's house can wait one more day."

I'm gearing up to push back, even though I *know* I'm going to make a meal of this and I'll have to face his hurt and resignation when I do. But Noah, who has been happily sitting in his high chair, chewing on a teething biscuit, makes a gagging sound and then a sickly, constricted cough. Hunter and I both react before I even have time to acknowledge what's happening. We shoot to our feet and we run, coming to a stop on either side of the baby. My heart is racing and my hands shake violently as I grab the biscuit and dump it onto the tray of the high chair.

My thoughts are a turbulent torrent, instantly bombarding me with worst-case scenarios and the most tragic of outcomes.

It's only when Hunter laughs softly and picks up Noah that I see the stunning disparity in our reactions.

"Silly bubba," Hunter chuckles, nursing Noah against his cheek and rubbing his back to comfort him. "You can't put the biscuit all the way down your throat, no matter how delicious it is."

"He could have *died* just now," I cry, staring wide-eyed at my husband.

"What? No, he just got a bit too enthused about the biscuit. He's fine," Hunter says, and he brings Noah with him as he walks around the high chair to rub my back. My husband's lack of panic is as confusing as it is frustrating.

"You're not taking this seriously enough!" I exclaim, stepping away from him. "He could have *choked*!"

"On a biscuit? Seems unlikely." Hunter motions toward the biscuit on the tray table of the high chair. "There's no way he could have kept that whole thing in his mouth long enough to obstruct his airway. He gave himself a fright, that's all."

But I'm staring at the same object, and I see all kinds of possibilities that very much feel like probabilities. He *could* chew on it for so long that it dissolves, but not all of it dissolves, and what if a hard bit gets stuck in his throat and he can't dislodge it? How do you even do first aid on a five-month-old baby? Why haven't we done a first aid course together? What if something happens to him and we don't know how to help him? What if we're not paying close enough attention and something bad happens and he's hurt or he *dies*?

I only realize I've voiced these thoughts aloud when Hunter carefully sets the baby back in his high chair and takes my shoulders in his hands to stare at me intently.

"Beth," he says gently. "Look at him." I glance down at the baby. He's calm but determined, his grubby little fist already reaching for the biscuit. Hunter squeezes my shoulders. "See? He's totally fine."

Hunter pulls me against his shoulder and I all but dissolve into him, sobs bursting from my lips as I struggle to dismiss a sudden and intrusive daydream of Noah blue-faced and choking, right there in front of me, while I watch on, helpless. The incident didn't play out that way. Things weren't as drastic and terrifying as all of that. But they could have been.

"Babe. You *need* to sleep," Hunter says. His brown eyes are fixed on me, his concern palpable. I'm sobbing hard now, even as I shake my head and prepare to argue with him some more. But it turns out that I can't even find the energy for fighting now, and I let Hunter lead me back to our bed. He arranges my limp limbs against the pillows and covers my body with the blankets. He tugs the blinds closed and quietly, gently, closes the door behind him.

I try to submit to my body's demands for sleep. I use every trick I know to try—I focus on my breathing; I consciously relax my muscles; I even try to bring back those wonderful memories of Grace, but that fails now, and I try to force my mind to conjure other peaceful scenes—family dinners, a peaceful forest, a calm blue ocean.

But hours later I'm still staring at the ceiling, reliving the sound of my infant choking, over and over again.

Every single time I force myself to think about something else, my mind returns to that biscuit, and all the ways that incident might have ended differently.

When I emerge from my bedroom three hours later, Ruth and Hunter are sitting at the kitchen table. Ruth is halfway through a sandwich, but she sets it down on her plate to pin me with her eyes. Hunter is staring into a steaming cup of coffee. I see guilt in the way he avoids my gaze and I'm immediately wary.

"We have a doctor's appointment this afternoon," Ruth says before I can even ask what's going on. Adrenaline spikes again, and I scan the room.

"What happened? Where is he?"

"He?" Ruth frowns, then her expression clears as she rises. "Jesus, Beth. Not for Noah. He's fine. He's at Chiara's house. The doctor is for *you*."

"What for?" I ask. I look at Hunter, and he picks up the coffee and sips it. Now his gaze is fixed on the dining room table, and suddenly I am conscious of the details I have missed. His eyes are rimmed red. He's changed out of his suit and he's wearing jeans and a sweater. His shoulders are slumped and he's leaning forward on the table as if he can't hold himself up. I look to Ruth, and my awareness continues to sharpen. Now I see the concern in my sister's expression, the little crease in the center of her forehead that indicates frustration, the irritating way her heels are tapping...tapping...tapping against the tiles on my kitchen floor. I'm not sure what this intervention is for, but I *am* sure it's ridiculous. "I didn't sleep well last night. That's hardly cause for a doctor's visit."

"Beth...a little insomnia isn't a problem. But you've hardly slept in weeks. And I'm pretty sure you didn't sleep at all last night, and..." Hunter finally looks at me. As his gaze scans my face, I see his expression fall further. "And you haven't even slept this morning, have you?"

"I... I slept a little..." I lie. The furnace is on too high and it's hot in here, too hot, and the air feels thick. I feel trapped by their concern, like they've cornered me. I'm not even sure why my sister and my husband are putting me on the spot. "One bad night isn't a reason to visit a doctor. You two are being ridiculous."

"Beth, you know I'm worried about you. We both are. Hell, we *all* are," Ruth sighs. "Will you please just humor us and come to the clinic?"

"And tell her what? A woman with a five-month-old baby is having disrupted sleep? Tell her a woman whose father is dying is upset? Lisa will laugh at us," I snap at her as I finally unfreeze.

I need to convince them I'm fine. I need to go back to Dad's house and keep looking for the notes—those notes might somehow explain everything.

I open the cupboard and withdraw a mug, concentrating hard on appearing calm and centered. The problem is that my hands are shaking and clammy, too, so inevitably, the mug slips and shatters against the floor. The sound of it breaking is unbearably loud, and I immediately cover my ears and take a step away, forgetting that my feet are bare, not even registering that there are now shards of shattered ceramic all over the floor.

Pain shoots through my foot and I cry out, then finally, belatedly, burst into confused tears.

Ruth is on me in an instant. Her arms envelop me and she pulls me tight against her. My sister smells safe like Grace and I'm shrouded in the very real scent of vanilla and roses and love. She is *shushing* in my ear and rubbing my back as she pulls me away from the broken mug and onto one of the chairs at the kitchen table. I'm vaguely aware of Hunter sweeping up the mess and tending to my feet, but I'm so tired. All of the world feels broken, and maybe I'm broken, too.

Just like Grace. And maybe, eventually, Grace couldn't take it anymore.

"Will you go to the doctor?" Ruth whispers when my feet are patched up and there's a cup of tea in my hands.

"Will you back off if I do?" I whisper back.

Ruth nods, and eventually, so do I.

Grace
March 11, 1958

Beth is a beautiful child—huge blue eyes, heavy chocolate curls, chubby in that way toddlers are supposed to be chubby. She's seventeen months old now and I'm ashamed to have only just noticed how extraordinary she is. Until a few months ago if you'd asked me to name one remarkable thing about my daughter, I'd have struggled to come up with even that.

But it feels like light is flooding over a horizon at dawn. Already, I can tell you all kinds of amazing things about Beth, and I could give you an endless list of the things I adore about her. Her ridiculously cute giggle whenever she does something mischievous. She can already count to six, and I've no idea how that happened, because I certainly didn't teach her to do it. She's brave, too. She still falls over a lot when she tries to run after the other children, but unless she's really hurt herself, she never cries. And even though I've not deserved it for the longest time, she gives me incredibly warm hugs that go on and on and on and bring tears to my eyes, and when she says Mama, *I know now that's who I am. It's not all that I am, of course, but it's a big part of what makes me me. And lately, it's a part of my identity that I actually love.*

That night at the Aurora Bridge was eleven months ago. Eleven cycles when we've been so careful for Patrick to finish away from me. Eleven months when my monthly came and I sometimes cried tears of joy at its arrival. But last month Patrick came home from work drunk and elated after completing a big project at work. I rolled my eyes and offered him some water to try to stave off the monster hangover I feared was brewing. He was so charming that night, flirting with me and making me laugh. It was fun and lighthearted between us as if our lives were fun and lighthearted, and we just got carried away, that's all. The next morn-

ing I prayed to God that He would grant me just a little mercy for this one mistake.

I've been waiting for my monthly for two weeks now. And then this morning I threw up, so it seems that God has not granted me any mercy.

But I will not go passively into the darkness this time. I will not walk through those endless days of sadness again—I can't.

I'm praying again tonight, just as I've prayed every time I realized I was pregnant. With Tim, I prayed for wisdom and strength and safety for my baby. With the twins, I prayed that things would be different. With Beth, I prayed for God to take the burden away.

And this time? Tonight I'm asking not for Him to intervene. No, this time I know it's up to me, and that's why I'm begging Him to give me the courage to do what needs to be done.

TEN

Beth
1996

"I spoke to Ruth and Hunter earlier," Dr. Lisa Gibbons says quietly as I take a seat in her office. "They've given me their perspective on what's happening, but I'd really like to hear yours."

I'm embarrassed to be here. Ever since I arrived at my family GP I've felt hot with shame and guilt.

Hello, I'm Beth Evans. Psychologist. Wife. Mother. Crazy person.

I know better than most that mental illness is nothing to be ashamed of. I also know better than most that in some professions, being diagnosed with a mental illness is the kiss of death to a career. That's why I'm just scared enough to come here today, but far *too* scared to admit why.

"They overreacted," I say, lifting my chin stubbornly. "Ruth has forgotten what it's like to have an infant. And Hunter has never had a child before. He just doesn't realize that it's normal for me to be a little strung out. And you know what's going on with Dad. I'm cleaning up his house, and it's stressful. There are genuinely overwhelming environmental factors weighing on my mind."

If I can convince her, I can relax. If Lisa believes me, then maybe I'm actually fine.

"Okay, then," Lisa says mildly. She leans back in her chair and links her hands behind her head—a picture of relaxation and ease. I desperately envy her. I'm sitting stiffly, knees and ankles close together, back ramrod straight. I've linked my fingers in my lap, but I hold my elbows locked tightly. I'm vaguely conscious my body language is sending a message I really don't want to send, but even so, I can't convince my limbs to relax. "Ruth feels that you haven't been yourself lately. And to be honest with you, I was concerned, too, after your visit with Noah a few weeks ago. I've known you a long time, Beth. I've never seen you quite so…distant. Withdrawn."

"Withdrawn?" I repeat the word, testing the feel of it in my mouth. Ruth said the same thing.

"Ruth mentioned she's noticed the same."

"My routine has changed. We both worked in downtown Bellevue so it was easy to see one another for lunch. Now getting out of the house with Noah takes me so long, and I still find it so stressful when he gets upset while we're out and about. I've still been going to Sunday dinners every week…but it's true that we don't always stay long after we eat these days because I always want to get Noah home to bed before it's too late. Once upon a time, Hunter would be dragging me out the door hours after we finished the meal, because Ruth and Dad and I would be drinking wine and chatting at a million miles an hour. But that's changed. Everything is changing." I'm rambling now, trying to distract Lisa's eagle eyes. It doesn't work.

"Beth, I was talking about the way you're interacting with us, not your routine. Do you *remember* that visit with me two weeks ago?" I think back to my last visit when I came in for a wellness checkup with Noah. My memory suggests that the visit was uneventful, and I don't remember doing or thinking or saying anything out of the ordinary. I shake my head. "You were concerned about Noah's weight. Remember?"

Ah, yes. Noah was on the fiftieth percentile for height and weight in the first three months of his life, neatly following the projected increase on the growth chart. And then in his fourth month, he suddenly dropped down to the forty-second percentile. I had a feeling that was my fault. Maybe I wasn't feeding him enough, or maybe my milk wasn't satisfying him.

"Yes, but perhaps you don't remember that there was a good reason for me to be concerned," I remind her stiffly.

"Beth, as I told you at the time, a drop of eight percentile on the growth chart is *nothing*. Most parents would take my reassurance when confronted by something like that, but I could see you were still anxious, and you weren't hearing me out. I actually made a note to check in on you next week. A first baby is an immense adjustment. It's okay to admit you're struggling."

"I'm not *struggling*," I exclaim, crossing my arms over my chest. "I'm *tired*. That makes me a little irritable. Taking a while to adapt is hardly a clinical condition."

"I'm not so sure about that," Lisa murmurs with a very gentle smile. "I know you work with children, but I'm sure you've heard of postpartum depression."

"I'm definitely not depressed," I say without hesitation. "I know what depression is. I'm not sad at all, other than a reasonable amount of *sad* because of my father. I'm just..." I'm not myself. I guess I am unusually irritable, but then again, I can't relax at the moment, so even that makes sense. And yes, I'm probably agitated, too, but that's just because everything that's happening with Dad. Plus, I'm running on so little sleep. Most of my problems are my circumstances, and the truth is, I've probably made the worst mistake of my life in having Noah, and I can't say it aloud because what kind of a mother admits she doesn't enjoy parenting? I chew all of these words up in my mind but I can't say them aloud, and because I have to say something, I just repeat the words that seem to be my new personal motto. "It's just hard, that's all."

"Sweetheart," Lisa murmurs softly. "I've got five kids myself, remember? I *know* it's hard, and no one tells you what a shock a new baby is to the system and so mothers often end up feeling like they're the only one struggling to keep their heads above water. But there's a difference between *that* level of struggle and the level Hunter and Ruth described. Depression doesn't always look like simple sadness. Sometimes its muddled up with anxiety and irritation and a general inability to manage your way through the ordinary world. Sometimes it's intrusive thoughts you can't shake, or feeling like the world has been drained of color. Sometimes it's like everything leaves you feeling inexplicably *flat*. Some depressed patients report that finding motivation to tackle simple tasks is completely overwhelming, or figuring out how to do things they've done a million times is suddenly impossible. Does any of that ring a bell for you?"

I clear my throat, but force myself to shrug nonchalantly.

Don't label me. God, Lisa, please don't label me.

"Sure. Some of that sounds familiar, but that doesn't mean I'm depressed. Any of those things can be explained by sleep deprivation, or genuinely stressful circumstances, or even just me attempting a task I'm not good at. Right? I mean, think about it. What if what Hunter and Ruth have decided is me being crazy is actually me just being a particularly inadequate mother? That's a *legitimate* possibility that you can't dismiss just because it's easier to slap a diagnosis on me and send me on my way." My voice breaks, and Lisa's expression softens.

"Do you trust me, Bethany?" she asks. It was Lisa who prescribed the pill to me when I was sixteen. Lisa who helped us navigate Dad's conditions, in between specialist appointments.

Lisa who helped Hunter and me through six long years of infertility. I swallow the lump in my throat.

"Of course I trust you."

"You're a wonderful, caring woman and your love for Noah is evident. You *aren't* failing here, even if it feels like you are. You know every bit as well as I do that depression isn't weakness. It's a matter of brain chemistry. Postpartum depression is no different. Pregnancy and childbirth are immensely taxing on a woman's body and it's not at all uncommon for a new mother to develop depression in the postpartum period. In fact, some studies suggest as high as ten percent of women suffer from it."

"I don't even think I can talk to you about this today," I whisper, suddenly breathless. "I'm just *so* tired."

A loud, humiliating sob bursts from my lips. Lisa leans forward to take my hand in hers.

"Let me give you some medication to help you sleep tonight. Everything feels worse when you're exhausted."

"But I'm breastfeeding..." I protest through my tears.

"I'll prescribe a drug that is safe for occasional use. And Hunter can feed Noah formula just for tonight so you can have a long stretch of rest. But I do want you to give the matter of his feeding some serious thought, because the next thing I'm going to suggest is that we try you on a low dose of Prozac, and that's *not* recommended for breastfeeding mothers."

"But..."

"I promise you, formula is totally safe. Sure, there are benefits to breastfeeding, but Noah has already enjoyed many of those benefits after five months, and in any case, *your* health is far more important than anything breastfeeding can offer Noah."

"The only thing that's working is the breastfeeding," I blurt hoarsely. "It's the only thing I'm actually good at when it comes to him."

"I know it feels true, but it's *not* true. You've got a healthy, happy baby and you're doing a terrific job."

"I can't…" I start to protest, but trail off. Lisa hands me a box of tissues and I take a handful.

"I hear what you're saying about your exhaustion, honey, so let's put a pin in this conversation," Lisa says quietly. "Let's get you some rest, and then tomorrow I want you to come back in so we can make a plan moving forward. Does that sound okay? You don't have to do anything you don't want to do, Beth. But let's not make any decisions until you've had some sleep and you're feeling rested."

I leave her office with a prescription for sleeping tablets. Hunter and Ruth are in the waiting room, side by side, both holding magazines they aren't actually reading. When they see me, they dump the magazines onto the coffee table and rise. The wariness in their gazes sends a punch of guilt to my gut.

"What's the plan?" Ruth asks me quietly.

"Sleeping tablets for tonight," I whisper. I'm still teary, overwhelmed and exposed by the events of the day.

"And then?" Hunter asks. I shift my gaze to his. I've found a home in this man over the past decade. Arm in arm, we battled to have this baby, facing miscarriage and infertility and heartache after heartache. *That's* exactly why it's so hard for me to lean on him now. But as he stares at me in this waiting room, I don't see judgment or disappointment. I see only concern and love in his eyes, and some of the resistance I feel to accepting his or anyone else's help starts to crumble.

"Tomorrow," I croak. "Tomorrow we'll reassess."

Grace
March 24, 1958

I've spent the past few weeks considering my options. Grieving, never once celebrating. I've realized that there is only one thing left to do but it is the worst, most drastic option. I just need to escape—I simply can't face this again. The fear looms big and bold, and I cannot even convince myself to live in its shadow.

There is only one way to outrun it. There is only one way to peace. It's bad enough that I've come back to this place—my children deserve for me to choose not to stay here. Even Patrick deserves better than this.

I know it is a mortal sin, and I have no idea how I'm ever going to convince myself to go through with it when I can't even bring myself to write the word, but I have run out of options, haven't I? It's death, one way or another, and at least this way I have control.

May God forgive me for what I have to do.

ELEVEN

Beth
1996

I sleep for fourteen hours. I sink into the kind of knockout dreamless slumber that only comes when you're utterly spent... or, I guess, medicated to the gills. I wake alone in our bed with the predawn light just filtering through the blinds. My breasts are engorged well beyond comfort—rock-hard and weeping milk and impossibly hot to the touch. I immediately check the cradle beside our bed, but Noah isn't there.

Yesterday Noah's absence might have spawned an out-of-control panic in me, but today, after an initial adrenaline spike, I console myself with logic. *Hunter probably took him into one of the spare rooms so I could sleep.* Yesterday such reassurance would have done nothing to calm me, but today I take a deep breath, and slowly leave the bedroom.

I find Hunter asleep on the mattress in the nursery we don't use. It seemed like the perfect room for a hypothetical nursery when we bought the house, but in practice, it's just too far away from our bedroom.

Hunter and I painted this room together when I was pregnant the first time. The walls are purple, the trim is white and the hypoallergenic wool carpet we splurged on is a pretty floral pattern that's a mix of the two. There's teddy bear artwork on the walls, and a matching comforter on the cot. The room was empty when I lost our first baby...freshly painted, but unfurnished. I called her Grape and I was convinced she was a girl, but we lost her so early, we never found out for sure. We closed the door to this room the day we found out she was gone, and we didn't open it for three years—not until I finally fell pregnant with Noah and we passed fourteen weeks and two days. That's when I lost Grape. I still think about her sometimes, especially around the key anniversary dates...the date we found out we were pregnant, the date we saw her on the first scan, the date we lost her, the date that should have been her due date.

I thought about redecorating when I fell pregnant with Noah. I thought about it again when we reached fourteen weeks and three days and I finally found the strength to open this door. I thought about it again as his birth loomed. Each time, I'd talk myself out of it, just in case I somehow jinxed this pregnancy, too. But I kept putting it off, and then Hunter had to race out to buy furniture when I was in the hospital after the birth.

Then we brought him home and he was so tiny...so fragile. No way could I sleep if he was all the way down at the other end of the house. We moved Noah straight into our bedroom, and this is the first time that crib has ever been used.

Right now Hunter is sprawled out on his stomach on a mattress on the floor, one arm tucked under his face. He's shirtless and the duvet is wrapped around his legs. He's snoring softly. I take a few very careful steps toward the crib, and there I find Noah. He's wriggled his way out of his muslin wrap and he's sound asleep with his hands in fists beside his rosy cheeks. I was going to wake him to drain my breasts, but I'm still not entirely convinced that the sleeping tablet I took is safe for him. After all, Lisa did say "safe for periodic use"...so *some* of it must get into the milk. Better not risk it. Besides, Noah looks so content in his sleep, and I can't stand the thought of waking him up.

Instead, I turn and slip out of the room, making a beeline for the shower off my bedroom, where I let the warmth of the stream ease the flow of milk as I send it down the drain. I watch the milk as it disappears. Breastfeeding was so painful at first, but I persisted, and it got easier. I didn't know to expect that. I didn't know that once I mastered it, the idea of stopping it would be devastating.

I'm sitting at the kitchen table with a cup of tea when Hunter emerges, a smiley, drooling Noah in his arms.

"How are you feeling?" he asks.

"Much better. Thanks. I'm really sorry about..." I trail off, not sure how to describe the events of the past forty-eight hours. Sorry that I'm flirting with madness? Sorry that I'm losing my mind? Sorry that I'm not coping with juggling all of these balls? Sorry that I'm letting you down? Sorry that this situation with Dad seems to have become the straw that broke this camel's back?

Hunter blanches, then shoots me an irritated look.

"Jesus, Bethany. You don't need to apologize. *I'm* the one who's sorry. I knew something was going on—I just didn't know it was this bad."

I swallow and look away.

"Lisa wants me to think about trialing some Prozac. I don't think I can do it."

"Why not?"

"I'd have to stop breastfeeding."

Hunter doesn't offer me Noah—instead, he sits him carefully down into the high chair and then busies himself making coffee and heating up some formula. After a few minutes he lifts Noah into his arms, then sits beside me to feed him the bottle.

"I know how much you wanted to breastfeed, babe. I know that it's important to you. And I don't want to influence you either way—but I do need to say this." He looks up from Noah's face to mine, and he blinks too fast, then looks away and clears his throat. "I don't really understand what's going on with you—I guess I can't. But I'm scared. *Really* scared. I want you to be happy, and I can see that you're not."

"I am happy," I say weakly. I can't be honest with him. The only way my husband could possibly respond to "I don't know what I'm doing when it comes to our kid" or "Is it possible we should have listened to Mother Nature and given up on a child years ago?" would be with platitudes and false reassurances I can't handle at the moment. "Okay, yes. I'm struggling a little."

"A little?" he repeats, giving me a wry look. "Honey, come on. I have eyes. I can see that you're in your own world at the moment, and I *know* you. That's not a place you want to stay. If you switch to formula, I can help more…take some of the pressure off."

"I don't get why everyone is so determined to stop me breastfeeding. First your mom, now Lisa and you. It's the only thing I'm good at these days!"

"The only thing you're good at?" Hunter blinks at me as if this statement makes no sense at all, and while I love him for it, I'm reminded only of how much he loves me, and how that makes him biased. "You're amazing at *everything*. Noah is a contented, healthy, happy baby and I'm at work fifty hours a week. Our son is incredible and *you* did that."

I wonder what he'd say if I told him about the time I left Noah alone in the house. Or the incident just two days ago when I left him crying in the attic at Dad's because I freaked out. *Amazing at everything?* Not so much.

"I'm going to think about it," I say stiffly.

"Okay. That's all we can ask."

I don't miss his use of the pronoun—*we*. So, it's me against "them" now. Hunter and no doubt Ruth are on Team Lisa, convinced this is all in my head, all of them failing to see what should be right in front of their eyes—*I'm struggling because I'm just not up to this task.* I try to stop myself from becoming defensive, but I can't help it. My mood sours so fast it's like an out-of-control brushfire, turning a peaceful morning to ashes in seconds. I push back my chair and stand.

"I'm not going to work today. I thought I'd take you back to the doctors," Hunter says quietly.

"I don't need you to treat me like an invalid. You don't have to patronize me."

At the sharpness in my tone, Hunter's gaze narrows.

"You can look at it like that, or you can see a husband who loves you and who's doing everything he can to support you. Either way, I'm not going to work. If you don't want me to drive you, I'll watch Noah while you go alone."

"Fine," I say, and I spin on my heel and go back into the bedroom. I manage to cling to my frustration and avoid Hunter all morning, until it's time to go to the clinic for my follow-up appointment.

And I do leave him and Noah at home. I give them a stilted goodbye and drive to Lisa's clinic. As I lower myself into the upholstered chair opposite her desk, I try to say what I think she wants to hear.

"I feel back to normal now. It was definitely just sleep deprivation."

I'm impressed with my delivery. It sounds fluid and convincing, and I think I've convinced Lisa, too, because she nods slowly then straightens in her chair.

"So everything's okay now that you've had some rest?"

"Yes," I say firmly. "I'm fine now." Fine, and ready to get right back to clearing out Dad's attic to find the rest of those notes.

"Let me read you something, Beth. I don't want you to say anything. I just want you to listen and see how this list lines up with your situation. Okay?" I nod, and Lisa selects a heavy textbook on her desk, then angles it toward her so I can't see the page. She slides her reading glasses on and reads, "Sleep disturbance. Lack of usual pleasure in activities. Depressed mood. Severe irritability. Unexplained agitation. Withdrawal from usual social activities and networks. Lack of interest in food. Hints at feelings of worthlessness and references failures others can't see. Apparent inability to concentrate." She looks at me over her glasses and says, "What do you think that was?"

"I'm guessing that's a list of symptoms for postpartum depression," I say impatiently. "But we already discussed this, Lisa. I'm not depressed."

She sets the book down on her desk and withdraws a piece of paper, then turns the page toward me. At the top, she's scrawled the words *Call from Ruth re Bethany Evans*. Beneath that, she's written *Call to Hunter, re Beth*.

The symptoms she's just rattled off to me are the notes she took in her calls with my sister and husband. My stomach drops. Lisa's gaze is fixed on my face.

"Have you had any thoughts of self-harm, Beth?"

"What? No!" Thoughts of running away, sure. Self-harm? No. The professional in me feels that now would be an excellent time to mention that my mother may have been a woman who really did have postpartum depression. However, I don't mention this to Lisa, mainly because my situation is not the same, and I cannot let her label me.

"Any thoughts of harming Noah?"

Does leaving him alone in his crib while I left the house count?

"Lisa, this is ridiculous."

"Can you answer the question?"

"No, of course I haven't had thoughts of harming Noah!"

"What about your anxieties about his health and welfare? Can we talk about those? Hunter said you reacted quite violently to an incident with a teething biscuit yesterday."

"Okay," I groan. "Yes. I overreacted. I *was* exhausted and seeing him choke like that was overwhelming."

"Any intrusive thoughts, Beth?"

Yes. That's exactly why I can't sleep. My mind is constantly engaged in *what-ifs* and I simply can't talk myself out of fixating on them. My body is on high alert—and it just won't turn off the adrenaline because it's convinced that danger is imminent.

"I don't want to stop breastfeeding," I blurt.

"I was hoping you'd agree to the Prozac, in conjunction with cognitive behavioral therapy. But if you're adamant about not taking the medication, we can try the CBT first."

How did I get here? How do I get back? What if I can't get back? What if I feel like this forever?

"I don't want anyone to know," I whisper. "Lisa, I'm scared of what my colleagues would think. I extended my leave but I told them it was just because I loved being at home."

"You don't have to tell anyone at your clinic, Beth," Lisa says gently. "We'll find you therapy somewhere else in the city if you're really concerned about confidentiality."

"Honestly, I'm certain I'm already doing everything a therapist would tell me to do."

"Oh, honey." Her gaze is gentle. "You *know* that's not how this works. You can't treat yourself."

"Can I think about this?"

"I'm going to give you the script today, and the name for a really fantastic psychologist in Seattle, right near Hunter's office. I'm also going to give you a fact sheet about postpartum depression. I want to see you in a few days, and you have my number and my on-call number. You can call me anytime—if I'm with a patient, I'll call you back as soon as I finish."

I leave her office for the second time in two days with a stack of paperwork. I stuff it all into my handbag and start the car.

For a while, I drive around the suburb on autopilot—up and down tree-lined streets and roads, stopping for a while at one lookout over the water, then another. I pass my own house and Chiara's house. I stop on her street and think about knocking on the door and going inside for a coffee with her, but I guess it turns out that I'm still embarrassed that I made her miss the recital, and maybe I'm not ready to face her in person yet.

Finally, I concede defeat and go searching for solace. It's no surprise that I find myself back at Dad's place, the safest house I've ever known. The first thing I do when I'm inside is to call Hunter to let him know where I am. We have a brief, terse conversation where he asks what Lisa said, and I act like a petulant child because I don't want to talk about it, and I tell him I'll be home when I've had some time to think.

I desperately want his comfort, and the last thing I actually want is to push him away, but I just can't seem to stop myself. Is this what Lisa and Ruth meant by *withdrawn*? I feel like there's an invisible force field around me and everyone who crashes into it is magically repelled with some force. It's awfully lonely in here with all of these secrets, especially when I'm not even sure why I'm keeping them.

Loneliness is worse than sadness. I've come to realize that's because loneliness, by its very definition, cannot be shared...

Cause of death unable to be determined due to body decomposition.

The notes. The notes might have the answers.

I draw in a deep breath and climb the stairs to the attic to keep sorting through the mess—not because I actually want to, but because I have no idea what *else* to do.

It's just after 6 p.m. when I leave Dad's house, after another fruitless afternoon of sorting through trash. As I step out of the car on our driveway, I catch the scent of fresh bread on the breeze and my stomach rumbles. Chiara taught Hunter to cook, and while he's usually too busy to do much of it, when he does step into the kitchen, the results are always spectacular.

"Hi," I say softly when I find him over the stove. He's sautéing Brussels sprouts and bacon, and there's a loaf of bread cooling on the table. On the countertop foil covers several other plates. I slip the breastmilk I pumped this afternoon from my handbag into the fridge, then walk around my husband to peek beneath the foil. When I find grilled pork loins and buttery potatoes, I moan in appreciation, feeling a burst of hunger that's become alien after weeks of lackluster appetite. "This looks amazing. Thank you."

"How are you feeling?" Hunter asks me, but he's watching the Brussels sprouts closely.

"I'm okay," I say. Hunter glances at me, then looks back to the frying pan. "Where's Noah?"

"He didn't sleep long this afternoon. He's already in bed."

I creep down the hallway to our room, but the cradle there is empty, and so I frown and go to check the nursery. Noah is in the crib, and Hunter has already made up the mattress on the floor, obviously intending to sleep here, too. I don't like this at all, and I quickly head back into the kitchen.

"Why the nursery?" I ask abruptly. Hunter sighs and starts plating up the food.

"Beth, I don't want to argue tonight. It's obvious you need to rest, and I just want to do what I can to help you. Okay?"

"That doesn't mean I want you to move out of our bedroom," I say, throat aching with the force it takes to hold back my tears.

"How could I possibly know what you want at the moment?" Hunter shrugs, sliding the Brussels sprouts onto each plate. "You're not exactly talking to me. I'm guessing at what might help because you're not giving me any guidance whatsoever."

We sit side by side at the kitchen table and begin to eat in silence.

"It's not that I don't love him," I say without even thinking about it. But once the words are out, I feel better, not worse. Hunter raises his gaze to mine.

"Okay."

I draw in a deep breath, and it takes some effort, but I force myself to keep speaking.

"I *do*. I love him so much."

"I know that, Beth."

"I really just thought I'd be better at this."

"You keep saying that… I just don't understand where it's coming from. You're doing everything right."

"But it's so hard," I whisper, eyes filling with tears. I set my cutlery down to pinch the bridge of my nose. "I thought all of this would feel natural. I thought I'd have some kind of instinct about what to do and when, but I just don't."

"Why on earth would you think you'd automatically know how to raise a kid?"

"It seems to be easy for everyone else."

"You're a good listener. Did that make you a psychologist?"

"You know it didn't, Hunter."

"It took you years of study and clinical practice, right?" When I nod, Hunter shrugs. "Well, as difficult as I know your job is, it's still easier than parenting. Your clients leave your office, and then it's up to *their* parents. With Noah, there's no line where our responsibility suddenly ends. When he's older, his well-being will be up to him, too, but for now it's entirely up to us…up to *you*, really, for most of the week while I'm at work. That's a lot of pressure. Hell, that's more pressure than either one of us has ever felt before."

"But you're handling it so well. You're *perfect*."

"Jesus, Beth. My wife has been suffering under my nose and I didn't do a thing about it for months. That's hardly perfect," Hunter sighs, running his hand through his hair. "It's going to take us time to find our way as parents, and it's the most important thing we'll ever do. We're supposed to struggle. We're supposed to make mistakes." His lips quirk. "We're going to mess him up real good, I promise, and one day *you* are going to have to untangle him because that's your profession. I'll be on hand for when he needs legal advice, but the psychological damage is all your department."

I smile weakly at his lame joke, even though he doesn't really deserve it.

"Thanks."

"So you've been feeling like you're not doing a good job. What else?"

"I think I'm probably wound up, like you said yesterday. I just can't relax. So when I lie in bed, it's like my mind is on high alert, waiting for something to go wrong. I haven't been sleeping."

"I know, babe."

"I didn't recognize it as depression because I haven't been *sad*. I mean, I have been sad, but the sadness I've felt has been understandable because of Dad. There's..." I suck in a sharp breath. "There's a *lot* going on with Dad, Hunter. It would be hard for anyone."

"That's absolutely true."

"But it's hard for me to be subjective about my own state of mind, like I would be for a client. And I think it is possible that maybe I haven't been coping as well as I should have. I *really* don't want anyone to label me, but I do think Lisa is onto something."

"Good. This is good, Beth. You're talking to me."

"You know, when we first started dating, I used to think I wouldn't mind at all if there was a way I could let you see into my thoughts," I blurt. Hunter chuckles and nods.

"We're both oversharers, normally."

"We always had the kind of relationship where we just shared whatever came into our mind. I had nothing to hide from you, and I hope... I think you always felt the same."

"I did. I do."

"But this feels shameful," I whisper, looking away. "Six years,

Hunter. Six years of trying to have a baby, and then we finally get one, and I have no fucking idea what I'm doing." I exhale shakily, then admit, "Some days I *hate* it. I feel so overwhelmed. I'm terrified of letting him down and letting you down. And I can't help but think he deserves a better mother than I know how to be."

"Beth," he says very gently. "We *do* have a safe, open relationship, and that's why I should have known something was going on when you pulled away from me. Since when do we disconnect in the tough times? We only made it through six years of trying to become parents *because* we leaned on one another."

"You know, I always thought that a psychologically unwell person would feel like something was wrong. I never really thought about it as such, but I guess I assumed that the negative feelings would feel distinct from typical feelings, so people would know they need help. But this hasn't felt like something in my mind wasn't working the way it should. It actually feels like I'm reacting in a typical way to the circumstances, so I've convinced myself the circumstances are the problem. I've felt frustrated and inadequate, and I've been thinking that was just because I *am* inadequate. Even as a psychologist, I didn't consider the possibility that those feelings were symptoms, and not a reasonable reaction to—" *an awful, bewildering, messed up* "—an extraordinary set of circumstances."

"When I suggested you talk to someone, you were concerned that it would negatively impact your career. Do you really think that's a possibility?" Hunter asks me quietly.

I rub my forehead, suddenly weary.

"Yeah. I actually think Alan will be okay." Alan is my supervisor, and he's incredible—empathetic, gentle, supportive. But he's not the only boss I have, and I have to be smart here. "I don't know how the higher managers might deal with this, given that I work with kids. They're understandably cautious about child therapists being in a good place emotionally themselves. That's why when I decided to take the extra leave, I just told them I was enjoying my time at home. There really is a stigma attached to mental health treatment, and it's still strong even in my profession. Maybe even *more so* for psychologists, which is silly, but there seems to be an expectation that we can just handle ourselves and that makes us immune to this kind of thing. I need to think this through…maybe get some advice."

Hunter gets out of his chair and crouches beside mine. He turns me gently to face him, and then stares into my eyes.

"I never want you to feel you have to shoulder something like this on your own. I won't judge you. We're in unchartered territory—as parents, yes, but also as partners. What's worked for us in the past has been communicating, and I think that's what's going to get us through this, too. Can you promise to *try* to keep talking to me?"

"There are things I'm not ready to talk about yet," I whisper, thinking about the attic and the notes and the death certificate I found in the bottom of that wooden chest.

"Do your best, Beth. That's all I'm asking."

I let Hunter talk me into taking another sleeping pill and catching up on some more sleep, but as a compromise, he and Noah move back into our bedroom.

TWELVE

Beth
1996

My siblings and I all qualified for "lapsed Catholic" status when we reached our teens. Dad let us decide for ourselves whether we'd continue to go to weekly church services, and we each gradually decided we'd rather sleep in. Even so, events at the St. Louise's Parish Church still seem to mark every important milestone in our family life. The sacraments are signposts for all of the major events in our lives: baptisms for infants, confirmations for the children, weddings and funerals for the adults. Sunday morning ten past ten, Hunter and I are tiptoeing down the aisle of the church to take the seats Tim and Alicia reserved for us. We're late, and everyone else is already safely seated in the pews, ready to play our part as witnesses in Ruth's eldest son's confirmation service.

St. Louise's isn't a big church, and the pews are short and so uncomfortable Ruth and I used to wonder if they'd been designed to keep the parishioners from nodding off. Confirmation services like this are big events in the parish and are well attended by the wider community, so we all cram in like sardines. Now Hunter is holding Noah on my left, Alicia is on the other side, Tim is at the end of the pew beside Dad, who sits in his wheelchair in the outer aisle, Ruth and her family are in front of us, and Chiara and Wallace are behind us.

"Remember that day?" Hunter whispers to me suddenly, during a particularly dry patch of the homily.

"Which day?" I whisper back.

He gives me a pointed look as he says, "The day we met."

I quickly do the math—over eleven years have passed since I met Hunter in this very church. I was living in Ballard at the time, having just finished my postgrad qualification and working in my first supervised position as a psychologist. I came home for Christmas, and Dad dragged me along to the Christmas Eve candlelight service. We had just taken our seats when I noticed the tall, extremely handsome man sitting with his parents right beside me. He flashed me a smile, and I smiled back, but then we discovered that our side-by-side seating arrangement was no happy coincidence.

"Wallace, Chiara," Dad had said cheerfully, leaning across me to greet the man's parents. "Fancy seeing you two here. This must be Hunter."

"Why, yes it is, Patrick," Chiara had said, a picture of innocence. "Lovely to bump into you. And this must be Beth."

It turned out that Hunter and I had been floating around in the same circles for years, even though we'd never met. Our parents were all active in the congregation at St. Louise's, and while mingling after the liturgy one week, Dad and Chiara cooked up a scheme to introduce us.

Somewhere between "Silent Night" and "O Christmas Tree," Hunter and I bonded over a mutual determination to teach our parents a lesson by not getting along well *at all*, but by the time the candle in my hand had melted down to a stub, I was smitten. But I was desperate to avoid encouraging Dad's meddling, so at the end of the night, I said a polite goodbye to Hunter and marched away before any of the parents could say something awkward.

"What do you think of Hunter?" Dad asked as soon as we were alone in the car.

"He was fine," I said, shrugging, feigning nonchalance, even as I kicked myself for not getting Hunter's number. "Not my type, but fine."

When the phone rang late on Christmas Day, Dad answered it, and he was grinning like an idiot when he brought me the handset.

"Sorry to call your dad's house," Hunter said. "I *really* don't want to encourage any more parental meddling, but I also couldn't live with myself if I didn't at least ask you out."

We arranged a date for when we were both back in the city a few days later, and that was it: we were inseparable from then on. We married in this very church eight years ago, and moved back to Bellevue a few months after that.

"Of course I remember." I smile to myself as nostalgia washes over me.

Hunter leans low toward my ear and murmurs, "That was the day my life began."

I flash him a small smile, then rest my head on his shoulder, turning to face the priest. This is Father Jenkins and he's been our parish priest for years—he's one of those compassionate types who seems genuinely overjoyed to see anyone at church and probably wouldn't care if Hunter and I had a chat during his homily, but I like to at least *look* like I'm listening. Thirteen years of Catholic education instilled a quiet terror of the clergy, and I guess old habits die hard.

"It hasn't been the happily-ever-after we thought it would be when we made our vows though, has it?" I whisper to Hunter. I was thirty-one when I married Hunter, but in some ways I was still a child, still thinking of marriage like a solution to some problem I hadn't quite identified. On some level I really believed that from our wedding day on, life would be smooth and easy.

Every now and again my siblings tease me about being the spoiled baby. I've never felt like I was, but at times like this I know that there's at least an element of truth in the accusation.

"I didn't want or expect *happily-ever-after* and I don't think you really wanted that, either. I wanted a partner—someone to share my life with. And I found the best woman on earth for the job."

"You still think that?"

"I still *know* that."

I brush my lips against his, a chaste and innocent expression of affection. There's a rap against the pew behind us, and when Hunter and I glance back, Wallace is giving us a pointed look through the thick lenses of his glasses. He points to the priest as if we need to be reminded that Father Jenkins is still there, but just as I turn to look away, I see my father-in-law smirking to himself.

When the service finally ended, Ruth and her family had the requisite photos taken on the church steps with Andrew in his suit, and then we all piled into the cars and came back to Dad's house. Ruth's sons Andrew, Mathew and David have all changed into casual clothes and are tossing a football around with Ellis and Jeremy in the backyard, apparently immune to the icy wind. Tim, Alicia and Dad are sitting at the beautifully decorated dining room table, and I can't help but raise my eyebrows when I see Tim and Alicia holding hands.

"What's up with you two?" I murmur under my breath when Tim gets up and approaches me to take Noah from my arms.

"Marriage counseling," Tim says wryly. "That's what."

"Really?" I say, surprised.

"God, Beth. You of all people should know that sometimes you just need a little outside perspective."

"*Me* of *all* people?" I repeat, scowling. He blinks at me.

"Because you're a psychologist? What else would I mean?"

"Oh." I wince. "Of course. Well, good for you."

Tim stares at me thoughtfully, then nods toward Dad and Alicia.

"Dad's a bit of a mess today."

"He is? I haven't had a chance to talk to him." I swallow the lump in my throat. That's at least in part because I'm avoiding him. I feel like I need to ask him about that death certificate, but I know he won't be able to answer me, and I know it's going to be upsetting for both of us. "Is his speech worse?"

"His speech is fine. Well, no worse than it usually is. But... look at him, Beth. *Really* look at him."

I drag my gaze to Dad and force myself to focus on him. He's engaged in a conversation with Alicia. She's talking quietly, her hands flying this way and that, and Dad is wearing that quiet smile that suggests he might not be following the detail of whatever it is she's saying, but he's happy to be talking to her anyway. He's slowly unwrapping gold-wrapped candies as he listens, and there's a growing pile of wrappers on the tablecloth in front of him.

But his skin has taken on an awful gray pallor, and he's so puffy today...his eyes look like they could disappear into the swelling. He's wearing lounge pants that I know used to be baggy, but are stretched around his swollen ankles—so tight I know they must be painful. Even seated with the oxygen supplementation, he's visibly panting. The dry, rasping cough he's had for months surfaces regularly between breaths. That cough has a rhythm of its own now. It's like the ticking of a clock—the audible mark of his last days counting down.

"He has ups and downs," I say, fumbling for optimism.

"Sure. But there's a trend here we can't ignore, and there's no point kidding ourselves." Tim draws in a deep breath, then murmurs gently, "He just doesn't have long left with us, Bethie."

"Today is about Andrew's confirmation," I cut my brother off abruptly. "I don't want to talk about this today."

"Make way, you two," Ruth calls, and we shift aside as she bustles past us. She's donned an apron since I saw her at Mass, and now she's carrying a huge tray of bread rolls. After she breezes back past us, Tim tickles Noah under the chin, then flashes me a sad look.

"Beth. I get it—it's hard to talk about. It's just... I'm just worried that we're not prepared."

He's not talking about funeral arrangements, and I don't even think he means it when he says *we*. He's prepared. Maybe Jeremy and Ruth are even prepared. But as for me...

"I can't *prepare*, Tim," I whisper back, looking over to my father. The tired smile is still fixed on his face, and the little pile of candy wrappers in front of him is growing by the second as he empties out the bowl. I move to intervene and suggest he eat something healthy, maybe redirect him toward some fruit or something, but then I stop myself, because for the first time, I really understand that it's too late for such tiny decisions to have *any* impact.

He just doesn't have long left with us, Bethie.

"Dad," I blurt, and I leave my son with Tim and walk hastily across the room to his wheelchair. "Daddy, can I talk to you? In private?"

The room has suddenly fallen silent, and the pause feels desperate and awkward. Everyone is staring at me. Dad wheezes. He coughs. Then he nods.

"Beth—" Hunter starts to protest, but I shake my head at him, and I take the handles to Dad's wheelchair and guide him out from the living area. I lead him all the way down toward his bedroom. It's still a mess, and the last place in the world I ever intended to take Dad today. But he's a long way past managing the stairs, and this is the closest room to the stairwell, so his bedroom is where we go. I park the wheelchair beside his bed and give him a pleading look.

"Just wait here, okay? Just for a minute." I'm crying, and wipe hopelessly at my cheeks, hoping he won't notice. But Dad catches my hand, and he's suddenly frowning.

"Maryanne," he rasps. "Don't cry, Maryanne. I'm sorry."

"Daddy," I choke, "It's *Beth*, Dad. Just wait here. I need to get something from upstairs."

I gently release his hand and sprint up the stairs to the attic. I scoop up the clipboard with the two notes on it, and run back down the stairs, almost tripping in my haste to get back to Dad before the rest of my family comes to investigate. I close the door behind us this time, and I sit on the piles of clothes on Dad's bed and rest the clipboard on his lap.

"Did Grace write these, Dad?"

"Grace…" Dad whispers, reaching down to touch the notes with a shaking fingertip. "Grace was beautiful. In the place… what's it called? With the roof."

"Daddy, I need to know *how* she died. It's very important," I choke.

"In the…" He picks up the clipboard, then he looks right into my eyes. "She went. I'm sorry."

"She didn't die in a car accident, did she? I found her death certificate. I saw about… I saw about the cause of death and it says…" God, this is even harder than I thought it would be. I can't say the word *decomposition*, so instead I say weakly, "The certificate says it was too late to tell how she died."

Dad closes his eyes, and a single tear runs down over the swollen skin of his cheek. He pulls the clipboard against his chest and shakes his head.

"She was beautiful in the place…"

"For God's sake, Dad, just tell me: did she kill herself?"

"I didn't…" Dad rasps. He takes my hands in his, and his desperate gaze bores into mine. "Maryanne. I didn't mean what I said. Forgive me."

"Daddy, *it's me*. I'm Beth!" I'm raising my voice despite my best efforts to stay calm. I'm so damned frustrated now, but so is Dad, and this is cruel and I know I need to stop, but I can't. Another tear rolls down his cheek, and his face is reddening, and the wheeze is coming harder and harder and spittle is flying everywhere as he speaks little more than winded gibberish.

"I took her away. I couldn't stand it. I was angry at myself. What she'd done to your mother. And I took her away from you. What's the word, Ruth? And I have to say please but I can't."

The door opens abruptly and Tim and Hunter are there. I rise, guiltily scooping the clipboard from Dad's lap, trying to wipe my cheeks as I do.

"What's going on, Beth?" Tim asks flatly.

"I just needed to talk to Dad," I say. I try to keep my tone light, but my voice is hoarse and I know I'm not fooling anyone this time. Tim looks pissed, but Hunter looks wary.

"Lunch is ready," my husband says cautiously. "Maybe we should all go back out there..."

"Hey, Hunter, could you take Dad out to the table?" Tim asks. I open my mouth to protest, but Tim's gaze narrows. Hunter waits for me to confirm, but when I nod, he takes my father from the room, and Tim closes the door behind them and pins me with a glare.

"What was that about?"

"I just needed to talk to him."

"Alone?"

"Yes."

"You upset him," Tim says furiously. "Do you still not get it? He's *dying*. I've told you it's pointless to argue with him—why on earth would you raise your voice at him today?"

"I didn't raise my—"

"I could hear you through the door!"

"What...what did you hear?" I ask after a pause. I sound guilty. I *feel* guilty.

"I heard you correcting your name," he exclaims. He shoots me a disappointed look, but then his tone softens as he says, "I know it's distressing and I know it's frustrating. But just let him *be*, Beth. Just soak up these hours, because we don't have many left."

I swallow hard, and then look at my brother and nod curtly. He sighs and throws the door open, then disappears into the hallway.

I tuck the clipboard beneath a pile of clothes on Dad's bed, wipe my eyes and follow him out.

THIRTEEN

Maryanne
1958

"Mail for you, Mary," one of my students called as she sorted the letters into their pigeonholes beside my office. I was tired that day—having been out until curfew the night before, and even after that, I raced back to the residential hall to talk until the small hours with the undergrad students I supervised.

My supervisor, Professor Callahan, had been to New York on a trip earlier that year, and he'd gifted me a copy of *The Second Sex* on his return. He told me I simply had to read it and report back with my thoughts. Well, several months later I was now making my own students read it, and the women in the residential hall were *still* discussing that now hopelessly dog-eared book long past midnight almost every night.

We were the generation of women born waiting for a gender revolution, and Simone de Beauvoir was the heroine we'd been praying for. We had granted ourselves permission to say the unsayable—we wanted more for our lives than "domestic bliss." It was an intoxicating freedom, and I felt the start of a momentum that I didn't fully understand, as if our discourse in the small hours were building something that might really change the world.

I was in a fog as I walked to my mail slot that day, exhausted but still intellectually buzzing from the night before, expecting only to find some piece of administrative mail. When I saw my sister's handwriting on the envelope, my mood improved immediately.

I made myself a cup of coffee and took the letter back into my office, closing the door behind me so I could have some privacy. Supervising the undergrad students in the dorm was fine, but every now and again I liked to close that door and pretend I didn't live in a dormitory that housed fifty-eight young women. As I held Grace's letter that day, I hoped for genuine good news. I'd seen her in person on just a few occasions over the years since I moved to California—her wedding day, one Christmas when Father unexpectedly sent me a ticket to come home, and just after the birth of her twins when I'd been in Seattle to attend a conference. The light had dimmed in my sister's eyes over that time, and in my youthful arrogance, I was certain that *Patrick* was entirely to blame.

I saw my sister as the victim of a dreadful epidemic: she had followed the script expected of her and married the first man who made her heart flutter. Now she was living out her life as a housewife, and whenever I thought about her situation, I couldn't understand how she could be anything other than completely unfulfilled and miserable with her lot. My life was exciting—jazz clubs and satisfying philosophical debates, earning my own money and controlling my own destiny. I worked hard, but my life was *fun*. I flirted with boys when I wanted to, kissed them or even more if the urge overtook me, and generally managed to feel like life was an endlessly thrilling game.

I loathed the distance that had grown between us, but even so, I felt powerless to close it. When Grace wrote me, her letters painted a bright picture of domestic bliss that I didn't for one second believe. And when I wrote her, I never really knew what to say in response. I was far from positive by nature, but I still believed that one day, Grace and I would connect again, and we'd restore our once-close sisterhood. Maybe once her children were older, and we found common interests. Maybe once she finally did as my parents so wished she would, and divorced that lout of a husband.

Every time a letter from Grace arrived, I thought the exact same thing: maybe *this* letter will herald the dawn of a new era between us. I tore into the envelope, and was startled to find the text was short.

> *Maryanne,*
> *Please call me at 7 a.m. on Saturday morning at the number below.*
> *This telephone number will reach the house of Mrs. Hills, our next-door neighbor. I am in desperate need of help and don't know who else to turn to. Grace.*

I set the letter down on my desk. For all those years, I'd wished for something *real* from Grace...and here it was, but I didn't feel relief at all. I felt scared. I could read the subtext, and it was evident that something was dreadfully wrong. I wanted to call her right away—but there was obviously a reason she'd given me such specific instructions. Instead, I sweated out the week, living a million worst-case scenarios in my mind over the sleepless nights that followed. What if she was ill? What if one of the children was? Or, as seemed most likely, what if Patrick had done something dreadful?

I called as instructed at precisely 7 a.m. on Saturday. Grace answered on the very first ring.

"Maryanne?"

"Grace? What on earth is going on?"

"I need your help."

"Anything," I said, and despite the years of strain between us, I meant it. "What's wrong? Why did I have to call you at your neighbor's house?"

"Patrick is still asleep at home with the children, and Mrs. Hills is out tending her chickens. Her husband is mostly deaf so I knew we'd have some privacy for a few minutes if you called now."

"Okay? But...*why* do we need privacy?"

"I'm pregnant," she said, then we both drew in a very deep breath. I quickly did the mental calculation. Seeing this pregnancy through would mean five children under five years old. I wasn't surprised at all when Grace then continued miserably, "And I need to *not* be pregnant. Will you help me? I don't even know where to start."

"Have you tried all of the at-home methods?" I asked her, gently.

"I've scalded my skin in hot baths. On Tuesday I drank bleach and vomited until I passed out. I threw myself off the back stairs. I carried Patrick's armchair around the house. I even tried to get some slippery-elm bark from the chemist, but he would only give me a tincture." She laughed bitterly. "Apparently, too many young women had been coming in buying sheets of bark to try to end their pregnancies."

It would have been much easier for me to find her help if she was in California. Abortion was illegal there, too, but I at least knew how to access it. I'd been living on campus for five years— I'd seen my share of girls go down that route. Pregnancy meant expulsion from university. Rubbers and diaphragms could be found if a girl was determined enough but they were expensive and notoriously unreliable, and while we'd all heard of trials of a rumored miracle pill that would prevent a pregnancy, it wasn't yet available to the public. My generation was at the mercy of their fertility, so accessing some kind of abortion *was* our primary form of birth control. There were few alternatives—our options were dreadfully limited.

"I just don't know who to ask for help, and I don't have any money," Grace sobbed.

"I'll get you money. And I'll help you find someone."

"I hate asking you, Maryanne. Truly, I do. We would have to be so careful…" I could almost hear the cogs of her mind turning as she thought it all through. "You must remember Betsy Umbridge?"

I did remember her. Betsy was in Grace's year at school, and when she got pregnant at just sixteen, her boyfriend, Henry, had stepped in to help—tracking down a backyard abortionist who ended the pregnancy. But Betsy developed an infection after her procedure, and at the hospital, doctors had immediately suspected that her story of spontaneous miscarriage was untrue and called the police. Arranging an abortion was a felony offense in Washington State, and both Henry and Betsy spent several years in prison. Even once they were released, they became social pariahs. It was a tremendous scandal for our whole community, and I remember being outraged that something that many of my peers were forced to do from time to time could actually destroy their futures.

"I'll come home," I finally said. It was a test. I was in my second year of a master's program, as well as working two part-time jobs. Grace knew I had commitments, and despite how frayed our relationship had become, I still trusted that she would never allow me to interrupt my life in California if she had *any* other option. If she had protested at the inconvenience to me, I'd figure out how to raise the money in California and wire or post it to her—but if she didn't…

"I'm scared," Grace blurted. "I don't want to do this but I have to, and I can't tell Patrick so I have to do it by myself."

"Why can't you tell him?"

"He doesn't get it, Mary. He just doesn't understand that I have nothing left to give."

When I hung up the phone, I went to pack a suitcase.

I knew Grace's address by heart, but I'd never seen the house she lived in. When the taxi pulled up at the front gate, I thought there had been some mistake.

"Are you sure?" I asked the driver. He grunted and held out his hand for the fare. I looked back to the house and saw the children running wild through the unruly yard. I squinted at the eldest of them, and when I recognized the shape of Patrick's eyes, felt my heart sink. Tim had grown up a lot in the years since I'd seen him, but there was no denying that this was my nephew. I paid the driver and let myself into the yard, only to be swarmed by filthy children. Little Beth was just a toddler, and she was wearing a ratty diaper that was so full, it hung almost to her knees. Her walk was little more than a waddle, and she stepped right up to me, right into my space, to stare up at me with curious eyes.

"Who are you?" Tim demanded, crossing his arms as if he could or would defend his siblings from me. "You look like my mother."

"I'm your aunt Maryanne, child. Where is your mother?"

"Laundry," Jeremy offered helpfully.

"Why are you here?" Tim demanded.

"Can you just get your mother for me?"

Tim surveyed me up and down, pursing his lips. The boy was no taller than my hips. His defiance might have been comical if the situation weren't so awful.

"Momma doesn't like it when we interrupt her in the laundry."

I sighed impatiently and walked around the house into the backyard. It seemed a safe assumption that I'd find the laundry easily enough—the house was tiny. I walked to the back door and went to twist the doorknob, only to find it was locked.

"Grace?" I called hesitantly. "Are you in there?"

I heard her fumble with the lock, and then she was there—all pale and wide-eyed, her face streaked with tears. It was eleven o'clock in the morning, but she was still wearing a tattered nightgown. Grace was thin and drawn and visibly drained.

"I'm having a bad day," she said unevenly.

I gaped at her.

"I can see that."

"It's the thought of it starting all over again, you see," she whispered, eyes wild as she glanced down at her own body. "It plays such tricks on my mind."

Over the next few hours I got a glimpse into the reality of my sister's life, and it seemed to confirm everything I'd ever feared about the pitfalls of married life for women. I knew that to Grace, her courtship and engagement to Patrick had been a fairy tale, but the reality of life after their wedding seemed to be a nightmare. Patrick had all of the power, Grace had all of the responsibility, and the pressure of that existence was crushing her.

The children were surprisingly self-reliant, helping themselves to water and quietly eating the sandwiches Grace served up for their lunch. They watched me with quiet curiosity but didn't speak much. But whenever they were out of the room, Grace spoke, and she rambled with the kind of energy that comes only from a long period of isolation. I was there at last to listen, and the verbal dam had broken. She told me that to her deep and private shame, each birth had brought a period of intense grief and emptiness that she couldn't explain.

I didn't want children of my own, but even so, I had always assumed that the birth of a child would be a happy experience for the mother, and yet I couldn't deny that when Grace spoke about these periods of her life, she was in an intense psychological agony. I didn't understand that at all, and I had no wisdom or advice to offer her. The one thing I could do was to listen.

Grace told me about long days at home alone, and how sometimes, entire weeks would pass without her having an adult conversation. She told me about financial woes and Patrick's drinking and the endless months with little to no sleep, until she was hallucinating and terrified, or she'd accidentally nap during the day and the children would be unsupervised for hours on end until she woke up with a start. She shook with shame as she described times when she found herself shouting at the children over the smallest things. Grace told me that they could barely afford to feed the children they had, let alone a fifth. She told me that the worse things got at home, the less time Patrick seemed willing to spend at the house, and she was genuinely scared he might leave altogether if they went through with this pregnancy.

"Would that be so bad?" I asked her hesitantly. "If he left, I mean."

Grace looked at me with alarm.

"I can't do it alone. How would I survive?"

"You *know* Mother and Father would help you if you divorced him."

"The thing is, I know this all sounds awful, but I do love him, Maryanne. And he does love these children. He just doesn't seem to know how to father them. No wonder, really. He grew up with his aunt Nina and he had no father of his own and he's still trying to figure it all out. I can't give up on him. I just can't." She cleared her throat, wiped her nose and then added in a very small voice. "But I also can't have this baby. It'll be the end of me."

She didn't need to convince me why she couldn't continue with the pregnancy, but maybe she was convincing herself. Over the next few hours, every time I told Grace I'd help her, she'd just keep on talking as if she hadn't heard me, justifying the decision over and over again.

Eventually, though, Grace seemed to run out of words. Her speech slowed, then stopped altogether. Tears still rolled down her cheeks and onto the nightgown. When her sobs had finally faded away, I squeezed her hands within mine. She looked at me with bleary eyes, and I smiled at her, confident that we both knew exactly what was best for her, even if I wasn't entirely sure how we'd achieve it.

"We'll find someone who can take care of it, and we'll fix this. I promise you."

At dinner that night, Father asked me why I had arrived unannounced midsemester. I was waiting for the question and knew exactly how to answer him.

"I'm in trouble," I said. "I'm starting to think you were right about some things, Father."

"Right about what, exactly?" He seemed wary, and fair enough, given how often we'd butted heads over the years.

"Well, when you said women shouldn't trouble themselves with matters of finances and careers," I sighed. "I seem to have made a mess of things and I'm in a bit of financial strife. I'm really reevaluating my future now."

It was just as I'd hoped—Father seemed smug at my failure, but he was still willing to help me fix it. Father and I had little in common, but I didn't doubt that he generally did have my best interests at heart.

"How much do you need?"

"Three hundred dollars should be enough," I said. It was a guess—based purely on the stories the girls back at the residential hall had told me. Father's eyes bulged, but he went into his study after supper and came back with a thick wad of notes.

After that, I waited until my parents were settled in front of the evening programming on the television, and I went into Father's study to use the phone. Women knew these things in those days. We talked about abortion and clumsy contraceptive methods in whispers, but everyone knew the codes.

After several careful phone calls with girls I'd been to school with, I had the name of a man in the city who would help us. He was reported to be an unregistered doctor who would perform the procedure at a secret location.

"It's all very cloak and dagger," my school friend warned me, dropping her voice. "You call him to arrange it, and he gives you a meeting place, then someone picks you up to take you to his clinic. They don't let you see where you're going because it's all top secret."

"How much did it cost?" I whispered back, only hoping I'd scammed my father out of enough money.

"Five hundred dollars," she said, and I gasped. "It's a lot, I know. I heard of a woman who does them in her kitchen and it costs less, but it's so much more dangerous—my friend ended up with sepsis. The doctor I saw really seemed to know what he was doing."

I knew I couldn't ask Dad for more money. I had some savings, about eighty dollars in the bank, but we were still going to be one hundred and twenty dollars short. I just had to hope that Grace could come up with the rest herself.

When I finished with my calls, I emerged to find Mother at the small table in the kitchen, sitting before a pot of tea in her nightgown. It was a similar gown to Grace's, only Mother's was, of course, in pristine condition. Her hair had been recently set and even at eight o'clock, she had a full face of perfect and expensive makeup.

"I visited Grace today," I blurted. Mother looked up at me in surprise, then her line-thin eyebrows knit.

"But you said you were at the university doing research."

"I finished early." Lies upon lies. "Mother, have you seen her house?"

"Not in the last year or two," Mother said stiffly. "Father is desperately displeased with Patrick."

"Why? What happened?"

"We never liked him. Right from the beginning."

"I'm aware, Mother, but you seemed to tolerate him for a while."

"Well, we tried to give him a chance to prove himself, but he blew it. He always wanted money. The phone bill. New work boots. Formula for the baby. The refrigerator shorted out. It was endless, and it was obvious from the outset that he'd only married her because he'd seen this house and he knew we were well-to-do."

I was hardly Patrick's biggest fan myself, but even so, I could see she was being unfair. I'd seen them on their wedding day, and the love between them had been so palpable, I might even have felt the tiniest bit jealous. "They were obviously in love in the beginning."

"Well, the final straw was when Patrick borrowed money from us for the phone bill that last time. The very next day, Father saw him out at the bar drunk with his friends. And Grace called us several days later to ask for money for the bill, she didn't realize Patrick had already borrowed it from us and drank it away."

"That's hardly Grace's fault. She seems to be dreadfully isolated."

"When she's ready to leave, we'll help her. I'd love to see the children more—I mean, heavens, I've only met the littlest one twice. But we can't condone her decision in standing by him."

"She needs us," I said. My heart ached for my sister—to see the innocence and optimism I'd so loved about her swamped by so much pressure and responsibility. "You're blackmailing her into making a decision she's not ready to make."

"I learned that tactic from you, Maryanne," Mother said with a shrug. When I gaped at her, she stirred her tea and gave me a mild look. "You were determined to go to college. Father was determined to stop you. You found a way to go, and then you refused to speak to him until he was ready to support you. And now look at you. He wouldn't even pay your way to California four years ago, and after just a few months of you ignoring him, he'd changed his tune. And how much money has he given you since? Another three hundred dollars tonight. Sometimes the only leverage you have over people is their presence in your life."

"That's *cold*, Mother."

"Perhaps, but you can't deny it's true."

"Grace's situation is entirely different. That house needs so much work, and she's just not strong enough to change her lot in life right now. She just needs a little help until she's back on her feet."

"I'll give her all of the help she needs," Mother snapped. "But only once she decides to leave that reprobate." She stood abruptly, and I noticed the way her hand shook as she reached up into the cabinet over the refrigerator to withdraw a small box of pills. She popped two out onto her hand, and swallowed them dry.

"Are you sick?" I frowned. She pursed her lips and shook her head.

"I've been under a great deal of stress lately. The doctor has given me some pills to help me cope."

"Stress over what?"

Mother stared out the window into the darkness for a long moment.

"Well, one of my daughters is disgracing the family name by choosing a life beneath her," Mother said very quietly. "And the other is married to a *man* who is beneath her. You have no idea the unkind things people say to me."

"Who cares what people think of us?"

Mother huffed impatiently and drained the last of her tea, then shot me a withering look.

"You never did understand, darling. All a woman has in this life is her reputation."

I probably understood that better than she realized. It was exactly why I was so determined to build a world where a woman could have something more.

Beth
1996

"How are you doing, Beth?"

Ruth decides it's intervention time again after lunch, probably because I'm acting like a crazy person. The kids and our husbands and brothers are all watching a movie in the family room. Alicia is in there, too, sound asleep on a sofa. Dad's half-asleep, sitting with his eyelids drooping in his wheelchair, just a few feet away from me and Ruth.

The dining room table and kitchen look like a party has just finished, and I guess it has. There's half-eaten food on every conceivable surface, empty wine bottles and beer bottles, and when the boys came in for lunch a cold breeze blew all of Dad's gold candy wrappers off the table, and they're now littered all over the floor.

I shouldn't have pushed Dad the way I did. He's so drained now, and it was all for nothing anyway. I feel like shit about it, and the last thing I want is Ruth to put me on the spot again.

"I'm fine. Doing better, talking to Hunter, thinking about seeing someone."

"And the antidepressants?"

"I have the prescription. I'm still considering my options," I say, glancing at Dad. His eyelids flicker a little, but he doesn't seem to react. Still, I drop my voice to a whisper and I add, "Ruth, I really don't want to talk about this now."

"What was all that with Dad about before?"

"Do I need some high stakes reason to talk to Dad?" I ask flatly. She sighs and raises her hands in surrender.

"I don't understand why you're so defensive about everything. I'm *trying* to help you."

I force myself to draw in a slow breath before I say, "I know. I'm sorry. I'm...everything feels very—" *Urgent. Awful. Hopeless.* "—strained."

"What *does* it feel like?" Ruth asks. I turn to face her, frowning. "I don't understand, and I want to. Are you sad all the time? Or is it more complicated than that?"

"It's *so* much more complicated than that," I say, battling to keep the defensiveness out of my tone. "Don't you think I'd have realized what was happening if I was suddenly sad all the time?"

"So...? Explain it to me."

"I just feel overwhelmed. On edge. I don't know... I just feel like everything is too much for me. And I've felt isolated." She opens her mouth to speak, but I lean toward her and add, voice fast and low, "Yes, I know if I'm isolated, I've done it to myself, but that wasn't intentional. I just felt like no one could understand, and I was embarrassed to be struggling to care for Noah the way I have been. Like everyone was judging me for being an awful mother. I know that wasn't really happening, but it felt...*feels* really real to me."

I settle back into my chair, but as I do, I glance at Dad. I'm horrified to find him staring right back at me, a concerned look on his face.

"I thought you were asleep, Dad," I say, my voice artificially bright. "Did you want to take a nap? Alicia is napping in the family room, maybe we could go in there where it's warmer, hey?"

Dad shakes his head and purses his lips. I glare at Ruth, and she rises and walks to Dad's wheelchair.

"Dad, I need some help with dessert. That's your specialty. Why don't you come and help me whip the cream?"

I think we've effectively distracted him. Ruth pushes Dad into the kitchen and he holds the electric beaters for a minute or two, starting off the whipped cream, but he tires quickly and she has to take over. I clear the kitchen table and reset it for dessert, and soon enough, we're all seated for round two of "food we're already too full to eat." Dad picks that moment of rare quiet to look right at me and announce, "I don't want you to…" He points upstairs vaguely. "The mess. Behind the floor."

"It's okay, Dad," I wince. "It's okay. We've got it under control."

"Time got away from me. The mess. I was going to clean it."

"I'll sort it out," I promise him.

"*We* will sort it out," Ruth corrects me.

"But the letters. With the scissors," Dad says, staring right at me. He's gasping for breath between words and his face is beet-red. "She wrote the letters with the scissors."

I hear Jeremy drop his voice to ask Ruth, "What on earth is he talking about now?" and Ruth replies with equally failed subtlety, "I have no idea."

"Dad, it's fine," I say firmly. "Everything is fine. You really don't need to worry about it."

"I wanted to paint the letters. And…the pictures." He raises his hand and indicates his forehead. "I kept the letters to remember. To do better. And then I could *see* the pictures when I read the letters. See her, so beautiful with the belly. I painted the letters so I could see the beautiful curve." A new thought seems to strike him, and he brightens for a moment. "The ring. Did you see the ring?"

"I saw it, Dad," I say softly. "It's a beautiful ring, and the painting is beautiful."

"I can't remember the word," Dad says, and he points to his head, visibly frustrated. "The colors. In my head." His voice has dropped to a hoarse whisper, and then he looks around and starts to cry.

"Right! That's *enough*," Tim exclaims, and he pushes himself to his feet, then kneels beside Dad. He adjusts the cannula in Dad's nose, fiddles with the oxygen tank, then scowls at the rest of us. "I don't know what any of this shit is, but he's *sick* and everyone needs to back the hell off!" He turns to Dad and softens his tone just a little as he adds, "You need to rest now, Dad. I think we should take you back."

"No." Dad wipes at his eyes with the back of his hand and then he points at me. "You…" He licks his lips, swallows and then clears his throat. "You…"

"She's Beth, Dad," Ruth gently prompts him. My gaze drops to the table.

"Beth. I wanted to…what's the word? I was going to…with the trash can."

"Throw away?" Ruth guesses.

"Throw away the letters. Paint the colors, throw away the letters and clean up the trash. But I lost the time and now it's too late."

"I'll throw them away for you, Daddy," I promise unevenly, forcing myself to raise my eyes to his again. "And if you don't want me to read them, I won't."

"What's this about letters?" Jeremy frowns, but Dad's gaze is locked with mine, and now I'm only vaguely aware of the audience. Everything disappears but my wonderful, fragile father.

"I took her away. She would have helped you," Dad whispers. Another tear slips onto his cheek. "*Write* them." He shakes his head, then clenches his jaw. "*Read* them. Read them." He chokes on a sob, and he stares right into my eyes as he whispers, "Beth, loneliness is *worse* than sadness."

That's when I know he did hear and understand my conversation with Ruth earlier. I rush toward him and nudge Tim out of the way so I can take Dad's hands in mine.

"I'll be okay, Dad. You don't need to worry about me, I promise. But how did she die, Dad? If you can just tell me that—just that." He shakes his head, and then his distress mounts as he stares at me. His breathing is harsh now, labored breaths between that awful, tortured cough. I'm crying as I squeeze his hands. "Please, Dad. Can you tell me anything?"

"I'm sorry." *Cough. Wheeze.* "I didn't know what I was doing." *Wheeze. Cough.* "I didn't mean it."

"Beth, this isn't helping anyone." Tim's trying to nudge me back out of the way, but I stay stubbornly in place.

"Dad," I whisper. "Was it suicide?"

There's a chorus of gasps and confused questions behind me, but I'm staring hard at Dad, and I barely even register the sounds.

"Beth," Tim says flatly, resting his hand on my shoulder. "For God's sake. *Stop* this."

Dad releases my hand and reaches forward to gently push a lock of my hair behind my ear. He's wheezing and coughing, but he offers me a gentle, calm smile.

There's chaos all around me—family members trying to distract Dad and even me, trying to defuse the oddly intense moment we're sharing. But Dad and I ignore them—and we stay right there, staring at one another. He won't let go of my gaze, and I can't make myself look away.

"You're a good girl, Beth."

I choke on a sob.

"I know, Dad."

"A good mom," he whispers. "Like she was."

It's just too late.

He can't explain, and I can't keep asking. All I have are the notes.

FOURTEEN

Maryanne
1958

I stopped at a pay phone on the way to Grace's house the next day and dialed the number my friend provided. The call was short and simple—all of three minutes from start to finish. I gave him a false name and pretended to be seeking the procedure for myself. He didn't give a name at all—only instructions.

I had to wait for him alone on a road downtown at noon on Friday. I was to come alone and bring cash, sanitary pads and a large bottle of disinfectant. The procedure would take two hours, and he would return "me" back to the same spot. I asked him what his training was, and he explained to me, in a thick accent I couldn't place, that he'd been a doctor back in Europe and he'd done thousands of these procedures.

"Why aren't you registered to practice medicine here?"

"English not good enough yet. I learning."

"How do I know I can trust you?"

"Is very safe," he told me, his tone curt and dismissive.

"But where will you take me?"

"Police watch all the time. Clinic location is secret."

"Will it hurt—?"

"You want abortion, you come to the city on Friday. Is no skin off my nose if you don't."

Then he hung up. I scrawled the address down on the paper and continued to Grace's house.

"We still need one hundred and twenty dollars," I told Grace miserably when I was finished explaining. "Do you have *any* money?"

She sighed, pinching the bridge of her nose. "I could ask Patrick to ask his boss for an advance."

"Could he do that?"

"We've done it before. We just finished paying the last one off, actually, a few months back. I would have to explain to Patrick why I need the money, though."

"Gracie, can you *really* not just tell him the truth?" I asked her hesitantly. "It's so unfair that you have to deal with this alone. He's the one who *got* you pregnant."

"I didn't have to go back to his bed," she said weakly. "It wasn't like he forced me." She straightened, then pursed her lips. "He won't like it. I know he won't. He wouldn't even agree to use rubbers. I know he's not going to agree to this. But it's me who has to pay the cost if I follow through with this pregnancy, so it should be up to me what happens next, right?"

"I'm right with you there. I just think that he should help you deal with the situation he created."

We sat in silence for a moment. In the backyard I could hear Ruth bossing Jeremy around, Jeremy getting angry and Tim playing mediator. Grace glanced toward the window a few times but didn't rise from her chair.

"I can't think of any other way," I admitted eventually. "I do think you need to ask Patrick for the money."

"It'll be so hard to convince him to ask Ewan for money again," Grace said, rubbing her forehead. "It was such a struggle for us to pay the loan back last time. I just don't know…"

"I'll pay it back for you," I said, brightening. "I could send you what I have left over for the next few months. That'll sort it out."

Grace gave me a sad look.

"I can't let you do that. You've done enough already."

"If that's the way we get the money, Grace, then tell him you need the money to help me, and tell him I'll pay you back. At least think about it. You don't have a lot of time."

I was already feeling jittery when I pulled into Grace's street on Friday morning. I couldn't stand the thought of breakfast, nor could I stand my mother's delight at my lack of appetite. She commended me on my decision to eat less, predictably noting that it might be easier for me to find a husband if I lost a little weight. Of all the days for her to make such a comment. I was so angry with Patrick Walsh that just bringing his image to mind was enough to make me shake, and by the minute, my resolve to avoid marriage was only growing stronger.

The children were in the yard again that day. Jeremy was throwing a ball at the other children, in a version of dodgeball that was slightly too mean to be innocent. There was no sign of Grace, so I parked the car at the curb and walked up the path toward the front door. The children noticed me as I reached the porch.

"You're back again," Tim stated helpfully. "Mom isn't in the laundry today. She's in her bedroom."

"Thank you," I said stiffly, and I waved the children away and made my way to the porch. The front door was open just a crack, so I knocked then let myself inside.

"Grace?" I called as I let myself into the house.

"I'm in here!" she called back. I followed the sound of her voice and found her sitting at a dresser in one of the small bedrooms. She looked so much better than the previous day, her hair styled into a low bouffant, with the ends curled upward. She was even wearing a little makeup, and a pair of costume earrings I remembered Mother gave her for her birthday one year. Her swing dress was navy with big white polka dots and a matching white belt, and although her shoes were worn, they were pretty—navy pumps with a big buckle on the side.

Grace looked beautiful, but it wasn't just her outfit—when she met my eyes in the mirror, relief had relaxed the tension from her features. I was still nervous for her and for what we were about to do, but the renewed calm in my sister's eyes was enough to reassure me that we were doing the right thing. Grace didn't just want to end this pregnancy. She *needed* to do so.

"Are you ready?" I asked her. She stood and smoothed her dress over her hips.

"I'll just run next door and get Mrs. Hills to come and watch the children."

While Grace went to the neighbor's house, I let myself out the back door to stand on the ramp and watch the children play. The game of dodgeball had ended, and now the boys were riding tricycles, while the girls played with some wooden blocks. Even Beth was better dressed today, wearing a floral pinafore, her hair woven into a braid.

Grace returned with Mrs. Hills, who seemed to be as old as the hills. She used a cane and had a severe expression on her face, suggesting that although she might not have known the details of what was going on, she was certain we were up to no good. Grace gave her a series of instructions, directed her to the sandwiches already prepared for the children's lunch and then kissed each child on their forehead.

"Where are you going?" Jeremy asked, blinking up at her with a confused frown.

"I'm just going out for lunch with Aunty Maryanne."

"Me, too?" Ruth asked hopefully. Grace flushed a little, even as she laughed and ruffled up Ruth's hair.

"No, silly. It's a grown-up lunch. But we'll play tea parties when I get home."

"Momma," Beth said, throwing her arms around Grace's leg. Grace bent down and picked her up, then kissed her cheek.

"Its Mrs. Hills's turn to look after you, okay, darling? I'll be back in a few hours. You be brave."

Beth blinked her big blue eyes, trying to hold back the tears. Grace kissed her one last time, then firmly handed her to Mrs. Hills, then all but bolted for the car.

"Do you have everything? Did you get the extra cash?" I asked her. She patted her handbag and nodded.

"He wasn't happy about it," she sighed. "We had a screaming argument. It was awful. And you know my husband will never forgive you now that he thinks we helped you commit a mortal sin."

"Gracie, I love you to death, but I don't care even one bit what your husband thinks of me," I snorted. Grace gave me a sad look, then glanced over her shoulder and walked a little faster.

"Let's get out of here. I've never left them all behind before. I'm a bit scared someone's going to cry."

"They'll be fine for a few hours."

"It wasn't them I was talking about," Grace sighed, and then we both laughed.

"You seem better today," I told her.

"It's funny what a bit of hope can do for a person," she murmured.

I was proud then, that I had become the kind of woman who lived what I believed. Wasn't this what it was *all* about? Helping others to live the life they chose, and not the life society dictated for them? Helping women to reach their full potential, and not to stay subjugated into the roles their husbands assumed they would adopt.

The roads were clear—we'd hit the sweet spot between the morning peak and the lunchtime rush. I drove in silence for a while, and then Grace asked me quietly, "You think I'm doing the right thing, don't you?"

"I think you know better than absolutely anyone else what's best for you, and it's strong of you to seek it."

She flashed me the closest thing to a beam I'd seen since my arrival back in Washington State.

"Tell me what your life is like down there," she said, adjusting her legs against the buttery leather of Dad's "weekend" car.

"I work hard. My jobs take up a lot of my week. But I fit in a lot of fun around that—clubs and dancing and talking with professors and the other students about exciting ideas," I said. "I feel like I'm right where I belong."

"That's lovely, Mary," she said, smiling at me with an odd sadness in her gaze.

I signaled to change lanes and move around a slow truck, then glanced at her and prompted, "Do you?"

"Do I what?"

"Feel like you're where you belong."

Grace picked at a knot in the fabric of her dress and avoided my gaze as she pondered this question, but she looked out the window while she answered it.

"We're very different, Maryanne. You're destined for bigger and better things than I ever was. I never had it in me to swim upstream the way you do. I was always going to marry young, have a bunch of children and see out my days wiping noses and changing dirty diapers."

"Do you really believe that?"

"Dad would say this is the ultimate honor for a woman. To be a wife and mother, I mean."

"Dad would also say that a woman pursuing a career is the

beginning of the end of society. Dad says a lot of things that he thinks are fact but that are, in fact, uninformed opinion," I muttered.

"Will you ever get married?"

"Never."

"Have you ever been in love?"

"I've met some lovely boys, but I've never been in love."

"Well, how can you say you won't marry if you've never even felt love? It's love that led me to marry."

"Love is a feeling. I value my thoughts far above my feelings," I said. "If I were to fall in love, I'd do my absolute best to override that emotion with sensible decision-making. I don't plan on becoming *any* man's property."

"I wish you would fall in love. I wish you'd love a man the way I love Patrick. I know you only see his flaws, but I still see his potential, and I know that one day he's going to be a great man," she sighed. "And for all of his faults, and I know he has many, I still love my place in his life. I know you two don't see eye to eye on a lot of things, but if you could see each other the way I see you, I just know you'd love each other."

"I don't want to find a place in a *man's* life at all. I just want to be in charge of my *own* life."

"You have such a unique way of viewing the world, sister."

"There are plenty of women who feel as I do," I assured her. "And they are finding the strength to speak out, more and more every day. A hundred years from now things will be very different."

She gave me a weak smile, then turned to look out the window again. After a while she reached across and took my hand and squeezed it. Hard.

"I don't know how I'll ever repay you for this. I feel like I was headed for a head-on collision with disaster, but you jumped in and intervened and now I'm going to walk away unscathed."

"Tell me about what it's like for you when you had the children. Do you think you're just prone to the 'baby blues' more than others?"

"I don't know what it is. But whenever I've been pregnant and had a child, I feel like an ungodly fog descends on me, and it takes me at least a year to claw my way out. Having Beth nearly killed me, and feeling like that with *another* baby? I wouldn't survive it." She drew in a sharp breath, then admitted very quietly, "I've been a terrible mother, Maryanne."

"Don't say that," I protested. "Why on earth would you think such a thing?"

"I let them down all the time when they were small. You have no idea how dreadful I was in the early days after each birth. Some days with the twins, I'd forget to feed one...probably both. Tim is four years old and he knows how to organize lunches now, because I've been through this twice since he was born, and he's had to grow up too fast. In the summer I let Beth crawl around some days without a diaper because I couldn't be bothered to change her. I had days where I cried from the minute I woke up until the minute I went to sleep. The misery just felt endless, even when I'd done this before and I *knew* it would pass if I just held on."

"Didn't you have friends to help? I know Mother and Father haven't been good to you lately, but surely there were others you could call."

She sighed and shook her head.

"I know it doesn't make any sense at all, but the sadder I get, the less I'm able to reach out and so all of my friends drifted away. It's like I curl up into a miserable ball, even when I know that doing so makes everything else worse."

"Why didn't you tell *me* about this?"

"I tried. I sat down to write you last year after Beth, but I was mortified to admit how awful things were," she murmured.

"Are you really telling me you'd cry *all* of the time? What was Patrick doing during all of this?"

"He took me to the doctor once, but the doctor just said I needed to be stronger. Patrick didn't understand—I'm convinced he thought I wasn't trying hard enough. He just wanted me to handle myself better."

"So you were on your own, depressed for months on end, with no relief?" I surmised grimly, thinking that the next time I saw my brother-in-law, we were going to have words.

"Well, I have found an outlet recently. I've been writing these notes to myself. It probably sounds a little silly, but just sitting down and scrawling my thoughts out on paper has helped me a bit since Beth. Even today I wrote one before we left…about what we're doing today. About how grateful I am to you."

"You wrote a *confession* letter and *named me* in it, then left it in the house for Patrick to find?" I gasped. Grace laughed softly.

"Maryanne, I've been doing this for over a year and he's never even come close to finding my notes. I keep them in the last place he'd ever think to look for them, believe me. And they help me so much, I do think it's worth the risk. It's like jotting those words down on paper gives me the chance to see them with fresh eyes, and sometimes once they're out, the bad thoughts aren't as big as they seem when they're locked up in my mind."

I was still unnerved, if a little relieved to hear this "note" wasn't sitting out in the open somewhere. And I knew she was probably getting nervous about the procedure as the city drew nearer, but I decided that later, when it was all over, I'd ask her to destroy that note. I couldn't risk my part in this coming out somewhere down the line—I wasn't at all ashamed of what we were doing, but the risk to my career was simply too great.

"Have you thought about what happens after this?" I asked her instead. "How you'll make sure you don't end up in this position again?"

"I just don't know. I'll be sure stay out of Patrick's bed for a long while after this. And…well, we did manage to avoid a pregnancy for some months just by…" She paused, then flushed furiously as she muttered, "Well, we found a way anyway."

"Was he pulling out?" I asked her.

"Maryanne!" she gasped. "Don't talk about these things."

"Oh, Gracie, there's no shame in it. Pulling out works some of the time, but if you really don't want another baby, then maybe you need to get yourself a diaphragm. Or better yet, find a doctor who will give you a hysterectomy. Then you *know* you don't have to worry about it anymore."

"Patrick always wanted a big family," Grace said softly.

"*Patrick* gets you pregnant and leaves you to deal with the aftermath."

"Maybe if some more time passes and Beth and the kids grow up some more…then maybe I'd be able to cope with another baby when one comes."

"Do you even want more children, Grace?"

"What I want doesn't matter," she laughed softly, slightly confused, more than a little bitter. "Babies don't come when you want them."

"You shouldn't have to keep having pregnancy after pregnancy until it kills you."

"I just have to hope that's not my destiny."

"You control your destiny. That's why we're doing this today, because you know what you want and you have every right to make it happen for yourself."

"Maybe," she murmured. I sighed and pulled the car over to park beside a clothing store. When I flicked the ignition off, neither one of us moved.

"What time is it?" Grace asked me. I glanced down at my watch and butterflies rose in my stomach.

"We have ten minutes to walk to the meeting point."

Grace breathed in, then exhaled.

"Okay."

"Are you scared?" I asked.

"Kind of. Mostly, I just wish you could come with me."

"Me, too," I said softly, but then I felt compelled to reassure her. "But everything is going to be fine, Grace. You'll see. A few hours from now we'll be home and it will all be over."

Grace and I walked slowly on our way to the meeting point, striding so close that our arms kept colliding. A heavy cloud cover had come over, casting shadows down onto the footpath, and the air felt charged with danger as we neared our destination. I could hear Grace's breathing was heavier than it should be, and when I glanced at her, she was positively green. I wanted to promise her that everything was going to be fine. Women had abortions every day. I wasn't sure why I couldn't say what I needed to in order to reassure her. It felt like the words were stuck in my throat, and no matter how I tried, I couldn't convince myself to say them. Maybe it was because, despite my bravado, I knew on some level that there was a very real chance that everything *wouldn't* be fine.

When we reached the mouth of the alley, we slowed to a stop, and we stood in complete silence for a long moment. Grace wrapped her arms around her waist, took a sharp breath in then exhaled slowly.

"You'll wait here, won't you?" she whispered, her gaze desperately searching mine. "Out of sight so he doesn't get upset with me. But I'll feel a bit better if I know you're here."

"Of course," I promised. I actually had every intention of following the car, but I didn't want to promise her that I'd be right behind her, because I knew that keeping up with him was a long shot in the busy city traffic.

Grace drew in another deep breath, then threw her arms around me. I hugged her back, my arms locked tight, feeling somehow that I could keep her safe just by embracing her with all of my strength.

But then in the distance, I heard a clock strike twelve, and we both knew she had to go. The alley was clear for now, but the man was due any minute. Grace disentangled herself from me, took a step back and offered a wan smile.

"I'll see you at two o'clock."

"Two o'clock sharp," I promised.

"I don't know how I'll ever repay you for this."

"Knowing you're well will be repayment enough."

"I love you, Mary."

"And I love you, too, sister. See you soon."

Grace nodded and turned and walked into the road, disappearing into the shadows and the dismal gray of a city road at noon on an overcast day.

I did as promised. I lurked just beyond the top of the alley, standing in front of a restaurant with a book in my hand. I hoped it looked as though I was waiting for someone to join me for a lunch date. Only a few minutes passed before I saw a faded lemon Ford emerge from the alley. A man was in the driver's seat and at first, I thought it must be a different car because I couldn't see Grace in the back. Only when he passed did I see the blanket over the backseat, and the unmistakable shape of someone beneath it.

I closed the book and walked briskly to my car. As the Ford waited for a break in the busy traffic, I opened the car door with shaking hands and slipped inside. On first attempt, the engine stalled, and I swore and shook a little harder as I tried again. Finally, the car spluttered to life, just as the Ford passed. I wanted to look calm. I couldn't afford to panic and drive erratically and rouse suspicion. Dad's car was already eye-catching enough—a near-new aqua Chevrolet Bel Air.

So my instincts were to pull out without indicating and to gun the engine to catch up with the man, but I waited until another car passed, and then in the smallest of gaps, slipped into the traffic behind it. For several blocks I managed to hang just a car or two behind the yellow Ford, and my heart rate was starting to settle and I was actually starting to think I'd be able to follow him all the way to wherever he was going.

Then a traffic light turned amber, and just as I prepared to flatten my foot to race through it, the car in front of me stopped dead.

I sat behind that car as the light turned red, watching as the lemon Ford carrying my sister disappeared from view.

It's no exaggeration to say that it was the longest afternoon of my life. By two o'clock I felt like I'd been waiting weeks instead of hours. I was already at the alley, tapping my toe impatiently against the concrete of the footpath, glancing toward the sky that was darkening ominously. I had a blister forming in my right heel and I'd been sweating so much that my nylon dress was clinging to me all over. I bought a sandwich at a nearby deli, but it now sat untouched in a nearby bin. I was hungry enough to feel a little light-headed, but I'd raised the food to my lips a few times, only to find my stomach was turning over so violently I couldn't manage a single bite.

By two-fifteen, I was pacing between a stack of trash bins and the roller door of a garage. I jumped at every sound, and when a car finally turned into the alley, my knees went weak with relief. But it wasn't the yellow Ford. It was an olive-green Chevy, and the driver gave me an odd look at my rapidly fading smile, then drove right past me.

By two forty-five, I could feel myself hyperventilating. She was forty-five minutes late and there was no longer any avoiding the "what-ifs," but once I opened that floodgate in my mind, I was quickly overwhelmed. I sank onto the curb and forced myself to take some deep breaths because I wasn't going to help anyone if I actually passed out.

By three o'clock, I'd returned to my father's car and found the tattered piece of paper with the unregistered doctor's phone number on it, and I was frantically looking for a pay phone in the blocks around the road, no longer trying to stay calm, and no longer trying to look inconspicuous.

I finally found a pay phone. It took me six attempts to dial the number because my hands were shaking so violently. The busy signal echoed in my ear, so I tried again, and again, and then I ran back to the road again, and I checked at the car in case she'd found her way there somehow, and then I ran back to the pay phone and tried again.

I repeated this cycle over and over, trying to convince myself that any minute now the call would connect and the "doctor" would give me a very reasonable explanation for the delay or that Grace herself would wander around a corner and tell me she'd simply gotten lost.

Grace is fine. I kept telling myself she was definitely fine. She had to be—she had four children at home who desperately needed her. *I* desperately needed her. The universe wouldn't be so cruel as to have her harmed when I was only trying to help.

When I ran out of change, I managed to convince the attendant at the deli that I'd had a family emergency, and he let me use a phone in his apartment upstairs. I sweated as I raced through the entries in the telephone book, calling hospitals, praying someone had information about my sister. My attempts at conversation were embarrassingly unclear because I was so flustered I could barely explain what I needed.

"Grace Walsh...but maybe she's not admitted under that name. Maybe she's just been dropped off injured and you don't know who she is yet. Have you had any unidentified women admitted this afternoon...? Do you have a women's ward? Could you ask them?" And then finally, when I grew still more desperate, "I don't know what you call the wards but I know you have places where women go. The women who've had failed abortions. Could you *please* check there?"

"We have two," the clerk said curtly. "The sepsis ward, or the palliative care ward?"

"Oh, God. Check *both*."

When my calls turned up nothing, I had started driving from emergency room to emergency room. One hospital did have a Jane Doe recently admitted and I waited half an hour to see her, but she turned out to be a stranger.

In the early hours, all I could think about was Grace. I was terrified for her—frantic only at the thought that she might be hurt...or worse. But as evening became night, a new realization was starting to dawn, popping up in my thoughts every now and again, then bursting like a bubble. It was becoming unlikely Grace wasn't coming home unscathed, and there was something new at stake for me *personally*. I hated myself for even thinking about the consequences for myself when I didn't even know what had become of my sister, but I had to be a realistic.

I arranged that abortion for Grace. She'd begged me to, and she'd wanted to go ahead with the procedure desperately, but that didn't change the reality that I had broken the law.

And if Grace had been seriously injured, or *worse*...then maybe I was criminally responsible for her fate. If Betsy Umbridge's boyfriend could spend two years in prison for arranging an abortion that had gone exactly according to plan, what would happen to me if Grace was injured...or never came home at all?

Beth
1996

I retreat to the bathroom to wash my face, and when I return to the table, everyone falls silent.

"I think you guys probably need to talk," Ellis speaks first, motioning vaguely toward the four of us siblings.

"I'll handle the cleanup," Alicia offers. There's a moment of stunned silence. Ruth's jaw actually drops.

"Seriously?" I blurt, and Tim glares at me. He's always been something of a leader in this tribe—and I've always been the most compliant member of our family. I've angered him more today than I have in decades, and I hate it.

"Thanks, honey," Tim says pointedly to Alicia. "That would be a huge help."

"Noah and I will take Patrick back to the nursing home," Hunter offers cautiously. "If you'll all be okay here." His gaze is on me, again asking me a silent question. I nod, then look away.

"And I'll take the boys back into the living room to watch another movie," Ellis says.

Our spouses scramble away. Ruth excuses herself and all but sprints to the kitchen, returning with a bottle of wine and three glasses. I reluctantly, awkwardly, explain to my brothers and sister about the hidden cavity in the bottom of the wooden chest. By the time I finish, they're all staring at me, slack-jawed.

"So...wait," Jeremy says, holding up a hand toward me. "Mom didn't die in a car accident?"

"I don't think so," I whisper.

"And you think she died in 1958?" Tim frowns, then shakes his head. "That doesn't seem right. She was definitely still alive when I started school."

"Us, too," Ruth says. They all stare at me.

"I'm just telling you what it says, guys," I say weakly. "It's not my fault it's confusing."

"Jesus Christ," Tim exhales, pinching the bridge of his nose. "What the hell are we supposed to do with all of this?"

"I didn't bring the photo album so I can't show you the death certificate. But the notes and the artwork are upstairs."

"Good. Let's see them."

I divert past Dad's room to retrieve the clipboard while the other three walk upstairs. By the time I catch up, they're all staring around the mess. My brothers are visibly horrified.

"You said there were paintings," Jeremy says stiffly, glaring at Ruth. "You forgot to mention it's an absolute fucking disaster zone up here."

"I told you it was a mess. I didn't realize I had to qualify that with an exact description," Ruth snaps. Tim hesitantly picks up a basket, then grimaces and sets it back down again. "What's in there?"

"Empty paint tubes, what looks like it used to be an apple core and I think maybe a whisk."

"It's all random. Just like that," I tell them. "There doesn't seem to be any pattern to the mess."

"Let's see these notes you found," Ruth prompts. I pass the clipboard to my nearest sibling, which happens to be Tim, and then I motion toward the dark canvas.

"The date on that canvas matches this first note," I say. Tim skims the page, then swallows and raises his gaze to the ceiling. Jeremy takes the clipboard next, and he and Ruth read it together.

"*That's* a suicide note, right? She talks about 'mortal sin.' That's suicide?"

"Everything is a mortal sin," Ruth scoffs, then sobers. "But yeah. That doesn't sound great."

"How do you even know *she* wrote these?" Tim asks. I lift the page to show him the other note, the one that refers to us and to Dad, and he exhales as he reads it. "Right. And downstairs, that stuff with Dad and you. What's going on there?"

"I was asking him about Grace because of these. And the death certificate."

"I meant why did he *tell* you to read these?"

"I think because he heard me and Beth talking earlier," Ruth says. "Lisa thinks she has postpartum depression." I look at her incredulously.

"No, Ruth, go right ahead and tell everyone my personal medical information. I don't mind at all," I say bitterly.

"I knew something was going on with you," Jeremy says, tilting his head at me. "Are you okay?"

"I—" I want to protest and to assure my siblings that they don't need to worry about me, but this time I don't. "I don't know. But reading *that*—" I point to the note in Tim's hand "—I can't help but wonder if there's a genetic component."

Tim hands the second note to Jeremy, and Ruth steps closer to him to read along.

"I just need to know," I admit, throat tight. "I just need to know what happened to her. If she…"

"You should have told us about this," Tim says abruptly. At my pointed look, he runs his hand through his hair, then says in exasperation, "*All* of this, Beth! The stuff you found in Dad's chest. These notes. *Christ.* And the depression."

"I don't get it," Ruth sighs, looking up from the note. "Why on earth didn't you tell us? This is…a lot."

"I didn't know how to explain," I say weakly. "I was worried you'd try to take over. I was worried you'd worry about me. It was overwhelming. Maybe I wasn't thinking straight."

"I get it," Jez sighs. "A few bits of paper and suddenly I'm questioning the entire way we've understood our upbringing." He points toward the clipboard, then adds, "I mean…this refers to Dad, but she isn't talking about the Dad we know. Right?"

"We don't even know if they're real," Ruth protests. "You can't let two random bits of paper—two *unsigned* bits of paper— make you question anything. Especially not the way you see Dad. That's completely unfair."

"It's not just the notes," Tim says heavily, glancing at me. "The death certificate Beth found raises questions, too. Why would he tell us she died in a car accident if she didn't?"

"It would be unforgivably disloyal to judge a man who can't defend himself, based on any of this," Ruth snaps. "He's so confused, and there could be a perfectly reasonable explanation he just can't share."

"Such as?" Jeremy says incredulously. Ruth opens her mouth to snap a reply back at him, but Tim cuts them both off.

"Squabbling isn't going to help, is it? The only hope we have of understanding this is if we find the rest of the notes."

"Well, that I can agree on," Ruth murmurs. Jeremy nods, too, and then they all look at me, and it suddenly occurs to me that we are, at last, a united force.

I wanted the truth, but maybe I didn't have the strength to find it until I had allies. Now, realizing that we'll be a team, I'm less afraid of what we'll discover up here, and simply determined to find it.

"Okay, boys, this is what we're going to do," Ruth announces, snapping on her project manager voice. "You two are going to handle the big items—boxes, baskets, furniture and so on. Empty them over here, and then take them up to that end of the attic."

"We're starting this today?" Tim asks, but he's already rolling back the sleeves on his shirt.

"I don't have anywhere to be. Do you?" Ruth says.

"The second note was in a pile of junk food wrappers," I tell them. "So check everywhere. Listening to what Dad said downstairs earlier, I think he probably planned to throw these notes away once he finished the paintings. So they might already be scrunched up, like the second one was, or even just dumped in some random place among the chaos."

"Got it." Tim mock-salutes us. Ruth turns to me.

"You and I will sort through the smaller pieces of trash. We'll make two piles—a keep pile, a toss pile. Jez, in between helping Tim, you can ferry the trash down to the dumpster."

"We won't get this whole space done today," Jeremy warns us. "Not unless we work till midnight."

"We don't actually need to get the whole space cleared out." Ruth shrugs. "We just need to see if there are any more notes."

Jeremy finds a third note under a discarded plate by one of the windows, the back smeared with paint. He reads it silently, and then offers it to me and Ruth.

"Is it like the others?" I ask, staring at his hand hesitantly.

"Yeah."

"Does the date match a canvas?" Tim calls from the other end of the room. Jeremy takes the note as he checks the canvases on the table, then nods.

"Put it with the clipboard, then, because we're probably going to find more," Ruth murmurs, returning to her sorting. "I'll read them in order when we're done."

"Beth?" Jeremy checks, and I nod.

"Yeah. I want to do that, too."

We have three notes now, three out of thirteen, assuming there's one for each canvas. Jeremy sorts carefully through the pile of Dad's canvases, then removes the relevant three and rests them on the floor. He pauses at the unique canvas.

"You said this looks like the ring you found."

"I'm sure of that much, at least," I tell him.

"And he said downstairs the others are of the curve of her stomach," Ruth says quietly. Jeremy picks up one of the other canvases and we all stare at it. Before, when I was looking at this series of canvases, it was difficult to know what to focus on—they are busy, with layers of different colors and materials. Now that Dad's given us a clue, it's easy to recognize the shape of a pregnant woman's belly and I can't believe I missed it the first time.

"These are beautiful," Jeremy says suddenly. He looks up at us, his gaze brimming with emotion. "I'm not really a fan of art, but there's so much emotion here. I can *feel* the sadness. His regret. Her isolation."

"The theory is that with Dad's kind of dementia, as the language centers atrophy, the visual centers of the brain overcompensate. I read a paper where a woman who was in decline like Dad described the way her imagination went into overdrive when she got sick," Tim says. "Neurologists think we can learn a lot about how the brain works from cases like Dad's—" He makes a sound of triumph, then lifts a note up out of a basket.

"There's a splash of paint on it, but it's legible. It's another of the early ones," he tells us as he carefully puts it in place on the clipboard, and Jeremy removes another canvas to the floor.

We get distracted for a while after that, when Ruth uncovers her Grade 4 report card, and we all chuckle at her teacher's comments about how she was *stubbornly determined to rule over her peers rather than to learn.* Jeremy finds a copy of a long-forgotten photo of a camping trip we all took to Gardner Cave when we were preteens—the trip that sparked his love of geology. Tim then finds what looks suspiciously like mouse droppings, and we decide to take a break, swarming downstairs around hot cocoas. Hunter reappears, with Noah in tow.

"Sorry it took me so long," he murmurs, embracing me from behind as I linger at the kitchen countertop with my siblings. I didn't even realize he was coming back—he's been gone so long I just assumed he'd just taken Noah straight home. "It took a while for your dad to settle back in at the nursing home. His oxygen saturation was far too low. The nurses had to call the doctor to adjust his medication."

"I shouldn't have upset him," I say, throat tight.

"He's *dying*, Beth," Tim sighs. "Look, I know I was harsh earlier about you raising your voice at him, but like I keep trying to tell you, we're past the point where any of these things will make much difference."

"I do know that," I mutter. When I think about the future, it's all a blur. I have no idea how much longer we have with Dad—I get that the end is looming, and that's why we had to move him into the hospice. But I don't dare ask about the time frame. I'm certain Tim has an idea, but I just can't bear to know if we're talking days, weeks, or months.

"I assume you want to stay, honey. I just came back so you can feed Noah," Hunter says quietly. "Maybe Jez can drop you home when you're done here?"

I check in with my brother, who nods, so I curl up in Dad's

armchair to feed the baby. Through the window I'm watching Ellis and the boys, who are back out in the cold, throwing the football—their faces red as raspberries now; the joy in their expressions as they play together is such a contrast to the heaviness inside the house.

Tim approaches as I'm burping the baby. He perches on the armrest of the chair opposite me, and says very quietly, "I've been thinking. Especially about what you said earlier."

"I said a lot of things earlier."

"About Dad. About…what's coming for all of us. About your postpartum depression." His tone is gentle, his gaze soft on my face. "Look, I'm a surgeon. I don't know much about mental health—just the basics. But I do remember colleagues talking about postpartum depression when it was added to the *Diagnostic and Statistical Manual of Mental Disorders* a few years back. I know just enough to know this is a big deal. You need to go home with Hunter and leave upstairs to me and Jez and Ruth."

"Tim, you've known for like two hours that I might have this condition, right?"

"Right. I mean, I suspected something was going on, but it didn't occur to me it was this serious."

"Okay, fine. I just need to point out the utter hypocrisy in you telling me what I can and can't handle when you didn't even know I was unwell three hours ago."

Tim opens his mouth, then closes it. His lips are pursed now. My brother is frustrated. *Good.* So am I.

"I'm just worried about you."

"Good. Thanks. I appreciate that." I hand him Noah, and then straighten my clothing as I shake my head. "I knew that when someone had a mental illness, they have to deal with the stigma, but it's even worse than that. As soon as anyone suspects you're mentally ill, they start treating you like you're fragile— like you could shatter if you're exposed to stress or even just a loud noise. And at the time in your life when you need emotional support more than ever, people try to force you *out* of the difficult moments…which of course, are the moments when a family grows closer." I don't want to be childish about this, but I can't help the bitterness in my voice as I mutter, "But *sure* I'll go home, if that'll make *you* feel better."

Tim gives me an irritated look.

"You've read the first two notes you found."

"You know I have."

"So you realize then that it's looking likely that you're suffering from the same affliction that our mother battled, and we can't rule out the possibility that she actually died by *suicide*. And you're wondering why I'm trying to protect you from stress?"

"I want to be here. I *need* to be here."

Tim sighs, then throws his hands in the air.

"Fine."

Ellis finally drags his boys in, promising to pick up pizza for dinner on their way home. Ruth hugs them all and promises she'll kiss them all good-night when she gets home.

I plant a peck on Hunter's cheek, touch Noah's chin with the tip of my finger and say good-night to my family.

And then we all mount the stairs again, ready to face whatever ugly truth is waiting for us.

The hours begin to drag. My siblings and I work in silence sometimes, broken only when one of us finds a note, or some random memorabilia that we want to share. The stack of canvases on the table is soon halved as we match new notes to paintings and move them to the floor, but the sun has dipped low. Soon the light fades, and we're working by the glow of the yellow bulbs that hang from the ceiling beams.

"I can't stay much longer," Tim sighs. "I've got rounds at seven tomorrow morning, then a full day of consults. Plus, I promised Alicia I'd be home by nine."

"What's the deal with her anyway? Did she have a personality transplant?" Jeremy asks suddenly. Tim stills, then frowns at him.

"Jez. Seriously."

"Not complaining," Jeremy says, raising his hands. "Today was just a pretty stark transformation from the woman who wouldn't even help us with Dad not so long ago."

"If you must know, asshole, we've talked through a whole heap of shit in therapy." I forgot how sweary Tim gets when he's tired. During his residency, my straightlaced brother had a veritable potty mouth. "One of the things that's come up is that this family is so close-knit she's always felt like an unwelcome outsider."

"We're close, but we're hardly *freakishly* close," Ruth says.

"How many other families do you know that still meet up every week for dinner?" Tim says pointedly.

"Well, we don't really meet *every* week," Ruth says defensively. "I mean, if you're on shift or Jez is overseas…"

"But *unless* I'm on shift or Jez is overseas, we're here every single week. We're close, Ruth. That's not a bad thing at all," Tim says. "It's just been hard for Alicia to find her place with us. She said when she tried to pitch in with Dad, you two were always finding problems with whatever she did to help, and sometimes at family dinners, she'd come along and find the three of you barely spoke to her at all." His words falls like a stone into the space between us. Ruth and I share a wince. I had no idea that Alicia even realized how much we didn't like her, and it never occurred to me that she would have cared either way. She always seems so bulletproof. "Once we talked about it, I think she realized she was being unfair, and today was the first time in ages I can remember her actually relaxing at a family dinner." Tim motions between me and Ruth with a paintbrush. "Surely your husbands have felt the same at some point?"

Now Ruth, Jeremy and I are all sharing guilty glances.

"Uh, sure," Ruth says, unconvincingly. Tim frowns.

"Maybe Alicia wasn't being unfair," I admit carefully. "We

don't really have much in common with her, and I guess we've probably been a bit hard on her."

Tim's frown deepens.

"She said you two were always all about babies." He points at Ruth. "You raising the boys—" his accusing finger points to me next "—and you trying to get pregnant, and now with Noah. She said she felt excluded because *we* don't want kids."

I cringe because there's definitely some truth in that. I know from experience that motherhood is an exclusive club—and any woman on the outside, by choice or by circumstance, knows all too well what it feels like to have her membership application to the Mommy-social-group declined. The worst thing about this conversation is that I remember how awful it felt to be on the outside when Hunter and I were trying to have a baby. It just never occurred to me that Alicia was on the outside, too.

"That's why me and Fleur broke up," Jeremy says suddenly. Ruth, Tim and I gape at him.

"Because of me and Ruth?" I gasp, instantly sick with guilt. I might not have found much affection for Alicia, but I *loved* Fleur and I loved her for Jeremy. The idea that Ruth and I might have scared her off is heartbreaking.

"Oh. No, sorry. You were always much nicer to her than you are to Alicia."

Tim scowls again.

"What exactly have you two been doing to my wife that I haven't noticed? If you had any idea how much we've fought about this the past few years..."

"We never intentionally excluded her," Ruth groans. "And now that you've told us she felt like we did, we'll both make an effort to include her more. Right, Beth?"

"Absolutely," I say. "Jeremy, back to Fleur. What's the story?"

"I meant that we broke up because of kids. Specifically, she wants them. Posthaste," Jeremy adds, grimacing. "I couldn't see how a kid could possibly fit into my travel schedule. She said since we both wanted kids we should try for a baby now and figure the logistics out later if we actually managed to have one. We fought about it for a year and then she decided she was getting too old to wait for me to realize she was right."

"You said you two grew apart," Ruth says with a frown.

"Meh." Jeremy shrugs. When he's self-conscious, he has this way of trying to appear *too* casual, and that's how I know that he's still pretty sore over all of this. "It was probably more like we were ripped apart because a giant hypothetical baby came between us."

"Do you actually want kids?" Ruth demands.

Jeremy shrugs again, but then says, "Yeah. Probably."

Ruth and I share a look.

"Fleur was the best girlfriend you've ever had. You need to get her back before it's too late," I tell him.

"Tim, do you think having two exceedingly bossy sisters has damaged you in any way?" Jeremy sighs.

"I think it prepared me well for having an exceedingly bossy wife, actually."

"See, you'd both be lost without us," Ruth snorts, then waves her arm around the room. "Have any of you noticed that we're actually making some progress? We're probably at as good a place as any to call it for the night."

She's right—the mess has finally taken shape. Furniture and baskets and boxes are all at one end; trash and paperwork sit in three huge piles at the other. But much of the floor is now visible, and we can move around freely as we sort.

"I'll come back and keep working on it tomorrow," I say. A series of meaningful glances flick between my siblings.

"And what happens if you find the notes and there's no satisfying answer? What if there *aren't* other notes to find? Or what if you find the notes and you don't *like* the answer?" Jeremy asks. I feel myself slump even considering those possibilities.

"I don't know," I admit.

"I'll meet you back here tomorrow night and we'll keep look- ing together," Ruth says. I open my mouth to protest, but she holds up a hand. "Look, I get it. This is personal to all of us, but you're identifying with her in a way the rest of us can't. That's *exactly* why you shouldn't tackle this on your own."

"Ruth's right," Tim murmurs, then his gaze softens. "There's not much we can do to make your situation better, but we can be here to support you with this. Please, promise me you'll let us. I don't know if I can be here every night to search with you, but if you do find the notes, I'll find a way to be here to read them with you."

"Me, too," Jez says quietly.

I look around the concerned gazes of my siblings, and my eyes fill with tears.

"Okay," I promise unevenly. "Ruth and I will keep looking, but when we find them all, we'll read them together."

FIFTEEN

Maryanne
1958

My heart was thundering against the wall of my chest as I walked from the driveway to Grace and Patrick's front door that night. Over seven hours had passed since the time Grace and I were due to meet in that alley. I had hung the last of my hope on the remote possibility that Grace might have found her own way home. I'd almost convinced myself that we'd inadvertently had some communication confusion somewhere along the line.

I paused at the door, and for the first time in years, I offered up a prayer.

Please, God. Please let her be inside.

I drew in a deep breath and pushed the door open to find Mrs. Hills sitting on the couch watching the television, wearing a deep-set scowl.

"Where is she?" Mrs. Hills bit out as she struggled to her feet, only to wave her cane vaguely in my direction. "She said three o'clock! It's nearly nine-thirty! My husband had to make his own dinner and he is *furious!*"

"Grace isn't here?" I whispered.

"No, she's certainly *not!*" Mrs. Hills said, raising her voice just a little, then glancing toward the boys' bedroom guiltily. She dropped it to a whisper before she finished, "And neither is *he*, the useless lout he is. He'll stumble in drunk sooner or later, mark my words."

"I'm sorry, Mrs. Hills," I said. When Mrs. Hills started walking toward the door and I realized she intended to leave me alone with the children, I panicked. "Oh, please don't leave. I have to—"

"Young lady, I have been here all day with those children. I am *exhausted.* If you think I'm staying here for one more second, you have another thing coming."

The door slammed behind her, and I found myself standing alone in Grace's living room. Panic once again began to claw at my throat but I had to hold myself together because I had no idea when Patrick would walk through that door. I needed a plan to keep looking for Grace, but I also needed to come up with *some* kind of story to tell her husband, because I knew that if I told him the truth, he'd have no qualms in handing me over to the police.

"Momma?" a tiny voice said behind me. I spun around to face the entrance to the bedroom, and there in the doorway stood Beth. She was clutching a teddy bear, wearing a green nightgown and diaper, and her little cheeks were rosy red.

She was utterly adorable, and I was absolutely terrified of her.

"No, not Momma," I croaked, shaking my head. "It's Aunt Maryanne."

"Where Momma?" Beth asked me. She dropped the teddy bear to rub sleepily at her eyes, and my chest started to feel tight. *Gone, Bethany. She's gone and maybe she's never coming back to us.* I waved her vaguely back towards her room, trying to school my features to hide my fear.

"Go back to bed. Everything is fine."

"Want Momma," Beth said, dropping her hands from her eyes to give me a stubborn, determined glare.

"Soon," I lied, and then I spoke far too curtly, "Now go back to bed!"

I'd had zero experience with small children. I didn't need to know how to interact with them, given I had no intention of ever being responsible for the care of my own. I was so naive that when Beth's eyes widened and she opened her mouth to wail, I was actually shocked by her reaction.

"Momma!" she cried, and I looked frantically around the room, trying to figure out what to do to make her be quiet before she woke the other children. I rushed to her, but this only scared her more, and the volume of her cry grew louder. I scooped her up in my arms and stepped out of the bedroom, pulling the door closed so Ruth wouldn't wake up, and then I walked briskly to sit on the brown upholstered couch.

"Listen," I said desperately. "Listen to Aunt Maryanne, Bethany. Mommy isn't here right now and you're just going to have to be brave because...well..." It hit me then—really hit me—just how much we all might have lost. "Oh, God. I just don't know what to do."

My voice broke, and Beth hesitated mid-sob. She was sitting on my lap, but she leaned away from me, so that she could stare back at me. There were still heavy tears in those huge blue eyes, but something had changed. Now Beth seemed almost curious.

I saw my sister in that face. I saw Grace's innocence and optimism, and I simply could not bear it because *what if Grace was dead* and this poor child had lost her mother because of me? I closed my eyes, and the tables were turned, because now it was me battling sobs.

But little Bethany Walsh knew just what to do. She wrapped

TRUTHS I NEVER TOLD YOU

her arms around my neck and her chubby little hand clumsily patted between my shoulder blades. She dropped her head onto my shoulder, and she soothed me with a whispered, "Shhh…"

At first, I saw Beth's natural inclination to comfort me as proof of failure on Grace's part. I wondered if Grace had cried in front of her children so many times that even her toddler knew how to react.

But then Beth's arms contracted around my neck, and I had a sudden, startling shift of perspective. If the world needed anything in those days, it was people who could empathize—people who cared. And it was easy to judge Grace, but it was also apparent that Grace had been harder on herself than anyone. Somehow, she'd taught a *toddler* to emulate the very best traits known to humanity. Beth couldn't speak fluently or read or drive a car, but that child already knew how to recognize pain and to respond to it with kindness. Something my own mother has yet to master. Something I myself had never really been good at. This child's easy compassion for my pain was a small miracle in the darkest hour.

And as I recognized the remarkable nature of Beth's comfort to me, I finally let myself wonder if Grace had, without even knowing it, taught her children her very last and most important lesson.

The front door opened several hours later. I was still on the couch, facing away from the door. Beth was curled up asleep on my lap now because every time I moved she woke up. Even so, I knew it wasn't Grace…mostly because I could smell Patrick long before I saw him.

"What's for dinner?" he slurred, walking unsteadily toward the small kitchen. His tone was rough, and the yeasty stench of beer rose off him in waves. Like his youngest daughter, he'd seen what he expected to see and mistaken me for his wife.

"Patrick," I whispered, glancing frantically down at Beth. He stopped his path toward food, and turned to face me. The surprise in his gaze quickly cleared, and was replaced with disgust.

"You," he said, his nostrils flaring. "*Baby killer.* Get your fucking hands off my daughter. And you dragged me and *my wife* into your filthy—"

"Have you seen Grace?"

Patrick blinked at me, the scowl clearing, and confusion taking its place. It was then that I realized he was rolling drunk, and this was going to be both easier and harder than I'd feared. I immediately abandoned my plans to ask him to put Beth to bed, fearing that he'd drop her.

"She's..." Confusion flickered over his features. "She took you to..."

"I came back from the...the procedure," I whispered thickly. "She wasn't waiting for me like she said she would be. I can't find her anywhere."

I was lying on the fly. Despite the hours I'd had to come up with a cover story, my panic had been so intense that I'd failed to script a plan for how to handle Patrick or even my parents. But as the words left my mouth, I realized that Grace's lie to Patrick could help me, and for just a moment I felt relief.

Until, of course, I realized that the only way my lie would actually help me was if we never found Grace, because if she turned up in a hospital injured from her procedure, the truth would be revealed.

I was already assuming that she was dead.

Subconsciously, maybe I already knew she was. I started to feel sick all over again and I was sobbing before I even realized there were tears in my eyes.

"Where..." Patrick shook his head, clearly trying to gain some clarity. He looked from me to Beth, then from Beth to the kitchen, then he pointed right at me. "Don't you dare fucking move."

He walked to the kitchen, and I heard him puttering around.

He ran the faucet. Soon I could smell coffee in the air. The fridge door opened and closed. The bread bin opened and closed. And soon he returned to the living area with a mug of coffee and a thick, dry piece of bread in his hand. He sat opposite me, gulping at the coffee between large, messy bites of the bread. The coffee was steaming hot—far too hot to drink—but I could see that Patrick was quite desperate to sober up, because he drank it anyway, his eyes watering with every sip.

When he'd finally finished, he stood and walked toward me. For just a moment I thought he was going to *hurt* me, and I made a sound like a whimper. But he ignored me, instead bending to take Beth from my arms and to walk her into her bedroom.

Then he returned, sat heavily opposite me and looked right into my eyes.

"Tell me exactly what happened."

The lie took on a life of its own after that. I told the truth about the day's events—only I swapped my role with Grace's. By the time I finished, he was sitting with his head in his hands.

"You're sure this has nothing to do with your..." He looked up, lip curled scornfully, and waved vaguely at my abdomen. "Your business."

"They didn't even know I was meeting her," I said thickly.

Patrick began to pace, tension in the heavy fall of his footsteps and the locked set of his broad shoulders. "I need to call the police, but I can't tell them what you were really doing because if they find her she'll be charged, too. And *Jesus Christ*, I gave her the money! We could all end up in prison!"

He stopped abruptly, and shot me a withering glance.

"I can't believe you'd get us involved in this kind of shit. Grace is a *good girl*. And she was so determined to help you and now look! Who knows where she is?" He ran his hand through his hair, and then puffed out a frustrated breath. "I don't even know where to start." He stopped pacing abruptly, then turned to me again. "You'll have to stay with the children. I'm going to go look for her."

"No," I protested, standing. "I know where she was last time I saw her. *I* should be looking for her. I don't know the first thing about children, so you need to—"

"It's time to stop playing games, Maryanne," he said, cutting me off. "I know you live in some fantasy world where you think you can do anything a man can do, but this is the real world. This is *our lives* you've thrown into chaos. You'll do as I tell you to do!"

He slammed the door as he went out, and I was left sitting alone in their dingy little house, and the hours began to drag past me.

I didn't know if my sister was dead or alive, but her ghost haunted me in those hours. Her scent was in the air, and her style was in the sparse decor, and it was her books on the wooden chest they used for a coffee table and her hands that had last touched the television set. Her life didn't seem like much to me, but in my terror and my grief, I had my first taste of humility.

Grace had struggled and she'd suffered, but she'd loved her children and somehow, she'd loved Patrick, and those aspects to her character that I had shrugged off as a "waste of a life" were the very things that *gave* her life worth and meaning.

I couldn't sleep, but I was too tired to keep my eyes open, so after a while I lay on the couch and I gave in to the pull of exhaustion to close my eyes. This made my anxiety so much worse, because without visual distraction, all I could do was let god-awful scenarios play out in my mind. But I couldn't prop my eyelids up, and so I lay there awake and let myself feel the sheer terror of my situation.

When Patrick came home at dawn, that's where he found me: lying on the couch, wide awake and shaking with grief and shame. When I opened my eyes, I saw that he was alone, and I knew for sure then that my worst fears had come true.

★ ★ ★

Patrick went to Mrs. Hills's house first thing the next morning and called the police, and two officers came about an hour later. They sat in Patrick and Grace's living room, one on the threadbare armchair, one on the end of the sofa beside me. When they asked us what happened, Patrick looked at me, and I spun the lie out further.

Shopping in the city. She went to look at shoes. I went to the diner to get a table for lunch. Separated. She never came back.

Patrick corroborated the story in dull, flat tones.

It was evident from the first moment of that interview that the police had looked around the ragged house, seen the four tiny children squabbling at the kitchen table, smelled the stale alcohol on Patrick's skin and assumed that Grace had decided to take herself on a little vacation. They assured us she'd turn up sooner or later, and advised us "not to worry too much" in the meantime.

I went back to Mrs. Hills's house as soon as they left and called the phone number scrawled on that now-tattered piece of paper. I was entirely unsurprised when it rerouted to the operator.

"Hello, the number you've dialed has recently been disconnected," the operator said brightly.

"Can you tell me who the number belonged to?"

"Of course I can't, ma'am. I don't have access to that information. Can I route you elsewhere?"

"No," I said hollowly. "No, thank you."

She was just gone—disappeared. When that man put the blanket over my sister in the backseat of that car, he didn't just hide her. He erased her.

I took Dad's car and drove to my parents' house after that, but I'd forgotten all about the promise I'd made—I had told Mother I'd be home in time for dinner. Father sat up all night, and when I opened the front door that morning, the look of sheer relief on his face was a punishment in itself. I was often hard on my parents for their focus on money and reputation, but that day was a vivid reminder that they did actually feel a depth of love for us. If I had forgotten that truth until I saw how happy he was to see that I was safe, I was entirely certain of it by the time I'd finished explaining that they'd been worried about the wrong daughter entirely.

Shopping in the city. She went to look at shoes. I went to the diner to get a table. Separated. She never came back.

Mother stopped me halfway through my explanation so that she could fetch a container of pills from the kitchen, and after that appeared numb with some combination of medication and fear. Father seemed to be on a roller coaster of emotions, and as soon as I'd finished spinning my story, he snatched up his keys and sprinted to the car to go look for her in the city.

For the first few days fear was a buffer. It insulated us from the real world and from each other. Father took off work at the bank, and both parents were soon lingering at Patrick and Grace's house, apparently still convinced that she was going to walk through the door at any given moment. Father went out and purchased three stretcher beds so we could all try to sleep there, and we jammed all four kids into one of the bedrooms so we could set the stretcher beds up in the other.

I slept in short spells. I'd drift off, then wake up and leap out of bed, convinced I'd heard her coming in the front door. The children cried constantly, especially sweet little Bethany, and I spent much of those early days trying to console them with hugs that didn't feel at all natural to me.

"You're hurting me, Aunt Maryanne," Tim protested at one point. The next time I hugged Ruth, I was apparently *too* gentle, because she leaned back and stared at me in disgust.

"Cuddle me," she said, frustrated. "Properly. Like Momma cuddles me."

My parents were no help at all, although they tried their best. They spoke to the children as though they were adults, and the children reacted by avoiding them at all costs. I knew that a big part of their distance from the children was self-inflicted due to their stubborn disapproval of Grace and Patrick's life choices. But my heart ached when I saw my mother watching with a confused, hurt expression when the children came to me for comfort, not her.

"They hardly know us," she said at one point, her chin wobbling. "But they don't know you, either, and you're not exactly the most maternal stranger they'll ever meet. Why are they so willing to come to you for a cuddle when they'll barely speak to me?"

"I don't know," I lied, because it was obvious that my mother's cool, formal engagement with the children terrified them. But she had always been that way, and she was hardly likely to change her mannerisms anytime soon, so there seemed no point explaining the problem to her, especially when she was already so distraught over Gracie.

Patrick, too, was in a fog, walking around as if he was half-asleep, barely reacting when the children spoke to him…not reacting at all when they asked after Mommy. Father snapped at him about that, and Patrick stared back at us with hollow eyes as he explained that he just didn't know what to say.

I'd felt confused and I'd felt guilty since Grace went missing, but her disappearance seemed to have broken Patrick entirely and it was an awful thing to see, even in a man I had long despised.

"I think you should try to explain to the kids what's going on," I whispered to him later, when my parents were out of earshot.

"I can't," he said, and his eyes filled with tears. "I just can't."

I took the children out to the backyard after that. I sat them in a little semicircle on the grass and I sat right there on the grass with them, heedless of stains on my beige cigarette trousers.

"I need to explain something to you all," I said. I scanned their confused little faces and blinked hard, determined not to cry in front of them. Timothy's gaze narrowed on my face. "Mommy is lost. We don't know where she is, but we're trying to find her. We all need you to be good little boys and girls until we do. Any questions?"

Tim's suspicious gaze cleared. The skin on his cheeks paled, but he didn't say a word. Jeremy reached for Ruth's hand. Beth looked from her siblings to me, then burst into noisy tears. Before I could comfort her, Tim stood, shot me a glare, then slipped his arm around her shoulders and led her away.

Days soon became weeks, but life couldn't remain paused forever and we fell into something of a routine. My parents and I would all climb out of our "beds" when the children woke. Mother and I took turns preparing breakfast, and then dressing the children and sending them into the backyard to play. Father and Patrick would pull out the street directory and agree on a plan, then each would go to their designated section of the city to show a photo of Grace around and to ask if anyone had seen her.

Mother made trip after trip to the department store in search of items to freshen the place up, as she put it, returning each afternoon with bags or boxes or deliveries of furniture and knickknacks. I couldn't help but wonder if we'd have been in this situation if Mother had paid such close attention to Grace's comfort and safety at any point over the recent years that had passed, but I couldn't discourage my mother's shopping sprees. I needed to be alone in the house during the day.

While the children played in the backyard, I searched high and low for Grace's notes. It did seem likely to me that she'd hidden them somewhere in her cleaning supplies or even the kitchen—after all, she said she'd left them in the last place Patrick would think to look. At first, I was optimistic—the house was small; there were only so many places she could have hidden them…but the days began to pass, and I had checked and double-checked every conceivable spot. I considered so many possibilities. Had Patrick found them already? Had my parents stumbled upon them? That seemed unlikely, too. They wouldn't have called the police, but they'd have certainly let me know about it. I decided the letters must still be there somewhere, only hidden in a place I hadn't thought to look.

I had to keep searching, just in case—I had no option to stop. Besides, searching for the notes and keeping busy with the children were effective ways of prolonging the immense grief and shame I knew would bury me the minute I let myself be still.

In the second week Father arranged for the telephone to be connected, and then he returned to work. I called Professor Callahan and explained my situation.

"The week after your grandmother died!" He clucked his tongue. "What rotten luck. Take another few weeks."

Mother's days at Grace's house became shorter and shorter over the third week. And then Patrick's boss, Ewan, came to the house, his hat in his hand, muttering something about needing Patrick at a building site.

Patrick, who was spending his days driving around the city searching for Grace and his nights sitting up pouring over maps to plan his next day's search, told Ewan he just couldn't. But the next day the postman came, and there was a stack of overdue notices in the mail, including a particularly fierce letter from Yesler Terrace estate management. He'd missed a month's rent payment.

"How did this happen?" I asked Patrick quietly. He scratched a hand over his scruffy beard and admitted, "I spent all of my last pay on gas so I could keep looking for her. And when I don't work, I don't get paid, so everything that's come due since has just had to wait."

I convinced Father to cut Patrick a check so he could at least cover the rent. He grumbled and complained but wrote the check and informed Patrick that this was most definitely a "one-off."

Patrick went back to work the next day. The vigil was over without a conclusion and I was about to learn yet another hard lesson: sometimes life demands that you to move on without closure. Grace had disappeared, we had no idea where she was, and the truth was we might never know. Maybe I'd have run away then, too—tucked my miserable tail between my legs and run back to California—except that I couldn't. I knew it was a little less likely with every day that passed, but I could not let go of the hope that Grace would resurface somewhere. And in the meantime, I simply had to keep searching for her notes. The last one she wrote now represented a threat to my entire future.

Fortunately for me, it seemed to make sense to everyone else that I'd stay. They all assumed I was sticking around at least in part to help with the children, and the only problem with that assumption was that it meant I was alone with four children all day, every day, and I had no idea how to care for them.

I gradually, painfully, figured out the basics on my own— diapers, simple meals, how to work the television, but I still felt like a bumbling fool. After five years of excelling in academic study, I was learning that domestic life commanded its own skill-set, one I'd never thought to respect. I forgot I put eggs on the stove to boil one morning and the pot went dry and the eggs exploded, sending yolk and white all over the kitchen walls and ceiling. I took the children to the grocer to buy food for dinner and Jeremy ran off—it took half an hour to catch him because he thought running up and down the aisles away from me was a delightful game. I discovered that Beth's diapers were almost impossible to clean properly if I didn't get to them quickly. Mrs. Hills started spontaneously delivering baked goods for snacks for the children and days later, I learned that she was only doing this because the kids had been sneaking through the fence to beg for food.

"I didn't realize children snacked so much," I told her, by way of apology.

She gave me an incredulous look and said, "This is what happens, isn't it? You girls go off to get your book learning and you don't learn common sense."

The worst indignity of all for me was that even as a twenty-three-year-old woman of the world with an honor's degree under my belt, I was now periodically forced to ask a four-year-old for guidance. Tim seemed to know how to manage the younger children best. He knew where their clothes were and when they needed naps and what foods they would and wouldn't eat.

"Do you know where Mommy kept her letters?" I asked him hopefully one day. He nodded confidently and took me to a drawer in the kitchen, but when he opened it, I found it was stuffed to the brim with old bills and overdue notices.

"Thanks, Timmy," I sighed, and I sorted through them just in case, but just like all of my other efforts to search, it was fruitless.

Beth
1996

When I wake the next morning, Hunter is still in his pajamas, speaking quietly on the phone. I feed Noah while I sip tea and nibble on some toast. When my husband hangs up the handset, he takes the seat beside me and gives me a hesitant look.

"Your dad really didn't look great last night so I thought I'd call and check in on him before I go for work."

"Oh?"

"They said…ah, they said maybe you should come in."

"Today?"

"As soon as you can, honey." Hunter reaches across and rests his hand on mine. "I'm so sorry."

"Dad's had his ups and downs for months," I say, more for

my own benefit than for Hunter's. "This is just another down. He'll pick up."

"Babe," Hunter says gently. "I get that you're trying to be positive, but you do realize…" I stare at him expectantly, and he winces and looks away. The end of that sentence hangs heavily in the room, and I push my chair back abruptly.

"I'm going to get dressed."

Forty minutes later Hunter has taken Noah to his mother's house and I'm at the nursing home. They've moved Dad from his original room into another, much larger space. This room is painted in a soft yellow, and Dad is resting on a much wider bed. There are comfy sofas and pastel artworks all around, and a little kitchenette stocked with a coffeemaker and snacks.

This room is setup to bring comfort, and I admire it for a moment, but then a shiver runs through me. This *is* a special room, but it's not an upgrade—it's a place to see out the last hours of a loved one's life.

"How did you get here so fast?" I ask Tim. He's stretched out on the bed beside Dad, focused on the chart in his hands.

"I called the nursing station at five," Tim says without looking up. "They told me about his bloods, so I did my rounds and canceled my day, then came straight in."

I look to Dad at last. He's propped up into a sitting position, which I know helps with his breathing. Even so, his breath is audible in a way that I've just not seen before. Even with oxygen and the drugs and the seated position, even in sleep, Dad is clearly struggling to get enough air.

"Is all of this because of the stress of yesterday?" I ask miserably. I lean over to kiss Dad's cheek, then I take the seat at his bedside, opposite my brother.

"No." Tim shakes his head. "I told you, Beth. Stress does make things worse, but we're long past the point where keeping him calm makes much difference. He's not sick because you upset him. He's sick because his organs are failing."

"And…" For the first time I let myself think the words. My eyes burn as I force myself to ask for confirmation. "So this is the end?"

"It's close, Beth. We're talking days at best now, not weeks. That's what I was trying to tell you yesterday before the shit hit the fan. His blood results were bad when we moved him, but they're catastrophic now—his kidneys are barely functioning."

"Can't they do dialysis?"

"To what end, hey?" he says gently. "To buy him another few weeks of pain until his liver goes, too?" I blink back tears, and Tim slides off the bed to walk around to my side. He sits beside me, his gaze soft on mine. "We're at the point where it would be cruel to intervene. I know this is hard, but it really is for the best."

"Will he suffer?" I croak.

"The staff will do their best to keep him comfortable."

My gaze tracks back to Dad. *Don't leave me, Dad. Not now.* But it's hard to ask him to stay when I can see him laboring for every breath. And it's hard to hope that he holds on if he's going to be in pain. The first of what I know will be many tears runs down my cheek.

"Will he wake up again?" I whisper.

"Maybe. It's hard to say."

"I'm just not ready to say goodbye," I choke. Tim sighs and pulls me close for a hug.

"It's time, Bethie. It's really time we let him go."

When Ruth and Jeremy arrive, we take seats close to one another on the sofa in the far corner of the room.

"I've been thinking," Ruth says quietly. "If Dad has only days or hours left, I don't want to spend that time trying to dig up the past. I know the notes…the death certificate… I know these things raise questions we'll want to answer one day, but I don't want to waste this time. I want us to promise one another that until this is over, we put everything else aside."

"I agree," Jeremy says, for once, falling into step with his twin. "We don't know much about their early life together and we don't know how Grace died, but what we know for sure is that Dad is an extraordinary man who lived an extraordinary life. We have a limited number of hours left with him after a lifetime of love. We owe it to him to love him in these hours as if we never doubted him." The words are rough, and Jeremy's eyes redden as he speaks. Ruth reaches across and takes his hand.

"Can you do this, Beth?" Tim murmurs. I inhale then exhale slowly, then nod.

"Okay."

"He raised us to care for each other, first and foremost," Ruth says quietly. "I think the ultimate homage to Patrick Walsh's life will be for us to focus on this family, even as he leaves us."

Tim reaches to rest his hand over Ruth's, as it rests over Jeremy's. I give a noisy sniffle, then throw myself at the three of them, initiating what soon becomes a messy, awkward group hug.

A day passes and then another. We are keeping vigil by roster under Ruth's careful administrative command—two of us here all the time, the other two home resting, waiting for the call to come. Hunter can't take off work because he's in court, so Chiara takes Noah. She brings him to the hospital sometimes, helping me to keep breastfeeding without any fuss, and I'm so grateful for that. When Ellis brings the older boys, they crowd around Dad on the bed, hugging him and telling him they love him. Dad's congested breathing seems to ease a little when the boys are with him, and so the next time Chiara comes, I rest Noah on the bed with Dad, too. On her next visit Chiara brings a camera, and she takes a picture of Noah beside his grandfather.

"I know it seems strange now, but this photo will be special to you one day," she whispers, giving me a sad, watery smile.

Dad wakes up sometimes for brief stretches, but he's often confused about where he is and who we are even when he does manage to speak. Tim explains to me that this is a sad interplay between his comorbidities—the dementia was already wreaking havoc on his brain, but now toxins are building up in his blood, too. He warns us to expect Dad's mental state to become more and more muddled as the end nears, and I hate every second of this. I'm endlessly torn between wanting Dad to stay, because I need him, and wanting him to go, so he can be at peace.

Sometimes I convince myself he's going to turn a corner. After all, he's been sick for a long time, and he's survived crises before. Dad's a strong man—he's always pulled through. Maybe he'll surprise them all and bounce back again. Maybe a week from now, he'll be back in the other room, watching black-and-white movies on the TV and cuddling Noah when we visit. I don't dare voice these hopes aloud. My siblings have all come to terms with saying goodbye, and I know that if I try to be optimistic, they'll keep me in check.

On Wednesday morning, Tim and I are about to leave to go home and rest, and we're speaking to Ruth and Jeremy in quiet whispers in the hallway, catching them up on what's been another long night of coughing and wheezing and morphine doses. Just as we say goodbye, I glance back at the room and see that Dad has woken up and is watching us through the doorway. My siblings keep talking, but I rush back to his bedside and kiss his cheek.

"Hi there," I say softly.

"Maryanne?" Dad says, peering at me with eyes that are glassy and hopeful, even as his cough emerges closer to a sob. "You came back." I'm about to correct him, but then his face crumples. "I need to say sorry." Dad is concentrating hard and visibly determined to get this out. "I was... I don't know the word. What's the word? I made you go away. I'm so sorry."

These words from him fall slowly and he enunciates them with care. I want to correct him and to make him see that it's *me* here—Beth, his baby girl. But at the deepest level of my soul, I feel my father slipping away, and I realize that it's just too late to do anything but to offer him comfort. For some reason he needs to think I am this mysterious Maryanne right now, and I have no choice but to play along.

I smile softly at my dad, and I stroke his forehead gently as I whisper,

"It's okay, Patrick. I forgive you."

"I didn't mean it. I just couldn't bear it. And I did a thing, I think," Dad says. There are tears in his eyes, and when he blinks, they roll down in a slow path toward his chin. "I did a good... what's the word?"

"You did so many good things."

"Job. I mean I did a good job with them."

Oh, God. He's speaking about us kids and I can't bear this. But he needs this, and I can see it in his eyes as much as I feel it in my heart.

"Oh, you did a wonderful job," I whisper.

"I missed you," he chokes. He's weak, and his eyes drift closed. For a moment I think he's asleep but then he speaks again. "Are you...happy? I don't know the word, Maryanne. Are you...what's the word? Are you...happy of me?"

"I am *so* proud of you," I say. Dad smiles at me, sad and tender, and he lifts his hand to my cheek. His swollen fingers are trembling violently.

"I didn't mean what I said."

"I know, Patrick. I understand." This hurts. Everything hurts—grief is a physical pain in my chest and I don't know how I'll ever survive it. These are my last minutes with Dad, and he doesn't even know who I am. I have clung to hope that he'd recover somehow because I couldn't bear to face the truth—but the man I knew as my father is already gone—all that is left is this tortured shell, and I couldn't wish him another minute of pain. "Everything is okay now, Patrick. You did a beautiful job with the children, but your work is finished now. You can rest. You can…" My voice cracks, but I force myself to say it. "You can go, Patrick. You can go."

His hand falls from my face to the bed, and he closes his eyes, slipping back into sleep.

"What was that about?" Ruth whispers behind me.

"I don't know," I choke. She sits on the edge of the bed beside me and rests her head against mine, then slides her arm around my shoulders to hold me close. "He thought I was someone else, and it just seemed cruel to keep correcting him when he obviously had something he needed to say to her."

"You should go home and sleep," Ruth whispers.

"No." I shake my head. "I need to be here."

"Are you sure?"

"Yeah. And I think…maybe it's time we call Father Jenkins."

In the end, Tim stays, too, and the four of us are there when Father Jenkins anoints Dad's forehead and administers the Last Rites. The priest stays in the room with us after that, taking one of the floral sofas to silently pray and offer his support.

But my four siblings and I cuddle up around Dad on that big, comfortable bed, and we're all speaking softly to him, right up until he breathes his last tortured breath a few hours later.

My father's arms have always been around us—holding our family together, keeping us safe. He releases us now, but I know that's only because the work is done, and the time has come for him to continue his journey alone.

SIXTEEN

Maryanne
1958

A week after Patrick returned to work, Mother and I were sitting in the garden sipping tea in silence, watching while the children played. She'd arrived that morning with a bag of clothes for the kids, and it was strange to see the four of them in their brand-new outfits instead of their usual, worn out clothes. Beth was so delighted with the ribbons Mother had gifted her that she was sitting aside from the others, stroking a ribbon with a grin on her face.

"I need to get them toys next," Mother mused.

"Oh, Mother," I sighed. "Please don't overwhelm them with *things*."

"All of these *things* are helping them get used to me," she said stiffly. Beth was certainly taken with her ribbons, but Mother didn't seem to have noticed that the kids would extend their hands for her gifts, then run to the other end of the yard.

I heard the sound of a car pulling into the drive, but from where we were, I couldn't see who it was, so I rose and walked toward the gate. We weren't expecting anyone, so I tensed right away, but when I saw the shape of the police car there, my body shifted into some hyperalert mode. Every beat of my heart against the wall of my chest felt too strong, the tea churned in my stomach and I heard everything—the birds in the trees around us, the tinkle of the children's laughter behind me, the officers' footsteps on the gravel as they approached me.

No. No. No.

Grace had been missing for almost a month. Father and Patrick had visited every hospital within driving distance, checking for Jane Does, and had spent hundreds of hours flashing her photograph all over the city, looking for leads. But perhaps some part of my heart had clung stubbornly to hope, because when I saw the policemen remove their caps, and when I saw the awkward sadness etched onto their young faces, I was forced to face a truth I still desperately wanted to deny.

"What's this?" Mother said, approaching behind me. I heard her give an awful squeak and I knew she'd quickly come to the same conclusion I'd reached. "No," she said, and then her voice became a wail. "No, Maryanne. Don't let them tell us."

"Mother, please," I whispered, taking her elbow. "We can't hide from this."

"Miss, Madam," the taller of the two policemen greeted us.

"Please," Mother said, her voice strained, her sense of etiquette apparently persisting even in the worst moment of our lives. "Please take a seat with us so we can talk."

If there was any doubt in my mind what the police had come to announce, it disappeared when they walked into the garden and saw the children. They exchanged an awful glance, and I wanted so much to weep then, but I knew I couldn't do it outside—not with the kids *right there*.

"Should we go inside?"

"No," Mother said stiffly. "We stay here."

So we all sat around the little table, and then one of the officers said very quietly,

"I am sorry to—"

"Can I get you some tea?" Mother interrupted him, her voice rising a little hysterically. "We need tea, Maryanne—"

"Mother," I pleaded. "Let them speak."

"Madam," the tall policeman said, very gently. "I'm sorry to tell you that we have recovered a body from Lake Washington last night. The body is in an advanced state of decay. However, some of the clothing was intact. It matches—"

"No," Mother said, standing. "I really need to get that tea—"

"—the description you gave us of Mrs. Walsh's blue-and-white polka dot dress. The medical examiner has concluded that it is almost certainly her."

Mother sat heavily. The birds in the trees kept singing and the children kept playing even while my heart was breaking in my chest. I started to cry then, the full weight of the decisions I'd made finally coming to rest on my shoulders. Those babies would never again know the comfort of her arms, and the tragedy of that loss alone seemed unbearable.

"Well?" Mother demanded hoarsely. "What happened to my daughter?"

"There's no way to be sure," the shorter officer said very quietly. "Of course, we'll do our best to find out who's responsible, but it's fair to say that a body dumped in the river is a somewhat reliable indicator of foul play."

Mother made another whimper in the back of her throat and shot to her feet.

"Excuse me," she said stiffly. As she walked to the house, she covered her mouth with her hand and began to run. Alone at the table with the officers, I gradually became aware of the sound of ragged breathing. I looked around to find out who was making the sound, and then I realized it was me.

"Do you have *any* idea how she died?" I asked. My voice sounded desperately high.

"It looks like she's been in the river for weeks, Miss," the office said awkwardly. "And with this hot weather...well, the medical examiner said he'd try to do an autopsy, but to be completely honest, I don't hold any hope you'll ever know for sure."

The worst of it was, I couldn't help but feel some relief about that, and as soon as I recognized the emotion, I hated myself.

The police wanted the address of Patrick's job site so they could deliver the news. They said someone would go to the bank to tell Father, too.

"You can't deliver news like this over the phone," one of the officers said as he straightened his hat. "Once again, Miss. We're so sorry."

They left then, and I went inside to find Mother so that I could comfort her, or she could comfort me, or at least so that I didn't have to be alone with the children while I carried the weight of the news. But I found Mother lying on the stretcher bed, staring at the ceiling. She was silently crying, her makeup staining the tears that ran down her cheeks and into her hair. She clutched the little pill container against her chest as if it were some kind of lovely, comforting teddy bear.

"Mother?" I asked unevenly. She looked up at me and I saw that she was seeing me through a medicinal glaze. I'd never felt as alone as I did in that moment.

Gracie. Oh, Gracie, what have I done?

I made myself a fresh cup of tea, having forgotten all about the tea that I was halfway through drinking when the police arrived. I took the fresh cup out to sit on the stairs at the back of the house and I watched the children play and I tried to fix a mask in place.

Be a grieving sister, not a guilt-stricken murderer.

Logically, I knew that I hadn't performed the procedure myself and I couldn't be held responsible for this outcome, but emotionally, I was entering the first phase of living under a cloud of guilt that would come and go for decades. Yes, Grace begged me to help her, but I found the doctor. I arranged the procedure. I got her most of the money. Oh, God, I even drove her there and when she was scared, I didn't tell her that she could still back out.

"Aunt Maryanne?" Tim climbed up to sit beside me on the stairs, his expression steady and very serious. I looked at him with bleary eyes, staring at him through a haze of shock, battling to resist an urge to beg that child for forgiveness.

"Yes?" I croaked.

"Did the policeman find her? Is Mommy coming home soon?" he asked me, his little face shining with hope.

It wasn't my place to tell him, but I knew intuitively that Patrick wasn't going to be in any state to explain it to the children. I wasn't nurturing or gentle or kind, not the way Grace had been. I wasn't motherly at all...but that day I was agonizingly aware that I was all that the four of them had. I opened my arms to him and he climbed up onto my lap, shooting me wary side glances as he nestled against me.

"Sweetheart," I said, straining to keep my voice level. "Mommy had to go away to heaven."

"But I don't want Mommy to be in heaven," he said, scowling. "We want her to come home."

"Sometimes God needs people in heaven even more than we need them here with us," I said, lying through my teeth because I didn't even believe in God myself, especially *that* day. But what else could I possibly say? *I made a mistake. I did everything wrong. She's never coming back and it's my fault.*

"But who will look after us?"

"I don't know."

"*You* don't even know how to make us eggs."

"I know."

"Grandmother isn't going to stay, is she?"

"No," I said, swallowing. "Grandmother won't stay."

"Will you?"

I shook my head, and my tears at last spilled over.

"Timmy, I can't stay, either. This isn't my life."

"I don't know what that means," Tim said, but his eyes had filled with tears. "I just want my Mommy."

Great, rolling sobs were now bursting from within me, and when Tim started sobbing, too, I could only hold him tight in my arms. The other children came to see what the fuss was about, and I had to have the same conversation with the little ones, who cried as soon as they saw us crying, and soon the five of us were all sitting on the back steps, sobbing as though the world had ended.

It felt so strange that after all those weeks of coming to the house every night, Mother and Father retreated immediately. Father came from the bank, but he set about packing up their belongings right away, and then he helped Mother up from the stretcher.

"Where are you going?" I asked desperately.

"Home," he said, jaw set and shoulders locked stiffly. "We need to go home."

"But...now?"

"Yes, Maryanne. *Now.*"

Patrick arrived home just as Father was leading my near-comatose mother from the house. His eyes were dry, his expression blank and I could see he was in some kind of shock. He shook Father's hand, and then pushed past me into the house without a word.

"Father, I don't know what to say to him," I choked. "Please don't leave me here alone with them."

Father closed his eyes briefly, then he helped Mother to stand by the car before he turned to me.

"We need to go home to grieve and to think this through. I've tolerated him for these weeks because I had to, but we all know where the blame really lies."

My eyes widened, and my nervous, guilty heart skipped a beat.

"Where?"

"With *him*, Maryanne," Father spat, pointing at the house. "She probably ran away. He never treated her right, and now she's dead, and..." His face was red, his hands in fists that trembled violently with the force of holding back punches he desperately wanted to throw. "Jesus Christ. In the *lake*, Maryanne. For a *month*. He should have taken better care of his wife."

I started to cry again and I wrapped my arms around my waist.

"Father, please believe me. This isn't Patrick's fault."

Father grunted, then he opened the car door and took Mother's arm, lowering her gently into her seat.

"How many of those damned pills has she taken this time?" he muttered.

"I didn't see how many, but I'm guessing it was a lot," I whispered thickly.

Mother gazed up at me, her expression completely blank.

"You'll need to help him, Maryanne," she said.

Father stepped out of the way, and I bent to kiss Mother's cheek, then croaked, "I will, Mother. I'll see you tomorrow."

I closed the door behind her, and Father cleared his throat once...twice...a third time. He was blinking rapidly now, still shaking with grief and an impotent rage, still glaring at the house behind us.

"That bastard barely looked after her and the kids when she was alive," he said. "How is he ever going to cope now?"

"I have no idea," I admitted weakly. "I just have no idea."

As I stepped back into the house, Patrick passed me on his way back along the hall. He was still dry-eyed, but he was carrying a bottle of whiskey now. He went straight into his bedroom and closed the door behind him without a word.

I found Tim behind the sofa in the living room. He was crying, rocking back and forth, rubbing his upper arms as if he was cold. The lovely new outfit my mother had surprised him with that day seemed ridiculous now, and I wanted to haul him out of there to at least hug him, but when I tried to coax him out, he shook his head and whispered at me, "I don't want to upset the children. They cried before when they saw me cry. I'll come out when I can be brave."

He was a little shy of four years old. I didn't want to leave him alone there, so I sat on the sofa in front of him and I tried to take his advice. *I have to be brave. I can't upset the children, either.* So I forced myself into a numb state of shock—promising myself I could weep later, in private once everyone was asleep.

The twins and Beth were tearing around the house and the yard again, apparently having already forgotten the awful news I'd delivered earlier. They asked me for snacks and I gave them some of Mrs. Hills's lemon slice, and after a while, Ruth came back inside.

"Mommy in heaven now," she parroted thoughtfully.

"Yes, sweetie."

"I want to go to heaven, too."

"You can't, Ruth," I croaked.

"Mommy will come back soon," Ruth assured me, patting my arm gently, and then she tore off again, no doubt to squabble with her twin about one thing or another. I had similarly awful conversations with Beth and then Jeremy as the hours passed, but Tim remained stubbornly behind the couch, and Patrick was still in his bedroom.

And I sat there on the sofa in the center of my sister's rundown house, surrounded by my mother's extravagant splurges, and wondered how on earth we were all going to cope now that Grace was really gone.

★ ★ ★

Eventually, I convinced the children to eat and then I bathed them and put them to bed. Only once the house was silent did Patrick emerge from the bedroom. His eyes had taken on the kind of intense bloodshot hue that only comes from hours of weeping.

I was washing up the dishes from the childrens' dinner, but I left the sink to serve him a plate of ground beef and vegetables. He was good and drunk, and as he sat there, he swayed a little.

"I'm sorry I was so awful to you that first day," he said suddenly.

You shouldn't be.

"You were under a lot of pressure," I replied, my voice weak with guilt I hoped he wouldn't hear.

"I couldn't have survived the past four weeks without you. And it can't have been your fault. Not really." He pinched the bridge of his nose and closed his eyes, his breathing suddenly shaky again. "She was a woman on her own in broad daylight, just waiting to meet her sister after shopping, at least as far as the world knew. You weren't even in a bad area of the city. What has the world come to that a woman can't even wander the city alone in broad daylight?"

"None of this is fair."

I meant those words to the very depths of my soul. In a fair world Grace would never have been forced to resort to such measures.

"I shouldn't have blamed you, Maryanne," Patrick whispered, and his face crumpled. "I still don't understand how you could kill your own baby like that, but you've been nothing but good to me and my kids. I should have done a lot of things differently in my life, but I can't change any of that now. Just…please believe me. I *am* sorry for the things I said to you."

I started to cry because as much as I'd never liked Patrick, his distress was so near to me and so raw. In that moment I wasn't sure I'd actually survive the guilt of my role in my sister's death. I sank down into the chair beside Patrick and patted him on the back, just as little Beth had done for me.

"You don't have to worry about that now, Patrick," I choked between whole-body sobs. "Please."

"But don't you see?" he croaked back. "We always think there's time to do better. I was always going to man up one day. I really was, I promise you. I was going to stop drinking and pay the bills and teach the kids how to use tools and to buy Grace nice things and I was going to love her the way she deserved to be loved. But I ran out of time and I let her carry this family all on her own and I told her she h-had to *harden up* and I…" He was a mess—his face was beetroot red, his expression twisted with grief and shame. He was leaking pure grief—tears and snot and even spittle as he spoke with such self-directed fury at all of the ways he'd let her down. And all I could do was to watch him suffer, because there was nothing at all I could say to make any of this better.

"I never even got to say sorry." His voice rose as if he was bewildered by life, and the way that it promises us happiness and delivers only heartache. "There is *no fucking* time, Maryanne. There's only now, and Grace isn't here now, and I won't ever get to say sorry to her. I can only say sorry to you." He was bawling like a baby, and fumbling for my hand. I let him take it, and he squeezed my fingers hard, then rested our hands against the cracked vinyl of their dining room table. "*Please* let me say sorry to you instead."

"You have to be brave, Patrick," I choked, thinking of Tim's sofa fortress, and how even the child had known to protect the littler ones. "The children are going to need you to be brave. You're going to have to put all of that behind you in the past and build a new future for them on your own. It's too late to say sorry to Grace, but you can do better for her kids."

And Patrick let go of my hand, pushed his dinner away and slumped onto the table to weep into his arms.

I decided I would leave a few days after the funeral—I couldn't wait to get back to California. I was going to positively *inhale* the freedom of my old life, and finally take some time to grieve. I was so busy with Patrick and the children that I hadn't found time to really accept that Grace was gone, let alone process my role in her death. I kept promising myself that as soon as I was on that train, I'd let the floodgates open.

But first, I had to find the letters. I told Patrick I was reorganizing the house to make it tidier, and I pulled things out of cupboards and closets and I searched through every single nook and cranny I could find.

I was searching through the children's clothes one afternoon when Father came around to talk to Patrick, and at first, I assumed they were discussing funeral arrangements. But then Father left the house in a huff, slamming the door behind him, and Patrick stormed back into his bedroom and I realized they'd actually been quarreling. I tried to ask Patrick about the incident, but he was in such a state, I didn't have the heart to force the matter. He'd run out of whiskey and there was no money for more, but after that day, he stayed in bed with the drapes drawn and for the most part, kept the door closed.

Ewan had given him a week of bereavement leave, unusually generous on account of his guilt at having dragged Patrick back to work just before Grace's body was found. When several more days passed with Patrick still essentially catatonic, I decided to leave him in peace. This gave me more time to search, and besides, soon enough he'd have to go back to work, so the least I could do was to let him have these short days to grieve before we laid Gracie to rest.

I kept things running in the household—tending to the children, doing the housework and such. I even decided I'd try to arrange care for them for after I went home. I saw Mrs. Hills out fetching the eggs from the hens in her backyard, and so I called her over to the fence.

"How are you today, Mrs. Hills?" I said as cheerfully as I could.

"Maryanne, I've been meaning to talk to you. After the funeral, this has to stop."

"What has to stop?"

"It's not right at all, love," she said, pursing her lips. "I know this has been a trying time, but you can't go on this way."

"I know," I said, still a little confused. I knew I wasn't the best stand-in mother in the world, but I really had been doing my best under extremely trying circumstances. "But…have I been doing something wrong?"

"I don't know about where *you're* from, but where I'm from, a man and a woman don't live alone under one roof unless they're married."

"Mrs. Hills," I gasped, then I scowled. "Are you really suggesting that anything untoward would happen between me and my recently deceased sister's husband? I suggest you think very carefully about what you're implying here, please."

"I'm just saying that if you're planning on sticking around, you should look for alternative accommodation," she said, her expression softening a little. "People talk, Maryanne. It was different when your parents were here, but they're gone now. I know you're focused on getting through the funeral, but as soon as it's over, it's time you made this right."

"I'll be going back to California after the funeral, for your information," I snapped, but then I remembered that I had come to ask for her help, so I pulled all of the animosity out of my tone and said very gently, "Actually, I was very much hoping we could count on you to help Patrick with the children once I'm gone."

"Are you crazy, young lady?" Mrs. Hills gasped. "Those children are *hellions*."

"Oh, they aren't that bad," I muttered, glancing back over the fence, just in time to see Jeremy push Ruth over so he could steal the cupcake she'd been eating. When I glanced back to Mrs. Hills, she raised her eyebrows at me. "The thing is, there's just not many people we can ask. Couldn't you take them at least a few days a week?"

"Your parents will have to step up," Mrs. Hills informed me haughtily. "That mother of yours will have to do it."

I piled all of the children into Father's car that afternoon and drove them to my parents' house. I couldn't help notice the way that the houses grew larger and the streets grew wider, until we were in a patch of paradise where every house had at least two stories and a late-model car in the drive.

The children hadn't been to Mother and Father's place since they were babies, and as we pulled into the yard, they stared wide-eyed at the expansive gardens and the huge house. When I parked and helped them all out, Ruth jumped up and down with glee.

"I want to see the princess!" she said.

"What princess?"

"She thinks it's a palace," Tim muttered.

"No, darling. This is Grandmother and Grandfather's home," I said, and I watched as all four faces fell in disappointment. "Oh, come on, children. They aren't *that* bad."

But as I sat with Mother in the living room to talk about the future, she started off the conversation by shrieking at the kids.

"Don't touch *anything*, do you hear me? We have nice things in this house. It's not like your place. You keep your filthy little hands to yourselves. Is that understood?"

"Mother," I whispered, shooting her a look. "They're unsettled because of...you know. And besides, you can hardly blame *them* if they don't know how to behave here."

Mother raised her chin stubbornly.

"We'll soon fix that, Maryanne. Don't you worry."

"I actually wanted to talk to you about what will happen after the funeral, when Patrick goes back to work. He's going to need your help."

"Father and I have spoken about this, and we have decided that the best thing for everyone is for the children to move in here," Mother said. I nearly dropped my teacup. It clattered against the fine china saucer and Mother's gaze narrowed on *me*. While her attention was off the children, Jeremy picked up a vase.

"Jeremy!" I gasped, reaching out to snatch it off him. "Please, Jeremy. Please just sit there on the rug and watch the television and I'll give you some candy when we go home, okay?"

He smirked, then dropped heavily onto his bottom, elbowing Beth on the way down. Beth immediately burst into tears and climbed up onto my lap. I gave up on the cup of tea, setting it carefully onto a coffee table so I could focus on my mother's shocking announcement.

"You're really going to let Patrick move into your house?"

"Oh, heavens no," Mother said, nostrils flaring. "The children will live here. He can visit them on Sundays."

"But..." It took me a long moment to digest what she was saying. "But... Mother..."

"Darling," Mother said, sighing heavily. "We had our concerns all along, didn't we? Even with Grace there to run the house he barely managed to keep that family afloat, and now it's just too much for him. Those children need more than Patrick can give them."

"Yes." I couldn't argue with that at all. "They absolutely *do* need more than he can give them. But he needs those children, and those children *need him*—now more than ever. If you really want to help, then maybe offer to babysit them for him—"

"I will babysit them," Mother said stiffly. "They'll be living here soon enough. I'll be babysitting plenty."

"Have you and Father even talked to him about this?"

"Father told him a few days ago."

It all made sense then. No wonder Patrick couldn't get out of bed. He'd just lost his wife, and it seemed that he was about to lose his children, too. My heart sank.

"This is a very bad idea, Mother."

"Well, if you can think of an alternative, I'd like to hear it."

"Help him find his feet," I pleaded with her. "Grace always believed there was a good man in there somewhere, under all the mistakes he's made."

"And do *you* think that?" Mother asked me pointedly. "Has he stepped up over these past weeks to show *you* what a great father he would be?"

I hesitated, then sighed.

"He's very sorry for letting her down. I do think we need to give him a chance—just a little support until he figures out how to manage on his own."

"It's too late for—"

"You did this with her, too," I interrupted. My temper was starting to simmer, and I tried to calm myself, but I had *so much* unprocessed pain just waiting to erupt. "You are so judgmental. The world is so *simple* to you, looking down on everyone from up here on your ivory tower. You were hardly perfect parents yourselves!"

"Maryanne Gallagher, you *will not* speak to me like that," Mother said. She was visibly hurt, and her total lack of empathy only enraged me further. Grace had felt empathy. Grace had even taught tiny *Beth* to feel empathy. But my Mother was too busy popping pills to numb her every emotion to think outside her own experience and to recognize other people's pain.

"He won't let you take his children," I snapped, standing.

"Well, that's where you're wrong, and you've clearly overes-

TRUTHS I NEVER TOLD YOU

timated him," Mother snapped. "He wasn't happy about it first, but even he could see that we were right about this."

"Come on, Timmy. Ruth. Beth. Jeremy, enough with the vase! It's time to go," I said, glaring at my mother and shepherding the children toward the door. She didn't even follow us out, and so I alternated strapping the children into their seat belts and firing furious glares back at the house.

Once they were all safely buckled in, I sat in the driver's seat and exhaled, then closed my eyes.

"Mommy," Beth said.

"Mommy's in heaven, Bethany," I said heavily.

"Mommy, hungry," she said.

I turned back to her, frustrated.

"Mommy can't get you something to eat. She's in heaven."

Beth extended her hand toward me and flapped her fingers impatiently.

"Mommy, *hungry*," she said, and her face was starting to redden with frustration. That's when a terrifying possibility occurred to me.

Was Bethany calling me Mommy?

"I'm Auntie Maryanne," I choked. "You know that, don't you, darling? I'm *Auntie Maryanne*."

"Hungry!" she cried, completely disinterested in my name. She just wanted something to eat, and she was in *no* mood to wait. I groaned and started the car.

"Well, we're not going back in there to get something now," I muttered, and turned the car toward home.

"Patrick?" I leaned my forehead against the door to Patrick's bedroom later that night, took a deep breath, then knocked. I was so weary. I wanted to crawl into my stretcher bed and sob for hours, but the funeral was the next day, and I needed to keep searching for the letters, and I needed to speak to Patrick before I faced my parents again.

For the first time I was starting to feel hopeless about the entire situation. My whole *future* rested on finding that note Gracie wrote, and I simply had to find it before I could go back to my old life, or Patrick was likely to stumble upon it, and then I'd lose *everything*. And the situation with Patrick and my parents was making me nervous, too. I'd been with the family for five weeks by that point, and I had to admit, the children had grown on me. I just couldn't bear the thought of them losing Patrick. And that's why I was standing in his doorway preparing for battle, even as my muscles ached with exhaustion.

"I don't want dinner," Patrick grunted.

I sighed and pushed the door open. He was in bed lying on his side, staring away from me. It felt strange to step into his bedroom that night. I'd searched every cranny of it while he was at work, but this was different. *He* was in there now, and I felt I was crossing some invisible boundary. But this conversation had to start somewhere, and I couldn't wait for Patrick to find the energy to get out of bed, because I just didn't know if he *ever* would without a push.

"I talked to Mother today."

He sighed heavily, then adjusted the blankets, pulling them higher toward his chin.

"I don't feel like talking about this now."

"Well, you don't have a choice," I said impatiently. "Is this really what you want?"

"Does it matter what I want?" he mumbled. I sighed and walked to stand in front of him. His eyes had sunk into his head, and his skin had taken on a gray pallor that frightened me. Patrick hadn't shaved in days, and the funeral was only twelve hours away. I had intended to interrogate him about his plans for the future but realized that it was going to be challenge enough to get him out of bed.

"Look," I said quietly. "Get up, take a shower and then come and have some soup."

"I'm not hungry."

"Well, it's not about you, Patrick. It's never been about you, but now more than ever. I know you are hurting, but if you want to keep them—"

"How exactly do I keep them, Maryanne?" he asked, sitting up at last. "Your father told me they've already spoken to a lawyer. A single man raising four kids on his own? Even if I figured out the logistics of childcare, if they take this to the courts, no one is going to side with me."

"That doesn't mean you don't *try*, Patrick!"

"Your father paid the rent last month, but I haven't worked enough this month for the next payment. Plus, I'm already behind with every other bill. I don't even know what I'm doing with them! I can't cook or clean and I don't know where to start with raising them. The kids will be better off in your parents' damned house with nice things and good schools."

"Those children just lost their *mother*," I whispered fiercely. "And if you stopped feeling sorry for yourself for more than five seconds and actually listened to me, I'd tell you that you can offer those kids something my parents don't even have the capacity to understand." He paused then, and finally met my eyes. I pushed on, emboldened. "My parents have more money than God, but no heart at all. And the past few weeks I've had this feeling that you…" I was frustrated by the tears that sprung to my eyes, and I kicked the bed out of sheer impatience. "*You miserable, pathetic excuse for a man*…despite *all* evidence to the contrary I just had this feeling you could at least offer them love. But if you're really going to let my parents take your children without so much as a fight, then I guess I was right about you all along."

I spun out of the room, and ignoring the sleeping children in the next room, slammed the door behind me. I took a bath and let myself cry for a while, because Grace and I had turned out okay, but my parents had only hardened as the years went on. The more I thought about it, the more determined I was that those four little urchins deserved *better*. Sometime over the month I'd spent with them, they'd burrowed their way into my heart, and the idea of my mother and father turning them into proper little statues was just too awful to contemplate. I didn't want Timmy and Jeremy to grow up to think that they were somehow better than the women in their life just by virtue of their gender. I didn't want Bethany and Ruth to grow up to think that a woman's only option was to stay at home. I tried to console myself by remembering that I had come out of that very environment and I'd seen the light, but I just kept thinking of Grace, and the life she fell into with Patrick, and how it never seemed to occur to her that she could choose something different for herself.

And I wasn't at all sure why I had convinced myself that Patrick was a better option for those kids than my parents, given the things I knew about his marriage to my sister. But her words in the car that final day just kept replaying in my mind.

One day he's going to be a great man.

She had seen something in him, and perhaps I'd seen glimpses of it, too, over those past weeks, when circumstances forced Patrick to be vulnerable. I appreciated that he'd found it within himself to apologize, even though he still believed I'd had an abortion, and no doubt he still judged me for it. It took real humility for him to thank me for my help, even though we'd never gotten along.

Maybe he had the potential to become something better than he had been, but I just couldn't do this *for* him. If he didn't even want to fight to keep his own children, then perhaps Grace had been wrong about him all along.

My heart was heavy when I climbed out of the bath. I pulled my nightgown on, intending to go right to my stretcher. But when I stepped into the hallway and saw the light in the kitchen, I followed it warily, and found Patrick at the table.

He was noisily slurping a bowl of the awful chicken soup

I'd made him. Steam rose from the bowl, so I knew he'd even heated it up for himself.

"Well?" he asked me, without turning around to face me. "Are you going to join me?"

I entered the room hesitantly but didn't sit at the table. Instead, I leaned against the countertop and crossed my arms over my chest.

"I don't want them to go," he said, his tone flat. "It'll kill me if they do. But tell me what options I have here?"

"I don't know," I admitted heavily. "But there has to be a way. Grace wouldn't want you to give up without a fight."

"Where do I even start?"

"Let's bury her tomorrow. We'll send her off and then we'll sit down and we'll figure this out."

"*We?* I thought you were going back to California any day now. That's what your father said, and that's what I figured was about to happen, too."

I raised my chin stubbornly.

"I know you don't like me, Patrick. I don't like you much, either. But we both loved Grace, and I think…" I cleared my throat a few times, then admitted, "I think that maybe we both love those filthy, noisy little monsters of yours."

Patrick nodded, then exhaled.

"Yeah. Okay."

"Get some sleep," I suggested. "Tomorrow's going to be a long day."

Beth
1996

Logically, I had expected that losing Dad was going to hurt, but I'm not at all prepared for the intensity of the grief. It crushes me, catching me off guard every time I don't distract myself for even a second. I stare at the TV for hours over the days that follow, but I don't absorb a word. I try unsuccessfully to go through the motions, but if Hunter wasn't off work and there to remind me, I'm not sure I'd eat at all, or bathe, or even feed Noah.

Walsh Homes shuts down on Monday for Dad's memorial service, and all of Ruth's staff and many of their family members come. There are people at the service who loved Dad simply because he built their family home—crafting the space that became their nest with such love and care that he earned a place of honor in their lives forever. Almost all of the regulars at St. Louise's Sunday Mass are there for the service, too, because Dad never missed Mass, and this community was his family almost as much as we were. Three retired priests make the journey back from wherever they've landed in old age to pay their respects. And when the time comes for the ceremony, a handful of Dad's golfing buddies and my brothers act as pall bearers.

Ruth, of course, has planned the service with militant precision. The four of us had lightly discussed it the day after Dad passed, and we agreed it should be a celebration of his life. Maybe that's what she organized, but I'm not at all sure because now that the time has come, I can't focus much on the words or the hymns or the prayers. I feel like I'm floating near my body, completely dissociated from the proceedings, a ball of tangled grief and loss and sadness. I don't even realize I'm sobbing until Chiara shifts along the pew, pushes Hunter out of the way and throws her arms around me.

"Darling," she chokes against my hair. "He loved you all, of course, but you were the light of his life. He's gone, but he's at peace now, and he's left behind a legacy I know he was so proud of."

I turn to her then and I press my face into her shoulder. I sink all the way into her embrace, and I feel for the very first time a simple comfort in her presence. I don't have the energy to wonder about the dynamic in our relationship or to analyze how to feel about her. All I can do is focus on the warmth of her arms around me, and maybe it's even that embrace that grounds me, because I make it through the rest of the Mass without dissolving into a puddle of pain.

We travel in procession to the cemetery for Rite of Committal. There are more prayers and more ceremony—the funeral Mass, the committal, then the wake. Despite my "lapsed" Catholic status, tradition provides a roadmap, and that roadmap unexpectedly offers me a path through the worst of the grief.

When Father Jenkins invites us to recite the Lord's Prayer as the graveside service concludes, I do so by rote, and I look around to my family as they pray. Everyone is in tears—Ruth and Tim and Jeremy unashamedly crying, too, now. When the prayer finishes, and Dad's casket is lowered into the ground, the four of us look to one another.

It's just us now, our gazes say.

We understand because we'll miss him, too, their red-rimmed eyes tell me.

We're going to be okay because we've still got one another, our common grief promises me.

And when the service ends, we gravitate to each other. There's more tears and hugs, but I feel the heaviest part of the grief lift *just* a little, and I mentally check back into the day.

This, I realize, is why we have ceremonies like funerals—not for the departed but for the living, to remind one another that even in grief, we don't have to be alone.

Ruth booked out a local function center for the wake, given the size of the crowd we were expecting. There's great food on offer and plenty of booze, and over the hours the people who loved him enthusiastically swap stories of Dad's life.

I find myself laughing at the antics his long-term staff members recount—about when he was first starting out on his own and desperate to save every penny, how he'd recycle even bent nails if he thought he could find a use for them. About the time he was building a house for a family, and right in the middle of the project the mother was diagnosed with cancer, and how Dad finished out the job for them without charging a cent for labor. About the day one young apprentice tried to hang a calendar with half-naked women on it in the workshop, and Dad set the thing on fire and gave the whole staff a lecture about respect for women.

I cry with Janet, who was Dad's secretary for two decades. I cry with Yuri, one of his best foremen. His golf buddies regale me and my brothers with unlikely tales about holes in one. We laugh about the "wild weekends" they'd plan; nights that would inevitably end with them all in bed early because Dad was nothing like a night owl, but he was also the life of the party. He'd turn in at eight or nine, and everyone else would get bored and soon turn in, too. His neighbors remind me about how until he got sick, Dad always helped them with their yardwork whenever life or health or family got in the way of it. Hunter's boss reminds me about that commissioned artwork on the wall of his office—and how customers and guests visiting *still* often remark at the sheer beauty of them.

My dad lived a big life and it was an important life, a life devoted to family and friends and his church and community.

And when all is said and done, *that* is who he was, and that's the legacy he left behind. It's enough for now for me to focus on that, and to put aside my confusion about his early years, and to grieve the man I knew him to be.

SEVENTEEN

Maryanne
1958

My parents seemed to assume there would be a truce among us all for Grace's sake, because when Patrick and I piled out of the car with the children for the funeral service, they both came to help us take our seats in the cathedral. For once in my life I didn't have it in me to make a scene.

Her funeral service was excruciatingly long because Father insisted that the priest send her off with the full Requiem Mass. I distracted the children with candy, and I was proud of them for patiently sitting around me, especially Beth. She seemed to understand that something momentous was happening, even if she couldn't really fathom what it was.

And then we all piled into Patrick's car, and drove to the cemetery. There wasn't so much as a breeze that day, and there wasn't a cloud in the sky. As we drove in near silence, I thought about how such an awful occasion shouldn't be allowed to take place on such a beautiful day. But life has no rhyme or reason sometimes, and when it all boils down, we really are at the mercy of fate.

There was quite a crowd around that gravesite, mostly Mother and Father's friends and executives from the bank who probably didn't know Grace well enough to care, but they certainly knew Father well enough to make the trip. Patrick's aunt Nina was there, and she held herself up against her walker beside the children. Mr. and Mrs. Hills were there, too, and Ewan stood within the circle of a small collection of people I vaguely recognized as Patrick's colleagues.

It was all dreadfully sad, and as they lowered my sister into the ground, I wondered how on earth I was supposed to carry on with my life knowing the role I'd played in her death. My guilt came and went in waves—some days I'd feel certain that it was all my fault, and if I'd just found some other option for her or refused to help her, things would have been okay. Other days I convinced myself that one way or another, Grace was going to end her pregnancy, and it was hardly my fault there were no safe alternatives. There at her graveside the day of her funeral, I felt for the very first time a balancing in those two extremes.

Grace was gone, and I'd certainly played a role in that. But I was only helping her to do what she felt she so desperately needed to do, and she had seemed quite sure that if she had gone ahead with the pregnancy, we'd have been burying her anyway. This was the start of me making peace with her loss, and when these thoughts struck me, I finally started to cry.

The priest was reading bible verses now and talking about "everlasting peace" and Grace's new home of heaven. This, the children seemed to understand, and I saw the shift in them. Timmy especially held himself so stiffly, refusing to spill the tears in his eyes. That beautiful boy stood there in one of my mother's expensive outfits, his hair freshly combed, with the weight of the world on his shoulders. When I looked past him,

I saw that Patrick was doing much the same, clenching his jaw in order to keep the tears at bay. I crouched next to Tim, ignoring my mother's questioning look, and I caught his shoulders in my hands.

"You can cry, Tim. You don't have to be brave."

"But..." He looked from the grave to his siblings and then back to me helplessly. "I want to be a big boy for..."

"Big boys cry sometimes," I promised him. Tim glanced up at Patrick skeptically, and Patrick looked down at us, frowning. "In fact, sometimes even *men* cry. This is very unfair and it's very hard, so it's okay to feel sad and scared, especially when you're with your family."

Patrick swallowed, then closed his eyes. Two heavy tears ran down his cheeks. When Tim looked up and saw his father crying his little face crumpled. He turned back to me, threw his arms around my neck and started to sob. Soon Ruth and Jeremy were crying, too, and I sat on the grass so I could hold the three of them at once. The priest kept looking over at us, and Mother was still staring at us as if we were tarnishing the precious formality of the funeral service by openly grieving the deceased. But we didn't do anything *really* scandalous until Patrick also dropped to sit cross-legged on the grass, too.

"Come here," he choked, and the twins and Tim ran at their father, the four of them sobbing audibly against the backdrop to the priest's ongoing monologue.

"Momma," Beth said, and she climbed onto my lap and wrapped her arms around my neck, then patted my back ever so gently. "Momma sad."

I'd suspected it the previous day, but here at the worst possible time was undeniable proof that Beth really was confusing me up with Grace. I knew that at least in *this* I had nothing to feel guilty about, but I did feel very guilty indeed. What if someone heard and assumed that I'd encouraged her to do such a thing?

"Yes," I said, for the purposes of anyone who might have overheard her. "It is sad that Momma is in heaven."

"So very sad," Mrs. Hills agreed behind us. "It's all so very sad."

The wake was held back at my mother and father's house—also known now by the children as "the castle"—and my parents' caterers had set out enough food and top-shelf liquor to fell an elephant. I helped myself to a generous glass of sherry, but when I glanced at Patrick, he was sipping water.

It was a dull function—more perfunctory than celebratory of my sister's life—and I could see the children were all bored and exhausted after the emotional moments at the cemetery. It wasn't long before Patrick and I exchanged a glance, and then by mutual, unspoken agreement, we made our farewells and left. All four children had fallen asleep before we were even out of Father's street, leaning into one another in a way that made my heart ache.

"You didn't drink today," I remarked to Patrick.

"Your parents would have loved it if I drank myself into a stupor," he said, dragging a heavy hand over his face. "I still don't know how I stop them from taking the kids, but I figure a good place to start is to get my act together."

"Good," I said, nodding. "That's good."

There was a pause, then Patrick added, "If you have any other ideas, now would be a good time to share them."

"I don't know if today is the day to talk about this," I admitted. I was utterly exhausted, already hoping the conversation would fade so I could nap as Patrick drove home.

"I don't have the luxury of time, Maryanne. If you have ideas, spit them out."

I sighed and sat back up, then rubbed at my temples.

"I think the first obstacle is childcare. Timmy will go to school in a few months, but there's the matter of the little ones to worry about, and your work hours are *much* longer than a school day anyway. But *if* we can figure out a solution for child-care, then that's surely half the battle."

"I was thinking I'd ask Mrs. Hills," Patrick said. I coughed delicately.

"She's not going to be able to help."

"How do you know?"

"I already suggested it." I cleared my throat again. "She was most unenthused about the idea."

"Okay. Then I was thinking about asking Aunt Nina to move down here."

"Your aunt *Nina*?" I repeated, horrified. "Patrick, no. That isn't going to work, either."

"I know she's frail, but—"

"She's more than frail. She couldn't even stand up long enough for the graveside ceremony."

"And she's lived in her house for sixty years," Patrick admitted, sighing. "Dragging her out of her home in Bellevue might literally kill her. The problem is that anything else is going to cost money I don't have yet. It's going to take me a while to catch up on the bills even after I'm back at work next week."

I closed my eyes, then swallowed the lump in my throat. *I still hadn't found Grace's notes*, and I knew that I couldn't leave until I did. I could almost feel my escape to California slipping through my fingers.

"I'll call my supervisor and ask for leave until the end of the semester."

"How long is that?"

"Six weeks. I could stay six more weeks to care for the kids. You can try to catch up on your bills, and we can try to find a long-term solution for the kids."

"And if your parents come for the children in the meantime?"

"Then we find a lawyer."

"With what money?"

"I don't know," I admitted. "I guess we have to hope they see sense before it gets that far."

"Mommy?"

"I'm Aunt Maryanne, Beth."

I had no baseline against which to compare her speech, but Beth *seemed* to be quite eloquent for such a tiny child. Still, she either couldn't wrap her mouth around the words "Aunt Maryanne," or my slight physical resemblance to my sister was just *too* much for her. Maybe it was some combination of both. All I knew was, every single time she called me Mommy I corrected her, and every single time I corrected her, she'd give me an odd look and ignore me.

"Mommy, drink," she said, and she took my hand and led me through to the kitchen, where she stared at me expectantly. I sighed and poured some water into a cup, then watched as she drank it. Beth passed the cup back and turned to leave the room.

"Uh-uh, Beth," I scolded. "Now, what do you say?"

"Thank you, Mommy."

"Thank you, *Aunt Maryanne*," I corrected. She toddled out of the room as if I hadn't spoken, and I watched her go, frowning as I tried to figure out exactly what to do about the confusion. In the weeks since we buried Grace, I'd tried firmly correcting Beth. I'd tried patience. I'd even accidentally snapped at her a few times, because although I wanted to be compassionate and her circumstances were heartbreaking, I was grieving, too. I had just lost my sister, and my own life was hanging in the balance, because somewhere in that house, my sister had left the death warrant to my career. Some days, it was a battle to keep a level head, and the constant reminder from Beth that her mother was gone was almost too much to bear.

"Mommy!" Ruth screeched then, tearing into the kitchen at a lightning-fast pace with Jeremy on her heels. "Jeremy hit me!"

"Auntie Maryanne!" I exclaimed, and Ruth and Jeremy both

came to an abrupt stop. "My name is Aunt Maryanne. Mommy is gone and she's never coming back and you have to stop calling me that!"

The twins stared up at me with wide, rapidly moistening eyes, and then Ruth burst into noisy sobs. Jeremy threw his arms around her and Tim came barreling in from the backyard.

"Why is everyone crying?" he asked with some exasperation. And in that moment I felt like the child, because Tim had this parental way about him that was both disturbing and adorable for a four-and-a-half-year-old.

"They keep calling me Mommy," I said, my tone both defensive and uneven. Tim frowned at me as he joined Jeremy to console Ruth.

"You're *not* my mom," he said, suddenly grumpy. "But she's not here, and they miss her, and you look just like her. Why do you have to be so *mean*?"

I guess that's when it really started—when I finally stopped resisting the mantle the smallest of the children seemed determined to thrust upon my shoulders. Maybe I just gave in. Maybe I decided it wasn't doing any harm.

And maybe I let them call me Mommy because I knew deep down that but for me, their mommy would still be there with them.

Patrick and I had both become so sick of waiting for an awful phone call from my parents that after a few weeks, we unplugged the phone altogether. Still, I knew that sooner or later they'd just come to the doorstep if they were ready to make a serious play for custody of the children. And besides, instead of warily watching the phone, now I warily watched the driveway.

Over the weeks after the funeral, I was genuinely run off my feet. I felt sure I'd checked every possible space in the house for Grace's notes, so I started way back at the beginning, doing a second pass of every nook and cranny. When I wasn't frantically searching, I made dozens of phone calls to day-care centers all over the city, only to discover that finding a solution to Patrick's problem was harder than I had anticipated. Childcare was far more expensive than I'd ever realized, but even if money wasn't an issue, the hours on offer were much shorter than his work-day. How on earth would Patrick manage to get to work for his 6 a.m. start if the day-care centers didn't open until eight? And how would he juggle picking the children up at 5 p.m., when he worked on job sites all over the city?

I didn't have the heart to tell him that my search was proving utterly fruitless, mostly because he was doing *everything* right. It was rare for Patrick to be late home from work in those days. He was always bursting through the door right when he said he would, covered in sawdust and dirt, making a beeline for wherever the children happened to be—usually bathed and in their pajamas, often snuggled around me as I read them a story. Those kids had such a voracious appetite to be read to, especially Beth. Some nights I'd read her a dozen picture books before I finally got them into bed, and we were walking to the library several times a week because I got so sick of reading the same books over and over.

Still, I made a point to extract myself very quickly from the circle of that little family once Patrick came home, retreating to "my" bedroom to read. It wasn't always easy—Beth had taken to me more and more, and some nights she'd cling to my legs or cry when I tried to say good-night. However, I was well aware that my time with my nieces and nephews would soon come to an end, so I made a point of quickly handing over responsibility to Patrick despite protests from Beth or anyone else. I'd walk to my room with my spine stiff, leaving that domestic bubble to go back to my own life in limbo.

But one night, as I went to bolt for the bedroom, Patrick called after me.

"Do you have to rush off?"

If he'd hinted for me to linger anytime over the weeks since Grace's death, I'd have been irritated at still more demands on my time. But this was New Patrick. This was the man who thanked me constantly, and who washed up his own dishes from dinner, and who noticed that Ruth needed new underwear and who tried very hard to catch up on his bills, even though that meant no money for whiskey. I wasn't sure I liked New Patrick, but I didn't dislike him, either, and I was conscious of a growing respect for the man.

"Is something wrong?" I asked him.

"Not really. Just felt like a chat."

The house felt like a completely different place without the stampede of little feet thundering against the floorboards or the television blaring too loudly, or the endless cycle of happy play that turned to raucous roughhousing that turned to the inevitable tears. The younger children all napped during the day, but rarely at the same time, and so I wasn't sure how I felt about being out of my room during the quiet hours. But then Patrick flashed me a tired grin and asked, "I'm guessing you cooked enough for fifty or sixty people, like you usually do?"

I laughed weakly.

"Yes, there's plenty there. Unfortunately, it's not very good."

"Maryanne, have I ever once complained about your cooking?"

"You have not," I conceded. "But you'll notice I don't ever linger to watch you eat."

"I'm the last person on this planet who would ever criticize someone else's cooking skills."

So we sat opposite one another at the dining room table with steaming bowls of the stew I'd made, and the silence was something like companionable. Patrick dove into the meal as if he hadn't eaten in weeks, and only when the bowl was half-empty did he pause long enough to say, "If things at work keep going well for me, I'm getting a promotion."

"Really?"

"Ewan said today he'd let me shadow him as foreman…to learn how to manage jobs myself so he can expand the business. It means a lot more responsibility—but also eventually, it'll mean more money. A *lot* more money, if I do a good job, and maybe one day I'll even be able to go out on my own. And once I finish training and my wages go up, I'll be able to fix up this house and afford proper day care and who knows what else. Anything else me and the kids need, really. I just never thought Ewan would trust me with an opportunity like this but he said…" Patrick hesitated, then cleared his throat and gave me a surprisingly bashful smile. "He said that he's been waiting for years for me to show some initiative, because he desperately needs another foreman."

Something about that smile endeared Patrick to me in a way I'd never experienced before with him. It took me a minute to grasp what it was. He had always been a little brash, a little too charming for his own good—but those awful months had humbled him. The sensitive side I'd seen hints of in the early days after Grace's death was now on full display, and it was a beautiful thing to see.

"My goodness. Congratulations, Patrick. That's fantastic."

"It is," he said, but then he hesitated. "Even if it complicates my situation even more."

"Oh?"

"Well, you're going to leave us soon, and besides, this new job will mean even longer hours—"

To my surprise, Patrick's voice broke. I stared at him, stricken, as the pride in his eyes faded and gave way to the gleam of unshed tears. He cleared his throat again, and a heavy silence fell upon us. I didn't know what to say.

"I'm sorry," he said. "But you have to admit, it's hopeless."

"Patrick," I whispered, reaching across to rest my hand over his.

"I won't turn the job down. I can't—it will mean a better future for these kids. But I've been calling childcare centers and…"

"I have, too. I know," I said heavily.

"One of the lads at work said maybe the wives could help, that maybe we could set up a roster system and the kids could go from house to house each day. But you know what Jeremy is like. He's such a handful since Gracie died and an arrangement like that is surely going to end in tears. And when Tim starts school next year, how on earth am I going to handle getting him to school and the kids to a different house each day, *and* make my early start? And then what if I get home late? And what about dinners?"

He sighed heavily and ran his hand over his hair in exasperation.

"I just keep thinking there's got to be a way, but maybe there isn't."

"I know," I admitted. "I've been trying to figure it out, too. It's just not fair."

"This really isn't your problem. You've done so much for me already. I wouldn't have even made it this far without you."

"Patrick," I said, my own voice rough around the edges now. "Thank you. I'm sure you noticed that caring for the kids is hardly my strength, but I've done my best and—"

"They adore you," he interrupted me. "You've been such a good influence on them as they grieved. I'm sure you've noticed the little ones have taken to calling you Mommy."

I hadn't realized he'd heard them saying that. I felt myself flush with a muddled kind of guilt.

"I've been discouraging them. But Bethany is still a bit confused, and the others are just mimicking her."

"It's understandable. They've bonded with you so well. You'll be an incredible mother one day." He paused, then cleared his throat awkwardly. "When you're ready, I guess."

I winced, shaking my head.

"No. I don't want children of my own. I'm more than happy to be a devoted aunt."

"So you won't marry, then?"

"No," I laughed softly. "Absolutely not."

"I don't understand you, Maryanne," Patrick laughed quietly. "You've always seemed so determined to break all of the rules."

"You do understand me, then. Because breaking all of the rules is exactly what I'm determined to do."

"What's so wrong with marriage and kids?"

"Nothing, if they were options instead of the default. I want more for my life than to be someone's housekeeper. I want a career and I want to see other women have the option to make choices, too, instead of operating as breeding machines for entitled men."

Patrick winced, and then I winced, too, and the quiet sense of "we're in this together" somehow evaporated. There was a long, strained pause before Patrick pushed his chair back from the table.

"I guess you better get to bed."

"I guess I should, too."

Beth
1996

I'm lying in bed the day after Dad's funeral, trying to will myself to get up and get dressed, when Hunter brings me the cordless handset. He's been off work since Dad passed, but he's got to go back into the office today, and he's already in his suit.

"It's Ruth," he tells me, and I give him a surprised look as I take the phone.

"Hi there. Everything okay?"

"Not really. I miss Dad and I hate feeling like this."

"Me, too," I say, softening.

"I'm taking today off. Want to meet me at Dad's place to do

some more cleaning?" She clears her throat, then adds, "And...
bring Noah?"

"Oh, I don't know——"

"I'll help with him, Beth. I just could really do with some
squishy baby cuddles today. Please?"

I meet Ruth at Dad's house midmorning, and as promised,
she takes Noah right off my hands. She sets up the playpen in a
clear space in the attic, and we work at bringing the boxes and
baskets to the dumpster and sorting through the rest of the loose
trash. We swap memories of Dad as we work, and ponder all of
our questions about Grace.

"I just keep thinking all of this would be easier if she was here.
I think that's why I'm so stuck on understanding what really
happened to her," I admit. "I *have* been fixated on these things."

"You're looking for closure, Beth. That's all it is."

"It's called *rumination*," I tell her, sighing. "Repeatedly pon-
dering a concept or thought without completion. Obsessing on
ideas. It's classic behavior from someone who's depressed and I
should have seen it for what it was."

"Right, Beth, we're going to stop talking about *should haves*
and just talk about moving forward. Everything is awful right
now—we just lost Dad, you've got postpartum depression and
all of this confusion with Grace and these notes isn't helping.
We can't do much about Dad, except give it time. But you *can*
think about therapy and medication, and you and I and the boys
can clean out this attic."

"Practical, as always." I give Ruth a sad smile. She throws a
paint rag at me playfully. "Do you have memories of Grace?"

"Yeah. I do," she says softly. "I remember lots of random
things. Her reading us stories, mostly. And she wasn't a great
cook, so we were forever eating her dreadfully bland eggs. Oh—
and Jeremy and I were desperately jealous because we thought
you were her favorite. You were always sneaking into her bed at

night and she'd let you stay there, but if *we* tried it, she'd carry us right back to our own beds."

"You were…what…*three* when she died?" I say, thinking for the first time in a week about that perplexing death certificate. "And I would have been two. It's extraordinarily young for us to have retained permanent memories."

"I know you think the certificate says it was 1958, but you really must have read it wrong. I know we were older than three." Ruth shrugs. "I remember her taking us to our first day of elementary school in 1960."

I sigh.

"I can check that death certificate when I get home, but I'm pretty sure I read 1958."

"Is it handwritten?"

"Parts of it, yes."

"Maybe the handwriting is poor. She must have died in 1961 or maybe even later."

"It would have to be pretty awful handwriting for me to read *1961* as *1958*," I laugh weakly. Ruth shrugs.

"Look, we were very young, but I do trust my memory. She definitely took me and Jeremy for our first day of school, and she can't very well have done that if she'd been dead two years by that point. Right?"

"Right," I sigh. Besides, if Grace did die in 1961, that means I was four when she died, and it makes a little more sense that I'd have memories of her.

We get back to work cleaning and sorting, and we're making great progress. Ruth finds several notes in a pile under one of the tables, and then I find another scrunched up in a clean, empty paint can. I leave Ruth and Noah and pick up some treats from the bakery a few streets over that Dad used to love, and when I get back, she has my son giggling hysterically as she pulls funny faces.

It's adorable, and I watch from the door for a while, not wanting to disturb them.

"Get in here," Ruth calls when she realizes I'm there, and I cautiously approach. When I come into view, a huge, joyous smile crosses Noah's face, and I feel something soft and warm inside...something close to affection. I scoop him up and hug him close to my chest, and I suddenly get what Ruth meant when she said she needed squishy baby cuddles.

Whether or not I'm providing Noah everything he needs is still in question, but in this moment, *he's* providing *me* with something new. I feel a flush of love and gratitude for my son as my arms close around him—the warmth of his body against mine, the softness of him in my arms—these things are a magnificent focal point for my thoughts, and I'm startled by a real sense of purpose for my life.

Dad is gone, but life must go on for the rest of us, and despite everything, a baby like Noah is the perfect representation of the way life works in cycles.

By late afternoon most of the loose trash has been dealt with. I never thought I'd miss the chaotic mess up here, but there's something particularly sad about watching the "to-sort" pile shrink until it's just a handful of wrappers, especially since there's still an unmatched canvas on the table.

"Maybe we've accidentally thrown the last note out," Ruth says.

"God," I sigh. "Wouldn't that be disappointing?"

We sit together to sort through the last of the trash, and soon we've cleared it all, without finding any more notes.

"We can check through the 'to-keep' pile again," Ruth suggests. I flip quickly through the notes, checking the dates against canvases, just in case we've missed counting one.

"We're definitely missing the note that goes with that really dark one," I say, holding up the bleakest of the canvases. "But the date is April fourteenth...maybe the canvas just represents her death. Maybe there isn't even a note to find."

"Maybe," Ruth sighs.

We hear the faintest ring downstairs, and Ruth grimaces as she climbs to her feet from the floor.

"Told you it was hard to hear," I say lightly as she passes, and she rolls her eyes at me as she sprints downstairs. I stare at that last, bleak canvas...and then at the clipboard, lined with notes. I pick up the clipboard and run my gaze again over that first note.

I know this desolate wasteland. I recognize the subtext of desperation and isolation. *Read them*, Dad said. *She would have helped you.*

I've been desperately curious about the notes, and the only reason I've managed to wait this long to read them all is that I promised my siblings we'd do it together. Even so, I haven't felt ready to read them. Not until now.

"Temptation getting to be too much?" Ruth asks me quietly as she steps back into the attic. I startle, and give her a guilty glance.

"I wasn't going to read them without you guys. Who was on the phone?"

"Jez. He was just checking in, but I told him we've finished. He's going to call Tim and they'll meet us here tonight to read them together."

I meet her gaze.

"Good. I think I'm ready."

She nods.

"Yeah, Beth. It's time."

Tim, Ruth, Jeremy, Hunter, Ellis and I gather around Dad's dining table that evening, passing yellowed pages around like a production line. If I wasn't already exhausted, seeing life through Grace Walsh's eyes would have wrecked me. I have felt alone, and I have felt lost and isolated, but even my experiences over these past few months don't compare to the life she describes.

Ruth and I are crying long before we get to the end, and at one point she drops a note onto the table and pulls me into a hug so tight, her muscles shake.

"Are you sure you can deal with this right now?" she chokes. I nod, squeeze her back and reach for the next one. I know I'm not the only one feeling strangely guilty, like I'm betraying Dad's memory.

"This isn't the Dad I knew," Ruth and Jez say again and again as we peek into Grace's world.

"Something doesn't add up," Tim keeps muttering.

But all we can do is keep reading. And by the time we reach the bottom of the pile, we're all in pieces. Maybe we should have waited longer before we tackled this—Dad's loss is still so raw—but by the same token, we won't move on until we put these questions to bed.

Hunter is at the end of our little production line, and when he finishes the last note I blurt, "Do you all agree...it sounds a lot like she took her own life?"

Tim hesitates.

"There's no way to be sure, is there?" my sister says cautiously.

"Oh, come on, Ruth," I groan. "She couldn't stand the idea of going through the depression again and she took herself back to the bridge, only this time she went through with it."

"Probably," Ruth says, but then she gives me a sharp look. "But we can't be sure. Do you really think Dad would have lied to us for all of these years if she killed herself?"

"Yes," I say immediately. "That's *exactly* why he would have lied. Especially if he blamed himself. And given the things he said before he died, and the fact that we know he read these notes, we can be pretty sure he did blame himself."

"There's a lot to process in all of this," Jeremy murmurs.

"So this note says that Mom had a sister. This Maryanne she talks about," Tim says suddenly, glancing around us all.

"Seems so odd that we might have an aunt out there some-where and Dad never thought to tell us about her," Ruth says, tilting her head.

"Doesn't seem odd to me," Jeremy shrugs, motioning towards the notes. "It's pretty obvious they didn't get on."

"Dad called me *Maryanne* a few times in those last weeks when he was really confused," I say, throat tight. "Remember that last day? When he apologized to me? He was calling me Maryanne."

Tim reaches across to squeeze my hand.

"You know, guys…we could…"

"Track her down?" I finish for him when no one else does. My throat is suddenly dry.

"It's probably not going to be easy," Jeremy says. "We know her maiden name was Gallagher like Mom's, but Maryanne is probably married by now and probably has a new surname."

"Leave it with me," Ruth offers. "I can at least try to find her."

"Can I…keep the notes?" I ask hesitantly. I feel heat on my cheeks as the moment stretches, with my siblings and husband all staring at me, each obviously waiting for someone *else* to talk me out of it. Ruth speaks first.

"Honey, obsessing on those notes is not going to help you—"

"Or maybe it will help me a lot," I interrupt her. I don't even know if this is true. I just feel like I want to read through them again, to feel her close to me again. I'm painting a new picture in my mind of the Grace I've always remembered.

Despite her depression. Despite her misery. She made me feel loved and she made me feel safe. Maybe I can do that for Noah, too.

Hunter gives me a thoughtful look, then asks quietly, "What was it she wrote about loneliness?"

"It's worse than sadness," I whisper because those words already imprinted on my heart. "Because by definition, the burden can't be shared."

"I'm tired and I'm grieving and I'm sad. I know you feel the same," Tim says suddenly. "But if there's one thing we aren't, it's alone. If those little notes remind you that you aren't the first woman to go through what you're going through, and if they remind you that you're part of a family who would never want you to feel as isolated as *she* obviously felt, then you take them. Even Dad seemed to think they could help you."

"So, good news," Ruth tells me on the phone the next night. "Not only is Maryanne still Maryanne Gallagher, she was also the third M. Gallagher in the first phone book I tried—she lives in Fremont."

"What?"

"I just called her up and explained who I was, and she wants to meet us. I invited her to Sunday dinner."

"But…"

"But this is tremendously good news?" Ruth suggests.

"Terrifying," I laugh weakly. "You just called her? Just like that?"

"Sure," Ruth says matter-of-factly. "I said 'Hello, my name is Ruth Turner, née Walsh. Did you have a sister called Grace? Because if you did, I think I'm your niece.' And she swore in ways I didn't know a person could swear. I mean, she didn't sound entirely displeased to hear from me, just utterly shocked. She's a professor, apparently. At the University of Seattle. I told her Jez is an academic, too, at Washington U, and *that* seemed to shock her more than the call itself." Ruth laughs, the sound light and melodic, then says drily, "So pretty sure she did at least meet Jeremy when we were young."

"Doesn't it make you wonder?" I murmur. "Dad raised us all on his own once Aunt Nina died. That must have been so hard on him. Grace seemed to think they weren't fond of one another, but given the circumstances, I can't understand why this Maryanne didn't help with us once Grace died."

"Yeah. That's one of the things I want to ask her on Sunday."

"I can't believe you found her," I say, laughing softly. "Ruth. You blow my mind sometimes."

"Well, you should know by now—I'm a problem solver."

EIGHTEEN

Maryanne
1958

With just two weeks left until my departure, I sunk into something of a funk. I'd swept the house for those notes twice more and still couldn't find any sign of them. Worse still, Patrick was no closer to figuring out how to keep his children, and I knew that my departure would mean the family could no longer stay together.

Day and night, these things were all I could think about. In fact, I was about to start a third search for Grace's notes when I heard someone thumping on the front door. The kids followed me as I ran to answer it and were right at my heels when I opened the door to my father.

"What do you want?" I asked him flatly. He sighed and reached into his suit jacket to withdraw a piece of paper.

"You know what I want. You're going back to college soon, are you not? This has gone on long enough, Maryanne. They've had time to grieve. It's time for them to get used to their new life."

"Father, this is *cruel*," I whispered, snatching the paper from his hand. My vision blurred as I read the notice—a letter of demand from some lawyer I'd never heard of. "So you're really going to go ahead with it?"

"Mother and I agree, this is for the best—" Father started to say, but he didn't get a chance to finish because I took a step back, gently shifted the girls out of the way and slammed the door in his face.

Mr. and Mrs. Francis Gallagher will be petitioning the courts for custody of their grandchildren, Timothy, Jeremy, Ruth and Bethany Walsh, based on their father, Patrick Walsh's, immoral character and his inability to provide for and care for them to a satisfactory degree. It is the opinion of this firm that based on the evidence supplied by Mr. and Mrs. Gallagher, Mr. Walsh is unlikely to win judicial support for his ongoing custody of the children, as the courts favor normal family arrangements and frown upon single fathers. We advise you to seek independent legal advice if you do decide to fight this petition, otherwise please deliver the children to the Gallagher family home by this Saturday, July twenty-fifth at 10 a.m.

"What does the letter say, Mommy?" Tim asked as I sat on the lounge weeping.

"Auntie Maryanne," I corrected him automatically, then I sobbed again. "It's hard to explain, Timmy. I'll let your dad talk to you about it when he gets home."

That night I watched Patrick as he read the letter. His face flushed as his anger rose, but his eyes remained dry. If anything, he looked frustrated but resigned, and when he reached the end, he dropped the letter to the table and gave me a miserable look.

"We knew this was coming."

"It's still very upsetting," I whispered.

"I'm out of options, aren't I?"

I racked my brain for the millionth time, but there was no solution that solved his problems.

"I'll call Ewan and go into work late tomorrow so I'm here when the kids wake up," Patrick said suddenly, raising his chin. "I should be the one to tell them. That's only right." He pushed his chair back and stood. "You'll have to excuse me, Maryanne. I need to go to bed."

I knew he was going to his room to cry. Even if I had doubted the changes in Patrick's character over those months, I faced irrefutable proof of it that night.

Even in failure, he was taking responsibility. It seemed bitterly cruel that just when Patrick Walsh pulled himself together, my parents were taking his family away.

Once again it was Timmy who understood the coming changes well before his siblings. Now though, Tim was unable to hold back his tears, and as Patrick tried to explain what was happening, Tim wailed in a way I'd never imagined he was capable of. He finally looked like a child in that moment—like a terrified, overwhelmed child.

"No!" he kept shouting, stomping his feet, red-faced and sweaty. "I won't go. You can't make me go. I hate the castle!"

"There isn't a princess in the castle," Ruth muttered, shooting me a look as if I had deceived her. Jeremy sat in silence, and Beth, who was sitting on my lap, just watched the television, which was on behind Patrick with the volume down low, as he paced and tried to explain.

"We've tried everything, Tim," Patrick said patiently, miserably. "There's nothing left of it but for you to go to live with

Grandfather and Grandmother. They *will* take very good care of you, and you'll still have each other. That's the most important thing, son."

"I *hate* you!" Tim shouted, making up for lost time with the childish outbursts, it would seem. He ran out into the backyard, and Jeremy silently stood to follow him, leaving me and Patrick with the girls. Patrick sighed and ran his hands through his hair.

"I have to go to work," he said helplessly.

"It's okay," I said, hugging Beth a little closer. "You go. I'll try to explain it to them over the day."

"And..." Patrick hesitated, then asked me reluctantly, "Mary, I hate to ask this, but could you pack for them, too? I just don't..." His voice wobbled, and he swallowed hard. "I just don't think I can do it."

"Of course. I'll see you tonight."

I tried my best to explain to the children that Daddy had done everything he could, but that they needed to live with their grandparents now. I told them a highly fanciful story about four wonderful children who went to live in a castle and had the best adventures ever, but halfway through Tim got up and went to sit behind the sofa.

I knew what that meant, and it nearly killed me to let him sit in there and grieve. On top of losing his mother, Tim really was about to lose his father and his home, and there was nothing I could do to make it better.

Ruth and Jeremy were starting to understand, and they were sullen and sad, holding one another's hands as they moved around the house. And Beth seemed oblivious, but then when she saw me packing her clothes away, she watched me, an intense look of concentration on her face.

"Mommy?"

"I'm Aunt Maryanne, Beth."

"*Mommy,*" she said stubbornly.

"What is it you want, child?" I asked her impatiently.

"Mommy, I *stay*," Beth said, climbing up onto the bed and pushing my hands away from the suitcase.

"I'm not...it's not up to me," I whispered, and then stupid, hot tears filled my eyes. I blinked hard and kept on with the packing. "I can't do anything about this. There's just no other way this can work."

"She's upset because no one wants us," Tim said from the doorway. I glanced back at him and found him staring at his shoes.

"That's not true, Timmy. Lots of people want you. That's the trouble. This is just the best way for you all to stay together."

"No. The best way for us all to stay together is for *you* to keep looking after us. Where are you even going anyway?" Tim said stubbornly.

I opened my mouth to explain it all to him—that my life was in California, that my career was the most important thing, that the world had to change and I could see that change and most people couldn't, so I needed to be a part of it. But he was six weeks shy of four years old. Asking most adults to think of the big picture beyond themselves was too much—how could I ask the same thing of a tiny child, and one who'd already seen such depths of pain?

"You'll still see Daddy every Sunday," I said unevenly. "And Grandmother and Grandfather have that beautiful house, re-member?"

"I hate the castle. Grandfather is mean. And Grandmother is mean, too. Why don't you want to stay?"

"It's not that simple."

"I don't want you to go. And I don't want to move in with those people."

"You *have* to," I exclaimed, and a tear trickled over onto my cheek. Tim looked up at me, confusion and hurt in his gaze. "There's just no other way."

But then I looked from Tim's miserable gaze to Beth's huge blue eyes and I saw Grace in those children and I felt it right in my gut—the unmistakable sense of belonging. These children were hers, but my sister was gone and they were scared, and my love and grief for her had somehow grown and evolved until it was now shaped like love and a fierce protectiveness for her children.

It seemed that in the ten short weeks I'd been in their home, I had inadvertently allowed myself to be dragged into this broken little family. I was a part of them now, and they were a part of me.

I couldn't just walk away and let my parents take these children away from their father. The four of them had been through too much; they had seen too much already that they couldn't understand. They needed comfort and cuddles and love and endless picture books each night, and sending them into that formal, oppressive atmosphere at my parents' house would change them in ways that couldn't be undone.

Somehow, through all that had happened, I'd been swallowed whole by my dead sister's family, and even if I'd wanted to extract myself, I didn't have a clue how to start doing so.

Tim slunk away, shoulders downcast. Beth slid off the bed and waddled after him. Ruth and Jeremy were still watching cartoons on the television.

I unpacked the suitcases, then I made a call to Professor Callahan to start the process of blowing apart every little thing I'd worked so hard to achieve back in California.

Beth
1996

"We still haven't figured out whether to sell the house or rent it," Jeremy says as we all sit around the dining room table on Sunday night, waiting for the mysterious Maryanne to make an appearance. This afternoon while Ruth and I cooked the meal, everyone else busied themselves packing up the rest of the house, and not surprisingly, the process moved much quicker when a whole team was there to work.

The house is all but empty now, other than some heavy furniture we'll probably sell. The kitchen area is last to be cleaned out, and I'll start that tomorrow—this will be our last family meal here. I'm nervous that the tradition will die, especially because it's often been a strain on Tim and Alicia and Jeremy to travel back here each week.

"The bill from the hospice will come any day now," Tim murmurs. "But let's face it—we can't hold on to the house forever. Let's just list it now and get this over and done with."

"And I still think we need to keep the house," Ruth counters. "This place is too special for us to cut our ties with it all together."

"Beth?" Jeremy prompts.

"I think that every time you three find yourselves feeling uncomfortable these days, you deflect your internal discomfort by raising the subject of what to do with the house," I say. "I suspect you do this because you know the subject of the house will cause drama, and the drama will distract you from your own feelings of loss. Unfortunately, once you start talking about it, you all *panic* at the first sign of drama even though you thought you wanted it, and that's when you try to handball the topic to me." Beside me, Hunter and Ellis both quietly chuckle.

My siblings all stare at me for a moment, then Ruth says wistfully, "Remember when Beth wanted to be a pop star?"

"That's right. She wanted to join The Monkees," Tim laughs.

"With her singing ability, The Monkees was probably the only band she would have been allowed to join," Jeremy says wryly. "You know...on account of them not actually singing their own songs. Get it?"

"Do you see what you're doing now?" I say, laughing in spite of myself. "You're still nervous, but now you're deflecting the nervous energy by making fun of me."

The doorbell rings. Our laughter immediately fades.

Ruth rises, and we all watch in silence as she walks down the hallway to the front door. We hear voices as Ruth and Maryanne greet one another. They stop on their way back through to the dining room so that Ruth can introduce Maryanne to her sons, who are playing Jenga in the family room. And then the footsteps come closer, and the silence at the dining table is broken as Ruth and Maryanne enter the room.

My aunt is short and thin, but even at first glance I see that she has a flair for the dramatic. She's wearing a black-and-crimson caftan and a startling array of chunky jewelry—enormous bauble earrings, a matching necklace of oversize beads and more bracelets and rings than I've ever seen on one human being at one time. Her hair is raven-black and cut in a bob, with pieces on either side of her face that hang just a little longer, dyed the same stunning red as the trim on her caftan. She's is wearing a full face of makeup over her pale complexion, including winged eyeliner that I couldn't pull off even if a professional helped me apply it, and red lips several times brighter than the red in her hair.

The whole look is artsy and quirky, but it's also severe. I can't even begin to guess how old she is. She's surely somewhere around Dad's age, but she doesn't look it. I don't know if that's a side effect of her style, or just that she's aged particularly well.

She scans the room with her bright blue eyes, and then her gaze lands on me, and I am suddenly overwhelmed by memories of my mother.

I'm lying in the bed, cuddled up beside her, under the heavy duvet and she's stroking my hair.

I'm curled up on her lap; she's reading me yet another book.

Burnt eggs for breakfast again. Hugs that smell like cake. Safety and comfort and love.

Intellectually, I know I'm having this reaction because Maryanne has the same pale complexion and dark hair that Grace and I also shared. And this woman—this *stranger*—is, in effect, a direct link to my mother, and this is the very first time I can remember meeting any of Grace's relatives. The rapid-fire stream of memories makes sense. Even the bubbling emotions make sense. I just didn't expect to find her so familiar, and I don't feel prepared to feel this way. It takes me a minute to collect myself, and just as I do, I think I see a flash of emotion cross Maryanne's face, too. Whatever it is, it clears in an instant, and then she's greeting us with a casual, somewhat formal tone.

"Hello, all," she says, and she lifts a hand to wave at us. My gaze drops to her long fingernails, painted in a glossy red, and the heavy bangles on her wrist that clang as she moves her arm.

Tim stands, hand extended to shake hers.

"Tim Walsh," he says. Maryanne quirks an eyebrow at his formal introduction, then shakes his hand.

"Lovely to see you again, Timmy," she says mildly. "Still taking the lead, I see."

"Uh, okay…"

I think I see something of a flush on Tim's cheeks above his beard, and he turns back to me and gives me a strained look.

"And you, Jeremy." Maryanne approaches my other brother, shaking her head incredulously. "Is it true?"

"Is what true?" Jeremy asks cautiously.

"Ruth tells me you're an earth sciences professor."

"That's correct."

"How surprising," Maryanne muses thoughtfully. "I've kept my eye on the papers over the years, half expecting to hear you'd been arrested for something."

I suppress a giggle, which Ruth and Tim altogether fail to do. Soon we're all laughing—except Jeremy, who's trying very hard to scowl. He drops the act after a moment or two and shrugs.

"Let's face it. We all know it could have gone either way."

As everyone laughs, Maryanne turns her attention to me.

"Bethany," she murmurs when I come close to her. "My goodness."

TRUTHS I NEVER TOLD YOU

For a moment she seems almost overcome. She rests her hands on my upper arms and stares at me, then she pulls me in for a hug. I let her embrace me, but I'm not entirely sure why I get this display of affection, and everyone else got a polite greeting. When I turn back to face the rest of my family, I see the surprise on their faces, too. I shrug, a little self-conscious, then introduce her to Hunter and Noah. Ruth takes over to introduce her to Ellis, and then Tim introduces Alicia.

"And where is..." She looks around as she sits in an empty chair at the dining table, and then says hesitantly, "Ruth, you said this is Patrick's house...?"

Tim, Jeremy and I all look at Ruth, who winces. In a surprising display of reticence, she doesn't leap to explain, leaving Tim to fill the gap.

"Dad passed away recently. Just a few weeks ago," he says carefully. It still hurts to hear those words, and I swallow the lump in my throat as the truth of that statement sinks in all over again. But compared to our muted reactions to what's still very tender news, Maryanne's shock is palpable. Her jaw drops and her eyes widen, and she grips the armrests in both hands, her knuckles turning white.

"My God," she whispers, blinking rapidly. We all sit in a horrible silence for several moments, until Ruth catches my eye and gives me a frantic *what do we do next?* look. I decide I'll try to break the awkwardness, but before I can, Maryanne gives a funny cough that I think might actually be a sob. I rise automatically, wondering if I should try to comfort her, but she rises, too, and says, "I'm dreadfully sorry. Could someone please direct me to a bathroom?"

Ellis saves the day, leading her down the hallway and away from the rest of us.

"Ruth!" Jeremy whispers. "You didn't think you should mention that Dad *died*?"

"It didn't seem to be the kind of news you deliver over the

phone. Besides, I didn't expect her to get so upset. I mean—
God, as far as we know, they haven't even seen one another in
forty years!" Ruth whispers back, but then she looks at me in a
panic. "Help. I don't know what to do now."

"Let's serve dinner," I say. "Let's just try to keep things casual. We can't leap right into an interrogation about her sister's
death after *that*."

"Good idea," Alicia says, rising. "I'll help."

I join my sister and Alicia in the kitchen, and we work in near
silence as we serve the casseroles Ruth has prepared.

"I'm sorry about that," Maryanne says, reappearing in the
kitchen doorway. Her eyes are dry, but her lips are pursed.

"I'm so sorry I didn't warn you about Dad," Ruth says, un-
characteristically hesitant. "He was sick for a long time, but his
passing is very new and I wasn't really..." She clears her throat.
"Honestly, I didn't realize you were at all close, but even so, it
seemed better to tell you face-to-face."

Maryanne looks between us, then asks carefully, "What *did*
he tell you about me?"

Ruth gives me another panicked look. It's almost a novelty to
see my sister intimidated. I'd be enjoying it much more if this
wasn't all so *awkward*.

"We didn't even know you existed until recently. But Dad was
very unwell toward the end and quite confused—he had a form
of dementia as well as serious heart issues. He said your name
a few times, but not much of what he said made any sense by
that stage. It took us a while to even figure out who you were."

Maryanne's gaze turns sharp.

"I see. So why did you look me up?"

"Well, we have a lot of questions..."

"About?"

"Ah...mostly about Grace's death," I say carefully.

"What would you hope to achieve by asking me about her?"
Maryanne asks. Her chin is high, but there's an incredible ten-

sion in the way she's holding herself—flared nostrils, overly stiff posture, even a crease between her eyebrows. I get the real sense that nothing about tonight is unfolding as she expected, and she looks more than a little shell-shocked.

"We just want closure," Ruth admits, and we share a sad look.

"Your mother's death was an awful business, and it's not something I like to think about even now," Maryanne says flatly. Her body language is increasingly defensive, and I'm painfully aware that we're losing her. We need to turn this around if we're going to have a real conversation tonight.

"We have a lot of questions about her, and Dad is gone now. We don't really have any one else to ask," I say gently.

"And why didn't you ask Patrick about these things while he was alive?"

"We didn't realize there were questions to ask, to be honest," I say. I'm noticing a pattern—she's defensive with Ruth, ignoring Alicia altogether, but watching me closely. I have to suspect that maybe, if she did know us once upon a time, I was special to her.

It seems like an awful thing to leverage, but I'm running out of options here, especially when Maryanne says abruptly, "If your father wanted you to have further detail, he'd have given it to you a long time ago."

"Did your family have some kind of falling out with Dad?" Ruth asks. Maryanne frowns at her, and she shrugs hesitantly. "It just seems so odd that we never even knew you existed, that's all. He was on his own for so long without any help at all. It never occurred to us that Mom had family, let alone a sister just a short drive away…"

Maryanne visibly stiffens, and I realize she's heard Ruth's question as an accusation of neglect.

"Ruth," I say, scolding her. "Why don't we all sit down and—"

"It was an exceedingly complicated situation and I have no doubt that every decision your father ever made was what he thought was for the best for the four of you." She inhales sharply, and then adjusts her caftan. "I really think I should leave. I'm not feeling well."

"Please stay," I say, although I'm unsurprised that she wants to go. She looks quietly devastated, and even if we do convince her to stay, I know we'll need to leave any potential questioning about Grace or Dad or anything else for another time. "I hate to think we've upset you, or even made you uncomfortable. We'll just get to know each other a little. Please."

Maryanne's expression softens a little as she stares at me, but then her eyes fill with tears and she waves vaguely toward her head.

"Migraine, sweet girl. I really need to go. I'm sorry."

It's clear that Aunt Maryanne is leaving. Ruth fetches her bag as I follow her to the door. Maryanne pauses and stares at me, and then at my sister. Her eyes cloud, and she stops long enough to gently touch my upper arm.

"When you think about your mother, all you really need to know is that she was a beautiful soul. She loved so deeply, and she loved you all more than anything. I see her in the both of you, and it makes me very happy to know that some wonderful part of her has lived on."

"Thank you," I say, and it strikes me all of a sudden that at least part of her awkwardness tonight is that she's a stranger to us, but we aren't strangers to her, given she obviously knew us at least a little, once upon a time. She's viewing us through a filter of grief and sadness, even after all these years. Maryanne must have loved her sister very deeply, just as I love mine. As soon as I recognize her pain, instinct takes over and I throw my arms around her. Within my hug, Maryanne Gallagher holds herself stiffly, and I pat her back gently, unthinkingly. Suddenly, all of the stiffness in her posture disappears, until she's almost limp in my arms.

"Goodbye," she croaks, and she pulls herself out of my embrace and disappears out the front door. Ruth and I walk back to the living space in silence, until she gives me an odd look.

"What on earth about that bewildering encounter suggested to you that she would want a *hug* just now?"

"I guess...she hugged me when she came in and she lost her sister and..." I'm still reeling a little myself, and I shrug. "Honestly, Ruth, I have no idea. She just looked like she needed a hug."

"Where's Maryanne?" Tim asks when we return to the dining room.

"We asked her about Grace, and she got teary, and ran away," I surmise, disappointment finally starting to sink in. When I look around my siblings, they all look every bit as crushed as I feel.

"Ah—do we call her again?" Jeremy asks.

"She has my number," Ruth sighs, rubbing her forehead. "I guess she'll call me if she changes her mind."

"I prepared myself for a lot of things tonight," Tim says slowly. He reaches for Alicia's hand, and I see him flash her a sad, fond smile. "The one thing I didn't consider was that meeting the mysterious Aunt Maryanne might be a dead end."

"Did she seem familiar to any of you?" Jeremy asks thoughtfully. "When she was scolding me...joking about me ending up in prison... I felt this odd sense of *déjà vu*."

"It's funny you say that. I know exactly what you mean," Tim says, frowning.

"Mom used to call me 'sweet girl,' and Maryanne used that phrase just now, too," I tell them all. "And her coloring—she looks quite similar to Grace. We're just confusing them."

"It was more than that," Ruth says quietly. "I thought I was imagining it, but she was so familiar and she obviously knew us. We must have known her when we were kids."

"Did you bring that photo album?" Tim asks me suddenly. "I wouldn't mind seeing those wedding photos."

"And we need to check the date on the death certificate," Ruth reminds me. I did bring Dad's wedding album—I thought we'd show Maryanne. I retrieve it from the car and hand it to Tim. He opens it while I'm still standing beside him, and instead of the wedding photos I looked at the first time I found it, he reveals a completely different photo.

He's opened it from the back, I realize. I didn't even check the other side—I just assumed the pages I opened to the first time were all it had to offer.

"Is that..." Tim says hesitantly. I stare down at the image until my vision blurs. It's of a couple standing on a set of concrete stairs, a large stone building behind them. Her dark hair is carefully done and she's wearing heavy makeup, including dramatic winged eyeliner and lips that look dark in the black-and-white photo. She's in a light-colored dress with ruffles all along the neckline, and her arm is linked through his. She's looking at the camera, a wild look in her eyes and a grin on her lips.

Beside her, my dad wears a suit. His shoulders are slumped, but his expression is subdued—he's smiling, but it seems forced. There's something else in his gaze. He looks almost ashamed.

"That's the front of the King County Courthouse," Hunter murmurs, approaching on the other side of Tim's shoulder. "Is that your mom?"

"It's Maryanne," Tim says suddenly. He looks back at me, brows knitting. "That's not Mom. It's Maryanne."

He turns the page, revealing another folded, yellowed piece of paper. He opens it and reads it silently for a moment.

"What is it?" Ruth asks. Tim gnaws his lip, then glances back at me.

"Where's that death certificate?"

I flip the album around and carefully slide Grace's death certificate out to pass it to him. He swallows, then exhales.

"Beth was right. Grace died in 1958."

"But I remember her taking us to school—" Ruth starts to protest, but Tim holds up a hand to silence her.

"And then a few months after Grace died, this happened,"

he adds softly, and he turns the album around to reveal a certificate of marriage.

Bride: Maryanne Frances Gallagher.

Groom: Patrick Timothy Walsh.

We all sit in bewildered silence for a moment, then Jeremy stands. We all look at him, and he points toward the liquor cabinet. "I need a drink."

"But what does this mean?" Ruth asks no one in particular.

"I had this feeling when she came in," Tim admits. "I had this feeling that…maybe once upon a time, we knew her well."

"Do you think…" I start to say, but I can't make myself continue.

Sweet girl.

"I think instead of speculating, we just need to get in touch with Maryanne again," Tim says.

"Because tonight went so well," Jeremy snorts, but then he gives us a bewildered look. "And speculating about *what*? What exactly are you two saying?"

Tim looks at me. His gaze is soft.

"Do you think you'd be up for meeting with her on your own?"

"Why me?"

"Because I have this feeling that once upon a time," Tim murmurs, his gaze sad, "you held a *very* special place in her heart."

"I'll get up to feed Noah tonight. But…maybe tonight's one of those nights when you should take something to help you sleep," Hunter suggests. We're home now—I'm sitting on the sofa, Noah sleeping in my arms. I have the TV on, but I'm staring right through it, mentally reliving every second of that brief encounter with Maryanne. Hunter has been winding down, reading a novel beside me. He closes the book and yawns, and then reaches to gently take the baby from me. "I'll put this little guy to bed. Are you joining me?"

"I'll be in soon," I promise him, "and yes, I'll take the tablet first." He gives me a surprised glance, so I offer him a wry smile. "You were expecting me to resist, huh?"

"Yeah. I was," Hunter chuckles quietly.

"I just want to look through that photo album one more time, then I'll come right to bed."

"You don't want company?"

I shake my head but rise to kiss him gently before he leaves the room with Noah. I take the damned medicine, knowing I'll never sleep otherwise, but while I wait for it to kick in, I sit at my dining room table with the album.

I've carefully slipped the notes from Grace into the front cover tonight, simply because I had no idea what else I should do with them. Now I flick very slowly through the photos of her wedding day to Dad. My gaze travels all over the page to avoid looking into his eyes. My loss is still so raw—it hurts more than I can bear to see his image right now. Instead, I stare at Grace.

Is it you in my memories? Or is it her?

I skim forward to the photo of Dad and Maryanne. The defiance in her gaze almost makes sense now that I've met her. Even after a five-minute encounter, I'm certain that she's always had a headstrong, bold personality.

Sweet girl. My sweet girl.

The memories rise again, of me tucked up close against my mother in her bed, of me curled up on her lap. I think of all the good things I drew from those memories, and the way they've shaped me over the years that have passed since.

And then, as clear as if she's in the room with me, I hear her voice in my mind.

I love you, sweet girl.

I flip back to Grace's notes, searching for a phrase my mind can only vaguely recall. When I find it, I close my eyes and swallow a lump in my throat.

...and I called them "darlings," because that's what I always call them...

The tablet is already working and sleep is tugging at me, so I close the album and retreat to bed.

Grace was my mom, and I know she wrote the notes I found in Dad's attic. I'm sure of those things—but I'm no longer sure how to place her in my mind. That series of beautiful childhood memories I've cherished stars the woman I thought of as my mother, but after tonight, I can't help but wonder if I remember Grace at all.

NINETEEN

Maryanne
1958

I waited for Patrick on the front porch that night, despite the icy wind. I wrapped myself in the blanket from my stretcher bed and nursed a mug of tea to keep my hands warm.

Patrick was a little late, but when I saw him climbing out of his car, I understood why. His footsteps dragged and his shoulders were slumped—he looked just as Tim had when I sent him away earlier that afternoon.

"I'm staying," I blurted as soon as he was within earshot. Patrick looked up at me in shock. "I still don't know how we'll make this work, but I'm going to stay. Between the two of us we at least have a chance of figuring it out."

"But how...why...?" Patrick blinked at me. "Why would you do that?"

"Grace had her troubles, Patrick, but the one thing I never doubted was how much she loved her family. If I leave, the kids lose you, and they need you now more than ever and you've more than proven over the past two months that you're the father they deserve. *She* would have wanted me to stay...and I can't see how you could possibly keep them if I go."

Patrick was staring at me in disbelief. He dropped his lunch pail to the ground and it clattered against the concrete, the sound jarring and unexpected—but not nearly as much as his next move. My heart was still racing when Patrick leaped over the fence to sprint up to the porch to embrace me. I found myself wrapped in the arms of my dead sister's husband as he squeezed me so tight I could barely breathe.

"Thank you," he said against my hair.

"This doesn't make everything better," I hastened to remind him.

"No, but it gives me a chance. Just a fighting chance, and that's all I really needed."

Grace's notes, for the first time in weeks, were the furthest thing from my mind. My decision to stay was a pure one—and for maybe the first time in my life, I'd made a decision to prioritize someone else's welfare above my own.

Patrick and I sat up that night and tried to brainstorm options with the new parameters of our situation, now that I was staying.

"I need to get a job. Maybe I can find a position at one of the colleges," I said thoughtfully.

"But... I thought..."

"I can't stay here and look after the house so you can work," I frowned. When Patrick hesitated, I shook my head fiercely. "My job isn't like yours. My days are shorter, and I won't be traveling all over the city to building sites—just to whichever campus hires me. I can be home in time to cook dinner and watch the children. I mean, we'll still need a babysitter, but between your wages and mine, we should be able to pay for some help."

"And where will you live?"

I blinked at him in disbelief, and Patrick's eyes widened. "Maryanne, my God. What would people say?"

"I could not care less what people say," I laughed softly.

He sighed and shook his head.

"Mrs. Hills was already scolding me about you staying here even this long. She said it's improper."

"She said the same to me," I said, shrugging. "I don't care."

"Look, it's not that I'm not grateful, because believe me, I *am*. But do you really think your parents are going to back off? If anything, your presence only strengthens their claims about my immoral character."

"That's it, Patrick!" I exclaimed, leaping up from the table and thumping my fist against it in triumph. "You genius."

"I don't follow…"

"That's the answer. All we have to do is get married."

"What?" He grew very pale all of a sudden, and I laughed.

"Don't flatter yourself, Patrick, I have no designs on you. But if we're married, then they can hardly say we're doing anything wrong living in the same house, and it settles their claim that you can't raise the children as a single man." He was still staring at me, gobsmacked, so I tried to clarify, speaking very slowly this time. "Because you *won't* be a single man. You'll be a married, gainfully employed man. Head of a complete household, in the eyes of the law and small-minded people like my parents. You might not be wealthy, but even so, I can't see a court ripping the children out of a proper family like that."

"But… Grace has only been gone a few months…" Patrick was utterly aghast.

"I'm not proposing we become husband and wife in real terms. Only in legal terms."

"Maryanne, I don't think you understand how much people will talk if we marry—especially now."

I flashed him a wink.

"You should know by now that I don't put much stock in

what people say about me. But in any case, you wouldn't be the first widower to hastily remarry so his new wife could care for his children."

"Isn't this shortsighted? What if you want to really get married one day?"

"I told you, Patrick. I'm never getting married. And do you really think you'll remarry for love anytime soon?" He hesitated, then sighed and shook his head. "Well, even if you do, we can just tell everyone I was unfaithful and I'll let you divorce me. It's all quite simple really."

"Jesus Christ," Patrick said, closing his eyes. "I need to think about this."

"Go right ahead," I said cheerfully. "But do let me know when you're ready to save your family."

The next morning I heard Patrick moving around the house and I decided to get up to see if he'd thought about my proposal. I rolled toward the edge of the bed, only to find a small human asleep beside me.

It was Beth. She was curled up in a little ball, her thumb in her mouth. I brushed her hair back from her forehead, and felt a rush of love so intense and unexpected it brought tears to my eyes. Oh, she was my favorite, all right—with those sad blue eyes and that complexion so like mine. I'd never understood the appeal of children and babies, but Beth had more than carved out a place in my heart. I relaxed back onto my pillows then, and cuddled her close for a while, listening to her quiet breath, inhaling the scent of her.

But after a long while, I still hadn't heard Patrick leave for work, and so I eventually pulled on my gown and walked out to the kitchen. He was sitting at the kitchen table, a resigned look on his face.

"Let's do it," he said without preamble.

"Excellent," I said, making a beeline for the coffee. "Do you want to tell my father, or can I?"

"You *want* to tell him? He's going to be livid."

"Oh, Patrick. Believe me when I say this: Nothing, and I mean this quite literally, would give me more pleasure."

I called Father at work the minute the bank opened.

"Father, I have some news."

"You won't change my mind, Maryanne. Patrick cannot raise those children on his own."

"You're absolutely right," I agreed, grinning to myself as I watched the children in question tear around the backyard. "That's why he's remarrying right away."

"What? But Grace is barely cold in the ground! Who is this strumpet he's supposedly marrying?"

"The *strumpet* is me."

I had felt for some time that having a relationship with my parents was a tenuous prospect at best. I had grown in the soil of their family home and thrived even though I did not fit there. But for some utterly bewildering reason, I did fit in Patrick's family now. Grief and heartache had forged a bond between me and those children, and I couldn't deny that their home now felt like my home.

And as my father cursed and sputtered as if I'd committed some heinous crime against him, I was certain that I'd finally rebelled enough to break the last ties I had with him and Mother.

Even so, I had no regrets.

After all, they had forced my hand.

We had to wait for Grace's death certificate to be issued before we could marry. It was an anxious few weeks—Patrick and I were both on tenterhooks, anxious that my parents might try to take the children before we could be married. And for the first time we squabbled a bit—including a few arguments that ended up with one or both of us storming off.

I was also petrified of what the death certificate would say.

The day it finally arrived, the postman brought it in the morning, and I couldn't bring myself to open it for hours. Logically, I knew that it wouldn't say *Grace died from an abortion gone wrong that Maryanne arranged on her behalf*—certainly if the police had any idea that an abortion had been involved in her death, they'd have come back to question us.

But that didn't mean the death certificate wouldn't give some clue as to the real cause of her death. And so I just couldn't open that envelope, even as the afternoon disappeared and Patrick was due to come home.

As I heard his car pull in, I finally picked up the envelope and opened it with trembling hands. My eyes scanned the page for any detail, and when I finally saw that it deemed her cause of death inconclusive, my knees went weak.

"You okay?" Patrick greeted me, just seconds later. "You look awfully pale."

I shoved the death certificate at him, and he read it, his face set in a grim mask.

"No wonder you look sickly," he sighed, shaking his head. "Jesus. It's hard to read that, isn't it?"

It *was* hard to read her death certificate. But it was also a relief, and I was starting to really believe that my role in Grace's death might never come to light. I was still looking for her notes in quiet moments, but my fervor had begun to die down. It seemed unlikely that they'd ever surface, given I'd searched the house high and low so many times.

Still, I was well aware that as I settled into this new life with Patrick and his children, I'd always be looking for those notes. In coming to love those children, I'd only raised the stakes. Now, if Patrick did stumble upon those notes, it wasn't only my career he'd take away from me...it was a part of my heart, too.

Patrick and I married a few weeks later, at the King County Courthouse on a sunny Friday morning. Ewan and his wife,

Jean, were our witnesses. Patrick and I discussed it and decided not to include the children in the ceremony—we didn't want to confuse them. But Mrs. Hills was pleased with this development, and agreed to mind the children for the morning. I'd once thought of Grace's wedding as a disappointingly simple affair, but my wedding day was entirely without pomp or circumstance. Patrick wore a collared shirt, and I wore a peach dress. I did set my hair and did a careful job on my makeup— but mostly because Ewan was bringing his camera.

There was no emotion in the ceremony. In fact, Patrick and I barely looked at one another as we made our vows. I just kept thinking of the children—there was no doubt in my mind by then that I was doing the right thing, even if I was still a little unnerved by the responsibility I'd willingly put on my shoulders. The girls in the residential hall back in California had packed up my things and they'd soon arrive by courier, and my old life was gone forever—replaced by this new one where so many unknowns still remained. In the days before the wedding, I had started inquiring about work as a professor's assistant at the universities in Seattle, but the response so far had been lukewarm. I had half a master's degree under my belt, and a million ideas for things I wanted to learn and say and do, but the professors I'd met so far had all been skeptical that I could balance family life and paid work.

Even so, I knew I'd find a way. I always had in the past.

"…you may now kiss your bride, Patrick," the celebrant beamed, and Patrick and I exchanged a horrified, awkward glance. He bent and kissed my cheek, and Ewan and Jean and the celebrant all clapped politely. We paid our fee on the way out of the courthouse, and then standing in the crisp morning light, I linked arms with Patrick and posed while Ewan took the photo.

"There, happy?" Ewan laughed.

"Absolutely. Could I please have a copy of that when you develop the film?"

"You're sending that photo to your parents, aren't you?" Patrick asked, amused.

"That's *exactly* what I'm doing." I smirked. My parents seemed to have given up on their quest to take the children from Patrick. We hadn't heard a peep from them since I'd informed Father of our impending nuptials, but I didn't need to speak with them directly to know they were intensely displeased.

By lunchtime, I was home with the children, and Patrick had changed into his work gear and left for a job site with Ewan.

I was now the second Mrs. Patrick Walsh, and officially a step-mother. As I formally adjusted to those roles, I was convinced the change was simply practical.

I was already somewhat used to my new responsibilities; now I just had to find ways to balance them with my true calling—my work. I knew there'd be barriers, but even so, I was determined that my new titles would never slow me down in achieving my goals.

"Professor Jackson?"

"Mrs. Walsh, nice to see you again."

Professor Jackson's expression and accelerated pace suggested it was anything but nice to see me again, so I knew he was just being polite. I chased him along the hallway at Seattle University's social studies department, clutching my satchel to my hip as I ran. I'd met him several times over the previous months, and Professor Callahan had sent him a personal recommendation about my work ethic and skills.

Jackson made it clear he was willing to accept my transfer into his master's program, but that wasn't quite enough. I also needed paid work, because without it, Patrick and I would never afford the cost of a babysitter. This was my fourth visit to the university, and each time, I'd sought Professor Jackson out to inquire about a tutoring position.

"I just wanted to talk to you about the possibility of work with your department—"

"As I told you last time, Mrs. Walsh, I don't hire married women as a general rule, because married women tend to have babies and leave me in the lurch. And you are not *just* a married woman, but rather, a married woman who is already responsible for a rather large brood of very young children."

"Professor, with all due respect, my family responsibilities are my problem, not yours. And if you give me even a little work as a tutor, then—"

"You told me last time you were here that you'd recently married a widower, correct?"

"That's correct, Professor, but—"

"Mrs. Walsh," Professor Jackson interrupted me, finally stopping his frantic pace so he could face me. "You have young children at home who have lost their mother. Your job for now should be seeing to the best interests of those children, should it not? What exactly would you do for childcare if you found yourself a job?"

"We'd hire a babysitter," I sighed halfheartedly. "We've thought of all of this, Professor. It's not an insurmountable obstacle."

"So you will outsource the care of the children you have agreed to raise, in order to fulfill your own ambitions?" Professor Jackson's tone left no doubt as to how he felt about *that* arrangement.

"Are you suggesting that because I'm married, and have stepchildren, that I should give up my plans for a career?"

"That's exactly what I'm suggesting."

"But you have plenty of female students—"

"We have female academics, too—several of my tutors are women. I'm actually supervising a very promising PhD candidate at this very minute who happens to be a woman. But you won't find any female academic staff in my department, or any others that I know of, who have a husband and young children at home. This is the way of the world, Maryanne, and so it should be. Society prioritizes the welfare of children over the ambitions of self-focused young mothers." His lips were pursed, and the deep wrinkles on his forehead turned down, too. He looked incredibly displeased, and I finally admitted to myself that this door wasn't just closed, it was locked.

"Self-focused?" I repeated, but I was almost too disheartened to feel outrage. Instead, I felt worn down.

On each of my visits to this university, I'd had pretty much the same conversation with the librarian and the staff in the administration unit. I'd had the same kind of response at Washington University, and an even icier response from the staff at Seattle Pacific. Plenty of women had jobs in those days, but even with employers who didn't have a formal "marriage bar" policy, women with office jobs tended to resign once they were married, and always once they had children.

"I apologize if I've offended you, Mrs. Walsh," Professor Jackson said. "But I won't change my stance on this."

The irony did not escape me. I had married Patrick at least in part because it was considered unacceptable for an unmarried woman and man to live together and if I was going to help him with the children, I'd have to live in his house. But that marriage had become an insurmountable barrier to the career I'd long dreamed of, and without work, I couldn't even afford to study.

Society seemed absolutely determined to define me as wife, and in doing so, to lock me in the cage that had driven my sister all but insane.

"So that's really it?"

"There's nowhere else to try, Patrick."

"And you're just giving up? Really? That's not like you."

We were sitting on the porch one night after the children

went to bed. Patrick was sipping a beer, and I was nursing my fourth sherry. He didn't want me to give up with my quest for academic employment. But I had been looking for work for months by then, and I'd come to accept that I'd accidentally backed my way into a corner. I was trying desperately to keep my chin up. I didn't exactly regret agreeing to stay, but I was a little panicked at the thought that I'd just destroyed everything that mattered to me.

I was trapped. I'd spend hundreds of hours looking for that note from Grace by then, trying to protect my career. All the while, I'd blown up my career anyway.

"I'm not giving up forever," I assured him. "Just until Beth starts school. That's only two years away, and I guess by then you'll have finished your foreman training, and you'll be able to afford a babysitter even if I can't find work. Right?"

"Right..."

Two years felt like an eternity, and I was miserable about it. I'd seriously considered seeking work and not mentioning the young family I had at home, but I knew inevitably that I'd need some degree of flexibility when emergencies arose. I knew women hid their marriages all the time so they could keep jobs they enjoyed, but hiding four small children was a bit of a stretch, even for me.

"I know I seem to say this a lot," Patrick said, tilting his head at me. "But I don't understand you. I keep thinking about the fact that you had an abortion because you didn't want a child, presumably because you were determined to have a career instead. And now here you are, assuming responsibility for *my* children, even though it effectively means your career has stalled."

Panic swelled, as it always did when I thought about Patrick finding Grace's notes. We had, against the odds, become something like friends over the months since our wedding and I couldn't bear the thought of how hurt and furious he'd be if he ever found me out. And, yes, maybe my career was temporarily on hold, but with every day that passed, I loved those children more and more. I was painfully aware that if Patrick ever found out the truth, this fragile truce we'd built for the children would be undone in an instant. But the panic faded, as it always did. *I'd looked everywhere*, and if I couldn't find the notes, there was surely no way he'd *accidentally* find them.

"Your children are an immense blessing, Patrick. I've come to love them very deeply and I can't even imagine my life without them. But that doesn't change the fact that a pregnancy isn't always the best thing for a woman. Childrearing is almost entirely a woman's responsibility, and pregnancy *is* entirely a woman's domain. For this reason alone I am absolutely convinced that a woman should have complete control over what happens to her if she falls pregnant. I don't think I should have to justify my decisions to you, or anyone else, for that matter."

Patrick sighed and ran his hand through his hair.

"What about the father of this baby? What were his thoughts on the matter? Did he approve?"

In this I could, at least, answer honestly, and I answered for Grace as much as anything.

"He didn't know. It wasn't his place to decide."

"There's at least one thing you've taught me in the five months since we got married," Patrick said after a pause. He glanced at me, then laughed softly. "I now know you don't have to agree with someone to form a very successful partnership with them."

Patrick was right—our partnership was a resounding success. We'd settled into a new life together, and career struggles aside, it was a life I was coming to love.

Beth
1996

It's not hard to track down Maryanne Gallagher's office now that I know she's a professor at Seattle University. Just after nine o'clock the next morning I call their switchboard, ask for her, and seconds later I'm speaking to her assistant.

"Professor Gallagher has office hours Tuesday afternoons," the young man informs me by rote.

"It's a personal matter. Is she available? I'd really like to speak to her."

"Oh." Maryanne's assistant sounds stunned, as if he's never had to deal with a personal call for his boss before. "Who's calling, please?"

"This is Bethany Evans. Er...maybe tell her it's Bethany Walsh."

"Hold, please."

The tinny hold music comes down the line, but only for a few seconds before Maryanne picks up.

"I had a feeling you'd call me today."

"I'm really sorry about last night."

"You don't need to apologize, Beth."

"I was hoping you'd be available for lunch today. I know it's late notice, but I'd really love to talk to you, if you can spare me the time."

"I'm..."

"Just me, Aunt Maryanne. Not the others."

Maryanne sighs heavily.

"I never could say no to you. Where and when?"

We make arrangements to meet at one of the cafés near her campus, and I pause, wondering if I should call Chiara and ask her to babysit. After a moment, I set the phone carefully down onto the cradle and go to pack the bag so Noah can join me.

I have no idea why I'm voluntarily dragging my son on an hour-long drive across the city, and risking taking him along for what's bound to be an uncomfortable lunch, but for some reason today, I just don't want to be apart from him.

I'm a full half hour early, but it turns out, so is Maryanne. When I get to the café to look for a table with space for Noah's stroller, I immediately see her in the corner. There's a book on the table, but she's staring at the flower arrangement in front of it, a vaguely distant expression on her face.

Maryanne is dressed in a similarly dramatic style today. She's wearing a navy blue dress in a stiff fabric, with a square neck and hugely dramatic bell sleeves.

I know you. I definitely know you.

I draw in a deep breath and check on Noah in the stroller, just to buy myself some time before I approach her. But when I look up, she's already seen me, and I have to force myself to walk across the room.

"I didn't have a migraine," she says, giving me a ruefully sad smile.

"I know," I say. My mouth is suddenly dry, and my heart's racing in my ears. I sit heavily, and blurt, "I have the most beautiful memories of my mother. When I was a kid, those memories seemed like some extraordinary gift from the universe, like some consolation prize because I had to grow up without her. I missed her, you see. I didn't miss the idea of having a mother. I missed *her*." Maryanne swallows and looks away, and I reach into the stroller beneath my sleeping son. "And I've missed her more than ever since Dad got sick…ever since Noah was born. I've thought about it all the time. And then when I was cleaning out Dad's house, I found these…"

I pull the jewelry box out from the stroller, and Maryanne tilts her head at it.

"Does this look familiar?" I ask her.

She frowns, then shakes her head and reaches to pick it up. As soon as she opens it, she bites her lip.

"Oh, that sneaky man," she whispers, then she blinks rapidly before she meets my gaze. "I didn't think we could afford this ring. He must have gone back to get it to surprise me."

"There's more," I say, then I pull the photo album from beneath the stroller and open it carefully up to the first page of

Grace's letters. I expect Maryanne to react with shock, but instead, she gives me a sad smile and reaches into her handbag. She withdraws a plastic sleeve and rests it on the table beside the album.

I recognize immediately the yellowed paper and beautifully flowery script of the page beneath the sleeve.

"That's Grace's note from April 14?" I whisper.

"It is," Maryanne says, eyebrows lifting. "And how did you know *that*?"

"It's a long story," I laugh weakly. "How did you get it?"

"Your father gave it to me," she murmurs, then she gives me a sad look and extends the note toward me. "Those notes blew up our whole lives, and this was the only one I ever got to read."

Grace
April 14, 1958

Last week I decided I had two options: I could give up without a fight, and let the darkness take me away from my family. Or I could take charge the way my sister would.

It was Maryanne I went to for help, because she's the kind of woman who can make things happen. When she arrived from California this week, she charged in to save the day and in no time at all, had organized an abortion for me, and even found most of the money so that I could pay for it.

I'm skeptical that Maryanne is right about the future—I can't ever see men giving up the reins to this world, but when I see the way that she's broken past every obstacle to help me, I have some hope. With women like Maryanne to lead the charge, maybe things really can change.

I'm up early because I couldn't sleep. I just kissed Patrick on the cheek and sent him off for the day, Tim and Jeremy are watching cartoons, and Ruth and Bethany are still in bed. And in this predawn moment, I stop and reflect on what I am about to do.

I didn't make this decision lightly; I don't suppose women ever do, *but sometimes, you just have to do things you never thought you would to survive. The cost of this sin is not nearly as great as I know the cost of my inaction would be. In the weeks since I realized I was pregnant, some part of my mind was already back at that bridge, staring down into the swirling ocean waters below, longing only for the pain to stop.*

I know what is best for me and for my family. I am proud of myself for finding the strength to do this—to do what's right for me, and for the children I already have.

I will be brave—I must *be brave. And when I come home, all of my mind will come home, not just the parts that aren't consumed with despair and grief and fear.*

I hate having to do this but there simply is no alternative. It's the pregnancy or me, and so I'll do what needs to be done to be a good mother to my children.

TWENTY

Maryanne
1959

I couldn't even say when my relationship with Patrick began to change. We worked side by side as colleagues over the year that followed, engaging only around family life, each of us playing the role we needed to play. I'd gradually developed a healthy admiration for Patrick—a man who bounced back from the depths of grief, a man who was clearly willing to do whatever it took to keep his family together and to raise his children well. He worked harder than anyone I'd ever known—and he'd clawed his way back out of a financial pit that, once upon a time, had seemed insurmountable.

We had our squabbles. Patrick could be hotheaded and proud, and so could I. Every now and again, we'd clash over some issue big or small—how to discipline the children, which school to send them to, how the repairs to the house should be done, whether it was time to move out of public housing and into our own place. I *knew* in theory that all these things were Patrick's domain and that I should let him make his own decisions, but I couldn't help express my thoughts whenever he came to a crossroads. We'd shout at one another, I'd storm off into my bedroom and then we'd both sulk around the house for a few days, refusing to be the first to speak.

But eventually, he always took my opinions on board. And over weeks and months, we started wearing one another down, because the ferocity of our arguments faded. Instead, we started coming to each other for advice...and a sense of true partnership began to form.

Once upon a time, I would hand off responsibility to Patrick the minute he walked in the door—even if I was halfway through a story with the children. But gradually, I started to linger in the family life each night, and this naturally lent itself to me and Patrick sharing dinner once the children were in bed. He told me about his day, about supplies that came late and laborers that frustrated him. He told me how embarrassed he was by his own work ethic over the first few years of his professional life.

"I hate to say it now, but I always felt like I'd been dealt a bad hand, being an orphan from such a young age," Patrick said one night as he reflected on the behavior of one young apprentice. "Aunt Nina is an odd sort. She was so much older than any of my friend's mothers, and she had some funny ideas about how men and women should be. I'm not blaming her, of course, but when I look back at my life with Grace, I really took your sister for granted. I grew up in a house where I was the only man, even long before I *was* a man. And being the 'man of the house' didn't mean that I had more responsibility. It meant that I had *less*. Aunt Nina built her whole world around me and I expected that Grace would do the same. Even at work, when my boss would get on me for doing something wrong, I'd feel this—" he gestured toward his chest in frustration, fingers stretched out "—this burning indignation. This entitlement. Of course, now life has beaten some sense into me, and I realize no one owes me anything. I see that same behavior from the young guys at work, expecting that things are just going to be made to happen *for* them. It's frustrating as hell to manage, and I don't know how Grace or Ewan ever put up with me for so long."

"She'd be so proud of you," I remarked. "I'm proud of you."

"Thanks, Mary." He smiled. "I think we're doing okay."

It had become an incontrovertible truth that the more time I shared with Patrick, the fonder I felt toward him, and instead of resisting those quiet dinners once the children were asleep, I began to eagerly anticipate them.

Patrick and I didn't do anything by the book. We started out with a forced partnership, then married and *then* became friends. I think that's why, at first, I didn't recognize the urge to spend time with him as affection. I thought it was the natural combination of proximity and a sense of me being out of place and a little lost there in Yesler Terrace, away from the life I thought I'd live. The fiercely arrogant young version of me had died a painful death after the loss of my sister. I was not the same girl I once was, but I had yet to figure out who I now was. And as I wandered around learning the landscape of my new life, I did so with a now treasured partner and friend in Patrick.

The first anniversary of Grace's death came and went, and we celebrated a birthday for each of the children without her. I mastered the art of keeping the house clean, and I set up a system for the laundry that I adhered to religiously. I even learned to cook—a little. The children still ate an awful lot of dishes that involved toast and eggs, but rarely complained. We really were doing just fine.

When I walked Tim through the gate for his first day of kindergarten, he was adorable in his little outfit, startlingly young, ready to face the world. I crouched right at his eye level and said,

"You're a kid now, got it? School is about learning, and learning is fun. You don't have to look after anyone while you're here."

He kissed my cheek and ran off to play, and as I walked the other children back to the car, I bawled like a bewildered baby, and when he settled in without so much as a hiccup, I was proud as if he were my own.

By the winter of 1959, Patrick and I had a well-established habit of sitting by the fire each evening for a drink and what was often a hearty conversation. Patrick was becoming well versed in early feminist ideology, and as much as I knew he still struggled with the idea that traditional gender roles might actually be limiting for women, he was open to discussion. He had revealed a surprising potential for intellectual depth. I loved debating him, and he seemed to love it, too. He'd offer me his thoughts, always prefacing his ideas with, "Well, Maryanne, you know I'm hardly an expert, but..."

I came to look forward to those nights. I came to long for them. Even so, I refused to let myself dwell on how good it felt to spend time with Patrick. I tried to convince myself that all I felt for him was admiration.

"Do you wish that you could have gone to college, Patrick?" I asked him one night, and he gave me a startled look.

"A fool like me? What would I have done at a college?"

"You are no fool, Patrick Walsh," I laughed softly. "I have a feeling you could have done anything you set your mind to."

"I barely scraped by in school," he said. "College wasn't in the cards for me. Aunt Nina wasn't big on education. My mother worked in a factory during the war, and my father was a mechanic. I suppose, if I'd had the option, I might've liked to study science. But I'm happy working with my hands. These hands earn me an honest living, and there's no shame in that."

He held his hands up as he spoke, palms toward the sky, fingers outstretched. That's when I saw the splinter in the pad of his right forefinger.

"That looks awful," I remarked, motioning toward his finger with my drink. Patrick rubbed at it ruefully.

"Occupational hazard. I thought my hands would get banged up less now that I'm in management, but I still seem to be wielding the tools a lot. It'll come out on its own."

But I could see that the splinter was starting to fester, and so insisted that he allow me to help him pull it out. We shifted into the dining room and Patrick sat at the table while I fetched the tweezers from my sewing kit. I cupped his big hand in mine to hold it steady, extracted the piece of wood without too much trouble and then dropped the tweezers onto the table.

We were supposed to part then, to go back to a conversing side by side. But neither one of us made any attempt to move. We were sitting at the table where we'd shared so many meals together, in the room where so many hours together had caused our partnership to turn to friendship and now…something deeper. Something more.

We were friends and companions and as far as the law was concerned, spouses. But for everything that we shared over the year and a half that had passed, we'd rarely had physical contact. A hug here, a consoling pat there, but never like this. We were still sitting at the table with my hand cupping his. And then, in a rush, he exhaled unsteadily, and turned his hand over and linked his fingers with mine.

My heart started to race, an incessant pounding against the wall of my chest—warning me of dangers untold. Someone had sucked all the air from the room, and when I raised my gaze to Patrick's, he was staring at me as if he couldn't bring himself to look away.

"Patrick," I started to say, but he snatched his hand back as panic flared in his eyes.

"We shouldn't," he whispered. "I'm so sorry."

He left me sitting at the table alone, heart pounding against my chest, feeling strangely stung that he'd walked away.

★ ★ ★

I barely slept that night. I turned the odd moment with Patrick over in my mind a thousand times—thinking about what it might mean, thinking about what it might cost. When Beth climbed into my bed at 3 a.m., I was still wide awake. She cuddled into me, sucking her thumb and mumbling something about monsters in the hallway, and her presence became another reminder of all I had to lose.

I tried to convince myself that Patrick and I simply would continue on as we had been. I told myself that it was nothing more than a moment of madness, one that he would want to avoid talking about, and so would I. To name something is to give it power, and I only wanted to starve *whatever* had happened between us of oxygen.

When my alarm jarred me awake the next morning, I did as I always did—clamored over Beth's sleeping form and stumbled to the kitchen. I was startled to find Patrick was waiting for me. He'd already prepared a cup of coffee for me, something he did most Sunday mornings. But this was a Wednesday, and it was already past six.

"What are you doing? You should be at work," I mumbled, and Patrick motioned towards my chair, indicating that I should sit.

"Take a seat, Maryanne," he said quietly.

Butterflies in my stomach sprang to life as I took the seat opposite him. I wanted to run back to my room, to pull the covers over my head and to pretend that none of this was happening. But cowardice was not my style, so I braced myself, picked the coffee cup up and gulped half of it down without pausing for breath.

"I think I've fallen in love with you," he said. I nearly choked on the coffee, and he rose hastily, thumping me on the back. "Sorry. Shit. I should have... I just thought it was better to come right out and say it."

"That's okay," I managed, still spluttering coffee as I tried to wrap my head around his declaration. *Love.* It made sense, in some bizarre way. Our family had been born in Patrick and Grace's love, but for well over a year, we'd been operating as a unit without her—Grace was gone, and the family survived because of the love that Patrick and *I* shared. Our love persisted when we were apart, it intensified when we were alone and it linked the six of us in a way I'd never thought possible.

If I were just in that house for the children, I wouldn't have been finding excuses to spend every spare minute with their father. The sight of him coming down the path wouldn't fill my heart with an incredible lightness. His gentle gestures, like making me coffee on Sunday mornings and including me on his outings with the children, wouldn't have meant so much. The way he complimented me as I cared for his children wouldn't have buoyed my very soul. The way he smiled at me for no reason at all wouldn't be enough to make my stomach flip.

"She's only been gone for eighteen months," he whispered now, dropping his hands from my cheeks. The words dripped with misery and guilt. "Whatever would she say if she knew? I'm letting her down again, even in her death."

I closed my eyes for just a moment and pictured my sister's beautiful face. I could only see her smiling, perhaps even smirking knowingly to discover that she'd been right all along. I thought I knew love, and I thought it was a creature I could tame and control. But it had snuck up behind me and pulled the rug from under me, just as she'd told me it would.

Even more miraculous, I felt in my bones that my sister had, inadvertently, given her blessing to this astounding twist in our fates.

I wish you would fall in love. I wish you'd love a man the way I love Patrick. I know you only see his flaws, but I still see his potential... If you could see each other the way I see you, I just know you'd love each other.

I rose from my chair and turned towards Patrick. I leaned in slowly toward him, until our foreheads were touching. I paused, waiting for guilt, but none came. I was somehow certain that if

TRUTHS I NEVER TOLD YOU

my sister could see everything Patrick and I had been through since her death, she'd feel only joy that he and I might find happiness in each other.

"You're wrong, Patrick," I whispered, heart racing. "If she knew that we took the mess that was left after she was gone and turned it into something beautiful, Grace would have been delighted."

He pulled away slightly. I opened my eyes and found him staring at me in wonder. It was magical and marvelous and somehow miraculous that we had taken a relationship so fraught with resentment and pain and turned it into something even deeper than affection.

"You feel it, too?" he asked me.

"I think I do."

And we stood like that in the kitchen, looking at one another like we might have on any other day, only this time we really were seeing each other for the first time.

Patrick and I found ourselves in the exceedingly odd position of being married and sharing the care of four children while courting one another.

In reality, the months of our courtship looked a lot like the months that had preceded it. We juggled daily life with the children together—arranging for the twins to start school in the spring, helping Tim with his homework, managing the house. When the children were in bed, we spent time alone, learning one another as individuals instead of parents. Life in those months was like a wonderful gift, and while Patrick openly talked with me about his guilt at finding love so soon after Grace's death, *I* only felt blissfully freed by this new phase of our relationship. We talked for hours each night, learning the depths to one another and exploring the connection between us. I even told him about that conversation Grace and I had in the car the very last time I saw her.

"She *wanted* me to fall in love," I told him. "I told her that I was never going to marry, and she told me that she wanted me to know how wonderful it felt to fall in love with someone. She thought that would change my opinion of marriage. To be honest, I think Grace felt a little sorry for me that I saw the world in a black-and-white way."

"And now?" he asked me quietly.

"Well, I still think inequality is a problem and I still think that marriage is an anchor around the neck of my fellow women sometimes, and I still think society should change...that society will change." I shrugged, but then I shot him a cheeky smile. "But I also think that the way you and I are together only makes me stronger. So maybe, things aren't as clear-cut as I always assumed they were."

"It surprises me that Grace would say such warm things about marriage," Patrick mused, frowning. "I wouldn't have thought she'd have had a positive opinion of it...after being married to me."

"She loved you," I said simply. He gave me a sad smile.

"Even when I didn't deserve it."

"Everyone deserves love, Patrick."

"I made so many mistakes," he sighed. "You were in California so you didn't have to see it. But I was a child with a man's responsibilities. I don't really know what it was about Grace, but every time she had a baby, she'd change. With Tim, neither one of us had any clue what we were doing and I really just thought maybe she didn't like being a mom. But with the twins, I could see it was more than that...some kind of mental problem she couldn't control. And it was worse than ever with Beth. And wouldn't you think her husband would see her struggling and step up to help? But I didn't. I didn't know how to, and after I took her to the doctor one time and he just told her she had to tough it out, I guess I panicked. It was easier to stay out with the boys from work than it was to come home and face the reality that I kept getting her pregnant and those pregnancies damaged her so much."

"I didn't know how bad it was for her, either," I admitted, throat tightening. "Not until…"

"Not until?"

I cleared my throat. Patrick and I had shared hundreds of hours of conversation by then, but rarely about Grace. It wasn't that we'd forgotten her; rather, we quickly realized that life would just keep marching on, and we had to look forward, not back.

"She told me about how depressed she had been," I said softly. "Just before she died."

"I don't know the full story and I probably never will, but there was one morning… I woke up and Grace looked as though she'd been hit by a bus. She had bruises all over her, and scratches even on her face, and somehow between me going to bed and waking up, she'd used all of the gas in my car. I think… I really think she tried to hurt herself that night. I tried after that to be around more. The thing is, she always perked up once the babies were a bit older, even if she was already pregnant again by then. It was something about that first year after she gave birth that messed her up." He glanced at me, his gaze intense. "You're *sure* you don't want kids, aren't you?"

I laughed quietly, then motioned toward the bedrooms.

"I'm sure I already have plenty of kids, actually."

"I mean it, Maryanne. I couldn't bear to see you suffer the way that she… I just mean, if we…when we… I'm not being presumptuous, but—"

"*When* we move into the same bedroom," I finish for him, laughing softly, "I'll get a diaphragm. Will that be okay with you?"

"I'd be fine with that."

"I truly don't want children of my own, especially now."

"But you love those kids. I can *see* it."

"I do. I feel lucky that I get to experience a taste of motherhood with your children. I just wouldn't want to start all over again with a newborn. Tim and the twins are at school now, and Beth will start next year—I'll be able to go back to studying after that. If we were to have another child together, that would mean still more years when I couldn't study."

"Good." Patrick nodded, satisfied.

"When *are* we going to…" I trailed off as the flush crept up Patrick's cheeks.

"…move into the same bedroom?" He finished the sentence for me. We flashed one another a slightly awkward grin. "I know you aren't one for tradition, but it still matters to me that we do this right."

"We've been married for over two years now, Patrick," I said, then I teased him. "What is your plan, then? Do you divorce me so we can remarry?"

"I've been thinking about this a lot," he said, and he ran his hand through his hair and looked away. "And I do mean a *lot*."

I laughed, delighted at his bashfulness, then turned him back to face me so I could kiss him. But all too soon, he pulled away, and said quite seriously, "I think I rushed your sister into life with me. I won't do that to you. When you're ready to marry me—properly this time—just let me know, and I'll figure out how we can do that."

"What does *properly* entail here, exactly?"

"The church. With Father Willis, not a registrant at the court house."

"Christ Almighty, that sounds dull."

"Maryanne."

"Okay, okay," I laughed. "But I'm *already* committed here, Patrick. Why do we need to wait?"

"It's not the arrangement I want you to commit to," he murmured. "It's *me*. This isn't you promising to help me out with the kids for the foreseeable future. I want to promise that you're mine, and I'm yours. That really means something to me, and despite your determination to blow up *all* traditions, everywhere, I have a feeling that this kind of promise will mean something to you, too."

"So now you're blowing up traditions."

"I am?"

"Well, now you're going to wait for *me* to propose?"

"I'd propose to you right now if I thought it was what you wanted."

I tilted my head at him.

"Patrick, I love you. I'm ready for this to be our life together."

Everything seemed to fall into place. Patrick and I were happy—happier than I'd *ever* expected to be. We were talking about "our" future, and the truth was, it had been a long while since I'd been able to imagine my life without him and the children in it. But at the end of the day, the man I loved also loved his traditions. If we were to be together as man and wife in every sense of the word, he wanted us to be married in the church.

This was what I failed to understand about love before I experienced it myself. Love doesn't just need compromise to survive— love, to its very essence, *is* compromise. It's genuinely wanting what's best for the other person, even when it trumps your own preferences. The idea of donning a white dress and walking down some aisle for a celibate man in robes to formalize our union in the eyes of his religion did not appeal to me at all. But it meant something to Patrick, and Patrick meant something to me.

So we set a date, and we planned a second wedding. Father Willis agreed to perform the service, and he made room for us in the church timetable just a few weeks later.

"There's no time to waste," he said, looking between Patrick and me with his lips pursed. "You two are already cohabiting, unmarried in the eyes of God. We're busy, but I'll fit you in."

I found an ivory lace shift dress in a store near the city, and we scraped together enough money for a new pair of shoes, too. Mrs. Hills insisted on baking us a cake. That was about the extent of what we'd planned for the celebration, but Patrick was counting down the days with obvious glee. I still thought his insistence that we marry again before we shared a bed was nonsense, but this did at least give me time to purchase a dia-phragm and to pay attention to my cycle so we could avoid intimacy midmonth.

And in the meantime, we sat the children down and explained to them what was happening.

"But you're already married," Jeremy said.

"Can I wear a pretty dress?" Ruth asked.

"I want to wear a dress!" Beth protested.

"Why do you need to get married again?" Tim asked, bewildered.

"It's so Maryanne can be your mom now," Patrick said, scratching his head and giving me a pleading look.

"She's already our mom." Ruth blinked at him.

Patrick sighed.

"But… I mean, she *is*, it's just that…"

"Sweeties," I said quietly. "This wedding means I'm never leaving. It means I'm here forever. And I always was, but sometimes grown-ups need to do these things just to make an arrangement official. So that's what it's about. And we get to have cake—everyone likes cake, don't they?"

The kids all nodded, and apparently that was just enough to satisfy them and they were ready to go back outside and play. Patrick puffed out a frustrated breath.

"I love how they've taken to you," he said. "But…"

"I hate it, too. I still want to remind them that Grace was their real mom and I hate that they've forgotten her. But if I do, they have to grieve her all over again," I sighed and met his gaze. "They are still so young, my love. It's too hard for them to understand that she was here, and then she was gone, and now *I'm* here instead."

"What do you think Grace would have wanted?"

"I think she'd have hated to miss any of this…any of their happiness, any of these years. But I also *know* she'd have wanted them to be happy," I admitted.

"That's what I think, too. We *will* tell them one day…"

"But just not yet."

We smiled at one another, as if that settled it, neatly stepping around the guilt that we both knew could not be avoided forever.

Whether we liked it or not, in the children's minds, I had replaced Grace, and we would just have to learn to live with it until they were old enough to understand.

Patrick worked a half-day on Saturdays, and that weekend when he finished for the week, we took the children for an outing to Alki Beach. I had packed a picnic, and Patrick and I sat on the sand while the older kids frolicked at the edge of the waves, and Beth built sandcastles nearby. It was a delicious, sun-drenched day, but when the children's cheeks were pink, and the sun was in the sky behind us, we packed up to go back to the car.

"There's a store we need to have a look at on the way home," Patrick said. He wouldn't tell me where we were going—instead, we drove in silence for a while, and then he parked the car and winked at me. We each took two children's hands in ours, and the six of us crossed the busy road toward the stores.

"Which do you like?" he asked me quietly, finally coming to a stop by the display window at a jewelry store. I peered through the glass at so many sparkling rings and then I laughed.

"The cheapest. Come on—"

"Seriously, Maryanne. We need to get you a set of rings, and we're never at the same place at the same time when stores are open. At least give me a clue what style you prefer."

I sighed, but looked through the window to scan the rows of rings.

"I like simplicity. I don't want something huge that will bankrupt us. Just get me a plain gold band—" But my gaze snagged on an engagement ring. It was a small oval aquamarine in a simple silver setting. It was hardly the most elaborate ring in the window, but I loved it on sight, even as I suspected it would be beyond our budget. I forced myself to look back at Patrick. "Just a plain silver band, okay? Whatever we can afford. Nothing more."

Patrick looked back into the window, then nodded, then offered me a smile and a peck on the cheek.

"Two more weeks, my love," he murmured softly near my ear, sending shivers down my spine.

"Two more weeks," I murmured back, and we shared a knowing smile before we turned the children back to the car and headed home.

Mrs. Hills and Aunt Nina insisted on taking me out for a bachelorette party the weekend before the wedding. I protested furiously at this, mostly because I wasn't exactly excited by the idea of suffering through two octogenarians offering me sex advice. But in the end, Patrick convinced me to go.

"You never go *anywhere*," he pointed out.

"I go to the park. And the library. And the grocery store."

"Okay. Correction. You never go anywhere *fun*."

"The library is fun."

"Christ, woman! Take the night off, get dressed up and go out for a nice dinner somewhere."

It was actually an uneventful meal in the end. I think my elderly friends probably figured out for themselves that I wasn't actually as innocent as they might have been just before their own weddings, and so instead of bombarding me with advice about marriage and sex, we talked about knitting and the weather and later, the way the world had changed over the decades since they were girls.

I went home, a little tipsy from the wine at dinner, and as happy as I'd ever been. It was a beautiful place to be. It was a miserable height to fall from.

As I stepped into the house, I skipped my gaze around the living room, looking for Patrick. I expected him to be waiting for me in front of the television, but the set was off. He wasn't in the dining room, either, so I peeked in on the children. I kissed Timothy's forehead, and put away the metal trucks that littered Jeremy's bed even though I'd told him a thousand times not to play with them when he was supposed to be asleep. I tucked Ruth in—she was forever kicking her blankets off. And Beth was missing from her bed, but I knew I would find her in my own bed instead. I was right—there she was, resting against my pillow, those beautiful dark eyelashes against the pale curve of her cheeks. I bent and breathed her in, soaking up the scent of soap and toothpaste and Beth.

And then I put the blanket up to her chin, and I left my room to find my love. There was only one place he could be: his bedroom...our bedroom, in just a few nights.

I was smiling as I walked to his room. I thought he'd be asleep, too; maybe he'd be under the blankets and I could pull them up to his chin, then kiss his forehead as I'd done for his children. But the light was on. Patrick was sitting on the bed.

His face was beet-red, his cheeks wet with tears, his eyes wild. I knew then. Even before I saw the wedding album on the bed, even before I registered the letters all over the bed cover, even before I saw my sister's handwriting on the piece of paper he clutched in his fist, I knew he'd found Grace's notes.

In the silence, I took the scene in, and my heart nearly broke when I realized that the "last place on earth" Grace expected her husband to look was in their wedding album. She was almost right—it took Patrick over two years to look at those photos.

"Where was that?" I asked him stiffly.

"In the bottom of the chest in the living room. I built it... I built a cavity so we could hide money. I went to hide your ring there last week and found the wedding album, but I didn't look at it until tonight," Patrick said. His voice was hoarse, but the words were wound so tight with fury that I winced and turned away. I'd watched him fight an attempt to take his children, but I'd never heard him so angry. I'd seen him lose his wife, but

KELLY RIMMER

I'd never seen him so hurt. "I promised myself I'd say goodbye to her tonight. I wanted to look at those photos one last time and say goodbye." I'd checked the chest, but I didn't know to check the base. How could I? He raised his eyes to me. "Did you know she wrote these?"

Patrick barely looked like the man I loved. He didn't even look like someone I knew. But I wasn't about to lie to him, and although I knew he held my future in his hands, I didn't think he would hurt me. I still trusted his love for me. I still thought that after everything we'd been through, we'd get through this, too.

"Yes. I knew."

"Did you look for them?"

"Yes."

His brows shifted down, then up and then he closed his eyes. "Is this why you stayed?"

"I stayed for the children," I said, but that was half a lie, and I was determined to tell him the truth. It seemed the only way we'd survive. "Wait. Yes—I did hope to find the letters, and that's why I stayed at first. I mean…" I was flustered and confused, bitterly regretting that last glass of wine as I tried to clarify. "Patrick, all that I knew was that she had written a note about the abortion. I knew you'd be angry and I was scared of what you'd do if you found it, but I also didn't think it would do you any good to see whatever else she—" I scanned the notes on the bed and my heart sank. "How many are there?"

God only knew what else was in those notes. If that last conversation I'd had with Grace had been any indication, her mental state over the years had been dire. I looked at Patrick again, and there were fresh tears in his eyes.

"So what really happened that day? I deserve to know that much."

I didn't want to tell him, but I knew that I had to. The time had come for honesty, and there was no avoiding the truth—no matter how ugly.

"It was exactly like I told you, only I lied about… I swapped our roles. Grace was pregnant, not me. I found her someone who could help, and I lied so I could borrow some money from Father, but it wasn't enough. That's why…that's why she asked you to get an advance from Ewan."

"She didn't *ask* me, Maryanne," Patrick spat out. "She insisted upon it. She manipulated me. It was so unlike her—I should have known it was all your idea." I winced, and he scrubbed a shaking hand over his face, then demanded, "And then?"

"I waited for her—"

"Where? Where was this?"

"On the alleyway. Downtown."

"And who did it?"

"An unregistered doctor. A man picked her up and she went with him."

"You didn't even go with her?"

"I couldn't. I wasn't allowed—"

"So you sent her off with a stranger who may or may not have had any idea what he was doing."

"He said he was a doctor, Patrick."

"Do you honestly believe a doctor would have met you in an alleyway?" He caught himself and dropped his voice, nostrils flaring. "Go on. What next?"

"Well… I mean, she just never came back. I looked for her everywhere. I tried to contact the man she went with, but the call didn't connect the first day and by the next morning the number had been disconnected. I assume something went wrong with the procedure and—"

"Procedure? You're calling the *murder* you ordered a *procedure*?" Patrick was bawling now, swiping hopelessly at his eyes.

"Patrick…" I started to cry, too, and I took a step toward the bed. "She couldn't handle another child. She just couldn't. She begged me."

"You *knew* I would never have allowed this—"

"It was her life!" I exclaimed. "Her body. Her *sanity*. I'm telling you now, she wouldn't have survived another pregnancy—"

"Well, Maryanne, nor did she survive the abortion that you arranged for her," Patrick interrupted me. The room fell heavily silent after that.

"I'm so sorry." What else could I say to that? He was absolutely right.

Patrick's emotions were now completely out of control. I hadn't seen him like this since the immediate aftermath of the discovery of her body. His grief and guilt were fresh and raw and all of the healing and progress we'd made over the years seemed to have disappeared in an instant. I had no idea what was in those letters, only that the last of them was something of a confession, and that Grace had found the experience of writing her thoughts down to be cathartic. I took a step toward him—wanting only to offer him comfort, but he raised a hand at me in warning.

"You need to go," he choked out.

"What? Go where?"

"I don't know. But I need to think…" He waved his hand around the bed, then wiped at his eyes hopelessly. "I just need to think this all through. I can't think with you here." He glanced up at me, then looked away and squeezed his eyes closed as a fresh burst of anger resurged. "*Jesus, Maryanne!* I can't even look at you knowing that you took her from us! You sent her with that man. You all but murdered her yourself!"

I'd been wary and remorseful since I stepped across that doorway, but as Patrick's distress turned to anger, I felt the first hot flash of my own temper. I was far too angry to shout; instead, I spoke with deathly, furious intent.

"What else is in those notes, Patrick? Does she talk about how she thought about ending her own life because you let her down? Does she talk about how your marriage was such a burden she could barely stand it? Does she talk about how she almost killed herself one night, while you slept in your bed, oblivious to her pain?" I crossed my arms over my chest and my temper ran free. "If anyone murdered my sister, it was *you*."

I regretted it as soon as I said it, but I was far too proud to apologize, especially when Patrick didn't even flinch. Instead, he scanned the notes on the bed, then scooped one up and waved it toward me.

"This letter alone would be enough."

"Enough for *what*?"

"Enough to prove that you arranged an abortion for her. She died alone at the hands of strangers, and you made that happen. Maybe you should pay the price."

We were getting nowhere, and things would only escalate if we kept speaking from our pain. I took a step back and tried to take a deep breath.

"This is absurd. I'm going to go to bed. We'll talk tomorrow—"

"Maryanne," Patrick said suddenly. His hand dropped to his side, taking the note with it. I glanced at him warily.

"What?"

"I don't care where you go, but you will leave this house tonight, or I will call the police and have you removed."

Patrick held all of the cards, and we both knew it. I had no idea how seriously the police would take a note like this, but I couldn't risk him trying to get Grace's case reopened.

"You said you loved me," I whispered.

"I…" He broke off, then ran a hand through his hair in frustration. "Don't you understand? How could I just carry on with you—letting you take her place in my life…in *our* lives…when *you* did this to her?"

We fell into silence after that. I didn't know how to make things right, but I was still sure there would be a way I could. We both needed time to think it through.

"I'll go," I said heavily. "Just for tonight."

I glanced back at him, and Patrick nodded, but his gaze was on the notes scattered all over his bed.

I told Mrs. Hills that Patrick and I had quarreled, and she made up the sofa. I stretched out and closed my eyes, but I slept very poorly. Somehow I knew Patrick wasn't sleeping, either.

Even so, I eventually talked myself around to hope that night. I wondered if Patrick's fury was rooted in guilt and shame, just as mine had been. Grace probably *had* revealed a depth of pain he wasn't aware of in those notes. I just hoped I'd get the chance to sit him down and to talk it all through in the cold light of the new morning.

"You'll see," Mrs. Hills said sagely as we nursed cups of coffee as the sun rose. "Young love is always volatile, but today you two will sort this out and everything will be fine."

"I hope so," I said. I knew our situation seemed simpler to her than it really was, but she was probably right. Patrick and I were both quick to anger sometimes, and as passionate as we were about one another, we also could be impulsive and temperamental.

There was a quiet rap on the glass in the back door, and I turned my head sharply to see Patrick standing there. As I feared, he looked so weary, but the exhaustion and sadness on his face renewed my hope. A man doesn't sit up all night torturing himself over a woman he doesn't love.

I flashed Mrs. Hills a knowing smile and almost ran to the back door.

I expected him to embrace me when I stepped outside. I actually expected an apology and a plea for a fresh attempt at a conversation, but what I found was something different. Patrick stood among a collection of boxes and bags that I immediately knew contained my possessions. My heart sank all the way to my toes.

"We can get past this—" I started to say as my vision blurred with hot tears.

"I won't go to the police. But you need to do something for me in return." He sighed heavily, then pleaded with me, "Maryanne, I need you to go quietly."

The idea of it was unbearable. To leave was already too much to ask, but to leave *quietly*? Without even saying goodbye to the children I'd come to love as my own?

"But I need to say goodbye to them—"

"You're *not* their fucking mother, Maryanne!" he snapped. I flinched as if he'd slapped me. He sucked in a sharp breath, then whispered fiercely, "Even if I could forgive the secrecy and the lies, I can't get around this one simple fact—you knew the truth about what happened to Grace that day, and you kept it to yourself. Who knows? If you'd gone to the police right away, maybe she'd still be here."

"But…honestly, Patrick, I thought she'd come back, and then I was so scared—" I was weeping now, barely resisting the urge to throw myself at him and to cling to him so he couldn't walk away. It wasn't just *us* he was tearing to pieces—it was our family, and I couldn't bear it.

"Last night you accused me of murdering my wife," Patrick said suddenly.

"I was angry—"

"And I accused you of murdering your sister."

"Patrick—"

"We can't just ignore this," Patrick said, his voice breaking. "Maybe we did the wrong thing all along, just pretending it never happened. But now that we know what we know, we can't just carry on, Mary. We have to go our separate ways."

He turned around then, and walked back across the front lawns and into the house.

I was far too stubborn to give up that easily, and I lingered at Mrs. Hills's house for several days. I got up early and watched out the window to see what he was doing with the children when he went to work. I was startled to see him loading all four sleepy children into the back of the car each day, and them disappearing down the street. After two days I had Mrs. Hills go to Patrick's house to ask him what he was doing for childcare. She returned with the news that he had temporarily arranged for the wives of the work crew to watch the children while he worked.

"He's still so upset, Maryanne," she muttered, shaking her head. "I don't know what you've done, but this isn't something he's going to get over quickly. I think you should consider looking for somewhere else to stay until you sort this out with him."

It was the last thing in the world I wanted, and so I resisted for another day. But the weekend was coming, and when Mrs. Hills pointed out that it was only a matter of time before the children came for a visit and saw me, I finally realized I had no option but to look into temporary accommodation elsewhere. With very little money on hand, there was only one place I could go.

"Maryanne?" My mother gasped when she opened her front door and found me and my meager belongings on the doorstep. "But—"

"I just need to stay a few days, maybe a week," I blurted.

She stared at me, mouth agape, then peered around me toward the drive.

"But where is Patrick? Where are the children?"

It was my turn to look at her incredulously.

"You actually thought I would bring them for a visit after what you tried to do?"

Mother's nostrils flared.

"I had their best interests at heart."

"No. You and Father were grieving and you felt guilty about how you'd cut yourselves off from Grace, and you tried to alleviate that guilt by taking her children. That wasn't fair. Patrick is a good man, and he was and is doing the very best he could with them."

"If that's true," Mother said slowly, "then what on earth are you doing on my doorstep today?"

To my horror, I felt hot tears in my eyes, and then the sobs just would not be suppressed. I hadn't cried on my Mother's shoulder since I was tiny, but even her stiff, perfunctory hug only reminded me of the children. Of Beth…sweet little Beth…who would surely be wondering where her "Mommy" was. Who was hugging her? Who was wiping away her tears? I resisted that job in the beginning, but I'd come to treasure it.

"Mother, I don't have anywhere else to go. But I swear to God, if you and Father try to disrupt that man's life again, that'll be it—I'll never speak to you again."

"Did you marry him?" Mother asked, and that's when I remembered that I'd never actually gotten around to sending her the photo of our wedding day. Life had moved on so fast.

"I married him," I whispered miserably. "And then we fell in love. But…we've had a falling out, and I can't go home until he calls for me."

I moved back into my family home that day, shifting my things into my old bedroom. To their credit, my parents didn't ask too many questions about Patrick; they simply allowed me to shift back into their lives as if we'd never argued. After a few days, Mother even opened up to me.

"What happened with Patrick after we lost Grace was my fault, not Father's," she admitted. "I wanted those children for myself. I was grieving and miserable, and I thought they'd offer me a distraction. It wasn't right, and I promise you, I'll never do it again."

"But…*why*, Mother? Why distance yourself from Grace like that when she needed you, then try to take the children as soon as she was gone?"

Mother stared into her teacup as she whispered, "I visited her a lot after she had Timmy, but I just couldn't stand to see her like that. It reminded me of what happened when you girls were born." She looked up at me, cheeks flushing. "I never wanted you to know. But... I had to stay in the hospital for a long time after I had you."

"After you had Grace, you mean. I know you had the hysterectomy—"

"No, Maryanne. After *you* were born. I..." She cleared her throat, then looked at the table. "I tried to harm myself. It was the strangest thing—it was as if I'd lost my mind, and then I took too many pills and...the housekeeper found me, luckily. We weren't going to have any more children, but then Grace came along, and it seemed I couldn't handle her, either."

"Mother," I whispered, looking at her in horror. "Are you saying you were depressed after Grace and I were born?"

"Depressed? No, that doesn't sound right at all. I can barely remember either of you before your first birthday. They said the electroshock therapy would probably damage my memories of that time, but it was more than that, I think." She stared at her lap, her expression pinched. "I wasn't just sad. I could barely function. I just wanted to be...gone. I was completely broken. Hopelessly broken."

"But maybe Gracie felt like she was broken, too, Mother," I whispered thickly.

"Father and I agreed we'd never tell you girls what happened. Heavens, he went to great lengths to hide what I'd done from our friends and family so I had at least a chance of coming back to normal life one day. And I suppose, when Tim came along, I couldn't bear to even consider the possibility that Grace was suffering like I had. It was easier to blame Patrick...easier to blame her for choosing that life, especially after I tried to help her leave him." Mother gave me a sad look. "It was a test, you see. I thought if she was as mentally unwell as I had been, she'd rush to come here for a rest. So perhaps she wasn't going through what I went through," Mother said, and for a moment she looked almost hopeful, but it passed quickly and her expression soon

TRUTHS I NEVER TOLD YOU

sank again. "Or perhaps she was, and I just underestimated her loyalty to him."

Mother rose from the kitchen table to walk, as if on autopilot, toward the medicine cabinet. She withdrew her little bottle of pills, swallowed one dry, then looked back to me.

"It's a good thing you don't want children, I think," she whispered, gnawing anxiously on her bottom lip. "I can't even tell you how frightening it is when your own mind turns against you. I really should go to bed now."

"Mother," I said as she went to leave the room. She glanced back at me uncertainly. "Do you think that maybe it wasn't your fault that you got sick after you had us? That maybe it was something biological?"

"The psychiatrist told me that it was just nervous tension. He said that I was simply too sensitive…simply too anxious. That's why they gave me the hysterectomy."

She then wandered out of the kitchen, leaving me with the feeling that I understood her, perhaps for the first time in my life.

I waited around for days hoping to hear from Patrick, and after a week, I couldn't bear it anymore. I called Mrs. Hills and asked how he was doing.

"They're moving, Maryanne."

"What? Where would they go?"

"I don't know. He won't tell me. But he doesn't look good at all. Now, you know I don't like to stick my nose into other people's business—" I'd have struggled not to snort, if it all wasn't so awful "—but if you were planning on trying to convince him to see sense, you'd best be doing it quickly."

I knew that by nine o'clock, the children would all be deeply asleep. That had been our magic hour, the time when the world rested and Patrick and I were alone. I was sick with dismay when I arrived at the house and glanced through the front window to see moving boxes in the living room, and then somehow felt even sicker as I approached the front door—uncertain about how I might be received. I knocked quietly, and then I walked to sit on the chair on the porch. Patrick opened the door, peered outside, and bathed only in the light from inside the house, I watched his expression shift.

There was frustration. Weariness. And then, to my surprise, an undeniable shame. For just a moment that shame gave me hope.

"Give me just a minute," he said heavily.

Patrick walked back inside, then came to sit on the porch chair beside me, leaving a gap between us that felt like an ocean. In his hands he held a folded piece of paper, but he made no move to offer it to me. Instead, he drew in a deep breath, and stared out at the road that ran past the house as he spoke.

"Grace was right about so many things...she was so much smarter than she knew. She said that I had been running from responsibility for my whole life. She said that I was a child in a man's body. I've read those notes so many times over this past week, and I finally understand just how badly I let her down."

"You were young..."

"Don't make excuses for me! You and your family do *not* get to pass judgment on me, and you sure as hell don't get to absolve me." He was frustrated, but so much more self-contained than he had been when we argued the previous week. Patrick drew in a deep breath, then glanced at me. For a moment he seemed to hesitate and I rushed to plead with him, feeling a delicious hint of hope that I might still change his mind.

"Please, Patrick... I love you. I love *them*. Please don't make me leave."

"You lied to me for *two years*. How could I build a life with you based on a foundation like that?" he whispered brokenly. "I'm absolutely certain that we've both made mistakes, and perhaps we temporarily outran the consequences, but we both have to pay for those sins now. Your penance is that you have to live with what you did, and you have to live without your sister and my family." A sob broke in my throat, and he turned away, his face set in a mask of agony. "And *I* have to be the man I couldn't be for Grace. I have to do it for my kids and for myself. And I have to do it without you, because that's *my* penance."

He passed me the note, then. Our fingers brushed, and I felt a shiver along my arm. Maybe I knew that was the last time I'd feel his skin against mine.

"What's this?" I whispered through my tears.

"It's the last note. The one where she talks about the…" He swallowed, then finished with obvious difficulty, "This is the note where she talks about you arranging the abortion."

I looked at him in shock.

"But why would you give this to me?"

Patrick looked back to the road.

"You need to read it. You need to face what you did to her." He sounded furious, but then he choked up, and he glanced at me, his gaze swimming in tears. "I'm so angry with you. I'm so hurt that you let things get as far as they did with this secret between us. But God help me, I love you, Maryanne. I want you to go back to the life you were meant to live, and not waste the rest of your years worrying that some note is about to bring it all down around you. And…her other notes were about how I'd let her down. This one…this is the only one that wasn't about me. It just feels right to give it to you."

We sat in silence for a while. I held the folded piece of paper between my palms, my fingers interlinked around it. Locking my hands together was the only way I could stop myself from reaching for him.

"How will you juggle it all?" I asked him eventually.

"I'll manage," he said. It was a calm statement of fact, and it was a promise I was instantly certain he'd keep.

"But where will you even go?"

"That isn't your problem anymore."

"Just tell me one thing," I choked, tears finally spilling over onto my cheeks. "Are the children okay?"

"They are grieving their mother," he whispered miserably. "Just as I *should* have made them do in the first place."

Beth
1996

"I remember how it felt when you hugged me," I choke out, eyes suddenly brimming with tears as Maryanne finishes her story. "I remember how safe I felt. How you smelled so beautiful. How you read me so many stories and let me sleep in your bed when I was scared."

"Sweet girl," Maryanne whispers unevenly, "I remember those moments, too. How could I forget them? I've done some extraordinary things in my life, but those times with you are some of my very best memories."

We've been talking for hours. Maryanne got up at one point to make a call back to her office to tell them she was taking the afternoon off, then returned to the table. She talked until her voice was hoarse, and then she kept on talking while I fed Noah and we walked to the restroom so I could change him. Now we're walking around campus to stretch our legs.

And she's right here. She's real, and she's alive, and it's not too late.

"Could you really have been charged?" I ask her when I've composed myself.

"Who knows?" she sighs. "Abortion was a felony offense, and people had been jailed for arranging them. I'm not sure how much an unsigned letter would have counted as evidence in a court of law, but the climate was so hysterically antichoice at the time, I may well have faced serious consequences, especially since Grace died during the procedure. At the very least, the letter might have ruined my academic career, and without your family, that's all I had left."

"You kept it for all of these years."

"Well, yes. Because what Patrick read as proof of my guilt, I came to see as absolution. I made so many mistakes, but my worst was lying to him. If I'd come clean and he'd read this with an open mind, perhaps he'd have focused on what Grace was really saying here—that *she* wanted this desperately, that perhaps she even needed it. I was only helping her to do what *she* wanted to do. But in giving me this note, he gave me a gift, because at times my guilt at her loss would crush me, and I could go back to reread this note and be reassured that Grace's mind had been made up long before she called me home to help."

"What did you do after you left us?"

"I stayed with Mother and Father for a few months. I didn't want to—but I had no alternative. They then gave me the money to set up on my own again, and I moved to the city so I could study. I finished my master's, and then eventually my PhD and I built that career I'd always dreamed of," she says sadly. "Father died suddenly later that same year, and Mother and I gradually rebuilt our relationship. When she got sick some years later, she came to live with me and I cared for her until she died."

I swallow a sudden lump in my throat, and my voice is small as I whisper, "I missed you all of these years."

Maryanne gives me a sad smile.

"I missed you, too, sweet girl."

I raise my gaze to hers, blinking rapidly as I ask, "Why didn't you try to track us down?"

Her gaze is surprisingly gentle as she murmurs, "You love your husband, don't you, Bethany?"

"Of course."

"I loved your father enough to let him go. I don't know if you can understand that, but it's the simple truth rooted in an exceedingly complicated situation. He always felt guilty that he'd fallen in love with me so soon after her death, and then learning just how badly he'd let her down and that I of all people had organized the procedure that killed her... I realized that I'd always be a reminder of what happened to Grace. I simply had to walk away to let him move on." Her gaze becomes guarded as she asks, "Do *you* blame me now that you know what happened?"

"Of course I don't." I frown. "And...I don't think Dad did by the end, either. Just before he died..." My voice breaks. Those moments are still too hard to talk about it, but she's been so generous sharing with me—I *have* to tell her about them. "He thought I was you, and he was obviously trying to apologize to you."

"When Ruth called," Maryanne sighs, "I thought perhaps Patrick was ready to clear the air..."

"Maybe if he'd remained well, he would have someday."

"He had a good life?"

"A wonderful life. We had to hire an event space for his wake because so many people adored him and wanted to pay their respects."

"I'm so glad," Maryanne says, offering me a sad smile.

"And what was life like after he asked you to leave us? Did you ever fall in love again?"

Maryanne straightens, smooths a hand over her hair, then raises her chin.

"Make no mistake, sweet girl—I'm not the victim in this sad tale. I'd never intended to marry in the first place. I only married Patrick to help him, and he was the last man on earth I *ever* thought I'd fall in love with. The five of you absolutely won my heart, but it was your family I loved. I've missed you all dreadfully and your sister's call felt like a dream come true, but even in my heartbreak, I wasn't about to go tie myself to another man in order to replace you." She shrugs in a way that reminds me of Jeremy when he's feeling self-conscious, and adds quietly, "The thing is, Bethany, if I couldn't be with you and your family, I had little choice but to go back to Plan A—change the world. And that's exactly what I did."

Maryanne tells me about her amazing experiences in the 1960s and 1970s, earning her doctorate and fighting for women's rights.

She tells me about landing the job she'd always dreamed of, and explains how her time with my family softened her once very rigid opinions on the dynamics between men and women and their children. She tells me about her work campaigning for abortion law reform, and her pride that in 1970, a referendum to legalize abortion passed with a 56% majority, enshrining the right to safe, legal abortion in Washington State law years before *Roe vs Wade*.

But most of all, Maryanne tells me about my mother, about a woman who struggled against the darkness just as I have, but who had to face those demons alone, again and again. The idea of this chills me to the bone, because even with the support I've had this year, I'm increasingly aware that I've only just made it through.

"It's hard to believe how different things were for her. I mean, I've been sexually active for..." I pause and do the math, then grimace. "God. Over twenty years. I was on the pill for more than half of that time, until Hunter and I started trying to conceive. It was actually quite easy for me to avoid a pregnancy until I was ready."

"Society moved on so fast. That's what we wanted, of course," Maryanne says and sighs as she pats my son to sleep. With her other hand, she smooths down her wind-ruffled hair. "But there's a cost in rapid progress like that, because women your age don't always understand how lucky you are. Don't want a baby? Go to the doctor and get contraception that's cheap and reliable, or go to the damned corner store and buy a packet of condoms for a handful of change. Develop depression? Take some Prozac, see a therapist. For your generation, these problems have names, and because they are defined, solutions can be found for them. But for my generation, we didn't have access to those solutions and it made life endlessly complicated... and for women like your mother, endlessly cruel."

Two weeks ago I stuffed a script for Prozac into my tote bag, and it's still there—resting between baby wipes and spare pacifiers and my purse. I clutch the strap tighter in my hand.

"Do you think it's that simple?" I ask her, my voice uneven. "Things like tackling depression, I mean?"

"Of course it is," Maryanne says dismissively. "If your mother was born now rather than then, she wouldn't have died at the hands of strangers. She could have accessed contraception and planned out her family. If she fell pregnant anyway, she could have accessed a safe, legal abortion. She'd have given birth to you children when she actually *wanted* to. I know she'd still have developed postpartum depression—because it's pretty clear that my mother suffered from it, too, and there was some genetic predisposition. But if she was facing that challenge now, she'd have been able to access treatment for it. She'd have been able to control her destiny…and that's *all* my generation dreamed of."

Sometimes moments of change happen during quiet conversations like this, when a simple shift in perspective empowers you to make a choice you just haven't been able to make before. I know in this instant that I'll wean my son, and I'll take the damned antidepressants, because I *want* to feel better—for Noah and Hunter, but also, for me.

I don't want to live like this, and more importantly, I don't *have* to. I wanted to be strong enough to overcome this illness. I finally understand that in this case, *being strong* means accepting help to find myself again. With a little support, maybe I really can become the mother I always thought I'd be…the kind of mother Maryanne once was for me.

"I'm really glad we found you, Maryanne," I whisper, staring at her.

She smiles kindly, then reaches to gently pat my back.

"I'm really glad you did, too, sweet girl."

EPILOGUE

Beth
May, 1997

A wise man once told me that everything changes. He's gone now, but his spirit lives on in the evolving patterns of our family life. Today is our second ever Walsh Family Sunday brunch. Jeremy and Fleur are back together, so last month we met at their new house in Pullman. But this month it's my turn. Hunter and I have been cooking all morning, and we couldn't be prouder to play our part in maintaining the tradition Dad started all of those years ago.

In the end, we sold Dad's house—it was much harder to justify keeping a connection to it once we'd completely cleared it out. Besides, Jeremy decided that he wanted his share of what was left after Dad's care fees for a deposit, so that he could set up his own nest with Fleur. Not one of us could have begrudged him that.

It's a beautiful spring morning outside—the air still bitter, but the sunshine gloriously bright. Outside, Ruth's kids are playing tag, and from Hunter's arms Noah is watching his older cousins make mischief—one of his favorite things to do. The rest of us—the sensible ones—are all enjoying the relative warmth of my living room.

There's change everywhere I look these days. It might still be cold outside, but emotionally, my family has marched into spring.

"I think this brunch arrangement is going to be good for us," Ruth murmurs, walking up to hand me a glass of champagne. Family brunch will happen once a month now, and it will rotate through each of our homes. I'm relieved that something of our old tradition exists, less worried now that I'll drift apart from my brothers. Jez set up email accounts for us all, and between those messages and phone calls, we're still in reasonably frequent contact.

"Yes, I think it's going to be great," I agree, knocking my glass against Ruth's. "We only have to cook and clean up once every five months."

Ruth grins and sips at her champagne.

"I already miss drinking," Fleur sighs beside us. Jeremy slides his hands around her waist and pats her nonexistent belly as he grins. "Only eight months to go!"

"It'll be over before you know it," I tell them, and I mean it. Time flies by so fast at the best of times, somehow even more so when there's a baby involved. Then again, my experience has hardly been typical. My first five months of parenthood were, in hindsight, something close to hell, and I've spent the past few months focusing on getting better. I still see a therapist every week, and once we got the dose right, Prozac has made a world of difference to my life and my parenting. Just like Grace once said, the dawn has come and the night is fading. It's fair to say that accepting the help I needed to get through that stage of my life *completely* changed my relationship with my son.

"Here's Mommy," I hear Hunter say from the doorway, and then my boys are approaching me—both sets of cheeks rosy from the cold, both of them beaming big, cheeky grins. My heart just about melts whenever Noah's face lights up like this, especially when I know that enormous smile is just because he's seen me. It hasn't been an easy road from where I was months ago to where I am now, but I'd walk it again in a heartbeat to be able to wake every day and *enjoy* the way this gorgeous, cheeky face beams at me.

"Maryanne's here," Hunter tells me, as I take Noah from his arms.

"Where is she?" I ask, peering back toward the door.

"She's playing chase with the boys."

"Seriously?" I say, then I pass Noah right back to Hunter and Ruth, Jeremy, Fleur and I all bolt for the window, catching sight of my senior citizen aunt just as she tackles Andrew, who is laughing so hard he's almost in tears.

"Should I go out there and tell them all to calm down a bit?" Ruth asks uncertainly. "I'd hate for her to get hurt."

"I think we all know Maryanne can take care of herself," I say wryly. She playfully tickles Andrew one last time, then rises and dusts off her black dress pants and sweater, before smoothing over her hair and carefully rearranging her fuchsia scarf. She sees us watching through the window and flashes us a wink.

Tim and Alicia arrive last. He's come straight from a night shift, and there are shadows beneath his eyes and a scruff on his cheeks. He scoops up a handful of crackers from Fleur's cheese platter before he approaches us. There's a manila folder tucked under his arm, but that's not what we're all staring at.

"Timothy Walsh, are there *blond tips* in your hair?" Ruth asks, eyes wide.

"That was my idea. They look amazing, don't they?" Alicia interjects, and Ruth and I both tense with the effort it takes not to laugh.

"I think he looks younger," I force myself to say.

"I think they really suit you," Ruth says in an admirable attempt at politeness.

"Timothy, they do not look ridiculous, and you definitely do not look like a forty-three-four-old man fighting off his midlife crisis," Jeremy says, and Ruth and I thump him. Alicia laughs, then rolls her eyes. These days she gives as good as she gets—and I know part of the reason why she's so much more relaxed around us is that we're all making an effort to include her, even in the good-natured ribbing.

Right on cue, she raises her eyebrows at Jeremy, and says drily, "We'll all come to *you* for fashion advice, Professor Walsh, when you manage to buy an item of clothing that's not brown or beige."

"Those colors bring out the sparkle in my eyes," Jeremy says defensively. "Fleur always says so, don't you, honey?"

Fleur grimaces, and we all laugh.

"What's so funny?" Maryanne asks.

"Just our usual childish banter," I tell her.

"In that case, I'm sad to have missed it. How is everyone?" Maryanne moves around the circle of my siblings and their spouses, planting a quick kiss on each of our cheeks, then slips right into the group. We've come a long way since that awkward dinner at Dad's place last year. Maryanne is as much a part of this family now as I am.

"Let's get the kids settled and take a seat," Tim says. "There's something I want to show you all."

Ruth and Ellis set their boys in front of the television while I fix a bottle for Noah, then the adults of the family meet back at my dining room table. I've made Dad's apple cake for dessert, and the air is heavy with cinnamon and apple. Between the noise and the crowd and the scent of that cake, it feels like Dad's spirit is alive in this house today, and I love it.

Hunter and Maryanne playfully fight over who's going to feed

Noah, but inevitably she wins, and she grins at me as she sits down to give my son his formula. Noah is old enough to hold the bottle himself these days, but he seems delighted to lie back and let Maryanne feed him instead. I chuckle at the blissed out look on his face as he nestles into her and starts to gulp, then chuckle again at the matching look of contentment on Maryanne's face as she stares down at him.

Tim opens the manila folder, revealing a thick stack of bank statements. He's highlighted some lines and Post-its are attached to some of the pages. Tim smooths his hand over the papers, then pushes the folder into the middle of the table.

"You can look through this yourselves if you're interested in the details, but I wanted to let you know that I found out where Dad's money went."

"Oh, God," Jez groans. "I'm scared to ask."

"No need to be scared," Tim says, then he smiles. "He donated it. All of it, it would seem—to Planned Parenthood. There were small amounts going back as far as I could find, but since he retired, more and more money every year."

"Wow. That's so sweet," Ruth says, eyes wide.

"Wait—do you think this means he felt guilty for *all* of those decades? Was he trying to make atonement for what happened to Mom?" Jeremy asks, frowning.

I shake my head.

"You read the notes. He probably did feel guilty, but I don't think that defined his life, and I don't think that's what this is about. I have a feeling that these donations were Dad's way of honoring Mom, and his way of quietly trying to make things better. For us...and for all of the women who come after her."

Maryanne looks up at me, and a gentle smile transforms her features. In this woman, I've found my mother—not just because of my childhood memories of her or because she can share her own memories of Grace with me, but because of who she is to me now. She's a living example of the kind of bold, brave woman I want to be.

"A beautiful gesture," Maryanne murmurs now. "From a beautiful man."

"I miss him," Ruth says softly. There are quiet murmurs of agreement from around the table.

"Everything changes," Tim says quietly.

"You're right about that. The whole family changed this year," Jeremy remarks.

"But can you imagine us any other way now?" I ask, and one by one, they all shake their heads.

If there's one thing I'm sure of these days, it's this: our chaotic, quirky family was built with love, and whatever comes next for us, that love will continue to grow.

That's the way Dad raised us, and I like to think that some-how, he knows we're continuing on in his honor.

★ ★ ★ ★ ★

A NOTE FROM THE AUTHOR

As is always the case with my books, I spent many months researching the subject matter, and I was so fortunate to have a lot of help in doing so. However, it should be noted that any mistakes in the content of the story are mine alone.

When I realized how key postpartum depression was going to be to this book, I asked friends if they knew anyone who might be able to share their experiences of the disorder with me. To my surprise, I had so many offers of help, I couldn't possibly interview everyone who was willing to chat with me. In the end, I spoke with more than a dozen women about their experiences with postpartum depression. To Monique, Lucy, Amanda, Victoria, Stacee, Ellie, Kym, Anne and others who did not wish to be named, thank you so much for your courage, your candor and your eagerness to share your stories with me.

My initial interest in frontotemporal dementia was piqued by a particularly brilliant episode of the podcast *Radiolab* (www. wnycstudios.org/story/unraveling-bolero). *Radiolab* is an amazing podcast! I've learned so much from it over the years. Thanks also to Dr. Melissa Madera of *The Abortion Diary* (www.theabortiondiary.com). Dr. Madera has captured hundreds of women's firsthand accounts of abortion across the decades in her podcast. There is nothing more useful in understanding a topic than hearing someone explain their own experiences of it, and this unique oral-history repository was key to my research as I sought to understand not only the social and political climate Grace would have faced, but also the thoughts and emotions she might have experienced. I also found Leslie J. Reagan's *When Abortion Was a Crime* and Jo Wainer's *Lost* invaluable as I was planning this book.

Thanks to all of my author friends for their support and encouragement as I was writing this story, particularly Lisa Ireland and Sally Hepworth for talking me down from the creative ledge several times when doubt struck.

Thanks to my agent, Amy Tannenbaum of the Jane Rotrosen Agency, and to Susan Swinwood and the team at Graydon House and Harlequin Books. I'm eternally grateful for everything you've done to polish my stories and to get them into the hands of readers. Likewise, I'm grateful to Sherise Hobbs and the team at Headline UK, and Alex Craig and the team at Hachette Australia.

A huge thanks must go to my parents for all of their help and support as I wrote this book, and always, to my husband, Daniel, and my children for putting up with the madness that is my writing process.

To readers—thank you, thank you, thank you for investing your money and your time in reading my stories. This book covers a few really challenging topics, but they are subjects I am so glad to have explored, and I so hope you've enjoyed reading it. If you did, I'd be grateful if you could take the time to write a review online. Your review really does make a difference; it helps other readers find my books.

I love hearing from readers. If you'd like to get in touch with me, you can find all of my contact details on my website at kellyrimmer.com. You can also sign up for my mailing list at kellyrimmer.com/email—I hate spammy newsletters as much as you do, so I'll only contact you when I have a new book coming out.

TRUTHS
I NEVER
TOLD YOU

KELLY RIMMER

Reader's Guide

GRAYDON
HOUSE

1. This book is narrated by Beth, Grace and Maryanne. Did you prefer one narrative over the others, or did you enjoy them all?

2. Grace, her mother and Beth all suffer from postpartum depression. How have attitudes and approaches toward this disorder changed over the last few generations? Do you have any personal anecdotes to share about postpartum depression, perhaps in your own family history?

3. Beth is a psychologist, but despite her training and expertise, it takes her some time to come to terms with her own condition. Did this seem realistic to you?

4. What do you think life was like for women before contraception was easily accessible and socially acceptable? Would the course of your own life have been altered by the accessibility or inaccessibility you had to contraception?

5. Abortion is a highly contentious and emotive topic. Do you think the author intended to take a side in the way she told this story? Did the story challenge your own thoughts on the subject?

6. Did you learn anything new as you read this book, and if so, what was it?

7. Early in his marriage to Grace, Patrick is selfish and entitled. The dynamic in their home is blatantly unequal, as was the norm in most households at the time, and he was unable to understand how desperately Grace was struggling. Do you think societal norms during that era excuse such behavior, or should Patrick have behaved differently?

8. Patrick eventually grows into the father Grace always hoped he would be. Do you think this same growth would have happened if she had survived? Why or why not?

9. Maryanne makes significant sacrifices to help with Patrick and the children after Grace's death. Was she motivated to stay by love, guilt or fear of the consequences to herself if Patrick found Grace's notes? Had she and Patrick not ended their relationship, do you think she would have come to resent the choices she'd made?

10. Which scene in *Truths I Never Told You* affected you the most, and why? What emotions did that scene elicit?

11. Were you satisfied with the ending? Did the various narratives come together the way you anticipated?

12. What will you remember most about *Truths I Never Told You*?